The Unbearable of Being Mitzy

Stone of Amun-Ra, Book 1

By Ephie Risho

THE UNBEARABLE LUCK OF BEING MITZY
Stone of Amun-Ra, Book 1
Copyright © 2025 Ephie Risho.

All rights reserved. No part of this book may be reproduced or transmitted in any form or by any means, electronic or mechanical, including photocopying, recording, or any information storage retrieval system, without permission in writing from the publisher, except brief passages for review purposes.

This book is a work of fiction. Names, characters, businesses, organizations, places, events, and incidents either are the product of the authors' imagination or are used fictitiously. Any resemblance to actual persons, living or dead, events, or locales is entirely coincidental.

For more information: info@theelementalists.net
ephierisho.com

Cover Illustration: Hampton Lamoureux, TS95 Studios
Editors: Daniel Edelman, Melinda Falgoust
Book Layout: Ephie Risho
Font Used in Book: Minion Pro

Bozeman, Montana
ISBN (paperback): 979-8-9894865-4-0
ISBN (EPUB): 979-8-9894865-3-3
Library of Congress Control Number:

First Edition

10 9 8 7 6 5 4 3 2 1

Chapter 1

Gonzo never did anything halfway. Which is why, at 1 a.m., we were driving to the middle of freaking nowhere in Montana to watch the Perseid meteor shower. Gonzo grinned at me from the driver's seat, flashing that devilish smile he always wore before dragging us into something insane. I couldn't help but laugh. That's the thing about Gonzo—he's like the brother I never asked for but can't seem to ditch.

He managed to convince all four of us from our weekly B-movie club, which had just finished screening *Curse of the Blue Lights*. When a movie gets *that* bad, we do my personal favorite activity and mute the volume, then provide the character voices, Gonzo doing the voice of every bad guy, of course. It always makes me cry with laughter, and that night was no exception.

Chrissy was all: "You must wield a sword against zombies, you fool!"

And I was thinking: *Holy crap! How did she know that dude was going to pick up a sword, of all things?*

She's brilliant. No doubt about it.

Then Gonzo said in a zombie voice, "Um... excuse me, sir. You have some peanut butter on your face. Mind if I have a lick?" as the zombie went ambling after the teenager. I just about split my gut laughing.

So, as I was saying, we crammed into Gonzo's beat-up, rusty 4Runner and took off to the boonies. Vee, as usual, claimed shotgun with a single glance, leaving Chrissy and me to wedge ourselves into the back with discarded bags of Fritos, crushed cans of beer, and crumpled two-year-old receipts. Somewhere along the drive, the clock melted away, blurred by the buzz of cheap beer and bad movie quotes.

I braced myself as we hit another bump, the old vehicle rattling like it was about to fall apart. "Gonzo, I swear, if you take us off another cliff—!"

Gonzo glanced back at me, eyes completely off the road. "You'll thank me, Mitzy. Just you wait."

"I believe you! Just watch where you're going!" I gripped the door, bracing for the next bump.

Chrissy giggled next to me. We sat in the back when Vee was with us, because I'd learned over the years, when Vee wanted something, it wasn't worth the bother trying to change her mind.

"Almost there," Gonzo called back. "There's a big old cow field up here. And look! You can already see them. I've seen like five in the last two minutes."

He pointed, and sure enough, shooting stars were streaking across the sky, igniting my imagination. Occasionally I think Gonzo's pretty cool, and this was one of those moments.

Vee's face was lit by her phone. "Over here." She'd triangulated the data from the NASA website to figure out how to find the spot where we'd see the most. "We can stop anytime now." Veronica Velasquez, or Vee as we called her, majored in math and worked as a personal trainer. I think people enjoyed having a smart, disciplined badass push them. It sometimes helped us, too, like leading us to where to see the meteors best.

I felt the thrill of finding the perfect spot to watch the show with my friends. Yeah, it was late, but whatevs. I'm actually deep down a huge fan of stargazing, not that it would influence Gonzo's sense of adventure.

When we got to the field, we piled out of the car to stand and watch. Every time a new streak passed before us, we alternated between saying "Oooh!" "Aaah!" and "Neato!" in unison, much to my personal delight. But soon enough, Chrissy, the skinniest member of our group, was hugging herself against the night chill.

"You're freezing." *I* almost started vibrating, watching her teeth chatter.

"I'm on it!" Gonzo called, ambling over to the creaky trunk and pulling out a few blankets (you always pack some blankets when you live in Montana, even in the summer).

We huddled in the blankets, shoulder to shoulder, eyes glued to the sky. Soon after, a meteor streaked across the field and dissolved a few hundred yards above our heads. I couldn't believe it.

Chrissy shrieked happily. "I'm going to paint that!" She was glowing with excitement. I smiled to myself. Typical Chrissy, always seeing the world in colors and brushstrokes.

Gonzo pulled out his smartphone and started filming. "Dude! I'm so glad you mentioned this was happening tonight."

I smirked. "I was *thinking* we could just walk the neighborhood."

Gonzo lowered his phone. "You *know* this is better. Admit it!"

Vee smirked. "He's got a point, Mitzy. This is pretty incredible. Have you ever seen one this close before?"

I grinned from ear to ear. The magic of the moment outweighed the late hour. Sure, it was going to be a sleepless night, but with Gonzo's relentless banter, none of us were going to fall asleep anyway.

We were mid-laugh when it hit. A blazing streak tore through the sky, slamming into the field with a fiery thud. The ground shook beneath our feet, and for a moment, none of us moved, eyes wide, hearts pounding.

Gonzo shed his blanket and lumbered off toward the field, first trying to navigate a barbed wire fence while continuing to film, which got his jacket snagged and scraped up his leg.

"Ah!" He grabbed his leg, then turned to me with a wink. "Okay, I've officially donated by blood to science. I expect a thank-you letter from NASA."

I should take a minute to tell you about my best friend and roommate. Gonzo's actual name is Gus Papadopoulos, and he's a slob of a roommate but makes plenty of money because he can code like a wizard. Probably weighs around 260, doesn't do any exercise I'm aware of, and when he does, he goes slow.

But not that night.

We heard a ripping sound as Gonzo pulled his jacket through, still filming. "Look! It's glowing." His steps slowed as he stumbled forward, eyes glued to the eerie light coming from the small crater.

Vee shed her blanket and dashed after him next, jumping over the barbed wire fence with the grace of a gymnast. Not a word, just pure focus—exactly what I'd expect from a martial arts expert who could probably crush me with one hand.

Now, at that point, it was me and Chrissy, the two most reasonable members of the group. Christina Grace is a Midwesterner, but stayed in Montana after graduating, barely earning enough to squeak by as a graphic designer for a boutique company downtown.

I turned to her. "Don't you want to check it out?"

She gave me her signature head tilt—her way of saying, *Sure, why not?*

I held the barbed wire for her to bend through the second and first rows, and then she did the same for me. Chrissy is the most practical and clear-headed member of our group. When the rest of us goofed off and did single majors at U of M, she pursued a double major in English and art and worked hard every night. Sadly, neither field pays when you graduate. So, yeah, brilliant, but probably makes less money than me, and I'm a part-time IT guy for YouFixIt.

My name is Stanley Mitz. I'm from a small farm town in Illinois. I suppose I'm fairly average in most respects—trending to pudge, but not too bad compared to a lot of Americans. Not super handsome, but not ugly either. Pale, five foot eleven inches, maybe 210 pounds, or 215, if I'm being honest. I majored in history, which apparently wasn't proving to be very helpful in the job market. But I had time to figure it out.

At least, that's what I used to think before all of this happened—before our lives were all changed forever by that freaking space rock.

Gonzo stood there filming the still-glowing meteorite from different angles. Its heat pulsed in the surrounding air, the smell of scorched earth heavy in my nose. "What the heck, Gonzo. You're not saying anything! Don't you want to let people know what's going on?"

Gonzo shook his head, then cleared his throat. "It's August 12th, and we're watching the Perseid meteor shower. We're here at a field in Montana, and... it's still smoking, so we're either very lucky, or in a *very* slow disaster movie."

The rock was still glowing, so he zoomed in to pick up more details, then lifted the phone up and waved me over.

"What?" I thrust my empty hands out.

"Get in the shot, Mitzy. We need someone to show how freaking big this is!"

"Okay, but I'm not touching it. That thing's still redder than Darth Maul's skincare routine."

I crouched down in the small crater that had been created by the space rock's impact. The grass was burned and smoldering, the air still crackling from the impact. Gonzo rolled his hand at me, urging me to talk.

I examined the rock. "So... as Gonzo said, this rock just fell from the sky, and... it's still glowing." I glanced up at the sky and pointed. "It had a trajectory from that way." Gonzo panned the camera to take in the majestic stars, and another shooting star streaked by. For a second, all I could do was marvel, my mind trying to process the sheer craziness of it all.

While he was pointing at the sky, something else caught my eye. Another rock, only this one was just a shard, half-buried near the larger glowing one. It was different... unnatural.

"What the heck is this?" I bent in to look, and everyone crowded around, with Gonzo filming up close.

The shard was not at all like the other rock. It was perfectly crafted, with crazy-looking intricate patterns all over it. Like an alien language. It was indented in the earth, much like the other one. My skin prickled as I realized it had landed at the exact same time and angle.

I hesitated for a second, then reached for the shard, fingers trembling. I could feel warmth emanating from it, just enough to be cautious. I did a quip tap of my finger to test the heat. As soon as I touched it, my whole body tingled. Like a surge of electrified willies shot up the arm and sizzled head to toe.

It's hard to explain, but I just felt... good.

Cautiously, I touched it again, then lifted the warm object, admiring every tiny detail. "This incredible shard—Gonzo, zoom in. Look at the patterns on it." The camera got close. "These aren't just random markings. It's a language."

My friends were wide-eyed as I glanced up at them, then at the camera. "This... this is what we've been waiting for our entire lives." My voice quavered. "Who'd have thought we'd find it out in the boonies of Montana? This is definitely not some random thing." Breathing shallowly, I turned it carefully in my hands. "This was crafted by intelligent beings. It's a piece of something. A piece of a puzzle. Intelligent life created this."

My eyes practically glowed. "This is a sign of life on other planets!"

Gonzo dropped the camera as he reached out toward it. He was so stunned that he didn't even care about filming. But it still picked up our audio.

Gonzo's shaky hand took the shard from me, but the moment he held it, his face paled. He swayed slightly, clutching his head. "Ugh! Can't hold it. Here." He wobbled, eyes glazed, and passed it to Vee.

She took it, and for a moment her face twisted in discomfort. Within seconds, she doubled over, vomiting into the tall grasses. "Take it!" She tossed the shard toward Chrissy. "My insides are turning upside down."

Chrissy picked up the shard and peered at it curiously, turning it over in her hands. "Do you guys hear that thrum coming from it?" Her voice was quiet.

I shook my head. I was the only one paying attention to her at that point. "What's it like?" I leaned closer, trying to catch the noise.

"It's kind of like…" She frowned. "It's like the constant hum when you're sipping a coffee at Burns Street Bistro outside. You know the trains are nearby."

She held it up to her ear, then shrieked and dropped it as if it had burned her.

"What's wrong?" I rushed toward her. "Are you okay?"

"Uhhhhhhnn." Chrissy groaned and clutched her ears. Her face twisted in pain. "Can't you hear that? It's unbearable."

I listened, but couldn't hear a thing. I hesitated, then slowly picked up the shard and put it to my ear, half-expecting something terrible.

Nothing.

For all their negative reactions, I felt great holding it. And the more I held it, the better I felt, like positive energy bubbling up inside and filling every pore. I noticed Gonzo's phone in the tall grass and picked it up, then turned it around to face me and finished the video.

My face was a mixture of awe and excitement. "I can't believe it, people. But this is it. A sign of alien life. And we've found it here in Montana. Everyone here had a negative reaction holding this thing but me." I panned the camera to get footage of my friends, one at a time. Gonzo plomped into the tall grass with an audible thump. Chrissy was baring her teeth in a huge grimace as she held her ears. And Vee gave me the finger as she held her knees, face obscured by the grasses.

I continued. "This... thing... is special. Who knows what the hell it's done to us? Let's hope it's not a big deal. If you want to know more, you'll have to follow Gonzo's channel. But he's obviously in no shape to keep filming tonight. So, that's all for now. Good night!"

I popped off the video, slipped the shard into my pocket, and walked up to my best friend sitting in the grass with a pained expression. I handed him his phone and squatted down, peering into his eyes. "Gonzo, are you good to drive?"

His eyes were unfocused. His face was pale. "No way."

I waited, but none of them seemed to get any better. For a moment, staring up at the shooting stars, I had a glimmer of a thought that this moment could be pivotal for us, and I soaked it in. We'd discovered alien life! Were our lives forever changed?

The shard in my hand pulsed faintly, and I wondered why it hadn't affected me negatively like the others.

Chrissy winced and stood next to me, hands on ears. "Let's get out of here."

I gave her a brief grunt of acknowledgement and looked at the meteorite. It seemed to have cooled off, so I risked touching it.

Warm, but wouldn't burn.

I bundled it up in my jacket, then helped Gonzo while Chrissy helped Vee back to the car. Vee was a retching mess. She dry-heaved a few more times, then sat in the back seat—a first—and instantly fell asleep on Gonzo's shoulder.

Chrissy had a pained expression as she dug through the cluttered storage console in the front. She found some tissue, ripped a bit off and put it in her mouth to moisten it, then stuffed a piece into each ear. Finally, her face relaxed.

"Better?" I asked.

She nodded. "Much." But she wasn't able to keep great company as I turned the car around and headed back.

As for me? I felt great. I felt better than great. I felt like a jolt of positive energy had been shot through my veins. For the first time in a long time, I felt like everything was going to go my way. I almost expected it.

Boy, was I wrong.

Chapter 2

Once Gonzo felt a little better on the drive home, he uploaded the video to YouTube. I dropped off the girls at their dilapidated house on the north side, then drove Gonzo and me home, where we crashed instantly.

When I staggered into the kitchen at eleven in my Pac-Man pajamas, Gonzo was beaming at me.

"What?" I rubbed my eyes. "You're never this chipper in the morning after a late night."

"Over a thousand views." He held up his phone as if it were a trophy.

I squinted at his phone. "Congrats. Now get out of the way of the cornflakes."

"One thousand one hundred and fifteen views!" He practically shoved the phone in my face. "Have you ever posted a video that got that many views?"

I shook my head. "Of course not. But seriously. How many views before you make money?"

He shrugged, and I scoffed. "I think it's hundreds of thousands. You're still small pickins."

"Whatever, dude. This is going to launch my video career. Cue the dramatic synth music." He grinned at me. "So, where's the rock?"

The larger space rock was sitting on the weathered linoleum kitchen table. I pointed at it. "Duh."

"Come on, dude. The cool little one that messed with me. The shard."

"It's probably in my pants pockets on the floor of my bedroom. Speaking of which, how are you feeling?"

He shook his head. "Still lightheaded. But not bad. How about you?"

I shrugged. "Feel great." And I did. I didn't quite feel as supercharged as the night before, but not bad for a Saturday morning after an extremely late night.

"Go get it," he urged. "I want to look at it in the light."

I set the shard on the kitchen table, and Gonzo leaned in, careful not to touch it. It was an earthy-brick-colored stone about four inches long, and just under two wide at the center, tapering at the top and bottom. Intricate patterns covered all three sides. It most definitely looked like writing.

I got close and squinted. "Does this look familiar to you?"

"How so?" Gonzo asked. He craned his head around, looking from side to side.

"I don't know." I flipped it over, looking at the side that had been faced down. There was something about it—something ancient. Like it was a relic from a forgotten time.

Gonzo clapped a hand on my shoulder. "This is it, Mitzy. Intelligent life from out there. We have the proof. But how the hell are we going to figure out what it says?"

By then, I was munching on my cereal and scrolling through the comments on his YouTube post. Some were wowing. Others, probably over half, called us fakers and scammers. I got sucked into one thread:

@Mac-Daddie-4: *This isn't proof of intelligent life out there. I've seen more convincing stuff in crappy sci-fi thrillers.*

@DB_Sleuth: *You're ignoring the imprint on the earth it created from the impact. That's legit.*

@Mac-Daddie-4: *Haven't you seen AI videos yet? Totally easy to fake.*

@George4490: *You two are missing the point. Those inscriptions look Egyptian to me, which means it's probably not alien at all.*

I cocked my head, intrigued. Egyptian? I was definitely going to want to do some digging into *that*.

I froze mid-bite, my spoon hovering over the bowl. "Gonzo, you're going to want to read this."

"What?" He looked up at me, his focus snapping away from the shard. "What is it?"

"Listen to this, from SecretSauce026: 'The rock looks an awful lot like something I saw in a little museum in France.'"

"What? What? Seriously?" Gonzo lunged for my phone. "What else did they say?"

"That's it."

"Wow." Gonzo scratched his head. "This thing is a genuine mystery. Look at all those comments! Someone's bound to give us some help to figure this out."

"Sounds good," I said. "In the meantime, something tells me we should check on the girls."

"Yeah. Yeah. Okay."

I couldn't explain it, but an uneasiness had settled over me. I couldn't sit still anymore; something told me we needed to go... now. I grabbed the shard off the table and hustled out the door, dragging Gonzo behind me.

Vee and Chrissy lived on the north side in a rental near the train tracks—a two-bedroom seventies special with peeling paint and less hot water than two grown women thought was appropriate. When we knocked on the door and no one answered, I said, "Come on. They're probably at the bistro."

Burns Street Bistro sat tucked away across from a trailer park in a quiet corner of Missoula's west side, a quirky haven for early risers and coffee aficionados. The building itself was unassuming—a simple brick façade with large windows that let in the morning light—but the personality of the place was undeniable. Outside, mismatched wooden tables and chairs were scattered across a patio framed by potted plants and old bicycles repurposed as décor, their rustling frames adding to the bistro's casual, hipster charm. Locals sipped lattes from a variety of vintage mugs, the steam curling up into the crisp mountain air, while the smell of freshly baked pastries and sizzling bacon drifted from the kitchen.

We found Vee and Chrissy sipping coffee with half-eaten pastries at an outdoor table, the rumble of a passing train blending into the chatter of the other tables. Chrissy waved us over, and we sat with them.

"How are you feeling?" I asked.

"Pretty similar." Chrissy pointed at her ears, now with earplugs rather than tissue. "My ears are still on overload."

Vee gave a sad shrug and nodded. "I kept down a couple of eggs, but I'm not right." She held her hand out, and we watched it tremble. "I'm off somehow." She clenched her hand into a fist and looked at us. "How 'bout you guys?"

I beamed. "Great. Gonzo's still lightheaded, though."

Gonzo nodded, eyes lighting up as he lifted his phone for all of us to see. "I've got almost twelve-hundred views now!"

"Congrats," Vee said nonchalantly.

Gonzo was undeterred. "And one of them said there's a similar shard in France!"

"What?" Chrissy sat up and peered at Gonzo's phone.

Something caught my eye, and I glanced up. Two guys wearing dark clothing were standing at the sidewalk, watching us. Without a word, they turned and started walking toward the entrance of the bistro. Something about them sent a shiver down my spine.

"Come on, guys. Let's go."

"What's the rush?" Vee sat back in her chair.

I glanced nervously at the two guys. "I don't know."

Vee folded her arms. "Not good enough. Chillax, Mitzy. You can get so uptight."

"Okay. I suppose you're right." I tried to sound calm, but the gnawing in my gut told me otherwise. Something about those guys was wrong, and I couldn't shake it.

A moment later, the two men walked up to our table. They had the rugged look of seasoned mountaineers—fit, weathered, and sharp-eyed, like they could take on anything and walk away unscathed. They were dressed in matching black outfits—clothing suitable for movement—with padded jackets and cargo pants. The man in back had dark hair and a swarthy complexion, with a well-trimmed beard. The one in front was slightly taller, clean-shaven, with blond hair and crisp blue eyes that seemed almost too bright.

"Are you Gonzo33?" the crisp-eyed man asked, his voice calm but sharp, like he already knew the answer.

Gonzo was puffed up, clearly thrilled. "How'd you find me?"

They glanced at Chrissy. "She mentioned this place in your video. Mind if we ask a few questions about last night?"

Gonzo opened his arms wide. "By all means."

"Do you have that... rock... here with you?" the man asked.

My buddy bubbled with excitement. "Which one? The bigger rock, or the shard with crazy patterns."

"The shard." He leaned slightly forward.

Gonzo shot me a look, and I gave a barely noticeable shake of my head. He hesitated, then turned back to them. "Naw, but we can tell you about it. What do you want to know?"

"What... did it feel like?" The man's voice was stern. For a moment, his piercing blue eyes locked on mine. He leaned in further, gripping the back of a chair with firm hands that reminded me of the time I'd seen my uncle wring a chicken's neck—strong, unflinching, and dangerous. I swallowed hard. Where did that thought come from?

Vee was the first to break the silence. "The thing made me puke my guts out."

The two men exchanged quick, knowing glances.

Gonzo said, "I'm still lightheaded from touching it. Mitzy here got the best feel. What do you say, Mitzy?"

Both men turned to me, and I tried to get the image of a strangled chicken out of my head. I put my hand in my pocket and felt the shard. It had a hum about it. A pulse. Like it was alive... like it was working.

Their eyes flicked to my pocket, where my hand was holding the shard. "It feels like... like... a rock." I forced the words out as casually as I could.

I was uncomfortable, but Gonzo was oblivious and continued yammering. "Isn't it amazing? It's a sign of life on other planets! Do you guys know anything about it?"

"No," the man said, still watching me, voice cool and even. "Nothing at all." The other man still hadn't said a word.

Gonzo grinned. "So, are you guys astronomy fans? It's pretty cool, huh?"

"Yes. Of course," the blue-eyed man said, though his tone lacked any genuine enthusiasm. His gaze flicked back to my pocket, and as I stared at him, something caught my eye—a faint, almost imperceptible spark of electricity dancing in the irises. My heart skipped a beat. The spark was blue, just like his eyes. It was barely there, but enough to send a jolt of fear through me. Something was seriously off.

That's when I knew for sure we needed to get out of there as fast as possible. But Gonzo was thrilled that he had fans—people in Montana, of all places—so he continued to badger them with questions.

"What's your interest? Did you see the meteor shower last night?"

"Oh, I'm a big fan." The blond man nodded calmly. He did *not* give the impression that he was a big fan of astronomy. "So, tell me more about the effect it had on you?"

"Hey, Gonzo," I said. "Let's order some food at the counter. Come on."

Gonzo blinked, clearly confused, but one thing I'll say about Gonzo, he trusts me through and through. He stood. "Sounds good. We'll talk with you guys soon."

We went around the corner, and I pulled him aside. "I've got a bad feeling about these guys. We need to get out of here. Now."

Gonzo's eyes widened, and he glanced back at the patio. "But what about the girls?"

"I'll text them—tell them to go downtown first when they leave and make sure they're not followed home. Something's going on. We need to figure it out."

"Okay. Okay," Gonzo sighed, clearly disappointed. We slipped out the side door, snuck back to his beat-up 4Runner, and took a long, circuitous route around the city.

Early on a weekend, driving through Missoula felt peaceful, the lack of traffic giving us time to appreciate how the mountains cradled the valley like a protective womb. Nature was everywhere—the Clark Fork River winding through town, the evergreens carpeting Blue Mountain to the west—making it seem as if civilization could vanish just beyond the town limits. We drove aimlessly, past the box stores on the outskirts and back through the slanted streets, supposedly laid at odd angles because of a feud between rival brother developers. Near downtown, college students in flannels and Patagonia jackets strolled past art galleries and cafés, the town's tight-knit familiarity palpable. But as I scanned the rearview mirror, checking for signs of pursuit, that closeness felt more like a trap. In a place this small, it wasn't hard to spot an outsider, and it wasn't hard to be found.

As the streets blurred past, I glanced down at my phone, thumbs tapping out a message to the girls. Vee's response came in short. Sharp. Like a punch. She was pissed, and I could feel it through the screen.

You just left us?

I could almost hear the fury in her voice, could picture her eyes narrowing as she read my excuse.

My gut twisted. The bad feeling about those guys still gnawed at me, but I told myself she didn't need me. Vee wasn't just tough—she was ferocious. Three days a week fighting, working out years of frustration through mixed martial arts, her black belt slung around her waist like a crown she'd earned with blood and sweat. I'd seen her in action once, at a competition—her opponent barely touched the mat before they were on the defensive, scrambling to keep up with her relentless precision. Watching her was like witnessing a storm take shape, unstoppable and precise. What could I do that she couldn't? Compared to Vee, I was just along for the ride.

As we were driving past the brand-new library downtown, I thought I saw an old classmate of ours entering. "Hey, is that Rich?"

Gonzo glanced over. "Maybe."

"He owes me fifty bucks. Let's stop."

Gonzo pulled over and we stepped out into the crisp air. The new library stood like a beacon of modern design, a sleek glass and steel structure that towered over the surrounding streets. Its large, floor-to-ceiling windows invited natural light to flood the open spaces inside, offering sweeping views of the mountains and nearby river. The exterior, with its clean lines and polished surfaces, was a sharp contrast to the rustic brick buildings in the area, signaling a shift toward the future.

Inside, the scent of fresh wood and new books hit us immediately—a distinct, comforting blend of paper and possibility. Sunlight streamed through the skylights above the open atrium, casting geometric patterns across the floors. I scanned the first floor for Rich but didn't see him, so we made our way to the second, then the third. Just as we reached the top, my phone buzzed.

Chrissy's voice was taut with frustration. "So, those guys turned out to be total jerks. When you didn't come back, they got pushy, and we had to ask them to leave."

My stomach tightened. "Did you learn anything about them?"

"Nothing," she snapped. "Except they were *way* too interested in that shard. What's going on, Mitzy? Why did you leave?"

I hesitated, searching for the right words. "I don't know. Something felt... off. One of them had these weird eyes, like electricity. Look, don't let them follow you. I think they will. Meet us at the new library. Fourth floor."

A heavy pause hung in the air, and I held my breath. "Chrissy?"

"They're following us," she whispered, her voice shaking.

My heart stuttered in my chest.

"What the hell is going on, Mitzy?" Vee cut in, sounding furious.

"Look, I don't know!" I forced the words out, my voice cracking as panic clawed at me. My thigh tingled, and I glanced down. The shard in my pocket pulsed faintly. Its cool surface pressed against my leg, alive in a way that made my skin crawl. My hand closed around it, and for a moment, I felt its energy thrumming beneath my palm.

"Here's what you need to do," I said calmly. "I saw this in a movie. Get on a busy street with two lanes. Drive slowly in the right lane. Then, when a car is passing, speed up and let the car get behind you. Get some cars between you. You can ditch them at a light. If you run a yellow or even a red light, you'll lose them. And if you get pulled over for running a red, tell the cops what's going on. That'll lose them for sure."

There was silence for a moment, then Vee said, "Damn, Mitzy. That's good."

By then, I was holding the shard in the light, observing it from different angles. My fingers traced the intricate etchings. I wondered if there were books in the library that might help me understand it.

Chrissy's voice was tight with concern. "What are *you* guys going to do?"

I paused before answering. A large book on a table caught my eye: *Historical Artifacts of Egypt's New Kingdom*. But it wasn't the name of the book that drew me in, it was one of the items, prominently displayed on the glossy cover. I wandered over and held the shard over the book. Not a perfect match, but the connection was obvious. The etchings on the shard matched the writing on a tablet of stone almost perfectly. And I immediately remembered my classmate Jim who'd done his senior thesis on translating ancient Egyptian writing.

I grinned and said into the phone, "Something tells me we're going to figure it out."

Chapter 3

I dialed Jim and he picked up immediately. The guy was a seventh-grade history teacher, so he was free on weekends.

"Stan-my-man! What's up?"

"Jim, I've got something incredible I want to show you. We found an item that has writing that looks a lot like Ancient Egyptian. How would we figure out what it says?"

Jim sounded intrigued. "Ah, I'm super busy right now, but let me give you the name of the key advisor for my thesis. He loves this kind of thing, and he'll be all over it."

"Thanks Jim! You rock."

A moment later, I got the contact info and blasted off a quick text to the advisor. *Hi professor. My name is Stanley Mitz, and I studied at UM with Jim, who said you'd be able to help. We've come across an item that appears to be Ancient Egyptian and could use your expertise understanding it.*

The professor texted back almost immediately. *Where are you? I'm free right now.*

Eight minutes later, Gonzo and I were scanning titles in the Egypt section of the library when an old man, probably around eighty, with a tucked-in checkered collar shirt expanded to his full belly's girth, and tan khakis with bulging pockets walked up.

"Stanley Mitz, I presume?"

I grinned. "That's me."

He held out his hand. "The name is Robert Georges, professor emeritus at U of M in ancient Egyptian studies and linguistics."

I smiled. "A genuine pleasure to meet you!"

After introducing Gonzo, he ushered us to a table. "May I… see the artifact?" His eyes gleamed with curiosity.

I pulled it out, then hesitated. "Um..." I glanced at Gonzo. "How about I hold it for now, and you can just look?"

"Of course." He pulled wire-rimmed glasses out of his plaid shirt pocket and leaned in. "These etchings are Hieratic, which is a language used in Egypt from around 3200 BC till the first century AD. Although..." he squinted, "the more I look at it, the more I wonder about that."

Scratching his clean-shaven chin, Robert removed his glasses and gestured grandly, like a professor mid-lecture. "Two of the sides are quite unusual and completely different from Hieratic. I'll have to do more digging. The remaining side, I could have sworn was Hieratic when I saw it, but I don't recognize a single word."

"So, what language is it?" I was riveted on the shard in my open palm, ready for it to reveal its secrets. A quick glance at Gonzo, though, showed he was gazing dreamily out the wide windows overlooking the view of Mt. Sentinel, completely mesmerized by the massive white "M" on the hillside like a tourist who'd never seen it before.

Robert lifted his wire-rim glasses and peered at the shard, then put them down and squinted, then up and down a few more times, lips puckered. He straightened. "It's like Hieratic. I'm certain I can figure this out. Shall we go look at some books?"

I beamed. "Of course."

He led us to a shelf in the back with an assortment of books on Egypt. He peered at the spines, occasionally pulling a large one off and leafing through the index before putting it back.

Offhand, while leafing through the pages, he pointed. "See this? Look at the interesting patterns in this man's hair. Do you know why they did that?"

"No." I shook my head.

"Because the Ancient Egyptians liked to use *hairyglyphics*!"

He looked up with a wry smile, and I gave a little chuckle. When he saw the faintest grin on my face, he broke out into a loud guffaw. "Ha! *Hairyglyphics*!" His voice boomed through the quiet library, and he laughed till his eyes watered. Gonzo and I exchanged a look, unsure whether to laugh or groan. But the old man's joy was infectious, and soon we were all laughing together.

After settling down and wiping the tears from his eyes, he pulled a book from the shelf and handed it to Gonzo, then looked for the next one. Once he had found three, we sat down at a table and opened the books.

He pointed. "See here. This is Hieratic. See how it's so similar? We have records for three thousand years. I should be able to find something more precise. Ah. Look. This word here looks quite similar to that one on your shard. I believe it means 'power' or something of the sort. I think I could translate the entire message of the Hieratic side, given enough time and resources."

Gonzo leaned in, eyes wide. "Dude, what if it says something epic, like 'Congratulations, you've unlocked Level Two of reality'?"

I chuckled and leaned in to see the page of the book more closely. I majored in history, and was pretty good with languages, although unfortunately I didn't know much about Ancient Egypt. But while my academic interest was piqued, Gonzo started getting loopy.

"This is it, Mitzy! It's like *Stargate*. Aliens and Ancient Egyptians working together all along."

Robert glanced at him. "And why would you say that?"

"The shard came from outer space!" Gonzo exclaimed. "It landed with a meteorite last night while we were watching the Perseid meteor shower."

"Did it now?" Robert put his glasses down and gave Gonzo an appraising look.

"Yes. Yes. How else would we have come upon something this incredible?"

Robert pursed his lips, then looked back at the shard more closely. "May I?" He held up a hand toward the shard, beckoning.

My mouth twisted as I considered. He seemed pretty trustworthy so far, nothing like the gut reaction I'd had to the two dudes in black.

"It..." I paused, allowing my thoughts to formulate. "Each of us experienced different reactions when we touched it. Gonzo's was pretty bad, the same as our two friends. So, we're being cautious."

Robert nodded his head, eyes slanted. "Curious indeed." He pursed his lips. "If you are willing, I am open to taking the risk to see for myself."

Slowly, I held the shard out toward him, watching his face closely.

The professor touched it with a finger and immediately lit up, his head rising an inch and his eyes widening. Then, he furrowed his brow and took the shard, angling it in the light in different directions. His eyes watered slightly, and he wiped them with the back of his sleeve.

Gonzo watched him closely. "What did you experience?"

Robert looked like he'd say something, then closed his mouth. He cocked his head, looking at the shard more closely before replying, "Itchy eyes."

I stared at him. He was withholding something from us. I just knew it. But what? And to what end?

He didn't give me time to puzzle about it, because he handed it back to me and turned to the book opened on the table with renewed energy. "Well then. This just adds to the mystery. More to solve!"

He set the first book aside and began going through the next one. "Ah-ha! Look at this here." The old man glanced from the shard back to a photograph of papyrus. "See, the sentence structure is the same. It's just so odd that there are no words I recognize. It's quite similar to Hieratic."

"What could it be?" I asked.

"There are many possibilities, as you can imagine. Is it from that era of humanity? Absolutely. Within six-hundred years, certainly. Is it *exactly* Hieratic? Possibly. It may be something obscure that I simply haven't encountered. Likely, it's a sister language of some sort. Intriguing. May I take photographs?"

Gonzo and I shared a glance. My friend shrugged and nodded. "Sure." I held the shard out, and Robert pulled a massive smartphone from his pocket. Not only was it the largest model phone possible—I think they call those *phablets*—it had a bulky Otter case with a second battery attached. The thing was a monster. Mystery of one of the bulging pockets solved.

He snapped a few pictures, then I moved the shard around for different positioning.

"What are you going to do with the pictures?" Gonzo asked.

Robert had his wire-rim glasses lifted onto his forehead as he peered at the pictures on his phone. "I'll analyze them more closely with my books at home. I have more resources than this library. Although not to put the library down. It's got quite an incredible collection here. I can also ask a few colleagues."

Gonzo had a thoughtful look. "Can you text us if you find out anything?"

"Of course." Robert was peering at the phone, zooming in on the characters. Then, he frowned and stared Gonzo in the eyes. "Do you have any other information on this that would be helpful?"

Gonzo teetered his head. "Not really. Although from the comments on the video I posted last night, somebody said they saw something similar in a museum in France."

"Well, if there's one all the way over here in Montana, it wouldn't surprise me for there to be one in France. That's much closer to Egypt than here."

Just then, the girls came up the stairs and saw us at the table. We did some quick introductions and caught the girls up on what we'd learned. While Robert went back to leafing through books at one end of the table, we sat quietly for a moment at the other end of the table, wondering what to do next.

Chrissy held her hand out. "Let me touch it again."

I passed it to her. She still had earplugs in. She held it up to her ear and winced but didn't put it down. Slowly, she used her other hand to pull out an earplug. She sat with gritted teeth.

"What's going on for you?" Vee asked. Robert had stopped reading and was watching closely.

"It's like my hearing's all messed up. Normally the brain filters out all the noise in the room, and just takes in what you want, but I'm hearing absolutely everything and I can't filter it out. It's awful."

Vee took a breath. "Give it to me." Her hand was out.

Chrissy passed her the shard, and Vee instantly paled. Her hand shook, and she convulsed for a moment, then tightened her whole body. Placing it on the table, she said, "Still bad. But not as bad as last night." She glanced at Gonzo.

He rolled his eyes. "What. Seriously? We're all doing this now? It felt awful last night. Why would I do that again?"

Vee just stared at him till he shook his head and reached for it. "Whatever."

He held it for less than a second before letting it clatter to the table, recoiling his hand as if it were burning. His eyes blinked rapidly.

"What happened?" I asked.

He steadied himself. "Well, it was better than last night. But it's messing with my head. I feel all lightheaded and like I'm going to disintegrate. Like, I was going to not exist if I kept holding it. Not cool." Gonzo pouted. "How come you got off so easily, Mitzy?"

I shook my head. "Not only that, guys. I don't know how to explain it, but when I hold it, I feel like things are just going to work out."

Chrissy was putting her earplug back in. "Like what? I don't get it."

"Like, my instinct to ditch those guys at the bistro. Or that we could trust Robert here. Or remembering that movie, which gave me the idea of how to lose those guys following you. All of that. It's like my gut instincts are going into hyperdrive."

"Lucky duck." Gonzo shook his head. "You get the bonus package. The rest of us get shafted."

"What sort of... *guys*... were following you?" Robert asked.

"Oh," Vee huffed. "Big, bold alpha males, wearing all black combat fatigues."

Robert's face paled, and he fidgeted with his fingers.

"What?" I asked. "Do you know something?"

The professor raised his eyebrows at me. "Sounds like some serious people you wouldn't want to mess with. I'd stay out of their sight if possible."

I puzzled, watching the old man's face. For the second time, I felt like he knew something he wasn't telling us. Before I could formulate my thoughts, he continued.

"This ancient fragment is indeed supernatural," Robert said.

"What do you mean exactly?" Gonzo asked.

Robert fidgeted with his glasses. "Not only did it affect all of us who touched it, it gave off a tingling sensation at the touch. This is a very special rock. You must guard it carefully until we learn more about it."

"Wait." Chrissy had both palms on the table with a serious look. "Guys, this thing is a big deal. But tomorrow we all have day jobs to get to. What the heck are we gonna do?"

Vee whipped her head toward Gonzo. "You need to take down that YouTube video."

Gonzo gulped. "Take it down?"

"Yes, absolutely." Chrissy stared at him.

He squirmed, then pulled out his phone, muttering to himself. Then he cringed. "One thousand five hundred sixty views," he said in a pleading voice. But after a quick peek at Chrissy's stern face, he tapped the screen. "Done. It's private now."

"Okay." Vee pointed at the shard in my hand. "Mitzy. You should bury that somewhere. Don't walk around with it. Too much risk."

I nodded. Admittedly, in that moment, I knew I wouldn't do as she asked, but I wasn't about to stand up to her with her giving me that look.

Gonzo said, "If we're going to be serious, then we all need to go incognito. Stay out of public places as much as possible, so those guys won't find us."

He glanced at Chrissy, whose eyes burned into him. He squirmed. "What? What?"

She pointed at her arms. "You seriously think a black woman working in downtown Missoula has any way of blending in? What planet were you born on?"

His face grew bright red. "Sorry. Forgot."

She sat with a stone-cold face.

Vee patted her arm. "I'll drive you to work. No walking. Pack lunches for now. You'll be fine."

"But listen, guys." I was trying to imagine this alternative lifestyle. "My job puts me around the public all the time. I'm always all over town. Gonzo can just work from home. But Vee, you're out all the time as well. And what if those guys get access to police records or something? There's got to be some way to find us. They know Gonzo's YouTube handle, and they know you girls go to the bistro."

Gonzo smiled. "Well, good thing the rental agreement's still in Rich's name. And my car is still registered in North Carolina. I haven't bothered changing the plates." He chuckled.

Vee shook her head at him. "What are you, stupid? Insurance in Montana is way cheaper than North Carolina."

He lifted a finger. "Ah. That is true. Unless your parents are still paying for it."

"Seriously? You're a freeloader? You make more than all of us."

He shrugged. "I think we've bought some time. The video is down, and I don't think anyone ever said our real names in it. Except... they saw your car, Vee."

Vee nodded slowly. "Depending on what resources they have access to, they might track me down." She glanced at Chrissy, who was pouting. "What? What is it?"

Chrissy was downcast. "I was going to go to a performance tomorrow. Do I need to skip it? One of my best friends is in it. It's a modern take on Shakespeare with disco music. Looks super interesting."

We nodded in agreement; it did sound super interesting. But Vee gave her a serious look. "If you do, be alert. Not to freak anyone here out, but if they're serious, they'll eventually find us. And they'll probably figure out where Chrissy and I live sooner than you guys. We need to learn as much as possible before then."

She scowled at Gonzo. "What are you grinning about?"

Gonzo started beaming. "Admit it. This is pretty freaking cool! I know you're all doom and gloom, but nothing's gone wrong so far, and we found a freaking space rock with sci-fi effects and some sort of connection to Ancient Egypt. I'd say this is one of the best things that's ever happened to me!"

I couldn't help but smile. "Gonzo's right. Careful is good, but I don't think we need to get overly worried. I, for one, am gonna go home and start researching Hieratic!"

Robert cleared his throat. "If that's the case, my dear Stanley, I have a few resources I could recommend. Do you have access to academic journals?"

I paused. "Not anymore..."

He considered for a moment. "I have a few books to get you started, anyway."

"Okay then." Vee wiped her hands. "Here's our plan. Everyone goes about their normal routines. Keep in touch if you spot those guys again. We'll see if the research digs up any insights and reconnect in a few days. Is that good for everyone?"

"Sure." Gonzo gave me a bright look.

I bobbed my head in agreement, feeling the shard's cool surface on my palm. I was drawn to it like a magnet, eager for the slight tingling that made me feel positive. I glanced at

Gonzo, but he didn't seem to notice. Then, the shard pulsed—so faint I almost missed it, like the flicker of a dying lightbulb. A chill swept over me, and for a moment, it felt like the air had shifted. This shard, or some aspect of it, was waking up—and I couldn't tell if it was friendly or not.

Chapter 4

By Monday morning, the city felt different. My routine hadn't changed, but there was something in the air, something that tugged at my every move. My schedule was booked with nearly a dozen different jobs all across town, which usually meant hours of sitting in traffic. Instead, every light flicked green as I approached, as if the universe were rolling out a red carpet for me. Even in the middle of the morning rush hour, it didn't seem to matter. The world was bending in my favor.

As I stepped out of a Thai restaurant after improving their Wi-Fi mesh network, I noticed something unusual and bent down. There, on the sidewalk, lay a hundred-dollar bill, crumpled but very real. I blinked and looked around. No one was in sight. I picked it up, shaking my head in disbelief. This wasn't normal. Things like this didn't just happen, especially in a neighborhood where money rarely stayed on the ground for more than a second.

As I pocketed the bill, a flicker of guilt ran through me. In an area like this, a hundred dollars could change someone's week, and someone was probably really missing it. And yet, here I was, gathering up luck like it was meant just for me.

But maybe it was.

My next job was with one of those McMansions on the west side, installing the audio for their new mega-cinema, and they tipped me four hundred bucks. Biggest… tip… ever.

Later that afternoon, I was called in to fix a computer at Best Buy. A little ironic. I know. I instantly felt a thrill of excitement as I saw the gorgeous brunette assigned to walk me through the problem.

"Deborah," I greeted, eyeing her name badge. "My name's Mitzy. What can I do for you?"

She smiled sweetly. "Oh, computer crap of some sort or another. Crossed wires or something. We need it up and running and our entire team is busy. Back this way."

She led me to a back room and plomped onto the desk, swinging her legs and chomping on some gum. She smelled like rose petals with a tinge of body sweat, reminding me of my last real girlfriend from three years earlier. I tried to be nonchalant—I hadn't dated anyone seriously since being dumped back in college.

I lifted the computer onto the desk, pulled it apart, and quickly found the fried motherboard. I lifted it to her playfully with raised eyebrows. "Got any of these around?"

She dismounted off the desk and pulled my arm. "This way." She led me to the aisle with the right components.

I gave her a knowing look as I found the right replacement and lifted it. "Just like humans, finding the right match is important."

"Is that so?" She puckered her lips and raised her eyebrows at me playfully.

I couldn't believe we were hitting it off so well. I kept worrying I'd say something stupid, and I was drawn to put my hand on the shard in my pocket as much as possible.

As I popped the new motherboard in, she asked, "Where'd you learn to do that?"

"Guess I just sort of picked it up. And where'd you learn to do *that*?"

"What?" She looked around curiously.

"Look so good in that dorky shirt," I said with a grin. Yeah, it was lame, but she liked it, apparently, because by the time I had to leave, I got up the nerve to ask her to dinner and she said yes! I got her number and drove off, humming the entire way. Things were finally going my way.

I got home and showered, then realized I hadn't set a place to meet for dinner. I picked up my phone to text her, and my fingers hovered over the screen.

"What's something casual, but not *too* casual?" I muttered to myself. I deleted and retyped the message three times before finally sending: *How about going to the Top Hat?*

Sure, she texted back.

I was standing out front when I saw her arrive. Dressed in a tight blue dress that revealed every supple curve, I gulped and wondered for a fleeting second if I was worthy of such a perfect-looking date. I'd dressed up, but for me, that meant cleaner jeans and a plaid shirt. My hand went into my pocket for the crutch the shard had quickly become. It hummed happily, and I relaxed, but still didn't have brilliant things to say.

"Hey." I waved.

She smiled at me. "I love this place. Best tapas downtown."

"I know, right?"

We sat at a table and made small talk. Thankfully, she had lots to say, which covered up my jitters.

"God. Jimmy is such a slob. Leaves out trash in the break room and doesn't put away any equipment when he's done."

"Sounds bad," I said.

"Yeah. And then there's Allen. What would it kill him to take a shower before work?"

"Huh." I nodded.

After hearing about the third issue she was having with coworkers, I clenched the shard, looking for help. Change the subject. But to what?

"So, are you from here?" I asked.

"Yeah. Born and raised. What about you?"

I smiled and leaned back. "I'm from a small farm town in Illinois. Came here to study history at U of M and stayed. I love this town."

She nodded. "It's a good place."

"Speaking of history, wanna see something amazing?"

"Sure." She shrugged.

I looked around for anyone watching, then pulled the shard out of my pocket. "Check this out. It fell from outer space. The inscriptions are ancient Egyptian!"

"Cool," she said, leaning in and peering closely at the etchings. "And you just carry that around in your pocket?"

"Yeah." I smiled sheepishly. "My friends entrusted it to me. We're trying to puzzle out what it means."

"Wow." She leaned back and appraised me up and down. "You're definitely more than meets the eye."

My heart lifted, but then her phone buzzed, and she pulled it out and started tapping at it.

I glanced around for watchful eyes and put the shard back in my pocket. Probably not the right place to show it to her, anyway. "Uh... what do you like to do for fun?" I asked awkwardly.

She shrugged and lowered her phone, but didn't put it away. "Oh, you know, dancing, movies, concerts. Wanna go to a concert? I think there's something going on at the Badlander tonight."

I smiled. "Sure! Sounds great."

The concert was mostly loud, thrashing guitars and drums, so we didn't talk much. We danced a bit until my ears hurt, and she looked at her watch. She leaned in to yell in my ear. "I have to go."

I walked her outside. She was about to go a different direction from me, and I grabbed her hand. "So... want to have dinner again?"

She shrugged. "Sure. Not tomorrow, though. I'm spending time with my besties."

"Okay. Wednesday it is!"

She nodded. "Okay. See you later, alligator." She let go of my hand and walked away. I admired her backside as she went, then with a sigh, headed home.

Gonzo was clacking away at a laptop on the sofa while watching an old Clint Eastwood flick. "What's up?" he asked nonchalantly.

I beamed. "Just had a date."

"Nice." He continued typing (it always amazes me how he can multitask like that). "How'd it go?"

"Great! We have another date for Wednesday."

He nodded slightly. "Guess you're not exactly lying low, huh?"

"Dude," I said, hanging up my jacket. "Everything is going my way. I mean, everything. This shard is working for me. I hit all green lights. And I mean all. I must have crossed town over ten times today, Gonzo. Think on that. Plus, I found a hundred bucks, got tipped four hundred, and got a date." I tried not to feel guilty for ignoring Vee's command to stay home as much as possible. Besides, as I thought about it, it seemed like she was overreacting. There was no sign of those two guys anywhere.

He stopped typing and peered at me, as if trying to see something. "I need to bring you with me when I ask for a raise."

"Exactly."

He stared back at the laptop. "So, now what?"

I pulled the shard out of my pocket. "Now, time to get into some history books and see what I can learn about this little bad boy."

That night, I crammed as much into my head about Hieratic as I could. It's a fascinating language, covering thousands of years. Written right-to-left, it replaced hieroglyphics, and there are vast amounts of preserved writings ranging from administrative and religious texts to literary, scientific, medical, academic, and correspondence. Despite its prevalence, a lot of it is untranslated or only partially understood because of the complexity of the script and the linguistic shifts over the millennia.

I also started digging into Egyptian history in that era. It was an incredible time spanning the building of the pyramids; the growing of a vast empire; the invention of writing, papyrus, and black ink; and other cool stuff like toothpaste, wigs, irrigation, clocks, calendars, and mummies. The time included some notable historical moments like when the Israelites were slaves in Egypt, and then Moses led their great escape, sometime around Ramses II, which was 1303–1213 BC. I daydreamed, wondering just when and where this shard had anything to do with that era.

The next day went similarly, little things going my way. I hit a few red lights, but it felt like nothing compared to normal. I even ran into Rich, who finally gave me the fifty bucks he owed me.

Later that night, Gonzo and I watched a show on the connection between aliens and Ancient Egypt. It gave me a bit of a laugh, but also some ideas. Nobody knows to this day how the pyramids were actually built, or their purpose. According to the show, they could have been big energy machines that could expand consciousness and were shut down after the great flood. The show also went into theories about a reptilian alien species, which we still see reflected in their portrayal of the gods. But the one that made me perk up the most was seeing the connection to the shape of the Nile with the buildings, and the exact correlation in shape and formation as the Milky Way. Likewise, the pyramids are laid out along the same path as Sirius, Orion, Aldebaran, and the Pleiades. Bright stars. Close stars. Coincidence?

On Wednesday, I was doing a network IT job for Washington Middle School when I ran into my old classmate Jim. I realized then I hadn't spoken with him since sending him that text on the weekend, so during his fourth period break we went to the teacher's lounge for some privacy, and I showed him the shard.

Holding it up, I said, "I want you to suspend your beliefs for a minute. This little beauty dropped out of the sky along with a meteorite a few days ago."

"Ha!" he scoffed. But when he saw my serious expression, his eyes widened, and he went to grab it.

I pulled it back. "Not so fast. It's not natural, Jim. It has effects on everyone it touches, and mostly not good."

He looked at me incredulously, but held his hands back. "So, what have you learned? Did you talk to Professor Georges?"

"Haven't learned much yet." I flipped it over. One side looked much like the Hieratic I'd been studying, while the other two sides were covered with writing that was more runic looking. "The Professor is doing some deeper digging."

"Let's get him on the line." He pulled his phone out and dialed before I could say anything, then put it on speakerphone.

"Hi, Professor, it's Jim. You'll never guess who I ran into."

"Ah," the voice on the other phone said. "Stanley?"

"Bingo."

"Wonderful. And perfect timing. I'd love to throw something past you, Jim. As you know, and for Stanley's sake, Hieratic is a difficult language because of seemingly endless orthographic variants. A word can appear in a dozen different ways, depending on the era and context. Now, you came up with a pretty convincing translation of the Papyrus d'Aussi, which was extremely hard to translate up till you used AI to aid your effort. How, exactly, did you do that?"

"Ah. It wasn't easy." Jim sighed. "I had a computer science classmate who programmed the AI to analyze every variant through history and extrapolate a dozen plausible options, then hone it down based on context. I still have the program, but it needs an updated AI server and—at the rate tech is advancing—things even half a year ago are out of date. I'm sure the newest tech would be far more effective."

There was a moment of pause, then Robert continued. "What would it take to get something like that rolling for us?"

Jim glanced at me. "I don't know. I've lost touch with my classmate completely over the last three years. He could be anywhere. But I'm sure it's possible."

My mind was racing. "What have you learned so far, Robert?" I asked.

"I have the general gist of the side in Hieratic. It's not a variant that I've seen exactly elsewhere, but it's similar enough that I've pinpointed the era to somewhere at the end of the New Kingdom into the Third Intermediate Period, around 1200 to 800 BC."

"Around the time of Moses?" I asked. I went to Sunday school as a kid. That story had always fascinated me.

"Precisely."

"And what about the other two sides?" I held my breath.

"I believe they're the language of magic used back then. Unfortunately, I would have no direct translation of them easily accessible. But I believe, with perhaps Jim's help, we could accurately translate the Hieratic side."

"You said you have the gist of it?" I asked.

"Yes. A bit."

"What have you got so far?"

The sound of ruffling papers came over the phone, then Robert spoke again. "Okay, again, this is early and rough. Here's what I've got: Among the... something or other... there lies a great... unclear... with the power to... something. The righteous holder of... something... must bring it to the... somewhere... to save... unclear... Are you sure you want me to keep reading this? Like I said, it's rough."

"Keep working at it," I said. "And we'll talk again soon."

Jim shook his head. "Too bad this is a one of a kind."

I felt a pulse from the shard and blurted out. "Someone who saw our video said he saw a similar one in a small museum in France."

"Really?" Jim leaned forward eagerly. "Where?"

"Ah. I never asked." I pulled out my phone to look for the comment, then remembered that Gonzo had taken the video down. "I'll have to get Gonzo to look into it. I can't see their username anymore."

I sent Gonzo a quick text.

Robert broke the silence. "Jim, I would appreciate it if you could look into it. I can keep plowing through this, but I've already hit some major blockers. I think your new tech approach would really help speed it along."

Jim grinned at me. "For sure, Professor. I'd love to help."

"Thanks," I said to Jim as he hung up.

"Don't mention it," he said. "This is some really cool stuff, Stanley. I love that you've let me be involved. I'll see what I can dig up."

When we parted ways, I was humming to myself. Three thousand years old. I tried to imagine what life was like back then, and how this shard might have been in outer space. Aliens. That was the only option. Except that Robert briefly mentioned the other two sides being the language of magic. What could that possibly signify?

That night, when I got home, Gonzo was alight. "He responded."

I instantly knew he was talking about the YouTube guy who'd left the comment. "And?"

"He doesn't live there or anything. He says it's in a tiny museum in Sainte-Hélène, which is in Bordeaux, France. I looked it up online and there's no mention of a museum there. But he says from what he remembers, the shard we found looks the same as the one he saw there. That's a common thing in France, apparently. Little museums in people's houses with a handful of stuff to look at."

"Let's call the girls," I said.

The four of us were soon sitting around the dumpy kitchen table with legs that splayed outward. Somebody was always knocking a knee on one of them. We caught the girls up on all the happenings of the day.

Chrissy watched me with narrow eyes. "How are you feeling, Mitzy? For that matter, how are all of you? My hearing is back to normal."

Gonzo shrugged. "I'm back to normal, too."

"Same," Vee said.

They all turned to me. I sighed and pulled out the shard, placing it on the table. "I didn't bury it. But here's the thing—I don't think I should. It's like everything's going my way when I keep it with me. I'm just super lucky now. I don't want to lose that. And frankly, that might be protecting the shard more than anything."

Vee scowled at me, and I averted my eyes.

"Huh." Chrissy eyed me, then reached out and touched the shard. She immediately winced, then gritted her teeth and took a breath.

"How is it now?" Gonzo asked.

She grew thoughtful. "Not as bad. It's like my hearing's in overdrive. Which hurts. But I think if I held it more, I'd get used to it." She squinted at the shard. "It has a hum, like the crackling of power lines."

She cocked her head, then grimaced and held the shard out to Vee and Gonzo. "That's enough for me. It's going to give me a headache. Anyone else?"

Gonzo waved it away.

Vee stared at it with a frown. Chrissy almost passed it back to me, but then Vee held her hand out. When the shard touched her palm, her hand clonked onto the table with a thud. She stared at her hand in wonder, then gripped the shard, and slowly, with difficulty, lifted her hand. She frowned and concentrated on her hand, then dropped the shard and the tension released. She eyed the shard warily.

"What happened?" Gonzo asked.

"This time when I touched it, not only did my stomach go all queasy, which I was prepared for, but this time my hand felt like lead. It's really wonking with me. I don't like it."

I shrugged and reached out to grab the shard. As soon as I touched it, I felt the hair on the back of my neck prick and I glanced at the window. "Uh oh."

"What?" Gonzo whirled to the window.

"I don't know... Have you ever had that feeling like you're being watched?"

"Shit!" Gonzo stood. "Do you girls think you were followed?"

"How the hell should *I* know?" Vee stood poised on the balls of her feet.

The window showed no movement. It wasn't terribly late yet, and Montana gets long days in the summer, so it wasn't so dark you couldn't see.

There was a knock at the door, causing all of us to jump.

Gonzo stood. "Don't panic." He started walking toward the door.

"Wait." I held the shard and glanced around the kitchen. I turned to Vee. "You do the talking."

She gave me a silent nod. She and Gonzo went to the door and opened it. The two men from the bistro were standing there, wearing the same matching black outfits as before.

"Hello," the blond-haired man said, lifting a hand in greeting. "It seems we got off on the wrong foot. I wonder if I could just ask a few questions."

"Like what?" Vee stood next to Gonzo with her ready-for-anything stance.

"That small rock you found…" He held his hands open as if to signify his friendliness, but all I could picture was Uncle Bill's hands killing chickens with a single twist. "The thing is, it's very curious for me and my partner here."

"And why is that?" Vee asked.

He turned to her with a fake smile that fell flat. "We're with NASA, and we monitor YouTube for these kinds of things. Our computer alerted us right away, and we were dispatched to you the very next morning."

Vee squinted at him. "Show me your IDs."

The man in front glanced at the man in the back. "Of course."

He pulled an ID from his pocket, and turned to the man in back, then handed the IDs to Vee.

Vee took them and gave them a look with sharp scrutiny, Gonzo peering over her shoulder. The IDs looked real, so Vee handed them back. Then, in a moment of awkward silence, she glanced back at me.

I was standing by the kitchen table, hand in pocket, clutching the rock, desperately hoping it would give me a clue what to do. But when no inspiration came, I just gave Vee a shrug.

She turned back to the men. "Okay then. We can chat about it. But you're not coming in."

"Of course," the blond-haired man said, trying to look friendly.

"I noticed your names are Barry and Bruno Marx. What are you, brothers?"

Bruno opened his hands. "Just got partnered randomly. So, would we be able to see the shard? We would have spent more time looking at the video, but it's offline now."

Reluctantly, I moved to the doorway and pulled the shard out of my pocket. I was watching their faces, not the shard, and I instantly knew they knew something we didn't, because they both showed flashes of eager excitement. It passed in an instant, but I saw it. One of them, "Bruno," started reaching for it and I pulled back slightly. He lowered his arm.

Vee had her fists on her hips. "What can you tell us about it?"

They were silent a moment, then the one in back, "Barry," said, "We are always on the lookout for signs of alien life. I'm afraid we're not allowed to disclose what we know about it."

"But you *do* know something." Vee was firm and authoritative.

Reluctantly, he replied, "Yes. But not much."

"Have you seen this kind of writing before?"

They shook their heads. "No. This is new. And I'm not at liberty to say more here. But I'm sure we could cover all four of you to fly to our headquarters and have our experts fill you in on more. How does that sound?"

Vee shrugged. "Interesting."

He glanced at me. "Would… you be willing to let me look at it more closely?"

Suddenly, I got a piercing migraine. Not the head-throbbing kind, but an eye-migraine, where everything is sparkling and you can't see or think quite straight.

"Oooooh." I held my head. "Sorry, guys. I've gotta lie down." I wasn't faking it, but Vee thought I was.

She started closing the door. "You heard the guy. That's all you get today. Thanks for your interest. If you want to get back in touch with us tomorrow, you're welcome to do that. But our comrade here needs to get some rest. Off with you, then." She brushed them away with her hands.

The men had looks of disappointment as they stepped back, and the door was shut and locked in their faces. As I staggered back to the kitchen table to sit down, I said. "Close all the curtains." I put head in my hands trying to clear my thoughts.

By the time the migraine eased up, everyone was at the table, curtains drawn, staring at me as if I could magically make some sort of meaning of all of this.

I sighed. "Those guys are *not* with NASA."

"Agreed. They're both trained to fight. I can tell." Vee had a firm set to her jaw. "Also, their clothing is loose and rugged, not quite combat fatigues, but the next best thing if you're ready for action."

"But…" Gonzo leaned forward. "They *did* see that video in the middle of the night and fly here immediately. That much has to be true. There's no way they're from Missoula."

"Hmmm." Chrissy pulled on a rubber band in thought. "I wonder if they're with another organization but don't want to give it away, and they were sent here, just not with NASA."

"That makes sense." Gonzo nodded. "Of course, that would mean there are folks somewhere out there who've been watching for this thing, and they're ready to move in an instant. How *much* they will do to get a closer look at it—we have no idea. What say you, Mitzy? You're the one with a feeling about them."

I recoiled. "Don't ask *me*. I have no idea."

Vee shook her head. "Come on, Mitzy. Don't shirk the duty when it gets hard. You jetted out of the bistro to get away from them. If those guys are bad news, we should all be in the know."

I shrugged. "Thing is, I don't know. Maybe they're awful. Maybe they're just super into this sort of thing. I have a weird feeling about them, but I don't actually know anything."

I sighed. "I'm winging it, guys. *I* wouldn't count on me. You guys shouldn't either. Vee, you were the best at Go from the club back at UM. You've got great strategic thinking. I'm sure you've figured out something already."

She scoffed. "I know enough to trust my friends when I may be up against something dangerous. Don't wimp out on us, Mitzy."

I squirmed and peered at the fake wood laminate of the table, feeling her eyes boring into me. "I… I guess I don't know what to say, Vee." I looked at her, pleading. "This shard is giving me some wild reactions, but I don't know what to do with it. If those guys are bad news, I'd need you to take charge. I have none of your tactical thinking or training."

She softened and patted my hand with a smile. "Ah, Mitzy. You're not so bad at Go. You nearly beat me a few times."

I chuckled weakly.

We sat in silence for a moment, imagining the worst, when Chrissy said, "This calls for a drink. What've you got, Gonzo?"

He grinned. "I just stocked the fridge with beer. And the bar still has a nearly full bottle of vodka."

"Perfect." Chrissy stood. "Vodka tonics first. I'll make the first round, since, as you all know, I'm the only one who makes them well."

"Ha!" Gonzo scoffed, then said, "I suppose that's true..."

Before long, we were toasting to grand adventures and mysteries to uncover. About four drinks in, Deborah texted. I freaked, realizing I'd told her I'd take her to dinner.

"What is it?" Vee asked, seeing my pale face.

"I stood up a date." I put the phone down and held the shard with both hands, almost wringing it.

Vee smirked and shook her head at me. "Ditzy Mitzy, never quite paying full attention."

I ignored her and tried to will the shard to do something for me. Nothing happened.

"What's it like?" Chrissy asked curiously.

"It's like a pulse, a vibration, and it feels good... *right*... when I'm holding it."

I sighed, then picked up my phone and wrote, then rewrote the text.

Sorry. Got pulled away. Can I make it up to you?

Sure. No prob.

Tomorrow?

I tacked on a fingers-crossed emoji.

WMF.

WMF? I ran through translations and landed on the most obvious. Works for me. Duh.

I sighed in relief and put the phone away. "Okay. All's well."

Vee chuckled. "Well done. Now, onto more important things." She gestured to Chrissy coming to the table balancing four full glasses on a funky art déco serving tray with a mirror top I inherited from my grandparents.

Vee took one and raised it. "Cheers!"

We all clinked glasses and proceeded to enjoy one another's company as we finished the bottle of vodka and broke into the beer. Even Chrissy was getting sloppy as the evening wore on.

Frankly, I don't remember a lot of details from that night. We drank a lot, and the conversation yielded no new incredible insights.

What I *do* remember, with one hundred percent certainly, is what happened at 3:23 a.m. that morning.

It was what changed everything.

Chapter 5

I fell asleep hugging the shard like a child nestles their teddy bear. And I'm certain that's what saved my life that night. At exactly 3:23 in the morning, all that drinking had caught up to me, and I had to pee. Half asleep, I stumbled into the bathroom, leaving all the lights off, and plopped onto the toilet.

My technique for peeing in the middle of the night is solid and works perfectly. If I turn on the lights and try peeing standing up, not only could I make a mess, but the lights could mess with my circadian rhythm and I'd never get back to sleep. That's all I need—to wake up at that ungodly hour! So, I've learned the layout of my house well enough to get out the bedroom door, down the hallway, and into the bathroom without seeing a thing, eyes mostly closed.

It wasn't until I was sitting on the toilet that I realized I was holding the shard. I gave a little chuckle at myself—how silly.

Before I stood up, my bare foot brushed against something. I touched it. The serving tray? Why was my grandparents' funky mirror-topped tray there? I shrugged. Chrissy probably had it with her when she went to pee at some point the night before and left it there.

As I walked past my bedroom door toward the kitchen to return the tray, my neck prickled and a chill went through my whole body. My bedroom window was wide open, moonlight spilling in through the curtains.

And standing over my bed, cloaked in shadows, was a man in black.

Now, I sleep on my side with a giant pillow between my legs. Between the body pillow and the crumpled blankets, it looked like I was still in bed. Thank God, I wasn't.

I watched in horror as the man pulled out a ten-inch blade and stabbed it into the pillow.

"Eep!" I squeaked from the doorway, instantly regretting it.

The man spun around, blue sparks crackling from his eyes, and he threw his hands toward me. A jagged bolt of electricity shot toward me, and I reacted on instinct, raising the serving tray like a shield.

With normal lightning, the electricity would have blasted through and electrocuted me thoroughly. But this had the opposite effect. The blue bolt hit the mirrored top and ricocheted back straight into the man.

The force sent him slamming into the wall, knocking down a picture of my younger brother and me wearing goggles at a swimming pool and ripping off a poster of a man in a large rowboat getting across the open seas with a rhinoceros. I don't know why I love that print. I just do. Now, it's only a memory. It was destroyed that night.

But I wasn't, thank God.

I dropped the serving tray with a clatter and ran toward the kitchen, heart racing.

Gonzo shouted, "What the hell, Mitzy! What's with the racket?"

"Intruders!" I shouted, stubbing my toe as I raced to the drawer with knives.

I found the longest chef's knife, a good eight-inch blade, not very sharp, but pointy. I gripped it with a shaky hand, heart pounding, fingers already slick with sweat. I stood frozen, breathing heavily, barefoot in my Pac-Man pajamas. I clutched the shard in one hand and the knife in the other. Gonzo peeped his head around the corner, eyes wide. I waved him over and whispered loudly, "Get over here!"

Gonzo tiptoed toward me, then reached out a hand and knocked a picture off the wall, sending it clattering to the floor. I winced and gritted my teeth. He was fully dressed. I could only imagine he'd just collapsed the night before without changing into PJs. Lucky thing, too, because he had his phone and wallet on him.

I jerked my head toward the front door. "Let's get out of here."

Gonzo gave a nod, grabbed his keys off the counter, and we bolted out of the house as fast as we could. We made a beeline to the police station, bursting in with wild eyes and gave rushed explanations to the poor, half-asleep woman at the desk.

Another police officer came in with a blanket. "Here, sir. Take this."

I whirled on him, still holding the knife and shard, with a crazy face.

"Please, sir. I'll take that knife now. You're safe here." He spoke calmly, and I blinked, lowering the blade and handing it over.

My toes were frigid, so I curled up in the blanket as they sent three squad cars to our house.

"Are they there yet?" I called out.

"I'll let you know, sir," the woman responded.

Gonzo stared with glazed eyes into the air, face pale. I glanced at him and curled up tighter. How was it so cold? My legs were shaking, so I called, "Can I get another blanket?"

They brought me another one, and I warmed up, but my heart didn't stop racing. "Are they there?" I said with a raised voice.

"Yes."

"And?"

She held up a hand. "Give us some time, sir. You're safe now."

I shouted, "Come on! Hurry! This is top priority! Someone tried to kill me!"

The woman at the desk was unfazed. "We have the situation under control, sir." The calmer she spoke, the more frantic I felt, but I clammed up and forced myself to wait.

It was nearly 4:30 a.m. when a police officer called us to the back to discuss with us in private.

"Nobody is at your house," he explained coolly. "We checked every corner."

"What about the attack scene? Did you see that?" I had a flash of concern that the intruders had somehow covered it up.

"Yes. The pillow and blankets are sliced up, as you described, and the wall in your bedroom is smashed up, as if someone flew into it. We've opened an investigation, but we have very little to go on at this point. For now, we can provide a police escort and can have a squad car posted outside until we learn more."

Gonzo, finally looking less pale, gave me a look as if he wasn't convinced. "Give us a minute to talk."

"Certainly." The police officer stood and left us alone.

"Mitzy," Gonzo spoke in a low voice, "we need to get this shard to someone who can explain more to us."

"Robert?" I asked.

He tilted his head. "Robert's helpful, but... I think we could learn more if we looked at the one in France. Besides, we should get out of town for a bit. Lie low."

I reeled. Until that moment, the shard had been fun and had fit into my life perfectly. Things were just getting good. I couldn't leave it all behind just like that. I sputtered. "France? I can't go."

"You can't?" He gave me an innocent look.

"No. Just... leave everything? I mean, you can bring your laptop and work from anywhere, but what about *me*?"

He shrugged. "I have a little saved. I could float us for a few weeks. And I'm sure they'd rehire you in a second."

Truth be told, I didn't like my job all that much, anyway. Not that I hated my job. IT allowed me to geek out and be on my own schedule, with nothing really pinning me down. But it didn't thrill me like the internship right after college would have. Educational software—and I was put in charge of content for elementary school history. Such a cool gig, and I was fired for making one lousy mistake. Sure, it was a big one, but still... what about second chances?

Most importantly, I didn't like the idea of walking away from what was just crystallizing with Deborah. Especially since she was the first relationship that had a snowball's chance of working out since college.

I looked at the shard in my hand. "I don't know, Gonzo..."

"Look. How much can tickets be, anyway?" He popped open his phone, then stared wide-eyed. "Damn."

"What?" I asked.

"Tickets are $1,700 each. I only have about seven or eight grand."

"See?" I shook my head. "We need to hunker down here."

"With those guys after you? He almost killed you!"

I felt my gut clench. He had a point. "Maybe you're right. But how will we pay for it?"

He frowned, then lit up. "Hey. That shard is like a big four-leaf clover for you. Just... I don't know. Can you make it work somehow?"

"No idea." I puzzled over the shard, deeply torn. It had brought me so much luck, but now people were trying to kill me for it. "What if we just give it to those goons?"

"Are you serious?" Gonzo shook his head, his curly hair whipping around wildly. "First off, they're obviously bad dudes. We can't have them walking around with it. Second off, where's your sense of adventure? This is the most incredible thing that's ever happened to me. Are you not seeing that?"

I sighed. "Admittedly, I'm super interested in learning more about what the heck it is and where it's from. Robert is on the cusp of figuring some things out, and that era of history is chock full—it was right before the Egyptian empire crumbled and got taken over by Libya and Nubia. You've gotta wonder, did this have something to do with that? How did it wind up in outer space? Who made it? And what was its purpose?"

Gonzo grinned at me. "So... I guess we'll give it to those bad dudes, then?"

I chuckled. "I guess not."

"That's my man!" Gonzo slapped my knee, his enthusiasm infectious.

I sighed. "Okay, Gonzo. Let's do it."

He stood and did a goofy dance, stomach jiggling. "Alright! We're going to France!"

He paused mid-dance and raised a finger in the air. "First stop: Paris. Next stop: accidentally uncovering a centuries-old conspiracy and getting chased by monks with crossbows. I've been training my whole life for this."

I couldn't help but smile. The big guy was kind of crazy, but that's also what made him so likable.

With a police escort, we went back to the house and packed our bags hastily. I kept glancing at my phone, wondering what I'd text Deborah, and when it would be a reasonable enough hour to call the girls. I looked at a photo of my mother and brother, wondering if I should pack it. How long would we be gone, anyway?

Nope. Leave it behind. Just pack the necessities.

"Necessities" required two extra-large suitcases, one for each of us.

By 6 a.m., I couldn't wait any longer and called the ladies. Chrissy didn't pick up. I cursed under my breath and tried Vee.

Vee's groggy voice crackled through the phone. "Somebody better be dying, Mitzy."

"They tried to kill me," I replied.

That worked.

"Get over here. Now," Vee commanded.

We hustled over to their house and, over coffee, we explained we were going to go to France to check out the shard there. They sat in stunned silence.

"Look," I explained, "you don't have to come with us. But you're probably targets too. If we bring the shard with us, they might leave you alone. But who knows?"

Vee gave me a light punch. "Are you kidding me, Mitzy? Of course I'm coming. I wouldn't miss an adventure like this for the world."

"Nice." I turned to Chrissy.

She had a furrowed brow. "I don't have any vacation days left. I'd have to quit my job."

"You're not the only one," Vee said snappily.

I saw the sting in Chrissy's eyes. Vee could probably pick up right where she left off. Same for me. And Gonzo wouldn't even need to quit working. But Chrissy... she'd had bad luck after bad luck landing a good job after college. Just getting a decent enough gig as a graphic designer had been a big breakthrough for her. But it was a pretty low-paying job. I always figured if she'd just risk a little, she could be freelancing. With her mad web-design skills, she could make a killing. I never understood why she didn't just go for it.

Finally, Chrissy sighed, her shoulders slumping. "I'm in. I'll call them when they open. But I doubt I'll get my last paycheck for leaving so abruptly. So, Mitzy," she added with a wry smile, "what's that lucky rock of yours got for money to get us there?"

I cocked my head. "I don't know. But something tells me we should text Robert and let him know what's going on."

Robert was not into long texting, although I suppose that makes sense for an eighty-year-old.

ME: *Hey. So, some guys tried to kill me for that shard. Do you have time to talk?*

ROBERT: *Tea. Liquid Planet. Will discuss further in person.*

ME: *Sure. When?*

ROBERT: *Now.*

We left the ladies to pack and headed to the café. Robert was already there, wearing a different checkered shirt and an angler's vest with stuffed pockets. He had an old-school briefcase on the floor.

When we approached the table, he gestured to the chairs, then leaned in eagerly. "Tell me everything."

So, we did—about the further effects the shard was having on us, and about the lame NASA cover story of the thugs. I mentioned we were thinking of going to France to see the one there. At one point, I pulled the shard out, and he quickly shooed it away.

"Put that in your pocket, Stanley. Don't show it in public again, do you hear me?" He was earnest, and I swallowed loudly.

Robert sat quietly for a moment before pulling out his briefcase. "I've also discovered something."

He fished around, pulled out a book and some papers, then slid the briefcase under the table. The stack of paper turned out to be a printout of a web article. At first, I scoffed at the thought of printing out a webpage, then realized how helpful it was, given our current circumstances.

He pointed at the headline. "Something was stolen from the National Museum of China in Beijing six months ago. I am unsure exactly what it was, and the translation engine I'm using is probably imprecise, but I believe it to be something similar to your shard."

He opened the book to a page marked with a sticky note. "See here. This is the item. It's tiny in the picture, but if you use your phone's built-in magnifying glass—"

Gonzo interrupted. "The phone has a built-in magnifying glass?"

Robert raised his eyebrows. "You didn't know that? How about you, Stanley? You do IT for a living, correct?"

I shrugged. "We may be geeks, but I guess we never needed it."

He scoffed. "It is a hidden feature. But it's there. Anyway, as I was saying, look here." He hovered his phone over the picture. It wasn't the clearest image, but it looked eerily similar—a shard, the same size, displayed under a glass case.

"From the article and the picture, I believe this is the item. The stolen item was an ancient Egyptian 'shard of pottery' with Hieratic writing, roughly nine centimeters."

I snuck the shard out and gave it a visual measure. About nine centimeters.

Robert grinned at us, eyes gleaming. "The article says it was the only thing stolen from the museum. Gentlemen. I believe these shards may be scattered all over the world, and you've discovered one."

"Yeah, but ours came from outer space," Gonzo interjected.

"Perhaps." Robert shrugged. "Regardless, the fact is, there are more of these on our planet. They're all over the place. And people are out to get them."

We sat in stunned silence, the gravity of Robert's words sinking in.

"What do we do?" I asked.

"Why, go to France, of course," Robert said, smiling. "I believe the shard is guiding you."

"Well…" I grew sheepish.

"What is it?" Robert asked.

"We said we're going to France, but I actually don't know how we'll pay for it."

"Pish posh. Least of your concerns."

Robert reached into a pocket and pulled out the largest wallet either Gonzo or I had ever seen. It was bulging with papers, cards, and money.

After leafing through the mess, he pulled out seven hundred dollars in hundred-dollar bills. He placed a credit card on the table. "Use the card… but be warned. They may be able to track credit cards, if they're as well-connected as I think. If they determine it's you using my card, and you think they're tracking you, ditch it. And keep in touch using encryption. No regular calls or texts."

Gonzo and I exchanged a look, the same question hanging between us.

Who the heck was this guy?

He explained which encryption apps he preferred, and we installed them on our phones. We'd take care of the girls later, ensuring we could message each other without worry.

Robert frowned. "I'm going to set up an encrypted emergency message system. You'll have to memorize the phone number. If all else fails, leave a message on the service. I'll give you the number as soon as I have it set up, and the passcode to check messages so any of us can do it."

He took a deep breath and pulled out his phone. "I'll buy your tickets on the next flight to Paris using a VPN and a different card. That should give you a head start, for sure. Can you write down everyone's full names?" He passed a piece of paper to me, and I wrote everyone's name on it.

He tapped at his phone as Gonzo and I sipped our tea nervously. Finally, he set the phone down. "Done. Your flight is at two o'clock. You should head over as soon as possible."

He leaned back in his chair. "Now, we just have to deal with the unfortunate situation of the man watching you."

"What?" I looked around wildly, then realized that was probably the wrong thing to do and turned back to Robert. Gonzo was still craning his neck.

"I suggest I give you a lift, then let you slip out unseen at the right opportunity, so he loses your trail. You'll have to be speedy about getting to the airport at that point."

He stood and gestured to the door. "Shall we?"

We followed him dumbly outside to his car, a Hyundai Santa Fe with the back seat completely full of books and papers. "Oh, just move that aside," he said, which was easier said than done.

We shoved and shoved, making just enough space for me in the back, nestled into old energy bills, academic papers, newspapers, books, and fast-food bags filled with leftover trash that filled the space with a slightly rancid odor mixed with the dustiness of old paper. Gonzo squeezed into the front seat with six thick books on his lap.

We drove off, and Robert was as pleasant as ever, as if nobody was following us and our lives weren't in danger. "Now, the trick to eluding him is to get several cars between us, and as soon as we're out of his view, you two jump out and hide for a good solid minute or two. Then, head out on foot back the way you came."

Not for the first time, I wondered who this man was.

As he turned down a major street, he gestured to us. "From what I would guess about the capabilities of your pursuers, you should have at least a good eight hours on them. Even more if they don't put two and two together. They shouldn't be able to track my purchase of the tickets, although if they think of looking into the airport passenger list, they could figure it out. You may be completely safe there, but I would be careful."

We drove for four minutes, passed the brick alley wall with beautiful artistic graffiti covering its length, and over the bridge to the hip strip. We turned a corner, and he quickly stopped.

"Good luck, gentlemen. And do stay in touch."

We jumped out of the car and hid behind a dumpster. Sure enough, a black sedan passed by half a minute later with one of the Marx guys. We waited another minute, then took an Uber to get the girls and headed to the airport. Thankfully, all four of us had passports. It was nerve-wracking, sitting at the gate, watching everybody with scrutiny, hoping we wouldn't see the two men.

I typed and then retyped a text to Deborah, finally landing on: *Hey, I got pulled out of town for a while. Sorry. I'll write to you when I'm back.*

I hit send and watched my phone anxiously until I finally got her response: *k*

I sighed, wondering how long we'd be gone, and how long she'd hold out before dating some other guy. But it was the least of my concerns, especially since Gonzo nudged me to point out a buff guy in black walking past. Nope. Not after us. But we were all on high alert.

When we finally boarded the plane, I sighed in relief. We'd gotten out of Montana unnoticed and were heading halfway around the world.

No way those guys would find us now. I hoped.

Chapter 6

Paris. The city of lights, romance, culture, gourmet food, and wine. And I was stuck inside the four bland walls of a hotel room. We were on the fourth floor of the Marriott, right on the Champs-Élysées—one of the most culturally rich spots in the world—and Vee wanted us to stay safe in our rooms.

Vee eyed the touristy map of Paris I laid out on the table of the girls' mini-lounge and waved it away. "We can't! How do you know we weren't followed? We need to sit tight first. And stick together." She gave me a glare.

I looked out the window of the hotel longingly. The Eiffel Tower beckoned in the distance, and closer by, the recently rebuilt Notre Dame. For a history buff, every corner appeared fascinating, not to mention the entire street was bustling with music, food, and thousands of people.

"Professor Georges said we have at least eight hours before those guys could find us. Probably even more. Let's put it to good use."

"No way. Too dangerous. What if he's wrong?" She folded her arms. Chrissy was nodding next to her in full agreement.

I almost caved in, but they didn't know what I felt like holding that shard. Nothing was going wrong for me. Unless you counted the people out to kill me. But otherwise, everything was going my way.

I took a breath. "I'm going. You can stay here safe. But I don't want to miss this opportunity."

Vee's eyes flashed. "You can be so thickheaded sometimes."

I gave her a weak smile. "And that's why you love me."

"Ugh!" She waved me off. "It's your funeral. Go ahead."

I smiled and glanced at Gonzo. He shrugged.

Without a moment to second-guess myself, I grabbed his arm. "Let's go."

He glanced at Vee and Chrissy, giving them an apologetic look before following me out the door.

As we rode in the elevator, I imagined Vee's fiery eyes. She'd probably throw a fit, and I winced, imagining poor Chrissy taking the brunt of it. But it was my first time in Paris—I wasn't about to spend it holed up in a hotel room.

The Champs-Élysées stretched ahead of us, a river of cobblestones flanked by rows of towering trees and bustling with life. At the far end, the Arc de Triomphe towered, watching over the street's mix of luxury shops, quaint cafés, and the ever-present hum of people embracing the rhythm of the city. Every façade was worth a further look, from ancient buildings of stone to modern floor-to-ceiling-windowed monoliths.

The street bustled with energy—tourists jostled for space near souvenir stands while locals, heads bowed over their phones, weaved expertly through the crowd. Street vendors called out their wares, their voices blending with the distant hum of traffic and the occasional clang of a passing bicycle bell.

Gonzo couldn't stop grinning, his eyes darting from one landmark to the next as if he couldn't take it all in fast enough. "Look at that, Mitzy!" he said, nudging my elbow and pointing at a twentieth-century theater building with a stone façade and sculptures of dance and music. "This place is like a postcard—every damned corner." He snapped a quick picture of the street with his phone, barely able to stand still.

Parisians smoking cigarettes passed us by, and I had a twinge of a thought that we were being followed. I turned to look. A serious-looking man in dark clothing was walking thirty feet behind us, and when I turned, he looked away. Unsure what to do, I grabbed Gonzo's arm, and we stopped.

Gonzo glanced at me, then breathed in deeply, taking in the scent of freshly baked croissants. He looked at the sign of the *boulangerie*. "Oh yes! Great idea." He beelined straight into the bakery.

Another glance over my shoulder showed me I was wrong—it was just a guy wearing black walking in the crowd. I chuckled at my paranoia and followed Gonzo into the bakery. The warm, buttery scent hit us the moment we stepped inside, drawing us toward the counter like moths to a flame. Behind the glass, golden pastries glistened, still warm from the oven, their flaky crusts promising sweetness with every bite.

"Um... *deux chaussons aux pommes, s'il vous plaît,*" I said awkwardly.

My accent drew a raised eyebrow from the elderly man behind the counter. He muttered something under his breath but smiled warmly as he handed us two pastries.

The first bite was an explosion of flavor, apple pocket pastries that put American apple pie to shame. We finished by the time we'd barely sat down, and Gonzo immediately went back to the counter.

"Ooh! Ooh!" He pointed. "*Un croissant aux chocolate,*" he said in an American-twanged version of French. The old man selected a croissant with tongs and lifted it up to a machine, then pulled the handle, piping chocolate right into it.

By then, I was standing next to him, drooling. "You have to let me take a bite," I said.

"Get your own!" he scolded.

So, I did.

And of course, we had to order two coffees to wash it all down. As we sat stuffing our faces, my phone vibrated.

I glanced at it.

Vee.

I picked it up on the third ring. "Yes?"

"Fine. You win. We're coming to join you. Where are you?"

I grinned at Gonzo and told her the name of the bakery. "See you soon."

I hung up and gave Gonzo a wink. "I *knew* they'd come around. Come on. Let's go outside."

Gonzo shook his head at me as we left the bakery. "You need to improve your French, my friend."

"Ha!" I scoffed at him. "Says the guy who barely knows a hundred words."

"Yeah, but *one* of us needs to be the interpreter. I'm on a personal mission to become fluent overnight. What are *you* gonna do?"

I glanced up and down the busy sidewalks. "Let's chat with some locals!"

I strode up to a middle-aged woman smoking and leaning against a wall. "*Bonjour. Comment ça va?*"

"Shit!" Gonzo exclaimed next to me.

"What?" I turned my attention to him, along with the woman.

"Literally, dog shit." He lifted his foot. "I've stepped in it. What's going on here? Don't people pick up after their dogs?"

The woman giggled. "No. Not like in America. But it's far better than it used to be."

"What do you mean?" I asked in English, my French attempt now thrown out the window.

"When I was a child, the men would pee on the walls of the buildings every night after all their drinking, and in the mornings the women would go out with bleach and clean them. My memory of the city is that it always smelled like piss and bleach. Disgusting. It's far more pleasant now."

We recoiled, and she laughed. I switched back to French. "Did you grow up here?"

"Oh yes…" she responded in French.

I had a great conversation with her, with Gonzo occasionally interjecting a word or two for fun. The whole time he looked around for a patch of grass to wipe his shoe on, to no avail. Stone and concrete were everywhere.

The woman's ride arrived right as Vee and Chrissy showed up. Chrissy's eyes were alight, but Vee was alert, eyes shifting to watch everyone in the vicinity.

Chrissy was bubbling. "Whatcha guys doing?"

"Practicing our French!" Gonzo beamed. "*Je sais Subterfuge… avec ma baguette de camouflage, à la garage!*"

Chrissy chortled. "Careful, Gonzo. Paris might revoke your tourist visa."

He just grinned. "Come on! We need to keep practicing." We continued walking, and Gonzo called out *"Bonjour!"* with great gusto, and *"Ça va?"* to anyone who acknowledged him. We had a great laugh as an older gentleman feeding the birds started having an actual conversation with him.

Gonzo didn't understand a single word. He just kept saying, *"Oui,"* with a nod when the man nodded at him, and when the man shook his head, Gonzo would say, *"No."* And then the man asked him a question, and he said, *"Je ne sais pas,"* French for I don't know.

I just giggled and giggled, and finally Gonzo grabbed my sleeve and asked, "What's he saying?"

I chuckled. "He asked what you think of the pigeons swarming on those breadcrumbs. He really thinks you speak French!"

Gonzo grimaced. "How do you say, 'Sorry, I don't speak French?'"

I laughed and took over the conversation with the man, then taught Gonzo a few more critical words and phrases. Chrissy and Vee also started getting into it. Chrissy's French was about as good as mine, and Vee was picking things up quickly.

As we walked into a park, Gonzo started humming.

I brightened. "I kind of recognize that tune—what is it?"

He grinned. "Ah. Just thinking about how great it is having your luck to protect us, all from our little falling star." Without warning, he belted out a song at the top of his voice.

"Catch a falling star and put it in your pocket.
Never let it fade away.
Catch a falling star and put it in your pocket.
Save it for a rainy day!"

I laughed and clapped him on the back. I didn't know the words, but I did little *boom booms* at the end of every line. The locals smiled at us as we passed, mildly amused by our tomfoolery. Even Vee lightened up.

A while later, there was another moment where I wondered if we were being followed. A serious-looking woman. Vee pulled on my sleeve, and I followed her into a small crowd. The woman passed by. False alarm.

But I was admittedly thankful for Vee's vigilance. Would we even recognize someone if they were with the Marx guys? How? Would the shard give me a clue? I gripped it tightly every few minutes, just to be on the safe side.

Before we left the park, Chrissy and Vee were shaking their heads, pointing at someone.

"What?" I asked.

Vee put her fists on her hips. "We need new outfits."

I glanced from her to Chrissy skeptically. "But you look so good already!"

Chrissy pursed her lips. "We look like Americans. We want to fit in." She eyed me up and down. "And you should too."

"Me?" I looked down to assess my clothing.

I was wearing baggy jeans and a t-shirt depicting a cat in an astronaut's helmet. A glance at Gonzo showed a similar outfit, only his shirt read:

¯_(ツ)_/¯ Works on my machine.

We definitely stood out.

"So, what do you want to do about it?" I asked.

Soon enough we were in a swanky shopping district, where everything was priced like any ridiculous fashionable trend. They dragged Gonzo and me along, since we had Robert's credit card, and we quickly found ourselves bored out of our minds. Chrissy just had to have a particular lightweight tan scarf, and Vee found a red dress with a sharp cut she said just doesn't exist in America.

Gonzo and I tried on a few different outfits. Admittedly, neither of us was an adept shopper when it came to clothing and trends, so we relied on the saleswoman, and soon enough, we each had a couple of outfits. Nothing extravagant, just trying to fit in. Gonzo looked quite sharp in dark slacks and a blue-and-gray-striped shirt. I found jeans (what can I say, I'm stuck in a fashion rut), albeit they were tighter, sleeker French style, and darker than my typical choice. I also found a well-cut black jacket that felt like it could be dressy or casual both. Stuff we'd never find in Montana. That's for sure. All of it was charged to Robert's bottomless credit card.

When the girls started heading into the fifth store, laden down with multiple bags each, I passed them Robert's credit card and said, "Gonzo and I are gonna go get a coffee over here." I pointed at a café.

"Okay. How much can we spend?" Chrissy asked.

I shrugged. "I dunno."

"What do you mean?" She frowned at me. "What did Robert say to you?"

"He didn't."

"So... you guys are just spending whatever you want?"

"Well..." I tried not to feel guilty, and glanced at Gonzo, who shrugged. I fudged the truth. "He said whatever the cost, it wasn't a big deal. So, don't worry about it. Just get whatever you want."

"Oh. Okay." She brightened. "That's great!" They turned into the store with renewed enthusiasm.

Gonzo glanced at me with raised eyebrows but said nothing.

"Let's go." I pointed at the outdoor tables of the café.

After ordering coffee and pastries and sitting at the table, Gonzo wiped his brow. "They broke me, man. One more boutique and I was going to see visions of my ancestors. I need carbs, caffeine, and possibly a therapist. Can I pick the next activity? How about we go to a vineyard or something?"

I stirred my coffee absentmindedly, adding the typical milk and sugar packets the French serve with every cup. "Could be worse," I muttered.

Gonzo took a contented sip. "Like how?"

Before I could answer, a flicker of dark movement down the street caught my eye. My gaze lifted, and my heart dropped.

My grip tightened around the cup. "Like that."

Gonzo's smile faded as he followed my gaze. Down the street, dressed in a sharp black outfit that screamed danger, was Bruno Marx. The man who had tried to kill me back in Montana. The electricity guy. His movements were slow, deliberate, predatory. He paused, his dark eyes scanning the surrounding shops. With a quick glance at his phone, he continued his steady, methodical pace in our direction.

He's tracking us.

The realization hit me in the gut. Every step he took toward us was a countdown to a confrontation.

"Shit." Gonzo's face turned pale as his head swiveled, taking in all our surroundings as if for the first time.

I desperately reached into my pocket, fingers fumbling for the shard. The second it was in my grip, I squeezed it tight, willing it to work, to give me protection and the luck I needed to get us out of this.

I glanced back at Bruno. He wasn't in a rush. That made it worse. He knew exactly where we were. He was in control, and we were sitting ducks.

"Mitzy," Gonzo whispered, scrunching down in his seat. "What do we do?"

I scanned the pedestrian-clogged street, my mind racing through options, but the clarity I'd grown used to when holding the shard wasn't there. Panic clouded my thoughts. My breath quickened. He was getting closer, his steps calm, confident.

"He's coming straight for us," I said through clenched teeth. "We can't stay here."

"But where do we go?" Gonzo's eyes darted toward the exit, his foot jiggling.

Bruno reached the boutique clothing shop next to our café. His hand slipped into his jacket. The surrounding air seemed to crackle, his power simmering just beneath the surface, a reminder of what he could do—what he *had* done in Montana.

"Okay, okay, think." I tapped the table nervously. "What if we slipped into the crowds?"

Gonzo's eyes darted frantically. "There's no way we could outrun him—"

"But we need to move," I said decisively. "Just… follow my lead."

I felt the shard pulse again, a dull throb that mimicked my racing heart. It was doing something. I just had no idea what.

Bruno stopped again, his gaze sweeping the mobs of people walking right outside of the café.

"Go inside," I whispered. "Now."

Gonzo didn't argue. We slid our chairs back, moving as casually as we could despite the panic clawing at us. I felt exposed. Every inch closer to the door felt like another second lost.

"Don't look back," I whispered.

But it was impossible not to. As I opened the café door, I risked a glance. Bruno Marx was watching us at the edge of the street with a triumphant smirk. His hand was still in his jacket. He hadn't made a move yet, but he didn't need to. The tension in the air was suffocating.

Inside, the café bustled with activity. People chatted, oblivious to the danger lurking just outside.

"What now?" Gonzo whispered, his eyes wide.

My eyes darted to every corner. The shard wasn't giving me any clues. "Let's see if there's a back door."

"Lead the way." Gonzo stumbled after me.

We weaved through the crowded tables toward the back door. I could feel Bruno's eyes on me, could almost *sense* the moment he spotted us inside. My palms were sweaty, gripping the shard like a lifeline. My heart was in my throat.

We burst through the kitchen door, and I scanned the area for another exit.

"There." I pointed at the back door, just past two people with white aprons. Gonzo didn't hesitate, pushing past a startled chef with a pan full of pastries.

We shoved open the door and emerged into the deserted cobblestone alley. It was lined with garbage bins and was barely wide enough for two people. I glanced over my shoulder, expecting to see Bruno storming after us into the kitchen, but he wasn't there—yet.

"Move!" I hissed, grabbing Gonzo's arm and pulling him forward. The shard in my hand pulsed again. It was working. Was it going to save us?

We sprinted down the alley, the sounds of the city muffled on the other side of the walls.

As we huffed along together, Gonzo knocked into a trash bin and winced. "It's like we're in a spy movie. Except no cool car... or gadgets... or, you know, *skills*."

I heard a distant shout behind us from the kitchen and risked a glance back to see a dark figure exit the bakery into the alley.

With a burst of speed, I grabbed Gonzo's arm and rounded the corner, yanking him with me just as an eruption of blue energy blasted the wall where we'd been seconds before. The bricks sizzled, blackened by the impact.

"He's toying with us," Gonzo gasped, out of breath.

I didn't respond. My focus was on running. I could feel the shard pulsing in my hand, working for me. But I knew the chase had just begun. Bruno Marx wouldn't stop until he had the shard—or until I turned the tables.

Chapter 7

I took a quick glance around the corner into the alleyway. Bruno Marx was jogging toward us casually, not in a rush. He was athletically fit, trained for combat, and with hands that still reminded me of my uncle Bill killing chickens with a single twist. Not to mention his sci-fi electricity powers. We were seriously outmatched.

"Shit!" Gonzo's eyes darted wildly, scanning the narrow street. "What the hell do we do now?"

I scanned the area for options. While the street we'd emerged onto wasn't busy, the pedestrian-packed shopping district was only fifty yards away to our left.

"I assume he found us through our phones, so let's turn them off." I pulled mine out to shut it down, and he did the same.

"Let's go!" I said, grabbing his arm and running toward the busy street. He huffed along next to me while I formed a plan. "When we get to the busy street, you go right and warn the girls. I'll go left and distract him."

"What are you gonna do?" Gonzo asked.

I grimaced. "I'm going to hope I'm lucky."

Trusting an entire plan to luck felt foolhardy. Reckless. But I didn't know what else to do.

Halfway down the street, Bruno emerged and started running faster. We made it to the intersection, wheezing. I waited for Gonzo to peel off to the right before turning to face my attacker. Bruno slowed to a walk as he saw me stop. He had an evil smirk on his face.

"Stanley Mitz." His voice dripped like acid. "No use running. I'm holding all the cards. It's just a matter of time."

I was frozen in place, watching him approach like an inevitable car crash. He was forty yards away. Every step he took filled me with dread. For a brief moment, the idea flickered in my head to just let him have the shard and be done with it, but then it passed just as quickly. No *way* I was letting this evil dude walk away with something this powerful without at least *trying*.

"Why do you want it?" I asked, holding it up.

He grinned when he saw the shard, and electricity crackled in his eyes. "You have no idea what you're holding, Stanley. It's the key to everything."

At that moment, the shard pulsed and sent a jolt of energy through me. Without thinking, I took off running down the busy street in the opposite direction. The people around me scattered. I barreled through them as quickly as my legs would take me.

My legs burned as I pushed myself harder, my lungs on fire, dodging dozens of pedestrians wildly. Every breath felt like knives stabbing into my chest, but I couldn't stop. I dared a glance over my shoulder and saw he was quickly closing the gap between us, dodging pedestrians far more smoothly than I was.

"Come on, lucky shard," I urged, clutching it tighter. It hummed in my hand. Part of me wanted to believe in it—that it could somehow protect me from the man chasing me. But the rational part of my brain screamed that this was just some ancient rock, and I was an idiot for thinking it could save me.

People were amazingly polite and stepped out of my way, making room. Not like America.

I stumbled on a cobblestone and almost bit it. I stumbled to my feet and glanced back. Bruno was much closer now, a mere twenty yards behind me. You'd think all those years of playing soccer would have helped, but a few years of a more slovenly lifestyle chucked that out the window. Meanwhile, this guy looked like he came straight from the Olympics 100-yard dash.

My brain was going into overdrive. Maybe in a public place he wouldn't kill me?

A woman on a standing electric scooter was coming right toward me. I jumped to the side and tripped on a protruding step. Twisting my ankle, I flew face-first onto the cobblestones. Pain exploded through my knees and elbows. My face scraped the rough surface before my head knocked into a post.

"Ow!" I shouted. "Ow! Ow! Ow!" I rolled over, cradling my head, to see dozens of people coming to my aid, including two police officers.

Bruno Marx stood among the crowd, panting, as one officer—a woman who smelled like cigarettes and salvation—flipped me over.

"*À quel point ça fait mal?*" she asked.

"It hurts everywhere." I groaned.

She looked at my ripped jeans and shirt, and the blood welling on my skin. She glanced at my face and my hands cradling my noggin. "You hit your head?"

I nodded, the pain throbbing. "Yeah," I said weakly.

She leaned in to look more closely into my eyes. "We must get you to the hospital. Can you stand?"

"Uhhhnn." I groaned. "Give me a minute."

The crowd was quiet as I took a few deep breaths. Then, with the officer's aid, I shakily rose to my feet. They all applauded, and the woman who'd been on the scooter came up to me, palms together, and said in English, "I am *so* very sorry!"

"No worries. I'm okay." I gave her a weak smile, trying not to look at Bruno. Although it was impossible not to notice his iron stare boring into me.

"Nonsense." She looked me over, and I glanced down to see what she was seeing. I was a complete mess. My brand-new clothes were ruined, full of new holes and stained with dirt and blood, and the left side of my face stung brutally. I wondered how bad it looked.

"How can I make it up to you?" she asked.

I glanced at Bruno. His piercing gray eyes were calculating and steady.

"Um. I don't know." I tried to imagine how she might help. I cursed, not knowing how this luck thing worked.

An ambulance wail came at us from down the street, and the people parted. The police helped me into the ambulance, and the woman from the scooter said, "I will go with you—to make sure you are taken care of."

"Yes. Wonderful." I wasn't sure how that would help, but I didn't want to turn down any possibilities.

The paramedics helped me lie down on a cot, then one of them stayed in the back with me tending to my wounds, while the woman loaded up her electric scooter, and we took off down the street. The paramedic wrapped my ankle and the flesh wounds and put a salve on my face, then peered into my eyes with a flashlight.

"What's your name?" I asked the scooter woman. She looked like she was around my age, slight of build, with stringy brown hair. Nobody in France wore helmets, and she was no exception.

"Rébecca. And yours?"

"Stanley." I didn't know why I gave her my first name rather than my nickname. It just sort of came out. Suddenly, I had an idea. "Do you have a paperclip?"

"No." She glanced at the paramedic.

He nodded. "I have one here." He opened a drawer and pulled one out.

I took my phone out, straightened the paperclip, and popped out the SIM card, although it took a couple of tries as the ambulance bumped over the rugged Parisian roads and my hands were still shaky from shock.

"This is what you could do for me." I passed her the SIM card. "There was a guy chasing me, which is why I was running and had the accident. I don't know why he's after me, but I think he has a way to track my phone. What I need most is for him not to find me. If you could put this card in your phone for an hour or two, that would help a lot. It would get him off my trail."

She looked at me with a smirk. "You're not sure why he is chasing you, eh?"

I gave her a sheepish look. "Actually, I do. He's after this." I held up the shard. "I need to learn more about it, and why he wants it. I need to get it to a safe place."

"Exciting." She cocked her head, considering. "I will do this thing. But how will you keep him from finding you at the hospital?"

I turned to the paramedic. "Can you just let me off here? Am I okay?"

He shook his head, eyeing me with pursed lips. "I need to check more fully for a concussion."

I held my hands out to him. "Please. My life depends on it."

He sighed. "What day is it?"

I recoiled. My life had been such a blur, I couldn't quite remember. "Look. I just got here from the States. I'm on vacation. I don't know. Is it Wednesday or Thursday?"

He smiled and began a series of quick questions rapid-fire. Name, age, where we were, then jumped into questions about nausea and dizziness. He shone a light into my eyes again, then gave a reluctant nod.

"I do not know how bad your ankle is, but the rest are mere flesh wounds, and it appears you do not have a concussion, only a knock on the head. Yes, we could let you off. But let me wrap your ankle more tightly first."

I exhaled in relief. "Thank you so much!"

A few minutes later, they dropped me off, and the ambulance continued to the hospital with Rébecca. I glanced around to get a sense of where I was. It was a neighborhood with restaurants intermixed with other retail taking up the ground floors of four-story buildings, and residential units on the upper floors.

I listened, barely making a sound. Only a dozen pedestrians were walking down the street I was on, while the hum of a much larger crowd came from the next block. I waited, imagining what I'd do if Bruno showed up. Body still throbbing, I knew then that I would do nothing. If he showed up, I'd give him the shard, no question. I'm not a fighter, and I couldn't run anymore. What could I possibly do?

But he didn't show. And I smirked, imagining him arriving at the hospital only to find Rébecca. Taking in my options, I headed to the busier street. I started walking and immediately winced as I put weight on my right ankle. I hobbled, wishing I had a crutch every time I put the tiniest bit of weight on my right foot. The whole time I clutched the shard, hoping desperately it would help. The only signal it gave was a slight vibration. I decided that was enough.

At the busy street, I immediately realized I had no idea what to do to get back. Paris is a massive city, and without a smartphone, every street seemed the same. In Montana, a friend had once told me, if you ever get turned around to use the mountains to help figure out where you are. I looked up, scanning the skyline. The only clue I recognized was the distinctive Eiffel Tower in the distance, but I realized then that it looks pretty much the same from every angle.

I wandered down the street till I found a small store selling maps of the city. I had enough euros to buy it and then held it up to the woman behind the counter. "Where am I exactly, and how would I get to the Marriott Champs-Élysées?"

"Ah. Is very easy from here." She pointed out the window. "There is a bus that goes there. It leaves from that corner. Two minutes' walk. Very simple."

I thanked her and limped my way to the corner bus stop. As I waited, I considered putting the shard back in my pocket but held on. I touched my face and winced. My mind traced over just how I'd gotten away—certainly not unscathed, but alive and safe—for now. The bus came, and I half-expected my attacker to be on it, but he wasn't. At every stop, I cringed, imagining him stepping on and having to give up the shard, but the rest of the ride was thankfully quiet.

When I finally arrived at the hotel, I was greeted with concerned wide eyes.

"What happened? Are you okay?" Chrissy reached a hand toward my awful-looking face and gingerly touched it.

I winced. "Yeah. Yeah. But you should see Bruno! I really took him down a notch."

Gonzo scoffed. "You did a number on him, eh? I'm guessing that number was your dental deductible."

I grinned at him. "At least the electricity killer dude is off our tail. Did you guys remove your SIM cards?"

"Not yet," Gonzo said. "But the phones are all powered off."

I pulled the paperclip out of my pocket and handed it to him. "Here. And see if you can figure out how to get new ones without using our real names."

Chrissy gestured to the couch, and I plopped onto it. Vee handed me a glass of red wine.

Gonzo sat down next to me and popped out his SIM card. "So what happened? How'd you lose Mr. Snap, Crackle, and Pop? I can't believe you survived a fight."

I shrugged nonchalantly. "Never fought him. I fell, dodging a woman on a scooter. Made a huge scene, and the police came and helped. An ambulance took me away. And the woman with the scooter said she'd put my SIM card in her phone for a couple of hours, to get them off my tail."

The three of them stared at me, and I glanced up at them. "What? What?"

"That... incredible," Chrissy said. "That's how your luck works?"

"Um... I guess so." I sank into the couch and touched my face. "It sure hurts, though. I would have preferred not running into Bruno in the first place. Or even just finding a cop right away. Why couldn't *Bruno* be the one who tripped and got all scraped up? Now, *that* would have been luck."

"Well, sure, but you got away. That alone is incredible." Chrissy watched me, eyes alight. Suddenly, they darkened. "But what about the rest of us? We're not lucky at all. What if they catch up to *us*?"

I sat in awkward silence and looked her in the eye. "We need to get rid of this shard." The words came out before I could stop them. My chest was tight, the weight of everything pressing down on me, crushing me.

They didn't answer. I looked up. Gonzo and Chrissy were slowly nodding, but Vee's eyes narrowed. "Where? Who can we trust with it? What is it actually capable of? And what do you think they would do with it if they got it? These guys in black are willing to *kill* you, Mitzy. Think about it for a minute. Can you, with any sense of the greater good of humanity, let them get away with stuff like that?"

I recoiled. "I'm not gonna give it to those goons. But are we *really* the right people to be holding this thing? Maybe *you* could take on someone in hand-to-hand combat, but a dude with electricity powers? *I* sure as hell can't stop him. And hell, they're probably the people who stole that one in China. Who's saying they're not already doing something evil with it? I say we figure out who can be a better protector of this thing and be done with it." My ankle was throbbing. "We just stumbled into this. We're a bunch of clueless, pathetic kids going up against big powers. We're not prepared for this. None of us are." I paused and fixed her with a stare. "Not even you."

She pursed her lips. "That may be true. But I'm not willing to let them walk all over me, and you shouldn't either. Why did you come to France in the first place?"

I stared into her eyes as her words sank in. "I guess... I came here partially to escape from them, which clearly didn't work. And I guess, for the excitement of this incredible magic shard, solving the mystery behind it, and the chance of finding another one. But... well, you're right. We can't let those guys get it."

I held the shard up. "And we sure as hell should make sure they don't get the other one as well."

Vee grinned. "That's the Mitzy I've been waiting to see all day. The one who gives a shit."

I smiled. "Glad to finally meet your expectations. Satisfaction not guaranteed, but hey—full money back if we all die."

Gonzo gave a little smile. "I've always loved a good puzzle."

I looked at my best friend, so fast to jump into anything—the crazy nut. I smiled with him. "Me, too." I glanced at Chrissy, who gave a barely perceptible nod. I turned back to Vee and took a deep breath. "Okay. Bordeaux it is."

She relaxed. "Good. What's the shard leading you to do next?"

I shook my head. "I don't think it works that way. It's not like I suddenly know what to do or something. Let's just take the first bullet train to Bordeaux in the morning and get out of Paris. I have a feeling this place is crawling with those thugs. It doesn't feel safe at all."

That's when we heard Gonzo's laptop ping.

He went over to look. "Hey, Mitzy. Robert is trying to message you in the encryption app. He just messaged me asking for you. What should I tell him?"

"Pass it here."

He gave me the laptop to see the message.

ROBERT: *I can't get through to Stanley. Is everything okay?*

ME: *This is Stanley here. We've been found out. One of those guys chased after me, and I barely got away. I think they can track our phones. We're ditching the SIM cards for new ones.*

ROBERT: *Good idea. Now we know the resources they have. You'll have to be very careful. Ensure none of you have any location tracking set up on your devices. Have time to talk?*

ME: *Sure.*

The laptop rang a moment later, and Robert's face appeared on the screen. "Stanley, you look terrible! Are you okay?"

"Yeah." I touched my face. "It was worth it. It's how I escaped that thug. He was chasing me. Almost had me, too. But when I fell, it made a big scene, and an ambulance took me away, safe and sound."

"Remarkable." Robert appeared deep in thought. "You truly have an incredible gift with that shard. More and more curious… So, what's next?"

I glanced at my friends. "We're planning on heading to Bordeaux on the train in the morning. Do you have any updates on your end?"

He adjusted his wire-rim glasses and held up a piece of paper. "Possibly. Two of the sides have similar etchings of some sort of ancient language of magic, not Hieratic, but I think I found a match—a papyrus with a magical incantation of sorts, allegedly attributed to Ramessesnakht, a high priest who served from Ramses IV to IX, in the 20th dynasty."

Vee scoffed. "I knew it! Magic!"

I tried to peer at the papers in his hand. "Is it something you can interpret?"

He shook his head. "I don't see how. This is one of the rare pieces that no one has been able to translate. Like the Voynich manuscript, or the Rongorongo glyphs from Easter Island. It's an unknown language, except that it was used for magic and spells."

I scratched my chin. "But you think it might be the Ramsesessess… priest guy?"

"Maybe not him, but most likely. The shapes of the glyphs are nearly identical. I would definitely place it within the 20th dynasty."

Vee smirked. "Mitzy, you're looking more and more interested. Looks like maybe you want to solve the mystery after all."

I grinned at her. "It's definitely getting more interesting." I turned back to Robert. "We'll do some digging of our own and send you images of the other shard if we find it. Any word from Jim?"

Robert shook his head. "He still hasn't tracked down his friend, and he tried his translation app, but it didn't work. Something about the server being deprecated. I'll keep you posted."

I nodded. "Sounds good. Talk to you later."

"You as well. Good luck finding that second shard."

After we hung up, Gonzo was peering at me curiously. "What was he talking about—servers being deprecated and such?"

"Oh, I guess I didn't tell you," I said. "My friend Jim had a software project back in college to translate Hieratic, but it's not working now."

Gonzo leaned in. "And you didn't think to tell me? Maybe I can help."

"Oh yeah! I forgot that's what you do." I slapped my forehead, and Vee rolled her eyes at me. "Something about using AI to help figure out what the orthographic elements are, because they can be written in dozens of different ways, even in the same era, and depending on context. It's very laborious. Jim had a developer friend who built something out a few years back, but I guess it doesn't work anymore. Probably because it was in the cloud and the tech has changed since then."

Gonzo nodded his head with gusto. "Sounds like a job for G-Man! Give ol' Jimmy a text and let's see what I can whip up."

I emailed Jim, but it was the middle of the working day for him. In the meantime, Gonzo researched how to get us new SIM cards. Turns out, France requires an ID to get a new SIM card, so Gonzo got onto some different chat groups and found someone—admittedly on the shady, cash-only side of things—who was willing to provide us some unlocked ones.

They were delivered first thing in the morning, along with an email from Jim with the credentials to download the software. Gonzo downloaded it to his laptop, then we packed up and took a taxi to the train station.

On the way over, I held my hand out. "Give me your phones." Everyone passed them over.

"I don't want to put the SIM cards in yet," I told my friends. "I want to make sure *all* location tracking is off. Not only does the phone company track you, but lots of apps do as well. The SIM cards fix the phone company issue, but we still have to ensure we're not tracked by anything else. Like Google, for example. If you do a search, they usually want to know your location for better results. So, we either need to set up new accounts to get local results, or we need to block it. Or just not use apps like that anymore."

Vee gestured to her phone in my hand. "Yeah. Yeah. Do whatever you need to do."

When we arrived at the train station, we tried to look nonchalant while also keeping an eye out for thugs. Three different guys stood out to me as possibilities, but none of them did anything other than have a certain look. The entire time, I held the shard in my jacket pocket, comforted by the strong vibration I felt.

The bullet train arrived, and we found four seats that were facing each other, two facing forward and two backward. I cringed when I saw a man with a "trained killer" kind of look also get on the train. Was he following us? It was hard to say. I sighed and gently touched the shard in my jacket pocket. As the train started moving, I pulled out my phone, powered it on, and started going through all the settings. I logged out of everything that had even the remotest possibility of tracking me, just in case.

Gonzo shook his head as he squinted at his laptop screen across from me. "This is a mess. It's compiled code, not the source. And the AI engine is old. We need to find a new one, which I'm sure will be better. But it's going to take me a while."

"No worries. Do what you can." All looked good on my phone, so I took a deep breath and put in the SIM card. I waited. The phone got a signal. I cringed. When a message popped up, I actually jumped a little.

"What is it?" Gonzo's eyes darted my way.

I chuckled. "Scared myself. Robert messaged me in the middle of the night. No worries."

"What did he say?" Gonzo was already focused back on his laptop, fingers clicking. Yet again, I found myself impressed with his ability to both write code and listen at the same time.

I read the message aloud. "I've done some preliminary interpretation of the Hieratic words on the shard. It appears they may be a bit of a warning or forecasting—maybe even instructions. Something to do with Amun-Ra, a person being righteous, and great calamity. I'll keep working on it, but the sooner you figure out that software, the better."

I texted back. *I'll do some digging of my own after we find the second shard.*

For the rest of the train ride, I went over everyone's phone diligently before inserting the SIM cards, then programmed all our new numbers in. I also double-checked the system Robert had set up for encryption. We just had to call a certain number, which we all memorized, and leave a voicemail, and any of us could check it. After being separated without working phones the day before, it seemed like a good idea to make sure it worked.

Thankfully, we arrived in Bordeaux with no trouble. We went straight to the car rental place across the street. I chose the Hertz, and the bored guy behind the counter said in a monotone voice, "Credit card and driver's license, please."

I stared at my license for a solid minute. Would they be able to track me through Hertz's computer system? How advanced were these folks?

Chrissy grimaced. "What are you thinking? Should we figure out another kind of transport?"

I shook my head. "We need to go an hour from here." I placed the ID on the counter. We'd have to take the risk. Besides, we'd be far away from the rental place.

It was 2:30 p.m., so we hit the road to the countryside in a tiny Volkswagen model they've never sold in America. Driving in another country takes some getting used to. At least in France, they still drive on the right side of the street, but the traffic rules are different. Not the spoken ones, but the unspoken. For example, the entire countryside is littered with roundabouts, and there's a particular etiquette everyone takes at them. You often go from two lanes to one, and the French people politely do a zipper formation, allowing every other car to go in smoothly. The entire operation is quite fast and painless. If it were Chicago, people would be in a gridlock, fighting to get ahead of the other cars.

It was also quite amazing to me that, although pedestrians have the right of way in crosswalks, they are quick to move out of the way for vehicles. It makes the entire driving experience much less stressful, especially considering pedestrians are teeming everywhere you drive. The biggest thing I found confusing was the speed limits. Not that they were in kilometers—the rental car only displayed kilometers—but because it constantly changed from 80 to 50 to 30 willy-nilly. An hour in though, I was getting a knack for it.

Sainte-Hélène is a quaint little town surrounded mostly by trees and filled with a few hundred quiet homes. We drove through in about five minutes, then back through again, taking a different route. No museums anywhere. We pulled over at a gas station and asked for museums, but they weren't much help.

We pulled into a supermarket for some snacks and inquired again. Same response. We drove past a cow in a small field. Gonzo rolled down the window and shouted, "Hey buddy. You got a more local version of Google Maps? Yeah, me neither."

I drove to a park, and we talked to as many people as we could find. No one knew anything.

Finally, Gonzo patted my shoulder. "Hey. The tummy's a rumbly. What's the plan for food?"

I glanced at Chrissy and Vee, who gave begrudging nods. "A quick bite at a café. No big sit-down," I conceded. "There was a small one just down the way."

We popped in and ordered coffee and sandwiches. While I was paying, Chrissy was peering at some tattered posters on a message board and said, "You'd think somebody around here would know about a museum in the area. Are we sure it's even real?"

Vee was peering at an old, printed sheet next to Chrissy. "Maybe they don't call it a museum. What other word could it be? That one looks promising. What's a *cabinet de curiosités*?"

Chrissy recoiled. "*Cabinet* means bathroom. Definitely not going there."

An old fellow behind us chuckled. "*Pas un musée, non... le cabinet de curiosités de Richard.*"

I blinked. "His bathroom of oddities?"

The woman at the counter laughed. "No, no. *Cabinet* also means a little room. A curiosity room. You Americans."

I perked up and turned to her with a grin. "Can you tell us where it is?"

She pointed. "Just north of here in Le Devès."

We sucked down our coffee and packed our sandwiches to go, then piled into the tiny car and drove a few miles into the countryside. A few houses and farms, no sign of a museum. Frustrated, I pulled into a gravel driveway and got out of the car. I walked up to the farmhouse door and knocked sharply.

No one answered. I walked around back and called out, "*Bonjour!*"

A woman emerged from a doorway in the back of the house.

"Good afternoon," she replied in lilting French. "How may I help you?"

"We're looking for *le cabinet de curiosités de Richard.*"

She beamed. "But of course! Richard loves out-of-town visitors." She pointed. "Go down the Du Devès, then take the third right, and then the first left. You'll see a sign for it there."

I thanked her, and we got back on the road. I was curious about her description until we found the place. It was a tiny French house with a hand-painted sign that read: *Le Cabinet de Curiosités - Entrée €2.*

Not a single person in sight.

With great eagerness, we put our eight euros in the box and walked through the unlocked door. The museum, if you could even call it that, was a large single room with hexagonal walls and large windows. There were pedestals and shelves everywhere, filled with oddities from all over the world.

Mounted on the wall was the head of a goat. Well, two half-heads.

Did that make it two half-goats, or one whole one?

Next to it hung several African masks with ugly long noses and their tongues sticking out.

A skeleton figurine with butterfly wings sat on a shelf.

Was that supposed to be a dead fairy?

And I didn't know what to make of the stuffed ferret wearing a party hat and polka dot shorts.

The candle collection was surprisingly large, stuck in elaborate holders of all shapes and sizes. There was an entire section of the room devoted to eccentric clocks, some looking archaic with wild springs pinging into gears, and the hands of the clocks somehow miraculously still moving.

The shelf Gonzo got wrapped up in is what I dubbed the steampunk wall. Everything there looked like some cool gadget or other from the early 1800s. Goggles. Sticks with buttons and doodads on their ends. A small musical box with a frog on top. But what was odd about that shelf was I was strangely attracted to an old, rusted skeleton key.

It looked like a metal skeleton hand with fingers. Useless as a key, but something about it drew me in. I picked it up, examining it with curiosity when my eye was drawn to a shelf with shards of pottery.

I inhaled sharply, and everyone turned to look. Next to a piece of a vase from China sat the matching shard under a small glass dome. At first glance, it looked *exactly* like the one I was holding in my hand.

Everyone gathered around as I held up the other piece in my hand. It hummed almost imperceptibly.

Vee spoke first. "Crap, Mitzy. You were right. Whatcha feeling?"

I didn't hesitate. "The pieces want to be together."

I vibrated with excitement and tried lifting the glass case, but it was locked shut. With a wry look at the key in my hand, I inserted it into a small keyhole, and the phalanges morphed and reshaped themselves, fitting perfectly into the slot. I gave it a little turn to hear a satisfying *click*.

Pocketing the skeleton key, I lifted the glass case and handed it to Chrissy. Then, I slowly stretched out the shard, and the closer they got, the more it felt like they were magnets pulling themselves together.

When it got within an inch, the other piece moved in and snapped perfectly next to the one in my hand. I held them up in awe.

I felt… fantastic. Like all the good vibes I had from the first shard, but even more. Double?

Gonzo pulled his phone out, took a few pictures, and sent them off to Robert.

Vee peered at it closely. "What do you feel, Mitzy?"

"It's like the same, only more of it."

Chrissy held out her hand. I passed it to her, and we all kept quiet, knowing how much loud sounds hurt her ears when she held it. Her eyes widened. "Guys. I hear stuff from way out there. That goat. Do you guys hear a goat?"

We all strained, then shook our heads. "This is crazy. I hear…" She looked at me. I was thinking, what could she possibly hear from me? I was barely even breathing.

Her eyes widened. "Mitzy. I hear your thoughts."

"What the hell?" Gonzo's face went white. Then he said, "Okay, what am I thinking?"

She giggled. "That scene in *Curse of the Blue Lights* where you were doing the lines about pizza delivery being late, and the zombies killing off the teenagers was the revenge."

"Ho-lee shit." Gonzo held his hand out. "Okay. Give it to me."

As soon as he touched it, his hands went up to his head, and the shards clattered to the floor, where they separated.

"What happened?" Chrissy asked while I bent to pick up the pieces.

"I felt like I was going to die."

"Seriously? Explain what it felt like."

"I don't know. Like I wouldn't exist anymore. Like I was going to dissolve. Not good, guys. You're getting cool effects, but not me. I'm done. I'll never touch that thing again."

The two shards connected again as before. I held them out to Vee. "Want to give it a try?"

She pursed her lips and slowly reached her hand out. But before she touched it, we heard a car coming up the driveway. She pulled away. A man emerged from the rusted red vehicle and started approaching the building.

That's when Gonzo muttered woozily, "Somebody look at my phone. Robert just messaged me."

Chrissy took the phone from Gonzo's weak fingers and read it aloud: "Did you notice how the words flow perfectly from one shard to the next? They're pieces of a larger item! And look. From the shape of the pieces, it appears to form a partial hexagon. That means there are six, and they need to be connected in a certain order."

We were all standing there in dumb shock when the old man walked in. He stood all of five feet tall, wearing an Irish tweed flat cap and matching vest. He saw us, looked at the connected shards in my hand, and gave an appreciative nod.

"Ah! I wondered about that one. So, it's a piece of a puzzle after all!"

Chapter 8

"Where did this come from?" I asked in my almost-good-enough French accent.

"Ah. That's from Juliette, down the road. She brought it in about half a year ago. A lovely piece, isn't it?"

"It fits perfectly with mine," I muttered dumbly.

"I see that." The old man was being so patient with me.

"We need to talk with Juliette."

"By all means."

I looked from the man to the shards in my hand. "Um... do you mind if we take this with us?"

He frowned. "Most definitely I do. But it belongs to Juliette, not to me. Speak with her directly. If she says you can take it, by all means, it is hers to do with as she pleases."

I nodded. So reasonable. I'd completely forgotten about the skeleton key in my pocket. It was almost like it had just leaped in there, it had happened so quickly, and at that point, what with everything else going on, it wasn't at all on my mind, and wouldn't be for quite some time, so I didn't even feel guilty looking at the owner straight in the face.

The shards separated easily, for how much attraction they had toward each other. After determining which was which, I placed the second one back on its pedestal and Chrissy returned the glass cover. Then, I got more precise directions to Juliette's place.

One thing I was quickly learning about rural France is the directions are not what Americans are used to. For starters, most of us use GPS these days. But we all have addresses and you can find them on a map!

Juliette's place, on the other hand, turned out to be quite the headache. "Right down the road" turned out to be almost fifteen miles, even more in the middle of nowhere than Sainte-Hélène, and the "easy to find" house was the fifth one we tried. Eventually, we found her house. By then, it was a couple of hours from getting dark, but we figured we could find a hotel or Airbnb back in the bustling city of Bordeaux.

When we finally knocked on the right door, it creaked open to reveal a stout middle-aged woman, about five-foot-three, her round cheeks flushed from exerting herself. Her dress, a faded floral pattern, clung to her in the wrong places, as if it had once been too small but had stretched over time. A dirt-stained, yellow apron was tied around her waist, as if she'd just come from working in the garden.

She eyed us warily, her gaze lingering over us as though she were weighing whether to trust us or slam the door. "Can I help you?"

"We're looking for Juliette."

She frowned, but only slightly. "That's me." She gave each of us a piercing look.

I pulled the shard out of my pocket. "We found this in Montana. In the United States. Across the ocean. Mind if we ask you a few questions?"

She peered at it, then put her hands on her hips and scowled. "That's mine. You took it from the museum."

"No. No." I tried my best to appear friendly. "It's nearly identical, but different. We came all this way from Montana because someone told us there was one here as well."

"Montana, you say?" She glanced at my friends, who all nodded eagerly. "A second piece that looks identical to mine?"

We nodded again. "Yes ma'am," I said.

"Well, then." She opened the door wide. "Please do come in." She said this last in a heavily accented English.

As we tromped inside, she gave a *tsk tsk*. "This is a shoes-off house, youngsters."

We apologized and quickly removed our shoes, then we walked into her cozy living room with flower wallpaper from the sixties and frilly lamps with tiny jewels dangling from them.

We took seats on weathered floral armchairs and a lumpy blue couch, then listened to her rummage around in the kitchen.

The aroma of aged cheese and rich wine filled the small room as Juliette gracefully balanced a tray filled with cheese, two bottles of unlabeled wine, and five glasses. Her movements were slow and deliberate, as though savoring each step.

She set it down on the ornate teak wood coffee table. Or should I say, wine-and-cheese table? Probably gets more use for that purpose, I imagine.

One thing I'd learned already in France was to hold off getting to the point as long as possible, so I waited for her to fill all five glasses and raise hers.

"*Santé*," we all said, and took sips.

After setting down her glass, I stared at the wine in surprise. "Before we discuss the shard, I'm curious about this wine. It's as good as some of the other wines we've had here, but there's no label on it."

"Ah." She beamed. "I made it myself, from my vineyards here."

"You made this?"

She spoke English with such a thick accent not every word was intelligible. "Yes. My family has had this vineyard for over a hundred years. But only this year have the wines turned out so lovely."

Chrissy took another sip. "Delicious. Well done. It's young yet full of depth. A perfect blend of smooth and dry, with a slight cherry finish. Usually, wines in this region take a few years to achieve this."

That was good enough for me. Chrissy was our in-house sommelier. The only wine I knew anything about came in a box.

I tried holding back but was just too excited. "We're so curious about the shard." I pulled mine out of my pocket. "Where did you find it? And what kind of effect did it have on you?"

She pointed her head slightly to the left. "Out there in the field. It's incredible I found it at all. I was digging a pit."

"Digging a pit?" Vee asked. "Why would you do that?"

"Oh, you see, my poor vines, they were suffering. My babies. And I wasn't sure why. A fungus? Not enough water? Poor soil, perhaps? My sweethearts! I looked on the... how you say, internet? Yes. And one thing you can do to... to learn the issue is to dig a big hole next to your lovelies and take a look. You can learn many things by looking at their beautiful little roots. You can also see the health of the soil, and if you have friends like Monsieur Gerard, you can have it tested. And of course, you can see how well-watered the darlings are. All important factors to a good, healthy grape!"

We all nodded appreciatively. She clearly loved her plants.

She pointed at the shard in my hand. "The piece was there, in the soil, about a meter down. When I found it, there were no... effects, as you say. I kept it around for many months before passing it to Monsieur Richard."

I smirked. "And your poor lovelies... they obviously recovered quickly, didn't they?"

"Oh, yes!" She smiled ear to ear. "It was an overnight miracle!"

"Explain what happened."

We all leaned forward eagerly.

"I went to every plant and sang to it. I was... how you say... inspired. No? *Oui!* Inspired. I sang over every sweetheart, and the very next day they were all strong, lovely plants. My dear Gerard never needed to be called upon after all."

Vee looked like she was on the edge of exploding. "Did you, perchance, have the shard with you when you sang over the plants?"

She frowned and scratched her head. "I do not recall. But now that you ask... it was probably in my apron. I didn't bring it to the *cabinet* for many months. I came across it again when I finally got around to washing my apron. When I saw dear Monsieur Richard at the goat cheese festival last year and mentioned it to him, he said it would be appreciated more greatly in his museum than on my counter." She turned to Vee with a curious expression. "Why are you asking about it?"

Vee tried looking nonchalant but couldn't conceal her excitement. "We've found it possesses properties that people… react to. Special properties. Perhaps your… effect was to nurture your plants to health."

Juliette pursed her lips. "It wasn't because my darlings loved my singing?"

"Oh, I'm sure they did." Vee waved her hand reassuringly. "But I think they liked it even more when you held the shard."

Juliette sat with a furrowed brow for a moment. She kept her hands folded neatly in her lap, then reached out a hand to me. "May I?"

I handed her the shard without hesitation. I figured if she'd already touched one, touching another would be more of the same. And frankly, I was incredibly curious about what would happen.

She held it for a moment, head cocked to the side. We sat quietly in expectant curiosity.

Then she sang. It was nothing amazing, a little French ditty I couldn't quite catch the words to. Something about a child strolling down the street and looking at all the different flowers. Her voice wasn't strong, and didn't stay fully in tune, but we all felt warmth and wholeness wash over us, like a mother tucking her children into bed. It was beautiful in its own quirky way, the way I feel sometimes when I hear a recording of some old blues musician playing on an out-of-tune piano.

As Juliette sang, the melody wove its way through the air like a soft lullaby, filling the room with a warmth that wrapped around us like a blanket. Her voice, though unpolished and wavering, held a strange, quiet power, and for the first time in days, I felt the knots of tension in my chest loosen. The world outside, with its danger and uncertainty, seemed to fade, leaving only the soft hum of her song and the comforting presence of my friends around me.

When she finished, I started. "My ankle…" The words caught in my throat, disbelief flooding my senses as I flexed my foot. The sharp pain that had plagued me all day was gone. I stood, gingerly at first, testing it, then jumping in place. No pain. No stiffness. Just… nothing.

"Sweet fancy Moses!" Gonzo's eyes widened as he examined me.

Chrissy stood. "Your face, Mitzy. It's—" Her voice trailed off as she stepped closer, her fingers grazing my cheek.

I raised a trembling hand to my face, running it over the skin that had been scraped raw the day before. Panic and exhilaration warred inside me as I stared down at the shard in Juliette's hands.

Everyone crowded around. Upon further inspection, all my scrapes and bruises were completely healed. Juliette sat subdued, watching quietly.

Vee spoke first. "You can't let anyone know about this. You'll be pulled into all sorts of trouble. It'll ruin your life."

Juliette's brow furrowed as she studied the shard in her hand, her fingers tracing its etchings with a newfound hesitance. "I… I always thought it was just a trinket," she murmured, her voice quieter now, laced with uncertainty. "But if what you say is true…" Her gaze flicked between us, eyes wide with a mixture of disbelief and fear. "What is this thing capable of?"

Vee leaned in, her voice low and urgent. "Whatever it is, it's powerful. And we can only assume it's dangerous in the wrong hands."

Juliette swallowed hard, her hands trembling slightly as she set the shard back down on the table. "*Mon Dieu…* what have I gotten myself into?"

Gonzo's phone alerted us that Robert sent a message. He fumbled in his pants pocket and pulled it out. "Uh oh." His face dropped.

"Now what?" Vee asked.

Gonzo wiped his suddenly clammy hands on his shirt. "Robert says... the scary guys... they just showed up asking about us. He didn't tell them anything, but... the jig is up." His voice cracked on the last words, and he looked to Vee for strength. "If they have the resources he thinks they do, they'll figure out we used his credit card and track us to the last time we purchased anything."

"Damn!" Vee frowned.

"Have a sip of wine," I said. "I'm sure it'll all work out."

She shook her head. "No, you don't understand. We just used the card in Sainte-Hélène. They'll come straight here."

"But we're fifteen miles from there," I said.

Vee gave me a hardened look. "Yeah, but the other shard isn't."

A heavy silence fell over the room, the air thick with dread. Vee's words hung in the space between us, and I could almost feel the walls closing in. Chrissy's face went pale, her hands trembling as she clutched her wine glass. Vee paced the room, her lips pressed into a tight line, while Gonzo rubbed his forehead, his eyes darting toward the window as if expecting the worst.

My stomach churned, the weight of it all pressing down on me. *It's only a matter of time before they find us.* The thought echoed in my mind, relentless and terrifying. We'd come so far, only to end up right back in their crosshairs.

Juliette's eyes darted. "What is going on? What is the problem?"

Vee turned to her. "The short story is we posted a video of our shard online just over a week ago, and literally the next day two men showed up asking about it. We got out of there without them learning who we were. But they did finally track us down a few days later, and that night they tried to kill Mitzy to steal it. We got out of Montana as fast as we could, and figured maybe we'd learn more here, with you and your shard."

Juliette wrung a napkin in her hands. "*Mon Dieu.* What are we to we do?"

Gonzo started pacing. "All of this depends on who we're dealing with. We know they have people in Paris. But do they have people in Bordeaux? If they're in Paris, they probably won't get here till tomorrow morning. But if they have people in Bordeaux…"

The tension rose in the room. Chrissy squeezed the napkin in her lap. "What if they only checked on Robert now, but they've known for a few hours?"

We stared at her blankly. I felt my stomach churn. We'd come all this way… was it for naught?

Vee turned to Juliette. "Can we get your shard from the museum? Now?"

She glanced out the window. It was nearly dark. "I am afraid Monsieur Richard will have locked up the *cabinet* for the night."

Vee grabbed a piece of cheese and took a nervous bite. "Do you know where he lives? Can we get him to unlock it?"

She cocked her head and lifted her hand. "I suppose so. It would be terribly inconvenient for him, though."

Vee paced fervently. "These men will do anything for the shards, *which*," she waved toward the shard on the table, "obviously have some sort of power." Her voice dropped, and the urgency of her words sent a chill through the room. "We can't let them get their hands on the shards. Not until we understand what they're capable of. These men—whoever they are—they're willing to kill for them."

Juliette paled, her fingers twisting in her lap as her gaze darted between us. "But… why? Why me? I didn't know. I don't understand."

"Neither do we," Vee replied, her tone softening. "But we know enough to realize this isn't just some relic from the past. It's more powerful than any of us can comprehend. And if it falls into the wrong hands…" Her voice trailed off, leaving the unspoken threat hanging in the air like a dark cloud.

Juliette swallowed hard, the color draining from her face. "*Mon Dieu,*" she whispered, "what have I gotten myself into?"

Chrissy's hands shook as she set her wineglass down, rattling it on the table. "What have we *all* gotten ourselves into? And what should we do?" She looked at me pleadingly.

I had no answers. No reassurances. All I could do was to meet her gaze and try to keep my fear from showing.

Vee put her hands on her hips. "It's obvious. We need to move. And now."

Chrissy looked sick. She gave me a pleading look, then a glance at the shard. "Mitzy. Should we escape now with our shard, or try to rouse Mister Richard and get the other one?"

I picked up the shard and held it for a moment, everyone watching expectantly.

I hesitated, the weight of the shard heavy in my hand, aware we could be walking straight into a trap. But then the shard pulsed, filling me with a sense that it would all work out. Whatever I decided would be fine, as long as I held that shard. I felt my confidence grow and held Chrissy's gaze calmly.

"Monsieur Richard's house sounds good to me."

Chapter 9

We piled into the narrow white Volkswagen rental and off onto dark, winding country roads. I was about to turn right when Juliette's voice came from the back. "Not that way! It's faster to the left."

I swerved and Vee grabbed my arm. "Mitzy! Get in the backseat, and let Juliette drive, for goodness' sakes! We're in a rush."

We quickly changed places, and I became immediately uncomfortable. Chrissy squirmed between me and Gonzo, her elbows digging into my ribs every time we hit a bump. Gonzo, oblivious as usual, shifted his bulk, pushing her even further into my side.

"I swear, if I don't get some air soon, I'm going to suffocate," she muttered.

The small European car rattled as we took a corner, and I felt the edge of the seatbelt dig into my hip. "Yeah, this isn't exactly luxury," I said, trying to give Chrissy more space but failing miserably for the ten-minute drive.

Monsieur Richard was surprisingly warm and welcoming when we showed up at his house unannounced. He asked if we'd like to come in for a glass of port, but Juliette quickly explained that we needed the shard, and that criminals now knew about it and were after it.

For a man who looked eighty, he bounded surprisingly quickly to his old, rusted car, kicking up black smoke as it started, and leading us at a breakneck pace on more winding back roads. Nobody else was on the road, although the headlights caught sight of the occasional rabbit. As we rounded the last bend and went up the dirt road to the museum, another set of headlights passed us the other way. I glimpsed an Asian-looking woman driving an old truck as she passed.

"So odd, seeing someone else out at this time of night," Juliette said nonchalantly.

My neck pricked. "Quick! Get to the museum."

We parked and went sprinting up to the front door. My heart skipped a beat as I caught sight of the door—a jagged hole where a pane of glass had been.

"No," I whispered, dread pooling in my stomach.

We rushed forward, my breath catching in my throat. The door creaked open. A bitter breeze pushed it inward, and the empty spot on the shelf where the shard had been stood out in the dim light.

"It's gone," I croaked, my voice hollow.

Mind racing, I looked around for ideas, saw Chrissy, and passed her the shard. "Quiet, everyone! Chrissy, what does that truck we passed sound like? Where's it headed?"

Chrissy closed her eyes, her brow furrowing in concentration as she clutched the shard to her chest. For a moment, all was silent. Then her head tilted slightly, as if she were hearing something far away, something we couldn't perceive.

"It's an old truck," she murmured, her voice distant, as though she were somewhere else entirely. "I can hear the engine—clunky, uneven. It's heading east… toward Bordeaux." She opened her eyes, the faraway look still lingering as she handed the shard back to me.

I took a deep breath, the shard practically humming in my hand. "Let's go, people. No time to lose."

"What—?" Juliette half-asked.

I flashed her a smile. "We've gotta get that shard back before it's too late. Who knows what those thugs will do with it."

As we were loading up, I had another thought. "Gonzo, you sit in the middle. That way, Chrissy and I can both sit with our backs to the doors, turned slightly inward."

It worked! I felt much more space with the new seating arrangement, angled slightly inward, back nestled into the corner of the seat and the door.

Gonzo nodded approvingly as we took corners quickly. "What do you think, Mitzy? Think we'll catch this thief?"

I grinned. "Only one way to find out."

Admittedly, I was feeling brazen and reckless. I was intoxicated with the lucky breaks that just kept happening, and the brief moments of inspiration.

Was it luck, or just a general sort of blessing?

Sure, I could get scraped up. But I'd be fully healed the next day. As we twisted down more country roads as fast as Juliette dared tempt the gas pedal, I took a moment to imagine ourselves from a bird's-eye view and marveled at how much my life had changed in a mere week.

When we got to a crossroads, I asked Juliette to pull over and passed the shard to Chrissy. She rolled down the window and listened while we all held our breaths. She pointed to the road on the right. "That way. A few miles, I think."

Juliette revved the engine. Suddenly, Chrissy shrieked and dropped the shard as she clamped her hands over her ears. I unbuckled my seatbelt and clambered past Gonzo's girth to fish for the shard down between their feet.

The car swerved, and the shard flew out of my grasp. "Suck your gut in, Gonzo!" I shouted.

"Sorry, bro." He squirmed, trying to help.

I had just gotten my fingers back on it when the car screeched to a halt.

"Which way?" Juliette asked.

I fumbled the shard up to Chrissy's fingers and stayed at her feet, not wanting to move for fear of making any noise.

She pointed. "Take the second exit of the roundabout." Then she quickly handed the shard back to me.

As the car started bouncing over some loose rocks, I wiggled back over Gonzo to my seat, just in time to see the taillights of the truck in the distance.

Vee was calm. "Don't go so fast that they think you're chasing them."

Juliette slowed ever so slightly, but still fast enough to catch up. Soon we could all see more details of the vehicle, a beat-up brown truck from the sixties. Her voice quavered. "Now what?"

My mind raced. I clutched the shard and traced my fingers over the etchings as if looking for an answer. "I have no idea."

Vee shook her head impatiently. "Get up next to her in the other lane."

Juliette swerved into the other lane and up next to the truck. That's when we got a better look at the thief. A lithe woman of Asian descent was driving the old clunker, with the windows down. She stared at us for a brief moment, then put her hand outside the truck, palm lifted, and a blue pulse of energy emanated from her.

All at once, the car went completely dead. As the car slowed, Juliette freaked and jerked on the wheel. We swerved directly into the truck's rear, sending both vehicles careening into the bushes on the side of the road, where they came to a jarring stop. I found myself uncomfortably splayed across Gonzo's lap.

Before any of the rest of us could react, Vee was out the door and dashing toward the woman in the truck. The woman was still partly dazed but had just enough sense as Vee reached for her through the open window to scuttle back across the bench seat, out of her grasp.

Vee scrambled into the front window and grabbed for her, but the woman kicked her in the face.

"Ouch!" Vee grunted, then swiveled to the side and blocked as the woman kicked a few more times and got the far door open. She rolled out and started running for the woods.

But Vee was faster and took off behind her. Twenty feet from the truck, Vee tackled her, then grasped for a rear face lock, but the woman rolled to the side and gave another kick, this time hitting Vee in the side and sending her rolling, before regaining her footing.

The two women faced off, both in martial arts stances. Vee took a step in and jabbed with her left arm. The woman pulled back, then kicked with her right. Vee blocked, then lunged, her fist aimed at the woman's chest. The woman dodged, barely missing the strike, and retaliated with a sharp kick to Vee's side.

The impact sent her stumbling back, but Vee recovered quickly, her eyes narrowing as she circled her opponent.

They moved in tandem, each anticipating the other's next move. Vee feinted left, then darted forward, catching the woman off guard with a quick jab to the ribs. The woman gasped, her breath hitching, but she stayed on her feet, her stance wavering.

In a blur of motion, Vee grabbed her arm and twisted, sending her crashing to the ground with a thud that echoed through the still night. She didn't waste a second, pinning the woman's arm behind her back and locking her in place.

By the time the rest of us got enough sense to get out of the car and see what was going on, Vee was standing there calmly, the other woman held captive in an armlock.

Vee nodded her head toward the woman. "I'd claim the shard, but I don't want to touch that thing."

I shook my head, still stupefied by the accident, and walked up to the Asian woman. "Where is it?"

She stood silent. I repeated myself in French. Then, when she was still silent, I patted her pockets and pulled out the shard she'd been keeping there. Without thinking, I connected the two shards—they just so clearly belonged together.

Her eyes lit up, and I instantly regretted showing her my shard. But what was done was done. Plus, they vibrated as if happy to be together, and I felt an extra boost to my morale.

Was I going to be super ridiculously lucky now?

"Who are you with?" I asked.

She grew smug. "You mundanes know nothing."

"Mundanes?" I glanced around at the others. They gave me blank stares, and I turned back to her. "What do you mean?" She stood resolute, unblinking, and I faltered for a moment.

The shards continued to vibrate, and I felt my confidence return even amidst her silence. "You think you're so smart. We're figuring you out." I leaned in, close enough to see the flicker of uncertainty in her eyes. "We know you're after the shards. And we know you have people watching us."

She stared straight ahead, her expression stone cold, but I could see her jaw clenching.

"Why are they so important?" I pressed, my voice low. "What do they do?"

Silence.

I sighed, shaking my head. "You don't want to play it this way."

She scoffed. "I will tell you nothing."

I stared at her stubborn face, considering our options. Should we just tie her up and leave her? But then Gonzo's voice interrupted us.

He was staring at his phone, his face pale. "Guys, we're screwed. She hit us with an EMP."

"What?" I whipped around. "Are you serious?"

"Yeah." Gonzo's voice was tight. "Everything's fried. The phones. The car. My laptop." He held up his useless device. "We're completely cut off."

My stomach twisted. No phones meant no way to call for help. No GPS. No communication with Robert. And the car... we were stuck in the middle of Nowhere, France.

"Damn it," I muttered, running a hand through my hair.

Vee, always the calm one, said, "What about her truck? It's old. No electronics, right?"

Gonzo blinked, as if snapping out of his shock. "Right. It could still possibly work."

Chrissy climbed into the driver's seat and turned the key. The engine started right up. As I watched her, a thought popped into my head.

"Chrissy, mind coming over here?"

I took her aside and whispered, "Do you think you can listen to her thoughts holding one shard?"

"Don't know," she whispered back. "I just figured it out with the two."

"Here." I passed her both. "Come on."

We approached the woman again, still under Vee's hold. She stood stoic, like a cold, stone wall. I considered what would help Chrissy the most and decided I'd just start talking.

"So, we know you guys aren't with NASA, that much is for sure. But you *do* have resources to track us down. You tracked our phones. And our friend's credit card. And you obviously have people all over the world, because how else would you have gotten here so quickly?"

I leaned closer to her, narrowing my eyes. "You must have at least one of these shards," I spoke slowly, watching for any flicker of recognition. "I wonder. Were you a part of the group that stole the shard from the museum in Beijing?"

Her eyes flashed, just for a second, but I caught it.

"I thought so." My voice held steady, but my heart was racing. "You think you're the only one with a claim to these things? You think we're just a bunch of clueless kids, don't you?"

She clenched her jaw, her lips pressed into a tight line.

"Here's the thing," I continued, lowering my voice. "We've figured out how to use the shards. You and your people aren't the only ones who know how valuable they are. Did you know they give power to mundanes like us?"

Her expression flickered, and I felt a surge of confidence. She hadn't known. I decided to ask more direct questions.

"Where do you live?"

Silence. I waited for Chrissy to nudge me.

"What's the name of your organization?"

Again, I waited. When she nudged me, I continued.

"How many shards are still out there? ... Where are they? ... Where is your headquarters?"

Chrissy held the shards, her face tightening in concentration. Her breathing grew shallow, and I could see the strain on her features as she tuned into the woman's thoughts.

Finally, she pulled me aside and whispered, "At first it was working. She was thinking about tracking us. About her group. And about the shards. But now..." Her brow furrowed deeper and she let out a small, frustrated breath. "She's blocking me. She's deliberately thinking about... cooking. Rum cake."

I blinked. "Rum cake?"

Chrissy shook her head, handing the shards back to me. "It's a mental defense. She's using it to drown out her real thoughts. I can't break through."

"Damn." I stared at the woman, who met my gaze with a cold, smug smile. She knew exactly what she was doing. "Did you get anything good?"

"Yes. I'll tell you later. Lots of information. Good thing I know some French."

I turned to the group. "Well, what do we do with her?"

Juliette spoke up. "Take her to a police station. She is a thief, after all."

"Okay." I shrugged. "Where's the closest one?"

"Bordeaux, of course."

Gonzo went to the trunk of the rental car. "I'm getting my stuff."

The rest of us followed suit, throwing all of our luggage into the truck bed. There was only a single bench seat in the cab, so Juliette drove with Gonzo riding shotgun, and the rest of us piled into the back.

As we drove toward Bordeaux, I couldn't shake the feeling that something was off. The woman, who had been stone-faced and silent for most of the ride, now had a faint, smug smile playing at the corners of her mouth. It sent a chill down my spine.

"Why does she look so pleased with herself?" I muttered to Vee discretely.

She whispered into my ear, "I don't know, but I don't like it."

Then it hit me. "She doesn't need the shard to create an EMP. She could do it right now—fry every car on this road."

Vee gave me a hard look and a glance down at the shards in my hand. "What do we do?"

I swallowed hard, my mind racing. "We can't let her do it. If she hits us with another EMP on a busy road…"

I didn't finish the thought, but I didn't need to. The result of killing the electricity of surrounding vehicles in the middle of traffic could be catastrophic. But also dangerous for her, so she wouldn't just do it without a strategy in mind.

Vee leaned into my ear again. "We're out of options. The deeper we get into the city, the worse this could be. Come on, Mitzy. What's your double-luck telling you to do?"

I bit my lip. I didn't have an answer. The city was just ahead, the lights growing brighter, but all I could do was keep my eyes on the woman, who sat next to Vee on the truck bed, her expression unreadable. She hadn't moved. She hadn't spoken. But I could feel the tension radiating from her. She was waiting—waiting for her moment to strike.

"Juliette, how much farther?" I called up to her, my voice tight.

"Two minutes," she replied.

I held up the pulsing shards. They were working, I knew it. But what were they doing? And would it be enough?

Chapter 10

The police station loomed ahead in the city lights, its thick walls and barred windows giving it an air of fortitude and strength—except for how much of its power would rely on electricity. I gripped the shard, silently begging for a spark of inspiration, but nothing came. Just the slow and steady vibration, assuring me everything would work out in the end.

So, I decided not to panic, but to go with the flow. With twice the luck, it seemed like the right thing to do.

We parked the old truck in a mostly empty parking lot, streetlights flickering as they lit the area. Chrissy lowered the tailgate, and I began getting down when the captive exploded with a sudden burst of energy, kicked off the side of the truck, and flipped over, Vee's grip slipping and eyes widening in shock as the woman landed on her feet.

In two quick steps, she reached me and grabbed the shards in my hand. A blinding flash lit up the area, and the hum of electricity vanished for a good city block. Streetlights instantly popped and went out, and a sudden eerie silence fell, punctuated only by the distant sputter of dying engines and yells from inside the police station.

My legs buckled and before I knew it, I was tumbling off the tailgate onto the pavement. The shards slipped from my grasp as I hit, clattering across the parking lot as I lay there dazed and breathless. The woman lunged at me, her fingers clawing at my empty hands in the dark, her breath hot and wild.

"Help!" I called, scrambling to protect myself, but there was nothing in my hands for her to grasp.

Vee shot forward, launching herself into the air with a swift, precise kick. Her boot connected with the woman's chest, sending her flying back into the darkness. The woman tumbled, then took off running. Vee dashed after her, hot on her tail.

I frantically felt along the pavement, searching the area for the shards, eyes slowly adjusting to the pale moonlight. "Come on," I muttered, then saw them, separated, one under the tailgate and one by the rear tire. I snatched them up and took off after Vee, with no idea what I'd do to help, but hoping my luck would lend a hand.

A hundred yards away, there was a flash of blue and the lights popped out within a thirty-yard radius. I stumbled after them, straining to see them in the darkness. My lungs burned with each step, and my legs felt like lead. I pushed myself harder, but the distance between us stretched farther with every stride. I silently cursed my jiggling belly as I passed by confused pedestrians.

A few blocks down the road, I felt like my lungs were going to burst, and I stopped, hands on knees. Sweat dripped down my face.

Have I lost them?

I glanced up just in time to hear the pop of streetlights going out. I saw the buildings go dark a block down and to the right. I took a deep breath and staggered after them, wishing I were in better shape.

A couple of minutes later I rounded the corner down a deserted alley, only to see Vee duking it out with the woman in the dark. The woman was holding a metal garbage can lid as a shield as they circled each other. Vee moved with precision, her strikes fluid and powerful. Each time her foot connected with the garbage lid, it rang out like a gong. The woman scrambled to keep up with her relentless attacks.

The clang of metal echoed in the alley as Vee's boot struck, sending the woman staggering. In a swift motion, Vee followed through with a sharp punch to the chest, her expression one of fierce determination.

The woman went tumbling backward onto the street, the dented lid clattering as it fell at her side.

Vee strode up confidently while I stood there catching my breath, hands on my knees, panting and sweating profusely.

That's when a loud *clap* rang out through the alleyway, stunning us both.

My ears hurt so badly, I wondered if they were bleeding.

What had happened?

Vee wobbled, then regained her footing and looked around.

Two men were running toward her from the other side of the alley. It was hard to make them out in the dark, but they seemed athletic. When they came upon Vee, one clapped his hands and another deafening sound filled the alleyway.

I cringed. My teeth ground together as I worried about Vee. She was stunned, but she defended herself fairly well as the men came in and punched. In her dazed state, she couldn't dodge at her normal speed, but she kept herself from serious damage until a familiar blue crackle of electricity filled the air from one of her assailants and rippled into her body.

With a deep grunt, Vee fell limp to the street and lay lifeless.

I almost cried out, but I held my tongue. I had to act fast, but what could I do? So far, they didn't know I was there, and if I exposed myself, they could easily steal the shards. Despite all the luck I'd been experiencing, even I wasn't willing to push it. The woman had grabbed the shards even as I gripped them tightly. If three of them ganged up on me, I didn't think I'd stand a chance.

Suddenly, Bruno Marx's familiar voice filled the air.

"You're alive. Good. I was hoping I didn't overdo it." He was gloating. He kicked Vee, and I heard a crack.

Oh God, was that a rib?

"Uhhhn," she groaned.

"Veronica Velasquez. The only line of defense of your bumbling crew. So, does Stanley still have the fragment? Or I guess it would be two now, wouldn't it? Where is he?"

"Go to hell," she spat.

He kicked her again. "Don't be that way." Bruno walked around her, then kicked once more. "You don't *have* to die today. Just tell us where Stanley is. We just want the fragments.

What would you do with them, anyway? To you, they're just little magical baubles. To us... they can change the world."

Vee tried rolling away. He kicked her head, sending it flying back onto the cobblestones with a sickening thud.

Oh, God! Oh, God! Oh, God!

My heart pounded in my chest, my mind racing. But what could I do? If I ran out now, I'd lose the shards. I was frozen, torn between the urge to help and the icy grip of fear. *Come on!* I urged the shards. *Work!*

But nothing happened. Would these goons kill Vee?

In a moment of desperation, I said a prayer, *God, please don't let her die.*

I hadn't uttered a real prayer in about ten years, if I'm honest. But that was as real as it got. I was at my wits' end.

I don't know about God, but miraculously, the beating stopped, and the guys stepped back.

The woman stood up and quietly conferred with the two men. They gave Vee one last kick, then leaned over and rustled in her pockets, as if looking for something. Then, they stood, and the woman pointed back toward me, and instantly I knew they'd head back for the truck to get the shards.

My eyes darted around the alley, searching for cover, and I practically threw myself behind a rusted dumpster, thankful for the dark. I pressed myself into the shadows, inhaling the smell of rotten eggs, and praying they wouldn't spot me. They jogged down the alleyway and passed me, then rounded the corner of the still-dark streets toward the truck.

I breathed a sigh of relief, then scrambled to my feet and dashed over to Vee. She lay there, bruised and broken, but alive. Relief washed over me, followed by a surge of guilt. I hadn't saved her. But she was alive, and that mattered more than anything. I wasn't sure whether to thank the shards, God, or anything at all, but I felt thankful in that moment.

"Vee." I gently touched her shoulder. "I'm so sorry. I didn't know what to do. I couldn't save you."

She opened her eyes and blinked a few times. "What could you have done, Mitzy?"

"I don't know. Something!" I felt myself tearing up.

Vee's lips curled into a wry smile and I saw blood on her teeth. "Ha!" she scoffed, then coughed and winced. "Do you have the shards?"

"Yeah." I held them up.

"Then you did the only smart thing you could have. They have no idea where the shards are. I heard them—they're heading back to the truck."

"Damn!" I glanced back down the alleyway. "Our friends are in danger!"

Vee shook her head. "Nothing we can do. And you've gotta hide. Come on. Help me up."

I helped her to her feet, then lent her an arm. "This way." She pointed in the opposite direction from where the three assailants had just headed. She staggered along as I supported her, and we moved down the alley as quickly as possible.

We came out into streetlights and scattered pedestrians.

"We need a taxi," Vee said, eyes darting nervously. "Do you have cash?"

"Yeah. Some." I patted my pocket with my wallet.

Cash or not, there wasn't a taxi in sight. I got worried as we walked down the street that was getting busier the closer we got to the intersection. We were drawing attention.

Unwanted attention.

People stared at Vee, clearly interested in her beaten-up state.

"We need to get off the street," I warned.

"What are you gonna do about it?" Vee asked wryly.

I paused and pulled out the shards. "How does luck work?"

"How the hell should I know?" she scoffed.

I frowned at the shards. "This is ridiculous. We need to do something." I spotted a convenience store and nodded toward it. "Let's go ask in there."

We walked in. It was the French version of a corner store like you might see in any large city—a few groceries, a cheese selection (it *was* France), lighters and cigarettes, wine (some of which cost less than the bottled water, I might add), and some French, tourist knickknacks.

"Excuse me," I began in my still-poor French accent. "How would we call a taxi here?"

"Are you buying anything?" the man asked, arms folded.

"Um..." I glanced around, then turned to Vee. "Need anything?"

She rolled her eyes at me. I looked around, then smirked and pointed at the sign behind the guy. "How about a lottery ticket?"

I mean, why not?

He nodded and began ringing it up when I glimpsed the rack behind me. "And one of these first aid kits." After paying, I asked, "So, about the taxi?"

"Yes. Yes. One block over that way. You will find many taxis." He pointed to our right.

As we struggled down the street, Vee leaned heavily on my shoulder. I felt desperation well up in my gut. "Those people. All three of them had powers. We don't stand a chance against them head-on."

"That's true." Her pace picked up, although she held her side with one hand as she leaned on me with the other.

I scrunched my face, imagining the pain she was in. "I saw them rummaging through your pockets after they'd clobbered you. I assume they were searching you for the shards."

"Maybe, but..." Vee frowned and patted her pockets.

"What is it?" I asked.

"It wasn't just a search," Vee uttered slowly, her brow furrowing. She patted her pockets again, more urgently this time, like she knew something wasn't right. With a frown, she reached into her back pocket and pulled out a little swirly transparent disc, ultra-thin and about one and a half inches in diameter.

"What is that?" I asked. My eyes widened. "Is that a tracker?"

Quickly, Vee dropped it onto the sidewalk and crushed her heel into it. "Come on. Let's get out of here."

We hailed the first cab we could find and took it all the way across the river to the east side, a good twenty minutes away. When we crossed the bridge, I finally felt the tension dissipate as I realized we were safe. I asked the driver if there were any good bed-and-breakfasts in the area, and he found us one pretty quickly using his smartphone.

There were two rooms left. I checked us in with a kind old woman, paid cash, and asked to use her phone. I quickly left a message with our location on the encrypted voicemail service, helped Vee up the stairs to her room, went into mine and promptly took a shower.

After I was feeling fresh, I knocked on Vee's door. "I'm going to run to the corner store and get some wine, baguettes, and cheese. Want anything else?"

I heard her weary voice. "Charcuterie. And a new outfit." She chuckled.

"I'll get the food, anyway," I said. "Meet you back here in fifteen minutes."

When I returned with two bottles of wine, a purple t-shirt that said *Bordeaux*, and more food than we'd probably need, my heart choked up seeing Vee's battered body in her ruined clothing sitting on a couch. I tried not to wince as I waved brightly. "Good to see you up after all of that."

"I suppose. I look and feel like a truck ran over me."

I nodded as I opened the wine. Although her body was clean, her face was bruised and red from scrapes, and her shirt was torn and caked with blood. I poured each of us a glass and cut her some bread and cheese. With no shame, she took off her bloody shirt and tossed it on the floor, replacing it with the new one. I winced as I saw the extent of her battered body under her sports bra.

While we loosened up, Vee started reflecting on the fight. "We need to be more prepared. We can't take them on like this."

"Yeah. But what we really need to do is avoid them. We have to figure out who we should give these shards to. Or get off the radar completely somehow."

She nodded. "Paying cash and no cell phones seems like a start. But I think we're under-prepared as a general rule. We need training. I can't be the only one of us who can defend themselves."

I set my wineglass down. "Yeah. Look at us. You're a complete mess."

She pursed her lips in a smile. "Are you trying to insult me?"

"Ha!" I laughed, and she laughed with me. We let loose, then, and guffawed till the tension was completely gone. Tears rolled down my eyes, and every time Vee laughed, I laughed all the harder.

Finally, I wiped my eyes and leaned back in my armchair. "Do you think luck and God can coexist?"

"Sure. Why not?"

"I don't know. I guess I grew up with the idea that God basically controls everything, so that would mean there's no such thing as luck."

Vee shook her head. "God controls *everything*? What, like, genocides? Hurricanes? Viruses? That's putting some heavy blame on God for a lot of awful stuff."

"Yeah." I shook my head. "I always wondered about that. Maybe that's why I gave it all up. It makes no sense."

Vee shrugged. "Why do you ask?"

I gave her a sheepish look. "When I couldn't do anything to save you, I prayed. I haven't done that for real in ages."

She smiled gently. "Thanks, Mitzy."

I looked away awkwardly. "So, when should we get off our asses and make sure our friends are okay? What if they're prisoners?"

As if on cue, the door opened and in walked Gonzo, Chrissy, and Juliette, carrying all of our luggage.

I stood. "You found us!" The tension I'd been carrying all day finally lifted.

"Yep." Gonzo looked smug as he turned to Chrissy. "I told you they were okay. But damn, Vee. You look awful."

Vee shook her head. "This is where I'm supposed to say, 'You should see the other guy,' but, well…" She shrugged and took a sip of wine.

I gestured for them to sit. "So, how'd you get away from those thugs?"

"Oh, that wasn't so hard," Chrissy began. "We were already in the truck with the headlights on. We were going to go looking for you, but then we saw them, and they started chasing us. So, Juliette here, the speed demon, pulled a U-turn and got out of there lickety-split. Electricity-dude sent a bolt at us. Juliette swerved, and it missed us. They seemed pretty pissed, I will say."

"Yeah." Gonzo shook his head and sauntered to a nearby shelf to grab three more wineglasses. "The real dilemma came trying to decide what to do about you guys. We must've argued for half an hour before I thought to borrow someone's phone and check the voicemail." He smirked at Chrissy. "And look. Here they are."

Chrissy rolled her eyes. "And if they hadn't been okay? We'd have wasted all that time."

Gonzo shrugged and poured himself a glass. "Once again, all has ended well. But Mitzy, get those shards to Juliette!"

"Oh, yeah." I fumbled the shards out of my pocket and passed them to her.

She smiled and sang *Au Clair de la Lune*, a sweet and gentle song about borrowing a pen to write by the light of the moon. Instantly, the entire room was awash with gentle, healing energy, and we all relaxed. Warmth and vibrancy flooded my senses, and I felt the exhaustion of the day melt away.

Vee gave a contented groan, "Ohhhh, yeah. Thank you, Juliette." Her bruises and scrapes faded, slowly dissolving into nothing.

Juliette sang brightly, holding the two shards and rocking back and forth with a spark of joy in her eyes. I realized then how thankful I was to have her with us, despite having yanked her from her home unexpectedly.

Nobody wanted to interrupt the song, but when it ended and Vee seemed happier, Gonzo said, "So, are there enough beds for all of us?"

"Yeah." I nodded. "Although Chrissy and Vee will have to share a queen."

"No problem," Chrissy said. "So, you got beat up. What happened exactly?"

Vee scowled. "It was an ambush. I could fight one of them pretty well, but two more joined, including Mr. Electricity. They all had powers. It wasn't a fair fight."

"Bruno Marx," I said. "At least, that was the name on his ID. Not sure why we haven't seen Barry yet, but I bet he's somewhere around here, too."

I turned to Chrissy. "So, what did you hear when we grilled that woman?"

Chrissy frowned. "It wasn't all clear, you can imagine. I just found out I can do this today, for goodness' sakes. I only got bits and pieces. But let's see... She lives here, in Bordeaux, but travels the world. There are lots of them in their organization. I mean, lots. I have no idea. But thousands and thousands? I didn't get the name of their organization, but she kind of thinks of them as the... non-mundane police, maybe. I don't know. It's so hard. She also thought a lot in French, which made it murky."

We sat patiently sipping our wine as she continued. "I don't know how many shards they have. Two maybe. Or three? And I think Robert was right about there being six total."

"What about the aliens?" Gonzo asked. "What did she think about that?"

Chrissy shrugged. "I don't know. Sorry."

Gonzo sighed, slumping back in his chair. "Great, so we're up against a secret magic police force, and they don't even have the decency to be aliens? I feel cheated."

She lit up. "She did have a flit of a thought about Chile when you asked her about other shards out there. I'm pretty sure about that."

"Chile." I nodded appreciatively, then reached for my phone, only to remember it was gone. "Let's do some digging on Chile. Anything regarding shards, or unusual news. And we need to get some new phones."

"Yeah, and a new computer." Gonzo shook his head. "I have to figure out how to write to my boss. I'll get fired if I don't explain myself as soon as possible."

"And then what?" Vee asked. "Head to Chile? Are we done in France?"

I glanced at Juliette. She was staring into the distance with a furrowed brow. "What are you thinking?" I asked.

She glanced at me, then fiddled with her hands absently. "Oh, I just… how to say? Can I return home safely to my sweeties? Is my life in danger?"

We all sat like fools, then, realizing how we'd uprooted this innocent woman from her home and put her life at risk, with nothing to give her in return.

"Um…" Gonzo fiddled with a napkin awkwardly.

Vee was stone-faced. "You probably shouldn't go back."

Chrissy put her hand on Juliette's. "Join us. We don't know what we're doing. But we're absolutely on a path of incredible discovery."

Juliette looked into Chrissy's eyes. "No, thank you. This… danger… is not for me."

"It's not for any of us," Vee said. "But we've been thrown into it. Do you seriously think, if those guys found you, they'd just let you be? Their group tried to kill Mitzy. Then, they beat me brutally, and I'm sure they left me alive just to track me back to you and the shards. I don't think they want any of us alive, to be honest. I get the impression they want any trace of their existence gone."

I gulped. Somehow, before Vee had said that, I'd figured I would just go home after getting rid of the shards. But if she was right... maybe I would never be safe.

A single tear ran down Juliette's face. "I packed nothing. And I'm not ready. I'm not..."

She gave a little sob, and Chrissy put her hand on her shoulder. "We'll work together. We'll all take care of each other. Right, guys?"

"Yeah." "Yes." "Of course."

Juliette sighed. "You are very sweet. I thank you."

There was a moment of awkward silence.

"So..." I said, "I guess we head to Chile on this fleeting idea? I don't think we can use Robert's credit card anymore, so we'll have to figure that out."

Chrissy lifted her hand toward me. "Makes sense to me. You're lucky. Let's just keep rolling with your inclinations."

I shook my head. "I don't know. It sure didn't help with a lot of stuff today. We nearly got killed. Vee got the crap beat out of her. And now we're on the run again. How's that lucky?"

She shrugged. "We have two shards, which are a really big deal to really powerful dudes. We're safe. And we have ideas for what to do next. Not bad for bumbling through all of this."

I looked at Vee. She was quite relaxed with wine by then and just lifted a hand. "Whatever the group thinks."

I looked at Gonzo. He seemed disturbed. "What is it?" I asked.

He sighed, running a hand through his hair. "I think... I need to quit my job," he said, the words heavy with finality. He looked down at his hands, as if the decision was still sinking in. "I can't do all of this and that at the same time." He sighed. "Yep. I'm quitting." He walked to the front telephone and made a phone call. Three minutes later, he returned with a grin.

I smiled at him. "Feel good?"

"Yeah." He bobbed his head. "Feels great! Twenty pounds lighter." He glanced at his belly. "Not literally, of course." He chuckled.

I bit my lip. "Okay. Tomorrow, first thing, let's head to Paris. When we get there, we can keep a low profile and get proper smartphones and a laptop for Gonzo to keep working on getting that software running to help translate the shard."

"Alright!" Gonzo said. "Man. This is great. I'm gonna have way more fun now. I should've quit before we got on the plane. Chile, here we come!"

I smiled. I decided I wasn't going to worry. We now had a plan, and we were going to make it happen. I just hoped the worst of the harm was behind us.

But as Juliette passed me the two shards, I felt a jolt of energy pulse through me, causing my stomach to churn and my head to grow light. It was just for a moment, but my whole body tingled afterward, as if every cell was being altered.

"What is it?" Chrissy asked, concerned.

"Nothing. Just... noticing how they're more impactful when together."

"Are you sure?" She leaned toward me, studying my face. There was a moment of awkward silence as everyone's eyes turned to me.

"It's nothing." I pocketed the shards. "We just need to move fast."

But a lurking suspicion began to form in my mind about the shards. Could they be fully trusted? What would happen if we held them for too long? Part of me wanted to find out, and part of me wanted to be as far away from them as possible.

Chapter 11

Fluorescent lights buzzed overhead at the corner store as Juliette and I wandered the aisles, picking out jelly, cheeses, croissants, and coffee, when I spotted the lottery scanner. At first, I hesitated, then fed my ticket into the machine. It gave a somewhat ambiguous message: "Contact the National Lottery Claims Department."

Juliette's eyes were glowing. "Mitzy. You have won!"

"How much?" I stared at the ticket. It wasn't a perfect match of numbers, so it wouldn't be millions.

She shrugged. "*Je ne sais pas.* But you must go there today, yes? And let us hope they pay you quickly!"

After breakfast, the two of us took a taxi to the Lottery Claims Department in downtown Bordeaux. We'd have driven the old truck, but it was conspicuous, and we were keeping it hidden in an alley.

When I showed up with the ticket, the people at the department became all smiles and sat us in a room with white leather couches and gave us champagne to sip, along with lots of literature on real estate, luxury cars, and fancy clothing. But in the end, we didn't win enough for all of that, only 40,000 euros.

I'm sure any country is like this, but collecting cash doesn't just happen. Put a name on the ticket, show ID, pay taxes, it's a check, not cash, and they don't pay right away. It usually takes a couple of days at the bare minimum.

Oh, and did I mention the name of the winner becomes public information?

I looked at the winning ticket and almost crumpled it up. We were so close to having the cash we needed to sustain us, yet it felt so far. If I gave them my name, we'd surely be flagged again. Plus, what good would a check in euros do for me? I had nowhere to deposit it.

"Are you okay, Mitzy?" Juliette asked.

Slowly, my lips twisted into a smirk. "How do you feel about winning the lottery?"

So, that's how *Juliette* won the lottery. It didn't change the fact that we couldn't leave right away. We took a taxi back to our friends and broke the news. Everyone was excited, but Gonzo got us thinking.

"Look guys. It's great that we won all that money, but we need new phones and a computer today. And we can't use credit cards. Do we have enough cash?"

"Can they trace using bank cards?" Chrissy asked.

I thought about it. "I imagine so. But I have an idea. If we all go to bank machines downtown and withdraw as much as our banks allow, then get out of that neighborhood, all they'll know is we're still in Bordeaux. And they already know we're here. I think it'll be okay. But it's one and done. One day only. And assume we need to leave the area right away."

Everyone liked that idea, so we found a block with lots of banks and withdrew what we could. Each of us had limits of $1,000 daily withdrawals, but Gonzo had had the foresight to call his bank and ask for it to be upped to $5,000 for the day. So, we had enough for phones and a laptop.

All three of the ladies wanted iPhones, so we went to the Apple store. It was in a four-story marble stone building, with curved corners and a first floor with arched doorways and windows. The building looked like something out of the 1800s with marble pillars, arched windows, so the sleek, high-tech gadgets inside felt jarring, like we'd stepped into two different worlds.

The store was in an open area next to a fountain, a sculpture, and an outdoor café in the heart of the pedestrian area of Bordeaux, where the streets are cobblestoned for miles in every direction and thousands of people constantly mill about. While much of Bordeaux is a weave of tight streets, the wide-open nature of the plaza layout made me feel highly conspicuous. Before, it had felt like we could blend into any crowd, but with all the vantage points here, the area didn't feel secure.

I held the connected shards in my pocket. "Let's be quick about this," I told Gonzo. "You help the ladies buy phones. I'll keep watch."

He furrowed his brow. "You think they'll be here?"

I sighed. "They used an EMP. They know our phones are fried, and we just pulled out a bunch of cash. This is where I'd look for us, if I were them."

Gonzo swallowed. "We'll make it quick."

I stood guard outside, watching the streets like a hawk. Every person wearing black caught my eye, but none of them seemed dangerous. And then—there he was. A man from the night before.

Super clap.

I tensed and turned to look in the window to see the four of them coming toward the entrance.

"Just in time." I pointed as they emerged. "He just showed up, but he hasn't seen us yet."

Vee's face darkened, eyes narrowing. "Damn." She scowled as she searched left and right. A couple of tracks ran through the square, with five-car mini-trains rolling through every few minutes. Just then, a train approached.

"Come on!" I called.

We dashed out of the building and jogged alongside the train, keeping the man out of sight. Gonzo stumbled, and I grabbed his arm, yanking him along.

Thankfully, the train stop was only a thirty-second jog, and we boarded the train, sticking to seats on the opposite side from the man in black. Heart beating wildly, I watched him from my seat. I clutched the shards and my hand vibrated, as if I were straining it. I felt a headache coming on and blinked it away. Every second felt like an eternity as I waited for him to look our way. But he didn't look, and the train started moving again. I exhaled in relief and released the shards. The headache disappeared a few moments later.

Juliette was pale. "This is terrible. How can we stay here for two or three days?"

I pulled the connected shards out. "These are keeping us one step ahead of them. I'm even luckier than before, now that there are two. I can feel it."

Vee gave me a stern look. "You keep holding those, Mitzy. And anything you say goes. You say hop, we say how high." She made eye contact with the other three, one at a time. "Our lives are in your hands."

I nodded in agreement, but sitting there on the train, my stomach clenched. How could *I* be responsible for all of them? And what was with the new headache side effects when I used both shards?

I didn't mention it. Not yet. I didn't want to worry them. And they'd each had much worse side effects from holding a single shard. I shouldn't have been surprised to have *some* reaction with two. Right?

Juliette sat next to me, staring out the window, then said quietly, "Yesterday my life was serene, surrounded by my vines. This… chaos… I don't know how you are so calm, Mitzy."

I smiled at her, happy for the break from my thoughts. "I don't know. You seem to have it together. Seeing you handle yourself so well gives *me* extra confidence."

She shook her head. "I may act like I have everything together, but it's exhausting. All of this… it is terrifying. I miss how my life was simple before you showed up."

I squirmed. "Sorry," I said, feeling stupid.

She sighed and turned to me. "There was a time when I thought I could handle anything—until my sister died. And I learned then that some things are out of our control." A single tear rolled down her cheek, and I turned away. "I decided, then, to do only the things that make me happy. To build a life that is full of many little joys. But now, how can I do that when we are facing so much uncertainty and magical villains?"

"I... I don't know." I looked into her troubled eyes. "But at least," I patted her arm, "at least we're in this together."

She gave me a soft smile, then wiped her eyes and looked back through the window. It broke my heart, seeing her struggle. But I had no other words for her, so I refocused on the next task at hand.

We got off the mini-train at the geek store, where Gonzo and I not only got proper smartphones, he got a loaded laptop, and we also got some surveillance cameras with software on our phones that would alert us to any movement. As long as we had internet access, we couldn't be surprised.

Chrissy insisted on stopping at the art store down the street to get some paper, paints, and supplies, including a small easel. "Don't you just want to paint everything?" she insisted. I couldn't argue with that, so we just let her do it. I bought a bullet pen for myself, one that could slide in and out of my pocket easily.

Since we were going to stay in Bordeaux for a couple of days, I asked Juliette to take us to the library. The library towered above us, its glass walls shimmering in the sunlight. I craned my neck, taking in the sleek curves of the building. It was a striking contrast to the ancient city around it. The sun reflected the old historical buildings on the face of the new. An impressive design, as if to say, "Yes, it's new, but it can still hold some pretty awesome history."

Once inside, I beelined it to the antiquities section. I found a few books on the eras of Egyptian history that felt relevant—from the New Kingdom to the Third Intermediate Period. While Juliette checked them out, I asked the librarian if there was another library that might have more resources to help us with this topic.

"You may want to try the Library Museum of Aquitaine," he said.

We headed there next, and the stone building with sculpted sides and ornate pillars struck me as a proper building for old things. Inside, it was easy to get lost among the books and the exhibits. The others ended up touring the displays of ship models, ancient firearms, and French historical items of interest, while I found an interesting section on Ancient Egypt.

Soon enough, I was at a table delving into the books and entering the world of the Ramses pharaohs. Their era was during a change of empires. Ranging from the 18th to 20th dynasties, Egypt grew to a massive force, then dwindled again. I was so entrenched in the history that a sudden giggling surprised me.

Chrissy was sitting across from me, making funny faces.

"How long have you been sitting there?" I asked.

"A long time." She grinned. "So, what's got you so engrossed?"

I lit up. "What an incredible time of history! And trying to imagine these shards coming into existence—or at least appearing at this time—is quite extraordinary."

"Explain." She leaned forward eagerly.

I pointed at a picture of a mummified pharaoh. "Ramses III was the last great pharaoh of Egypt, from 1186 to 1155 BC. He was a warrior pharaoh and held off many invasions while most civilizations declined around them. Now, get this."

I pointed to another open book at the table. "Near the end of his reign, Hekla III erupted in Iceland, in 1159 BC, and the ash and ongoing emissions lasted twenty years! Sometime around there, Ramessesnakht was the high priest. Who knows if he was around during Ramses III, but he *was* the high priest from Ramses IV till IX. Robert thinks that's the match of the magic runes on the shards. So, here's the thing… did the shards have something to do with the volcano? Or the chaos that ensued?"

"What chaos?" Chrissy was skimming the page I'd passed to her.

"With all that active ash filling the skies, the empire dwindled. Food was scarce. The tree rings from that time show that their growth slowed massively until 1140 BC. So, of course, there was a major economic decline. Ramses III was murdered by one of his sons and his second wife. His body showed signs of a great struggle. We can see he lost his big toe from an axe."

"Wow."

"But that's not the best of it. Look here." I presented a picture of the mummy. "His body was buried with six... magical... stones."

"What!?" Chrissy turned the book toward her and read the words for herself. She flipped the book over to the cover and back again.

"Yeah," I said. "That's coming from some mainstream academic book. This is getting really interesting really quickly."

"So... then what happened?" Chrissy asked.

"Hard to tell. The next pharaohs didn't last long. Ramses IV did a lot of major building and mining, and it seems like Ramessesnakht was heavily involved in overseeing the entire operation. But the fourth Ramses only reigned six years. Ramses V had to defend against a lot of outside warring and only ruled for four years. Ramses VI held things off better, but by then Egypt was shrinking."

Chrissy was staring wide-eyed at the image of the six stones. "And you think this is all related to the shards?"

"Yes." I pointed at a page. "And that's not the craziest of it. During the reign of Ramses IV, it is said that Ramessesnakht prophesied about significant things to come, and that it is something that has been translated."

"What does it say?" Chrissy's voice was almost a whisper.

"I don't know." I sat back and shook my head. "I can't find it."

She gripped the table. "No! We have to find that."

"Yeah." Inspired, I pulled out my new phone and messaged Robert. *Do you know anything about the prophecy of Ramessesnakht? Can't find it in the books here in the library.*

"So, now what?" Chrissy asked.

"Keep digging," I replied, and turned back to the book.

She nodded. "Good thing you like history."

I chuckled and flipped the page. As I skimmed the contents, I asked casually, "Have you done any digging on Chile?"

"Actually, yes."

I paused and looked up. She pointed at her phone. "It wasn't hard to find, actually. Once you type in supernatural or unusual occurrences and Chile together, there have been quite a few things over the last week in greater Santiago."

"Like what?"

"Well... someone apparently rescued a child trapped down a deep pit."

"How is that weird?"

"They don't know how he got out. He didn't use ropes or a ladder." She raised an eyebrow, daring me to explain it.

"Oh. That's curious. But not so crazy." I cocked my head. "What else?"

"Something about a bunch of chickens. Everybody thought they were killed by coyotes, but they all appeared again the next day. And a few other things like that. But never anything concrete, and no details on who was involved. Not even with the child rescue story."

I shook my head. "Seems minor. I wonder why that woman thought about Chile when I asked her about other shards still out there?"

Our discussion was interrupted by Gonzo, who had just walked up. "Hey guys, it's wine-o'clock. Time to visit a vineyard."

I glanced at the clock. Three-thirty. I raised my eyebrows. "Really, Gonzo?"

"Well," Gonzo said, a grin spreading across his face. "If we're stuck in Bordeaux for a couple of days, may as well make the most of it."

I chuckled. That sounded like a great idea to me as well. "Let's drop off these books and change."

We regrouped and headed out of the library, but I realized I'd left my new bullet pen on the table. "Wait, guys. Be right back."

I walked over to the table to get my pen, and when I returned, everyone was wide-eyed and quiet. "What? What happened?"

Vee's voice was tight. "We saw him." She gestured out the door. "One of the guys who beat me up. He just drove by in a black car, real slow." The tension in the air grew. She shook her head. "If you hadn't asked us to wait, we'd have walked right out the door in front of him."

My mind raced. I patted my pocket. I had both shards. Did my luck just save us all again? In some ways, I felt relieved. It meant I didn't have to be directly holding the shards for them to be effective. But it was still scary to think the people in black were that hot on our trail.

"How do you think they know we're out this way?" I asked.

Vee glanced at Juliette. "Maybe they're onto you. You checked out books at the main library. Maybe they went there first, and they're planning to scope out this one, assuming we'll be here. Come on. We've got to get out of here. Now."

Gonzo was grimacing at me. "Do you think they can somehow track the shards?"

I rubbed my fingers along the shards in my pocket. "No. I don't think so. If they could do that, they would have found us easily over the last week. I think they're just persistent."

"So, just a recap," he said thoughtfully. "The magic space rocks saved us, *again*, because you forgot your pen. I swear, Mitzy, if the fate of the world ever depends on you remembering where you put your keys, we're all screwed."

I chuckled, but didn't let go of the shards as I led the way out the door. As if by some miracle, a taxi van rounded the corner just as we stepped outside, large enough for the five of us. We piled in and took a circuitous route back to our lodging.

On the way, I asked the driver the best mode of transportation for us to get to Saint-Émilion, which was where Gonzo wanted to go. At first, he said there was no easy way, but then I flashed some money at him, and he agreed to take the rest of the afternoon off and be our personal driver for 300 euros.

As we drove, I turned to Juliette. "Can you try to convince the lottery office to release the winnings tomorrow? We really need to get out of here."

She shrunk down a little. "How could I do that?"

"Um…" I glanced at Gonzo.

He lit up. "Tell them you have to visit your dying sister in Paris, and it's urgent that we go there in the morning."

She shook her head. "Deception?"

"Do you have a better idea?" Gonzo asked.

"No." She sighed. "I can do this thing. But I hate it."

She dialed the lottery office and was soon speaking with them in French so quickly I couldn't follow. When she hung up, we gave her expectant looks.

"Well?" Chrissy asked.

"Yes. We can go to Paris tomorrow morning. There is a lottery office there. We can pick up the winnings in two days' time."

"Ah." I scratched my head. "I suppose that's better, anyway."

As the cityscape faded into vineyards and open fields, I felt the tension slowly drain from my body. The weight on my chest lightened, and I let out a breath I hadn't realized I was holding.

The taxi wound through endless rows of grapevines, their green leaves shimmering in the afternoon sun. As we climbed the hill, a towering stone church came into view, perched at the top like a sentinel overlooking the sprawling valley below. "We are here," the driver told us.

We piled out of the van and marveled at the majestic building jutting out of the countryside. The wide stone steps led up to massive wooden doors, flung open as if beckoning us inside. Something about the quiet grandeur of the place made me want to lose myself in its history. Instinctively, we walked up the stone steps, over the courtyard, and into the massive gothic building.

My eyes were drawn up to the stained-glass windows by the ceiling. The ceiling boasted dramatic arches and made me want to keep looking up. Toward God, I realized.

I'd never studied architecture, but as I gazed up at the soaring arches and intricate stone carvings, something clicked. This place wasn't just a building, it was a conduit, pulling your eyes and soul upward toward the heavens. These buildings were created during a time when people didn't have Bibles, so this was their connection to the divine. This place. No wonder they made it tall, with spires. It all pointed upward.

I gazed up at the stained glass, the light casting colorful patterns across the stone floor. "What do *you* think of me being lucky?" I whispered under my breath, unsure if I was talking to God, the universe, or just myself. "Does it make prayer redundant?"

Of course, there was no answer to the question. I wandered around quietly, lost in thought. Although I was immersed, I also struggled, thinking how the Bible I knew was too stiff and formal to have space for sci-fi objects with magic powers. I noticed an open courtyard to the right and strolled through the opening, only to stop rigid, eyes wide, mouth agape.

"What the hell is that?" I wondered aloud.

A mural stretched across the entire courtyard wall, an explosion of color and chaos. Figures twisted and clashed, monsters with too many teeth, men on horseback wielding swords of fire—it felt like stepping into a fever dream.

There was a Jesus-like dude holding a scroll, and then monsters with lots of teeth, four horsemen, one of whom was definitely Death (I recognized that much), and then as I walked along, there was Jesus again riding a horse with fire coming out of his eyes and a sword out of his mouth. I kept walking.

There was a lamb who seemed important, uplifted and shining with light next to what I could only imagine was Mother Mary. Nearby was an evil-looking woman, who looked pretty but was veiled in shadows and ominous. And it just kept going. Skeleton-demons with tiaras and unicorn horns, and next to them leopards with similar horns. One figure—a bare-chested woman holding a goblet overflowing with money—caught my eye. There was something unsettling in her look, like she knew a secret no one else did. And then there was a yellow ladder going up to wild tendrils and a guy with a super long horn. Cricket-looking tanks. Rectangular warriors. It was wild. Wacky, even.

I stood there, mouth agape, wondering whose outlandish idea it was to put a mural like that on an ancient church, when a small tour group came in. The guide was speaking English to nine folks following along.

"This is a mural taken from the Book of Revelation, also known as the Apocalypse. As you can see from the imagery, it is quite the vivid vision that Saint John had…"

I stared at the mural, my mind struggling to reconcile the images with anything I'd ever read in the Bible. "This is… all from the Bible?" I asked the guide, my voice tinged with disbelief.

"Yes, sir. You can read it for yourself," he said before turning back to the tour group.

I wracked my brain, trying to remember what little I remembered. The Bible, to me, had always seemed stuffy and detached from reality. But this? This was something else entirely. It was raw, visceral, like stepping into someone's most outlandish nightmare. I'd always thought the Bible was boring, and this was anything but that.

I couldn't help but look at the lamb again. Amidst all the craziness, its simplicity was stark and beautiful. What was up with that? All the crazy imagery, and we're talking beasts with thousands of eyes kind of crazy, and then that.

The group was moving along, but I just had to know. "Excuse me," I said. "What's with that lamb? Doesn't that represent Jesus or something?"

The guide shrugged. "I don't know what's with most of this, to be honest, but yes, everyone agrees the lamb is Jesus." He turned back to the group. "And as we move along, you'll see the trumpets being blown…"

I tossed that idea around in my head. The only story of a lamb I remembered from the Bible was Passover, where people had to sacrifice lambs in Moses' day in order to not have their firstborn killed by the Angel of Death. Something about the lamb seemed important to me, but I couldn't put my finger on it. I wondered if perhaps I should crack open a Bible.

That Passover story *did* happen mere decades before the Prophecy of Ramessesnakht, right in Egypt with Ramses III. Was it a coincidence? Was Moses confronted with the power of the shards?

I stood quietly, contemplating, when Robert called.

"Professor. How's it going?" I asked.

"Fine, fine. Stanley. I have news."

"Do tell." I walked out of the covered courtyard to leave the sanctity of the space and was greeted by a breathtaking view of the town below. Stone houses clung to the hillside, their red-tiled roofs glowing in the afternoon sun. It dropped dramatically down from the backside of the church building, overlooking a glorious courtyard with outdoor dining and all sorts of shops and homes.

Robert was excited. "I tracked down the name of a publication that has the Prophecy of Ramessesnakht. It's called *Mystic Secrets of Egypt: Prophecies, Magic, and Secret Societies*. However…" He paused dramatically. "Not a single copy is available."

"What?" I frowned into the phone.

"You heard me, Stanley. Every… single… copy. I can't check it out from any library. I can't purchase it online. It's like the entire book has been removed from society. Someone doesn't want this knowledge getting out."

"You can't find it anywhere?" I scratched my head.

"I do believe there is one copy that cannot be removed."

"Where?"

"The Library of Congress, in Washington, DC. Unless someone somehow got in and stole it, there will be a copy there."

"Well then. I know where we're headed next," I said.

"Yes. Good. Good. We need to see that book. What other answers to our riddle will we find in it? I can only hope it's a wealth of information. But Stanley, consider this: How much effort would it take to remove a book like that from *everywhere*?" He paused, to let it sink in. "That's who we're dealing with, here. Be cautious."

I swallowed hard, Robert's words hitting me. A shiver ran down my spine. "I will. I guess we're not going to Chile, then."

"Chile? Why there?"

"Oh, I forgot to tell you, we interrogated one of those thugs, and holding both shards, Chrissy can now hear thoughts, so when I asked where other shards were, the woman thought of Chile."

"Ah. Well then, this isn't so simple a decision, is it?"

"What do you mean? We have no idea where in Chile we'd go. It's a huge country."

"Yes, Stanley, but you're lucky. And from what we can tell, they're not. Which means you may very well find it, where they won't."

I gulped. "I want to get *away* from those goons. And you're saying I should go straight toward them?"

"Well, when you put it that way, no." Robert paused. "But don't discard Chile just yet. *I* can always fly to Washington."

"Okay. Thanks," I said.

"Don't mention it. Keep me updated."

When I caught up with the others and told them Robert's news, they buzzed with excitement. But before we could start planning our next move, Gonzo's eyes lit up.

"We need to try some wines," he said, grinning. "We can save the world tomorrow."

The narrow cobblestone streets had wine stores everywhere, or *caves*, as the French called them, each offering free wine tastings of local wines. So, we picked one at random and the nice woman lined up twelve bottles.

"These are all 90% Merlot, 10% Cabernet Sauvignon, right from here in Saint-Émilion."

Chrissy was beaming with delight. With every wine we tried, she described its nuances perfectly—this one had more vanilla, this one blackberry notes, the next, more red fruit. Laughter filled the small wine shop as we sampled bottle after bottle, the rich flavors dancing on our tongues. By the time we left, arms full of wine bottles, the weight of the day had finally begun to lift. We made our way to one of the outdoor restaurants and hunkered down for a delicious meal on the cobblestones.

And although we enjoyed the evening together, carefree, a knot of anxiety sat heavy in my stomach. The thought of facing the thugs again at the train station gnawed at me, refusing to let me relax. Everyone was counting on me, and the weight of it felt suffocating. Barring when Vee was getting beaten the day before, I hadn't prayed in years, but as the anxiety swelled in my chest, I whispered a quiet plea.

Just in case.

Chapter 12

Chrissy's fingers drummed on her leg, her eyes darting between me and the window as the taxi jostled down the narrow streets to the train station. I tried to ignore her, but in the end, I had to say something.

"I've got both shards," I said, holding them up.

She glanced down at her hands fidgeting in her lap. "Thanks, Mitzy."

As we stepped out of the taxi, I could sense them all close behind me. Their footsteps echoed mine, and a knot of awkwardness tightened my chest. Nobody usually follows me anywhere. Ditzy Mitzy. That's the nickname some of my college buddies gave me. But now, our lives depended on these shards doing their luck thing through me, and I felt the weight of it.

Even so, in some ways, it felt good. It'd been a long time since anyone truly counted on me for anything.

I went to the booth to buy tickets with cash rather than at a kiosk. No way we were going to let them trace us buying tickets to Paris.

I checked the time. "We have twenty minutes. Let's grab a croissant and a coffee at that café." I pointed and everyone followed like ducklings sticking to their mother, or maybe more like slinky coils, never leaving much space.

We ordered, then sat at exactly the same time at a small round table in the corner. The silence between us felt tight, like we were holding our breath, waiting for the next move. I was feeling a little claustrophobic. But then Bruno Marx strode past, eyes scanning the crowds of people. He didn't see us at the café but kept going to the platform.

Chrissy grabbed my arm. "Now what? He'll spot us getting on the train."

"I don't know." My stomach did a flip-flop. On the one hand, it felt great knowing I was lucky, and that was most likely protecting all my friends. But on the other hand, I had no idea what to do to keep us safe.

"Ten minutes," Vee said, looking at a clock. "Train's leaving soon. What's the plan, Mitzy?"

I scowled. "I don't know!" I tried not to raise my voice. "What am I supposed to do? Do you think I know how this works? It just does. I'm not any smarter, and I don't have any clue what's going to work. I have *no* control over it. At all!"

Vee, Chrissy, and Juliette flinched, eyes widening at my outburst. They exchanged uneasy glances.

Gonzo leaned in, his hand resting on my arm, steady and reassuring. "Hey, no worries, Mitzy." His voice was calm. "Just go with your gut. We'll tag along. Won't we, guys? No pressure."

I looked at him and sighed. "Okay. Go with my gut." I glanced in the direction Bruno had gone. "My gut tells me to get as far away from here as possible and bury those shards."

Gonzo smirked at me. "But...?"

I smiled. "But… since we're going to *Paris* today, we have a train to catch. Come on. Let's go."

I stood, and everyone stood with me. I held the shards tightly in my pocket and strode out the door to the ticketing area. My hand was throbbing, and I felt the beginnings of a headache set in, but I ignored it.

As soon as we stepped into the open area, a large group of Japanese tourists came walking into the train station, chattering away. We fell in amongst them and walked toward the platform. My heart raced with every step, the weight of the shards in my pocket a constant reminder of what was at stake.

I glimpsed one of the guys who'd beaten up Vee and ducked my head a bit to hide with the Japanese group. Gonzo followed suit. We walked along with the group all the way till they boarded the bullet train. We slid into our seats, sinking low, trying to make ourselves invisible. My neck was tight, and my eyes darted nervously until, a few minutes later, the train took off for Paris.

Gonzo grinned widely, eyes twinkling with amusement.

"What?" I said.

"Nothing." He nonchalantly opened his laptop. "Just sayin'. If this were D&D, we'd have gotten, like, triple XP for that stealth check."

Halfway to Paris, I got a call from Robert.

"Professor, what's up?"

There was silence on the other end of the line for a moment, and my heart fluttered. "Robert? Is everything okay?"

"Yes, yes." He cleared his throat. "There's something I've been meaning to tell you."

My eyes widened. "Of course. Please. Do tell." What secrets was he hiding that he'd finally reveal? Gonzo instinctively turned from his laptop to watch my face.

Robert sighed. "I... let's just say I have something I should let you know about."

"And?" I was on pins and needles.

"And... here's what I'd like you to do. When you get to Paris, there's a cozy bed-and-breakfast tucked down a quiet street half a block from an English pub called The Purple Unicorn. Go check in there and have your dinner at the pub. When you're done, call me, and we can chat."

When I was silent, he cleared his throat again. "That's all for now. Best of luck to you."

I put the phone down more confused than before. What did Robert have up his sleeve? When I explained the professor's cryptic message to Gonzo, he just shrugged. "The prof's been studying hieroglyphs so long he's talking in cryptic squiggles instead of words."

"Something like that," I replied. But my mind was wandering. What was Robert Georges holding back from us?

When we got to Paris, we found the bed-and-breakfast just as Georges had described it. We dropped off our bags, and headed to The Purple Unicorn, a pub with an old-style English vibe to it, complete with a wooden sign dangling from chains that read *The Purple Unicorn,* and an etched illustration of, you guessed it, a purple unicorn.

I was half expecting some huge surprise when we stepped inside, but it was just a normal pub where the patrons spoke English. We sat at a round table, ordering fancy dips and a round of beers, when Chrissy got an alert on her phone and pulled it out. She got sucked in, then quieted us down and said, "Hey guys, you're going to want to see this."

She lifted her phone, and we all squeezed in for a better look. It was a news feed of a guy in Santiago, Chile, who had performed a feat of superhuman strength, lifting a truck off a young woman.

I know people have lifted vehicles to save someone before. Usually it's a few inches—just enough to let the person get out. And it's fueled by adrenaline and whatever other natural chemicals get the body to do superhuman stuff in times of need. But what stood out was that this guy was very short and skinny. Tiny—that's the word I'd use for him. And he'd lifted and moved the one-ton truck a good four feet.

Gonzo elbowed Vee. "Hey, his name's Miguel Velasquez, and he's from Chile. Any chance you're related?"

Vee scowled at him. "That's like saying, hey, you're from Canada and your last name is Smith. You must be brothers! I'm from *Argentina.*"

"Ha!" Chrissy grinned. "But you never know."

"True." Vee shrugged and gave her a smile back.

"They probably already have it, guys." I shook my head sullenly.

Gonzo was looking at his phone. "There's a direct flight to Santiago in the morning."

"No. Seriously. We'll never beat those guys to Miguel." I shook my head. "They already had their eyes on Chile."

"Yeah. That's weird." Chrissy shook her head. "How did that woman know something was going on in Chile?"

"Maybe..." Gonzo started picking up excitement, "they're aliens, living amongst us, and they were waiting for these shards to land. They knew which countries, or general areas, but no specifics, so they've been waiting till things show up online."

"Not a bad theory," I mused. "Perhaps the shards were sent down for them to do something here. They're definitely not what I would call 'good guys,' which makes me agree with Vee that if they get the shards and put them all together, it'll be for something nefarious."

"I've been thinking about it." Chrissy set her beer down and gestured for the shards. I handed them to her, and she winced, teeth gritting with pain, but she held on tightly. "Every thug, whatever they call themselves—non-mundane, maybe—has powers that are useful. And that woman seemed surprised that touching the shards gives us powers. I'm guessing each of us, if we touch them, gains a power of some sort. Gonzo, Vee, I know you're having bad reactions with them. But I bet if you push through that, you'll figure out something useful, like me. I can hear *so*, so much right now, even though my body is thrumming. And I bet with practice—I could really hone it down."

Gonzo shook his head vehemently. "Not interested."

I shot Gonzo a teasing smirk. "Who'd have thought the biggest sci-fi nerd among us would cop out with real sci-fi."

"No, it's not like that." Gonzo was serious. "You don't get it, Mitzy. It's like I'm going to dissolve completely."

"Like, turn invisible?" I gave him a mischievous smile. "That would be a pretty cool power."

Gonzo frowned, staring at the table. We all watched as he sat like a statue. Then, with a sudden *humph*, he reached out to Chrissy and took the shards from her.

My eyes were glued to Gonzo as he held the shards. Anticipation buzzed in the air. He winced, and his face paled. Then, suddenly, his eyes went wide. His hand trembled, but he kept holding. Then, the hand clutching the shard began to disappear—the shard along with it. With a wince, he dropped the shards, and they clattered onto the table. He steadied his hands, now solid again.

With a deep breath, he reached out and scooped up the shards again. His eyes were wide as he watched his hand slowly disappear again, followed by his arm, then shoulder. Gonzo was breathing heavily but remained calm as it eventually took over his whole body, and he was completely gone.

We sat watching the spot where he'd been. Was he still there? Had he turned invisible, or had something else happened? What if his instincts that it would harm him were accurate?

I felt a moment of panic. "Are you there, Gonzo?"

A disembodied voice replied. "Yeah. I'm here."

"Ha!" I celebrated and raised my beer. "You're invisible! I knew it."

An invisible beer glass clinked against mine. I grinned and took a big swig.

"That's one mystery solved," Chrissy quipped. She turned to Vee. "You're next."

Vee nodded. "What do you think, Mitzy? It made my hand feel like a forty-pound weight."

I shrugged. "Gonzo. You're as much into superhero stuff as anyone. What do you think?"

"No idea," said the detached voice of my friend. "But I've already found the first problem of being invisible."

"What's that?"

"I can't see the screen of my phone."

"Ha!" We all started laughing, and Gonzo reappeared looking clammy and pale as he put the connected shards on the table. "It's the weirdest thing. Anything I hold disappears with me. But my chair was still visible. I wonder if I could make that turn invisible too? I've got to play with this. But it took a lot out of me. I feel awful."

I held up my mostly empty beer glass. "Here's to Gonzo tackling his fear and figuring out his power. A mighty useful one at that!"

Chrissy smirked. "And to the newest superhero: Invisaguy!"

Everyone laughed, raised glasses, and finished their beer, except Juliette, who was just taking tiny sips. I ordered another round, then we turned to Vee.

"Ready?" Chrissy asked.

Vee gave a thumbs up and picked up the shard. Just like last time, her hand plonked onto the table, a heavy weight, but this time, she gritted her teeth and kept holding it. Then, with a trembling arm, she slowly lifted her hand.

Chrissy leaned forward. "Maybe you can control how heavy your hand is?"

Vee gave a tiny nod and gritted her teeth. She stared at her hand fiercely. And then, suddenly, it was like the weight was released, and she moved her hand normally again.

We watched in fascination as she moved the hand around in the air, then it sunk, but not all the way as before, then lifted again as normal. She pushed her chair back and stood, separating the shards, one in each hand. Then she turned in a circle, hands out. She spun twice, then took on one of her martial arts stances.

Vee stood for a moment, eyes darting and muscles straining. A quick grin cracked across her face before she hopped lightly, landing on the balls of her feet. She bounced a few more times, wiggling her arms like she was warming up for something big. Coiling down, she suddenly launched herself upward, soaring five feet into the air, her head narrowly missing a rafter. For a breathless second, I almost believed she might stay suspended there, but gravity reclaimed her. She dropped back to the floor and spun with her usual effortless grace.

Grinning with triumph, Vee gave us a deep, theatrical bow before sliding back into her seat at the table.

Gonzo grinned. "That was awesome! You basically unlocked the 'double jump' skill from every video game ever."

Chrissy applauded. "Tell us about it."

Vee's eyes were sparkling. "I can control my body's density, or something." Her voice was full of wonder. "I can make it super heavy, or as light as a feather." She stared at her hand as she flexed it. "And I can control parts of my body or all of it. It's going to take some serious practice. And I still feel like I could puke at any second."

"What a cool power," Chrissy said. "Gonzo, will we have time to practice before we fly out?"

He looked at his phone. "Well, if we can get the lottery money by noon, we can take the one-thirty flight. Fourteen hours on a plane. Not sure how you'd practice in flight..."

"Right. Let's talk about our plan." I held my hand out to Vee. She passed the shards to me, along with the weight of everyone's trust. I gestured to Chrissy's phone. "We're all assuming another shard's in Chile, right?"

I waited for them to nod. "And as I told you last night, Robert said he can go to Washington, DC." I paused. "Now, I sure don't want to run into those thugs again, but something tells me we should try to get that third shard before they do."

"Yeah, of course," Gonzo said. The others nodded.

"Are there five empty seats on that flight?" I waited for Gonzo to nod. "Then tomorrow, we need to figure out new IDs, how to buy tickets without being found out, and pick up our lottery winnings before we head to the airport and get on that flight." I paused, then smiled. "Totally doable."

Just then, a middle-aged man in a gray suit came by our table and said, in a British accent, "Enormous day, eh?"

We exchanged confused glances, unsure how to respond. Vee narrowed her eyes and said, "What the hell are you going on about?"

The man's brow furrowed in confusion. "Sorry... I—"

He turned as if to leave, then came back and pointed at Gonzo with narrow eyes. "I saw you disappear, correct?"

Gonzo gave a sheepish smile. The man whirled on Vee. "And you. You leaped up nearly two meters."

"Yep. What of it?"

He glanced at everyone at the table. "Did you... are you affiliated with Professor Georges, perchance?"

"Yep." I straightened in my seat. "That's us."

He looked reluctant, so I pulled an empty chair over. "Please, friend. Take a seat. We're looking for answers, and something tells me you may be able to answer them."

He glanced at the empty chair, then at my oh-so-innocent face. He edged back ever so imperceptibly.

I flashed my best innocent smile, trying to keep things light. "Pretty please? I promise we won't bite. I'd love to buy you a beer."

He smiled and relaxed. "You do speak my language, it would appear. Lovely." He sat down in the chair, and I waved at the server to bring another beer over.

He steeled us all with a stare. "You have questions. Fine. But I will go first. Something is amiss at The Purple Unicorn, and I want to get to the bottom of it."

Chapter 13

"First things first. The name's Edward Peacock." The man spoke with a British accent as he fixed us with a stare. "But the real question is, who the hell are all of you? And why do you take turns with your traits instead of having them all at the same time?"

Everyone stared at me, waiting to follow my lead. I held the shards under the table and looked him over. He had a mustached, weathered face and graying hair. He was the opposite of a fit thug. It looked as if the toughest thing he'd ever tackled was a thick book. I decided to just go for it.

"The name's Stanley Mitz," I said, trying to sound friendly. "I'm an American, and I work in IT. We came here looking for answers about our powers."

He nodded and turned to Vee. Everyone said their names and offered a little about themselves. Nobody mentioned the shards.

When Juliette had finished, Edward said, "So, what's bringing you to the Dunbody House? And without the secret phrase."

My friends looked at me, and I felt my hand grow clammy holding the shard. "Um. The professor, uh..." I studied his face. Could we trust him? He had calculating, intelligent eyes, and I got the sense that he was the kind of guy who could make things happen. I realized then that he was our first connection to someone who appeared in the know who wasn't chasing or trying to kill us. I sighed and plunged in. "The people in black clothing are pursuing us. The, uh, underground police. They've been following us since Montana."

"The Preservation Society?" He raised his eyebrows. "What did you do to get them upset?" His eyes darted. "You definitely don't want to be on their bad side. Hoo-boy! That would be a real stinker."

"No. No. It's not that… it's just." I hesitated. I wanted to find the right people to give the shards to. Maybe he could help. *If* he were trustworthy.

But then Gonzo jumped in. "Tell us where you're really from. What solar system? How many of you are there?"

"Solar system?" He looked puzzled, then took another swig of his beer. "No idea what you're on about, laddie."

I waved Gonzo down and pulled out the shards. "Okay. Look. No need to hold back. Here's the real story. The… Preservation Society is after these. The reason we take turns with powers is that they give us power when we hold them."

Edward eyed them with one raised eyebrow. "Eh? What's that?"

"I was hoping you'd know."

He pursed his lips. "May I?" He held his hand out, and with just a moment's pause, I handed one shard to him.

He peered at it curiously, holding it up to the light.

Finally, Gonzo couldn't contain himself. "Well? Tell us about the shards, then! We've been patient."

"Have you now? I daresay that's the case, seeing as I just met you lot." Peacock eyed them once more, then placed the shard on the table. He leaned back and took a sip of his beer. Every eye was glued to him.

He held his hands out. "Ancient Egyptian, perhaps? Gives off an aura of power. Other than that, I have no idea."

"Aw, come on!" Gonzo slapped the table. "After all that?"

Peacock shrugged. "Indeed. But…" He leaned forward with a gleam in his eyes. "I can tell you some things that may be of service to you. Ask away."

"Oh, good." Gonzo leaned back. "How long have you been living among us?"

Peacock teetered his head. "Whatever do you mean? I've lived here for almost a decade. And before that, Bristol."

"I mean, how long have your kind been living among us *mundane* humans?"

He fluttered his fingers together. "Oh, dear me. I don't know that I can answer that one. I would imagine thousands of years. But I don't have an exact number for you."

Vee steeled him with a stare. "So, who are those thugs exactly? The Preservation Society."

"The name doesn't sound so bad," Chrissy quipped.

"They are not bad. They preserve our way of life in the Theurgica," Peacock said calmly. "And most agents *do* work for the good of our people. So, either you've done something to upset the Society and our way of life, or..." His fingers drummed against the beer glass.

"Or what?" Chrissy asked.

He sighed. "Just as with any group, some can be swayed for selfish outcomes. I can only imagine—if you are truly innocent—then whoever is after you is leveraging their power within the Society to pursue you." He glanced at the shards. "Those relics must be special indeed to risk leveraging the Preservation Society's resources like that."

"About that." I grew eager. "What's with all the powers we get when we hold them?" My voice was sharper than I intended, so I softened it. "Every time we touch them, something happens. Any idea why?"

I was disappointed when he shrugged and said, "I have no idea. I've never heard of mundanes getting powers before."

"But—" Gonzo searched for words. "Do *you* have more power when you hold them?"

His eyes sparkled. "Perhaps. I can see that they're special."

"Wait." Gonzo started shaking his head. "What's your power?"

Peacock scoffed. "Such an American. Asking outright what my power is. That's very impolite, you must know. And by the way, we don't call them *powers*. We call them traits."

"Such a boring word for such cool stuff." Gonzo was getting exasperated. "So, I know I'm being impolite—I *am* an American after all—and I'm asking, what's your *trait*, then?"

Peacock gave a tight smile. "I can read between the lines."

All five of us looked confused—Juliette, because she didn't understand at all what he was talking about with her more limited English, and the rest of us, because, well, yeah, not very helpful.

"What—?" I didn't quite know what question to ask.

"Let's just say that lying to me would be foolish. I see through everything."

I was suddenly relieved I'd been honest with him.

Vee leaned in. "The Preservation Society—they must have people all over the world, and vast resources, right?"

"Yes. That is correct."

"If someone high-up in their ranks were against us, and could leverage all sorts of power against us... well... Is there anyone who could stand up to them?"

He tapped his fingers on the table. "The Great Houses, of course, stand apart. They typically influence who they want in their local Preservation Societies. But many Theurgicans have great resources at their fingertips and can handle what you're describing with ease. They act like they're peaceful, but don't be fooled. The Great Houses have *darts*—assassins—and spies, all of them. Which is why the Theurgica Leadership is important. They preside over all of us and have ultimate authority in all matters."

"What is this Theurgica, anyway?" I asked.

He paused. "This is a difficult thing to answer. Perhaps it would be easier to show you?"

We exchanged glances. Great. Up to me.

"What the hey," I concluded. We paid the bill and got our jackets. Vee sidled up and asked for a shard to practice. I offered both, but she wanted me to hold on to one.

"Keep that lucky streak going, right?" she chuckled nervously.

We followed Peacock out the back door of the pub. Only, we didn't walk out into the alley we were expecting, but a narrow, dimly lit corridor. And then, Edward punched in some numbers on the door keypad and led us through another door into a room with a table and a few wooden chairs and flickering light from floating old-style lanterns.

Not suspended. Not hanging. Floating.

The lamps hovered in the air like something out of a dream, their flames flickering with actual heat. I couldn't take my eyes off them, too amazed to process what I was seeing. As Peacock turned down a staircase, a lamp moved off the wall and floated in front of him. Surprisingly, but proudly, none of us were freaking out.

This was way cooler than any sci-fi movie any of us had seen—and it was *real* life.

Gonzo's heavy footsteps echoed in the quiet corridor, each scuff of his shoes a reminder of how out of place we were. His face was pale, his hands twitching nervously at his sides. I remembered then that he could get claustrophobic. I hoped he'd be okay. As soon as we started walking down the dark stairs, even with a lamp hovering along lighting the way, Gonzo started scratching himself nervously.

"Excuse me, Edward," he said. "But just how far down does this go?"

"Why is that?" Peacock glanced over his shoulder at my pale friend. "It goes on quite a ways. We need to get to Old Paris to enter the Theurgica. At least, that's how it works here. It works differently in different cities."

"Oh... um... nothing."

I looked back to see Gonzo gripping the worn wooden handrail tightly.

We walked down the stairs quietly. A thought occurred to me. "So, you said there are Great Houses. Are you a part of that?"

"Me? Ha!" He scoffed. "But one of the most powerful is right here in Paris, in fact. Maison Lumière. They control much of the Theurgica globally, as well as the mundane world. But there are quite a few French houses, and even more British ones. The Dunbody House, where I'm taking you, is pretty small compared to those, but large enough to have representation here in Paris. Although we're in Old Paris, like most of the smaller houses. Only the Great Houses have vast estates among the mundanes. They have enough resources to keep their true nature hidden, regardless."

"Wow." Chrissy had a tremor of excitement in her voice. "There's so much we don't know."

"Are there other Great Houses here in Paris?" I asked.

"Oh yes. Of course. The biggest all have representatives here. This is one of the major hubs. The House of Eldritch has the largest presence, as you can imagine. They're from London, and they're also one of the most powerful. And as Americans, I'm sure you'll appreciate that the Fulton House has a major operation here as well." He gave me a sideways look. "Always about the money and resources, that one."

"Uh-huh," I agreed, nodding. I had no idea what he was talking about but marveled at how he communicated in a way that filled us in, while also acting as if we were already in the know.

He stooped to touch a small knob on the wall as we continued. "As far as Great Houses, you'd probably be interested in the House of Wellington, from Hong Kong, the Dynasty of the Dragon, from Shanghai, Guild of the Sword, from Tokyo, and House Gottingen, from Frankfurt. Among others, of course. But those are the major players you need to pay attention to, if you care about such things."

Peacock turned to me and shrugged. "They're all the same in my book—scrambling to be on top and impress the others. A waste of time, of course. As for my house, we specialize in doing things behind the scenes, keeping things running smoothly, so everybody calls on us. We don't threaten anybody, so we wind up everywhere. If everyone uses your services, you end up with no enemies and lots of friends. Not like those bloodthirsty houses, always looking for more power. Ah, here we are."

I'm not sure how many steps down we'd gone, but it felt like about eight flights of stairs before we stood in front of a locked wooden door. Peacock gave three raps—two slow, and one quick.

The door opened immediately, creaking on ancient iron hinges, revealing an expansive chamber that seemed to hum with magic. The walls were lined with weathered bricks, their surfaces transformed by breathtaking graffiti. This wasn't the hastily scrawled tagging you'd find in the world above. This art seemed alive. It shimmered faintly, as if lit from within. Swirling galaxies painted in vibrant blues and violets stretched across one section, their stars twinkling in and out of existence when you tilted your head. A phoenix in mid-flight arched across another wall, its fiery feathers glowing as though they'd been painted with liquid sunlight.

Elsewhere, intricate designs flowed seamlessly into one another: a serpentine dragon coiled around the frame of an old iron sconce, its scales catching and refracting light from no apparent source. Next to it, a garden of luminous flowers seemed to grow directly out of the brick, their petals softly waving as though swayed by an unseen breeze. A mural of a vast enchanted forest stretched across the far wall, and if you stared long enough, you could swear the trees shifted, their branches reaching out like arms.

Three passages extended from the chamber, each marked by ancient, weathered street signs etched with names in old scripts and symbols. The ceiling loomed thirty feet above us, arching gracefully, and even that had been painted with constellations that winked and shifted, as though charting the movement of some forgotten sky. The air was thick with the scent of damp earth and something floral, something alive.

A row of cacti lined one wall, their spiny forms casting sharp shadows on the floor. As we stepped in, they stirred, unfurling tiny eyes that glinted like polished marbles and mouths that curved into broad, toothless grins.

"Hello there," one of them said, its voice gravelly but warm. The others chimed in with a chorus of "Welcome," their smiles somehow both eerie and endearing.

It was a place defying time and reason, where every surface told a story and every shadow hinted at secrets yet to be uncovered. As I took it all in, I couldn't shake the feeling that the walls themselves were watching, waiting, and maybe even listening.

Peacock waved us on. "This is the beginning of the Theurgica. Come this way. I'll show you a nice courtyard."

We walked through the corridor, then through another, admiring occasional graffiti art along the way. At one point, the graffiti art moved with us—a lizard surrounded by plants scurried along the wall and hid behind another painting of plants. The entire area we traversed was lit with occasional lamps, although they were sporadic, so there were plenty of shadows and times I was thankful for Peacock's floating lamp.

Vee broke the silence. "Tell us more about the Preservation Society. Just how much do they know about us? What resources do they have?"

"Oh, pretty much everything you could imagine." Edward glanced at her apologetically. "They have members all around the world, and people in most world governments. However," he turned around to face us, "the Great Houses control the Preservation Society, so they don't *really* work as one cohesive unit. There are plenty of cracks, which is how my house can be so successful. We know where the cracks are. Which is why we're crucial to inter-house liaisons."

"The agents," Vee began thoughtfully. "What sort of power do they have?"

Edward responded quickly. "Preservation Society agents go through significant training, and their position opens up many doors, no matter where in the world they are."

I frowned. "If we were to, say, try to leave the country, and they were after us, would they be able to track us?"

"Probably." He thought for a moment. "It depends. If those after you have representation in Maison Lumière, then yes, more than likely they will find you. If it's the Fulton House, it's iffier, only because they have much less control here. Either way, I'd get fake passports if I were you."

"Can you help us with that?" I asked.

"Of course." He glanced at me. "One favor for another."

"What type of favor would you like?"

He beamed. "Ah. Now, that's where the Dunbody House shines. No favor is necessary today. You will repay us in due time, of course."

"We have plenty of money. We could pay you now," I said.

"Ah, but what use would we have for money?" He paused and cocked his head at me with an expectant look. "So, what do you say? One favor for another?"

I slowly nodded. "Of course." I wondered briefly what ramifications it might cause, but I was just going with the flow, and it felt right.

A branch went to the left with a sign that read: Bradbury House. Ten feet into the branch, there were large wooden double doors with metal ribs. They looked hundreds of years old, as if they could withstand a battering ram. We kept walking, then saw another sign to the right.

Maison Bernard.

The double doors in that corridor were elegant and white, while still being large and imposing. The next set of double doors was to the left.

Maison Dubois.

Finally, we came to one that said Dunbody House, and we turned into the entryway.

Peacock went up to the stout-looking double doors and stood in front of them for a few seconds. The doors creaked obediently inward, to reveal a delightful cobblestone corridor about thirty feet wide that felt like a side street in downtown

Bordeaux, complete with shops and residential buildings that went up to three stories tall, and glowing streetlamps every fifty feet, giving the entire area a warm feeling.

Most of the stores were closed, but a café was open just down the way, where a dozen people were sitting outside at tables on the cobblestones, smoking and drinking as they chatted in English. As we walked toward it, I gazed at the signs above the stores: Grace's Pottery. Speedy Exterminators. Jiffy Delivery. Morning Brew. Knitter's Paradise... They were all quaint-looking shops you might see in any European town.

A yellow dog was walking down the street and stopped to pee on the nearest lamppost. I stared at the dog. Something was off, but I couldn't place what. That's when the dog turned to me and said, in a female voice, "What, never seen a dog pee before? Want a picture?"

"Sorry. Sorry," I mumbled and looked away.

Chrissy giggled. "Mitzy's heading to the doghouse."

Gonzo guffawed. "Dude, you didn't just go to the dogs. You got verbally neutered by one! Ha!"

They both laughed, and I rolled my eyes at them. I tried to ignore the dog as we walked past, but wondered, was it a person who could turn into a dog, or just a smart dog?

My head was spinning.

We walked past the café, coming to a four-way intersection, where we turned right toward the sound and lights in the distance. Walking down the street, we passed three more open-seating bars and restaurants filled with small groups of young adults chatting and drinking, then came to a spacious round courtyard, with four more eating-and-drinking establishments boasting outdoor seating scattered around the edges, and a large statue with a fountain in the middle. Buildings lined the courtyard, all two stories tall, with retail on the bottom floors and what appeared to be mostly residential above.

Besides the few dozen people eating and drinking, there were about ten people milling about in the courtyard, and two dogs ran around, as if it were a normal spot above ground in Paris.

At first glance, nothing about the scene seemed out of the ordinary. Just any old place to walk around in Paris. Upon closer inspection, I realized one guy at a table was glowing faintly red. I also noticed a woman with what I had assumed was a hairband with cat ears, until I realized her face had a very catty look as well, with wide slitted eyes, a tip for a nose, and a wide mouth that crossed most of her face.

A child was in the courtyard, running around with a helium balloon on a string, then released it with a look of glee on her face. An adult nearby, who was nonchalantly chatting with another woman, casually pointed at the girl, and she floated up into the air after the balloon.

Chrissy's eyes were glowing with excitement. "This is amazing!" she declared. "An entire magical world below ground."

Edward Peacock turned to face us. "I apologize in advance for not being a fantastic tour guide. I'm uncertain exactly what you'd like to know, so feel free to ask questions."

Vee pointed. "What about that child's bedtime? Isn't it, like, midnight?"

I thought it was an odd question, but I was curious as well.

He shrugged. "We obviously keep time differently down here without the sun. But yes, it seems a bit late for kids to be out. It's much busier during the day, you can imagine."

Chrissy was peering at the child, who had nearly caught up with the balloon. "Do people live down here? Do they go up to the regular world?"

Peacock tapped his chin. "There are all sorts. Many live down here. Some commute above for work. Others live above and come down here to do business."

Gonzo scratched his head, glancing around. "Okay, but the real question—where does all the *sewage* go? You're about as low as it gets. And if I don't get a decent answer, I doubt I'll be drinking the tap water."

Edward contorted his face for a moment in thought. "I daresay I haven't the slightest idea."

"Ha!" Gonzo folded his arms and eyed the people drinking nearby with a suspicious glare.

I gestured toward the people socializing on a nearby patio. "You said some people live down here full time. But *why?* What makes someone choose this life over one above?"

He considered. "Good question. I suppose it removes the risk of being discovered by mundanes. It's safer. Predictable. And when you're from England, you spend most of your time indoors, anyway. But I wouldn't know why, to be honest."

Vee looked at him with narrowed eyes. "You said your house specializes in keeping things running smoothly. Do all the houses have specialties?"

"Oh, yes," he replied. "Usually, it concerns their traits. You see, there are families of traits that all go together, and they're passed down through the bloodline. Bradbury House, for example, is known for manipulating temperature and weather—heating, cooling, and winds. My house is known for its keen insights and ability to smooth over any situation, hence its somewhat innocuous role of being the go-betweens of society. The larger houses..." He considered. "Well, they have their specialties, but those who want more power or influence can join them—usually by marrying in—so they are often more diverse."

"And the Preservation Society..." I glanced around. "What role do they have here?"

"Oh, they're always monitoring, always ensuring our safety."

Gonzo's face paled. "*Always* monitoring? Like, right now?"

Edward gave us a look, then his face lit up with understanding. "Ah, yes. You're trying to avoid them. I completely forgot. Oh, dear."

"What?" I gripped the shard in my pocket and found it thrumming insistently, as if working hard, and I felt my insides churn.

Edward scrunched up his face apologetically. "There is a possibility that the people after you won't come after you here, but there is also the possibility that they will. I'm so sorry. There are hidden cameras at all the entrances. It depends on whether those after you have requested help from the entire Society or not."

I grew alert and eyed the dozens of people around us. As I scanned the courtyard, something gnawed at the back of my mind. Everything seemed… fine. But the feeling in my gut told me otherwise.

As I turned around the courtyard, I felt my stomach clench. I could just *feel* that something was up. But what? I cursed under my breath.

Come on, luck! Work!

Just then, a stern-looking man, all in black, emerged, scanning the area. He saw us and lit up. My heart lurched in my chest. He looked exactly like the other Preservation Society agents we'd seen so far—someone who could kill me in my sleep without blinking.

I realized with a moment of deep panic that we were confronting the Preservation Society on *their* turf. Stuck in a confined space.

And standing out in the wide open.

Chapter 14

The Preservation Society agent jogged toward us, and I shot a quick glance at Vee. Her hand clenched tighter around the shard, knuckles whitening. A muscle in her jaw twitched, but she didn't make a move. I felt the weight of my shard grow heavier and my hand tingle, like it sensed the tension building. But he didn't look like he was pursuing us so much as approaching Edward, so I waited to see what would happen.

The agent stopped when he got to us, puffing. "Edward. Do you know who these people are?"

Edward stood calmly, not batting an eye. "They owe me a favor. Why? Who are they?"

The man's eyes darted toward the shadows at the edge of the courtyard. "Top Preservation Society agents from America are after them." His voice dropped a notch. "They're at the top of the Most Wanted list."

My pulse quickened.

"Does it say why?" Edward asked.

"Not really. Pretty vague. It's the Fulton House, so I take everything with a grain of salt."

"I'd say that's best." Edward nodded sagely.

The man glanced over his shoulder. "If you're helping them, they've got to get out of here. Two Fulton House agents are less than a minute behind me." He pointed toward the entrance at the back, and Vee immediately started running toward it.

She barely arrived at the wall next to the entrance just as two dark-dressed men emerged and pointed at us. The agent next to Edward grabbed his arm and pulled him away.

"Scatter!" I called out, running in the other direction.

A bubble appeared out of one of the agent's fingers and sped to where we'd been, growing and growing as it went. An unlucky woman in the courtyard didn't see it, and when the bubble came upon her, it captured her inside.

Vee launched herself through the air, her boot crashing into the man's arm with a thud. In one smooth motion, she grabbed his shoulder and twisted, flipping him hard onto the cobblestones. His back hit the ground with a dull crack, and he let out a strangled groan, the air driven from his lungs.

The other agent darted behind Vee and raised what looked like a ray gun at her. She whacked his arm so he couldn't get a bearing on her, then punched him in the gut. He staggered then aimed the gun again.

Only Vee wasn't there. She'd leaped six feet into the air, and flipped over the man, grabbing his shoulder sleeves as she flew, and pulled him backward. He toppled and fell but still managed to fire off a shot before he landed with a thud.

There was no big sound, just a pulse of energy that emanated out. The pulse shot out and hit Vee mid-motion, and she instantly froze. Her muscles locked, her eyes wide with fury, and her body held in an unnatural stillness, like a statue on the verge of collapsing.

My breath caught. I had to act quickly.

Both men stirred, groaning and struggling off the ground. I grabbed Gonzo, handing him the shard. "Try to steal that guy's gun."

Gonzo's eyes were wide, pupils darting from the frozen Vee to the agents lying on the ground, then back to me. His hands shook, and I could see the panic rising in his chest. "But how?" His voice was thin, almost pleading. This wasn't what Gonzo was made for. Stealing a gun from an armed man? It was madness. But we had no choice.

"I'll distract them. You go invisible." I whirled and dashed to the immobile Vee, both guys stirring and trying to get up. The one she'd attacked second was moving more quickly and looked like he would be on his feet in a few seconds. I reached Vee and ripped the shard out of her hand, then moved behind her, so her poised but frozen body was between me and the guys.

"Now listen," I said to them. "We don't want any trouble."

The standing man was now fully focused on me, and the other was nearly on his feet. I heard Gonzo running clumsily toward them and raised my voice. "Maybe you could just tell us what this is all about, and we can come to some arrangement. Hmmm? What do you think?"

I was being obnoxiously loud, and everyone else in the courtyard who wasn't seated at tables was edging away. I was hoping desperately that the thugs wouldn't hear Gonzo's loud clomping.

The one with the gun opened his mouth to answer, and then the gun disappeared right out of his hand. "Hey!" he shouted. And then he froze in place.

The other man struggled to his feet and put his hands on his knees, giving me a look as if to say, *I'm coming for you.* My mind raced.

Why wasn't Gonzo freezing him yet?

He straightened and glanced left and right, then started running toward me. I gripped Vee's frozen shoulders, unsure what to do, when he suddenly froze mid-stride and toppled to the ground.

Gonzo appeared out of nowhere, looking wobbly, but holding the gun with a wide grin. "Did you see that, Mitzy? I did it!" He stared at the gun as if it had performed a magic trick. "It's gotta recharge between shots, or I'd have got him sooner."

"Nice work, Buckaroo!" I gave him the thumbs up, my heart still hammering in my chest. I took in the situation. The immediate threat was taken care of, but we were sitting ducks.

I turned to Peacock on the other side of the courtyard. "Edward. Can you get us out of here?"

"Yes. Yes. Of course." Peacock fumbled with something in his hands.

Gonzo peered at our frozen friend. "But what about Vee?"

"Give me a hand," I said, picking her up. She was surprisingly easy to carry, stiff and easy to grip, so unlike a regular body. It was more like carrying luggage. Gonzo, still woozy from using the shard, grabbed her legs, and I grabbed her front as we made our way out of the courtyard. Some people were watching us but didn't look surprised or upset. Most of them had already turned back to their late-night drinks and conversations, as if all the ruckus was commonplace.

I turned so that only Vee and Gonzo could hear me. "I wonder if that gun has a reverse setting."

Gonzo was huffing along behind and said, "Hey, I can check."

"No. Just wait," I said.

He didn't respond. I glanced back as we entered the courtyard. Sure enough, Gonzo was trying to look at the gun while holding Vee, and a second later it went off. He froze, toppling over while holding Vee.

"Gak!" I exclaimed, jerking into place. I groaned and put Vee's top half gently down on the ground, then walked over to the frozen Gonzo and reached for the second shard, hesitating for just a moment before pressing it against the first. Double the luck seemed like a good idea right about now.

As soon as they touched, a jolt shot up my arm, making my hand tingle. But I also felt something ominous, perhaps even dangerous. Something was happening to my body the longer I held them together. But what?

I pulled the gun out of Gonzo's hand and peered at it. It was silver blue and looked a lot like a toy ray gun I had as a kid—all silver with a wide barrel and red lights. There was a knob with three settings, all of them in French. I realized then that my French was lacking, because I couldn't translate any of the words.

"Edward. Do you know how to use this thing?"

Peacock came over and peered at the gun. "That setting there says freeze. This one says stun, and this one says unfreeze."

The Preservation Society agent came up and shook his head. "Yes, it works as expected. But you must leave immediately. More will be on their way, and we do not want Edward to be seen associating with you."

"You got it." I set the knob to unfreeze and pointed it at Gonzo. Giving a slight wince, I pulled the trigger. He unfroze, and I breathed in relief, then did the same with Vee.

"Finally," she said, stretching. "No thanks to you, blockhead." She backhanded Gonzo.

He just shrugged and stretched with an exaggerated groan. "Ugh. That was the worst power nap of my life. Zero dreams, zero rest, and I think I have freezer burn on my soul."

Vee snorted and tried to hide a smile with her hand.

"Before we leave," I said, eyeing the agent, "can you tell us more about who's after us?"

"I'll have to check." The agent pulled out his phone, thumbs tapping quickly. "Looks like the order came all the way from the top in the States. Commander Jet Su, Inter-House Investigations Directorate."

He grimaced. "I've heard of this guy. He's got sway with all the houses, big or small. His job is to hold all of them responsible." He shook his head. "He's got a reputation as a tough nut to crack. Gets the job done by any means possible. People are afraid to stand up to him, so he gets his way pretty much all the time. He's one of only two commanders in the U.S.A. Whatever his trait is, I've heard bullets pass right through him. If he's the one after you, you don't want to meet him face to face."

He held up a picture of the man for all of us to see, a middle-aged Asian man with a stern look on his face. The five of us stood silently. A few thugs with powers after us were one thing, but someone high up in what appeared to be the most powerful secret organization in the world... it made me go cold. What could we do?

Chrissy turned to me, as if looking for support, and I felt my resolve strengthen. We would take things one step at a time.

"Peacock." I fixed Edward with a stare. "Show us the fastest way out of here."

"Right. But..." He held up his hand. "Before I commit to this... your favor has doubled."

I looked into his eyes and understood how his house had become so successful. But I couldn't think of other options. "Done. And... we also want your help if there's any trouble getting our lottery winnings in the morning."

He cocked his head. "Not a problem. That's easy enough we'll call it two favors, in total." He paused, then gestured with a wave. "From the lot of you."

"Done." I nodded.

He turned with a flourish. "This way."

We walked back into the main corridor, then turned down a tiny slit of a corridor we hadn't noticed on the way in, with a ladder going straight up.

Gonzo stared up the ladder into the darkness above. "There's no way I'm going to make it up that thing. It's eight stories."

I looked up with a furrowed brow. Gonzo was right—it was going to be a lot. But then I had a thought. "Vee, do you think maybe you can make Gonzo lighter, just like you do for yourself?"

"No idea. Worth a try, though."

I passed her a shard, and she closed her eyes and swayed, breathing deeply, hand on chest. When she recovered, she put a hand on Gonzo's arm and asked, "How's that?"

Gonzo grinned, bouncing lightly. "Whoa! I feel like a helium balloon. Vee, you are officially my new favorite person."

With Peacock leading the way, we started climbing up the ladder. But even with Gonzo's lightened state, it was painfully slow progress. There was a landing to rest thirty feet up, which helped, but Juliette and I were in terrible shape as well, so Vee had to swap who she was helping. By the end, all three of us were sweaty, and Gonzo's legs were shaking as he cursed everything.

We finally arrived at the top landing, and Peacock opened a door for us to breathe the crisp, outdoor air of Paris. By then, it was 1 a.m.

I turned to him. "We'll head to the lottery office at nine, when it opens. How can we reach you?"

He grinned and handed me a card, which had his name and number, and that was all. As I took the card, I wondered what he would ask of us. How big a favor did we now owe him? I squeezed the shard in my pocket for luck, just in case.

After shaking hands with Edward and promising we'd be in touch, we slipped away into the night. The streets of Paris felt quieter, darker, like they were closing in on us. I imagined Bruno Marx or Jet Su lurking behind every corner, and it made me jittery.

As soon as we were back at the B&B I dialed Robert and put him on speaker phone. He picked up on the first ring.

"Stanley. I trust you have more questions, now."

"Yes, Robert, we do." I looked into the eyes of the others, who watched me closely. "What do you have to do with the Theurgica?"

He sighed. "I am a member of the Theurgica. I've known from the beginning that the men after you were Preservation Society agents. But I don't have the resources I used to, nor the ability to do much, and I didn't want to get your hopes up."

"What *can* you do for us?" I asked.

Robert's voice brightened. "I can help uncover this puzzle, as I have been. And point you to someone in Santiago to get you at least tied in with the locals."

"Who?"

"His name is Mario Camiletti. I'll send you his information and let him know to be expecting you. He has been doing some digging on the Preservation Society, so he should be able to help you know more about them. And hopefully, how to avoid them."

I nodded and looked at the others. Juliette and Gonzo looked so tired, I had pity on them. "Thanks, Robert. And thanks for pointing us to The Purple Unicorn. We met Edward Peacock."

He laughed. "How's the old timer doing?"

"Fine, I guess." I paused. "How bad is it that we now owe him two favors?"

"It—" He seemed to struggle for words. "It depends. Most of the time, it's not a big deal."

We sat there, letting that sink in. "And do you know anything about Jet Su? He's the Commander of the Preservation Society who gave the order for all the agents around here to look for us."

"No. But Mario may be more help with that."

I sighed. "Thanks for your help, Robert. I think we all need to get some rest."

"Of course. And Stanley…" His voice grew tender. "I've heard Chile is an interesting country, with pockets of free-standing Theurgica communities not under the influence of the Preservation Society. If you can find one, they may be able to help you."

In the morning, I held both shards as I accompanied Juliette to the lottery office, and everything miraculously worked out perfectly. They wouldn't announce the winner to the world until later that week. I felt like my luck was holding out.

We took the check to a Paris branch of her bank and asked to have it changed into euros. They asked for her ID, and I cringed. This was it. How soon before the Preservation Society would be onto us? Days? Weeks? Minutes? My skin crawled, imagining someone coming through the doors any minute.

The bankers took far too long to get us the 40,000 euros. They asked how we wanted it, and Juliette asked for thousand-euro bills for most of it. A single envelope arrived, and I marveled at how inconspicuous it appeared. More money than I'd ever held in my life, in that one small envelope.

On the way back to the hotel, the shards pulsed the whole way, and I tried to stay calm. I checked over my shoulder constantly, but it seemed nobody was after us. I hoped the double-luck was doing what I really wanted—making us so lucky they didn't even have a chance of crossing paths with us.

Back at the hotel, we moved fast, shoving our belongings into our bags. Every creak from the hallway made me jump, and I kept glancing at the windows, half-expecting agents to be watching from the shadows.

We spread out the euros among us, eight thousand each, then I texted Edward.

How soon can we get the passports?

He texted back immediately.

Now. Go to Rue Georges Bizet, the store I mentioned last night.

From the outside, it looked like an ordinary fashion store with belts, purses, and women's clothing. Vee took charge, stepping up to the woman behind the counter with her usual authority.

"Edward Peacock sent us here."

"Back there." She waved toward a white door that said *Employees Only* in French.

We went through the door, down a corridor, and into a back room with computers and a photo booth. A guy with a beret and a dark bushy mustache got to business taking photos of each of us. The process felt painstakingly too long, and we had to wait a solid thirty minutes while he worked, but finally he handed us five new passports, all British.

I was impressed. They looked legit.

With deep curiosity, I flipped to the first page and read my new name.

Joseph Cunningham.

I could live with that. We thanked him and made a beeline to the airport.

On the way there, Gonzo pulled the freeze gun out of his bag. "What about this? There's no way we're getting this on a plane. Should we check it in?"

I shook my head. "It's our best protection. What if we're followed to the gate? We need to keep it with us."

I considered our options. "How would you feel about sneaking past security?"

"Seriously?" Gonzo paled. "I don't like where you're going with this."

"You can turn invisible."

"Yeah. I know. But... I'm not exactly small. Or nimble. Or... used to breaking the law."

"It's not a problem. I'll be right next to you, bringing you luck." I smiled and patted his arm. "If Vee can pass her powers to someone she's touching, I bet we all can. Hold my hand."

He looked at me like I was crazy, and I passed him a shard, so we were both holding one. "Okay. I'll make you lucky, and you make me invisible."

I actually didn't know how to make him lucky. I just said that, so he'd worry less. Regardless, as soon as we held hands, the world shimmered around us, and then—nothing. I looked down and couldn't see myself. My stomach lurched, and I felt a dizzy spell coming on. I understood in that moment why Gonzo didn't take to it right away. My seat belt showed my body shape, but my clothing and everything I was holding were completely gone—right along with me. It was surreal.

"Perfect." I released his clammy hand and talked with more boldness than I felt. "I'll sneak in with you. I'll give you my luck, and you give me your invisibility. We're a perfect team. There's no way we'll have any issues."

Gonzo reappeared looking shaky. "I guess so. But Mitzy. If it doesn't work... that's *French* prison."

I looked into his eyes. They darted all over the place. He was pale and sweating. I realized then he didn't have the last couple of weeks of lucky streaks to bolster his confidence like I did. I knew my plan had a thousand holes in it, and I tried to imagine another option. But none came. Luck seemed like the best approach.

When we arrived at the airport, we bought the tickets using our new identities, and Gonzo and I checked our bags along with the other luggage, so we wouldn't be encumbered with them. Chrissy put Gonzo's laptop in her carry-on, so he'd have it on the plane. Then I told the ladies to go through security and let us know what to watch out for. Gonzo and I sat at a restaurant and had a coffee while we waited to hear from them.

Gonzo was nervously tapping the table with his fingertips and constantly glancing over his shoulder. Did I mention he never wins at poker? Yeah. Terrible bluffer.

"Dude. Chillax. We're just having a coffee. We're not breaking any laws."

His eyes darted. "Not yet. Not yet."

I had to do something. The guy was a complete mess. "Maybe instead of coffee, we should have stiff drinks. That'll loosen us up."

He frowned. "But then we might make mistakes."

I held up the shard and wiggled it. "Not with this. You're worrying too much. Come on. Let's switch to Bloody Marys."

He nodded noncommittally, and I ordered us a round. We were halfway through when Chrissy called.

"What's the word?" I asked.

"Not good."

I muted and turned to Gonzo. "She's got a good plan for us." I nodded. Gonzo slowly followed suit. I unmuted. "Go on."

She explained. "It's in super lockdown, just like an American airport. They're taking people aside for individual body scans and going through lots of luggage. Something's got them on high alert."

I put on a bright face. "Okay. Thanks for the call. See you soon." I hung up and turned to Gonzo. "Give me a minute to see what she's talking about. Be right back."

"Okay," he said weakly.

A quick walk past security showed four lines. The general line, the pre-check line, the pre-pre-check line, for those who've paid extra, and the line for airline staff. That was the line I keyed in on. To get through it, we'd have to pass through a swinging gate—potentially obvious if we were to stroll right through on our own. But what if we did it at the same time as others? We just had to hope that Gonzo could suck his gut in.

I went back to Gonzo with a bright smile. "Plan's all set. Let's have another drink and loosen up. *Serveur!*"

After we drank down our second round of Bloody Marys, Gonzo stood, shaking and sweaty.

"Okay, amigo. Let's hold hands. Get some of that luck into your system." I spoke with false bravado. "This way." I led us toward a restroom, then just as we walked into the entrance, I said. "Now."

Gonzo obediently turned us invisible. Obviously, we couldn't give any gestures to communicate, so I gave a little hand squeeze. "Just follow me. We're going to head to security now."

He stumbled after me. I tried walking slowly, and he gave me a flat tire, making my right shoe pop off at the heel. I quickly scrambled with one hand to put it back on and Gonzo bumped into me again.

"Look," I said, trying to be calm. "I know we're both invisible, but you're gonna have to trust me to guide you. Hold tight." I had a sudden image pop into my head of him falling into me and letting go of my hand at a critical moment. My heart did a double flutter.

There are so many dynamics involved in sneaking past security invisible holding hands.

How did we ever think it was possible?

Communication without talking. No visual gestures. Be of the same mind.

I realized then what a fool I was to think he wouldn't constantly run into me. I quickly came up with a plan.

"Okay, here's what we're going to do," I whispered. "One squeeze means stop. Two squeezes means go forward. Follow me slowly. I won't go too fast. And try to keep the same amount of distance between us the whole way."

I hoped that would be enough.

We waited till there was more than one airport staff person in line and walked in behind them. They went through the swinging gate and we went through after. Darn Gonzo. He kept the gate open for too long. Fortunately, somehow nobody noticed, and there we were right in the middle of security.

The airport staff walked behind the scanners, and we followed them as best we could. We made it behind the people reading the X-rays.

Just a little ways to go.

And that's when Gonzo stubbed his toe on the leg of the scanner and let go of my hand.

Chapter 15

I blipped into existence right in the middle of Paris airport security, fully visible for the entire world to see. My stomach plummeted. Every instinct screamed "run", but I froze, heart hammering in my chest.

Prison, here I come.

I took in my surroundings. Two security guards sat mere feet away, peering at X-ray screens, their backs mercifully turned. My breath hitched as I scanned for anyone else who might have noticed. A young child waiting in line by the body scanner blinked at me, eyes wide. For a brief second, I thought he might yell or point. Instead, he just stared—silent, shocked.

I gave him a look. *Please, kid. Keep quiet.*

I snapped into action, darting back toward the last place I'd seen Gonzo. I waved my arm through the air, hoping to make contact.

Nothing. He wasn't there.

My skin prickled with panic. I crouched low, eyes darting as a guard cocked his head. His gaze slowly drifted toward me, frowning, as if I'd caught his attention but he wanted to finish scanning the screen in front of him. Sweat slicked my palms. I clenched my teeth, bracing myself for him to turn fully.

Desperately, I groped at the ground, trying to find Gonzo before it was too late. My fingers finally brushed against something—an arm. Gonzo.

He was crouched, clutching his foot in pain. Relief washed over me, and I fumbled along his arm until I found his hand. I squeezed hard, and just like that, the world shifted, and I vanished again.

I breathed a sigh of relief but was still worried. I watched the security officer. He glanced toward us, frowned and looked a little closer, then with a furrowed brow turned back to the screen.

Gonzo's hand was dripping sweat. I pulled him up, gave him two squeezes, and guided him out. Nobody called. Nobody stopped us.

Slowly, we passed through security, then past the people putting their stuff back in their luggage. Finally, we rounded the corner to the restroom, and I let go of his hand.

"We did it!" Gonzo was pale and shaking visibly. He held out a wobbly hand, then clenched it into a fist. "I think I need another drink."

"Yeah. Yeah. Okay." I took a deep breath, feeling shaky myself.

I texted the girls, and we stopped at the first restaurant we could find. Gonzo downed a Bloody Mary, then ordered another. When his hands finally stopped shaking, he hit me with a steely, serious look.

His voice dropped as he stared at the people passing by. "Mitzy, this is next-level stuff. I love adventure. Love it. I mean, who dominates *Call of Duty*? Yours truly. But this is real. Am I really cut out for this? Really?" He gave me a pleading look.

I felt myself soften. "I get it, man. Sometimes I've wondered what the heck we're doing on this crazy adventure. But... I can't picture doing any of this without you."

Gonzo nodded. "Thanks, man. I... Are we ever going to go back to our old lives? Our simpler lives?... Or are we too far gone?"

I considered, then raised my glass. "I couldn't say. But cheers to how far we've come, whatever the future holds."

We clinked glasses, and he took a sip. He smirked. "Well, if we are too far gone, I just hope the next plot twist involves less running and more all-inclusive beach resorts."

We lightened up and tried to enjoy the moment. By the time the ladies joined us, Gonzo was bubbling with excitement and told them every detail of what had happened. As the story went on, it gained embellishment and energy.

"Quiet down," I scolded. "You don't want the entire world to know." I was keeping an active watch on all the people passing by, hoping not to see any Preservation Society agents.

He smiled at me sheepishly. "Sorry. So anyway," he continued quietly, "there we were right behind security, when *poof!* Mitzy appeared. And there I was—crippled, betrayed by my toe, on the verge of never walking again. And Mitzy... he crawls his way over to me like an overachieving insect, scurrying to find its food. I was in so much pain I could barely think." He smirked at me. "As soon as he grabbed my hand, he was fine, but for a minute there, I thought we'd completely blown it."

Chrissy smirked. "You might even say you were *invisibly* shaken, am I right?"

We both groaned at the awful pun.

Vee was hyper-alert, watching the crowds, barely touching her drink. "Plane's boarding soon."

I nodded at her thankfully, glad I wasn't the only person being extra watchful.

When we got to the gate, the wait for the airplane felt far too long. I was eager to leave Paris as quickly as possible, but the flight was delayed by twenty minutes. Every minute that ticked past felt like an eternity as we stood out in the open. I hoped desperately that we wouldn't have to use the freeze gun and clenched the shards like a lifeline. The more I gripped them with intent, the more I felt an unnatural force shifting inside me. I noticed myself sweating more than usual, head throbbing, and I was breathing more raggedly. *Maybe two shards are too much to hold for long periods?* I wondered.

When we finally boarded, I breathed a sigh of relief. By then, my head was pounding, and I figured I should take a break from the shards, so I passed them to Chrissy and Vee to practice using their traits on the flight. I just wanted to sleep, anyway. And I did. I slept for ten, almost eleven hours. Enough that when I awoke, we only had a few more to go to get us to Santiago.

Gonzo was sitting next to me, busily clacking away on his new laptop, building out a new AI translator program.

"How's it going?" I asked.

He gave me a nod, eyes shining brightly. "I think I've figured out how the software was built. But I'm basically rewriting the whole thing. Good thing I'm an excellent coder."

"And good thing you're so humble about it." I grinned at him.

He raised his eyebrows playfully. "You're just jealous. Go on. Admit it. IT is like the little brother to coding. I'm the guy who builds the core systems, and you're the one who messes with them after I get all the hard parts done for you."

"Is that so?" I asked.

Gonzo wagged his eyebrows. "Coders create magic out of nothing. You IT guys just stand there waving a screwdriver like it's a wand, hoping if you turn it off and on again, it counts as a spell."

"How many developers does it take to screw in a lightbulb?" I asked.

Gonzo groaned. "Here we go..."

"One... but the bulb will only work on their machine."

He rolled his eyes at me, and I perked up. "*Or* the answer is 'zero.' That's a hardware problem."

He shook his head and went back to his computer.

When we landed at 9:30 p.m. local time, I had Gonzo give me the gun before going through customs. We walked through security without a problem, and I looked around. Not a single person looked out of the ordinary. I felt lighter. We were free and clear from the agents after us—at least for now.

"Now what?" Gonzo asked.

I pulled out my phone. "Let's see what this Mario Camiletti has to say."

I found Robert's message with Mario's contact info and sent him a message. A moment later, Mario replied. *Hire a driver for your time here. Meet me at 1:30 p.m. tomorrow at Café Literario in Parque Balmaceda, Providencia.*

I replied with a thumbs-up emoji, then turned to the group. "We need to hire a driver."

Chrissy started tapping at her phone, then held it up to me. "I just did a search. Look at them all. There are dozens. You choose."

I scrolled through for a bit, then randomly picked a guy named Roberto Vega. Two minutes later, he was on his way to pick us up.

Cars came and went, picking up arrivals. Vee and Juliette popped off to change some euros for pesos, and the minutes crept along.

Gonzo scratched his curly hair. "So, we have someone coming, but where will we go?"

I turned to Chrissy. "Let's turn in early tonight and do some digging with the strange anomalies you've been researching. We've got half a day tomorrow. We may as well see if we can track down the shard."

When Roberto pulled up in his relatively decent minivan, I gave him a hundred thousand pesos (worth about a hundred euros) and said, "Take care of us, and there will be more where that came from."

He grinned brightly. "You got it, boss!"

He insisted we call him "Bobby V," which Vee didn't like, but whatevs. He took us to a nice-quality twenty-story hotel nearby and promised to pick us up first thing in the morning.

The next day, after we all loaded up, he said, "Where to, boss?"

Of course, Vee was in the front seat, and she gave him the address of the incident with Miguel Velasquez lifting the truck. We swerved into traffic, and everyone politely slowed to let us in. Bobby V was a fairly calm driver compared to many of those around us darting in and out.

As we entered the heart of Santiago, I marveled at the vivid contrasts of the city. The towering Andes mountains loomed in the distance, their snow-capped peaks standing out starkly against a clear sky, while the sprawling metropolis below hummed with life. The streets were a chaotic dance of cars and buses, honking and weaving through narrow lanes, framed by a patchwork of gleaming modern skyscrapers and timeworn colonial buildings. For a moment, despite everything, it felt like we were in the right place.

The street from the incident felt like a relic from another time, its narrow sidewalks lined with aging storefronts and industrial garages. Faded signs hung crookedly over the entrances of small auto repair shops, corner stores, and family-run bakeries, their windows clouded with years of dust and grime. The buildings, a mix of cracked brick and peeling stucco, leaned into the streets as if they had weathered decades of noise and commotion. The air smelled faintly of engine oil and fresh bread, with the occasional sharp tang of cleaning chemicals wafting from a nearby laundromat.

As we got out, a delivery truck rumbled down the uneven street, kicking up dirt. Locals gathered outside the shops and cast curious glances at us as we walked to the site of the incident. Vee, of course, was fluent in Spanish, so she took the lead. I could make do, and Chrissy and Juliette knew some as well, so we spread out. We asked passersby if they'd seen anything or knew about it, then went into different businesses and did the same.

Everyone we spoke to was friendly and had their own version of the story, but nobody knew who Miguel was, or any details of real value. Finally, at a hair salon, we found a lead.

A young woman spoke to us as she cut an older woman's hair. "It was very exciting," she said in Spanish. "He lifted the entire truck. News was here, and our little street was famous for the day."

"But do you know anything about the man, Miguel?" Vee asked.

"He's my sister's cousin's handyman," said another hairstylist.

We turned to see who had spoken. Rita was rotund and pleasant. Standing around five feet tall, and somewhere in her fifties, she was easily approachable and spoke to Vee as she snipped hair with practiced care. "He was coming to the auto supply shop to see if they had a part. That's when he came upon Julia pinned under the truck and lifted it."

"What do you know about him?" Vee asked.

"Nothing. But not a big man. It was a miracle."

"What's the place where he works?"

"I'd have to ask my sister's cousin."

So, we waited till she wrapped up the haircut, then she got on an old phone hanging on the wall and chatted for a bit. She nodded and smiled, then turned to Vee. "He does handyman jobs on the side. His primary job is with *Construccion Javier Central*. He's been working on a big build south of Santiago down *Avenida Santa Rosa*. You're welcome."

"Thank you so much!" Vee responded and passed her some pesos.

We piled back into the minivan and drove another forty minutes down Santa Rosa until we saw an enormous construction site. The site sprawled on the outskirts of Santiago, where the city's edge blurred into the countryside, the nearby buildings an eclectic mix of old and new. Half-finished concrete structures, all sharp angles and steel, stood beside crumbling facades with chipped paint and iron balconies sagging under the weight of time.

Vee pointed at a small building with cars parked next to it, and we went inside. A frazzled-looking woman sat at an old computer at one of the two desks, both cluttered with a disarray of papers.

"Hello," Vee said as we walked in. "We're looking for Miguel."

The woman behind the counter frowned.

"What's wrong?" Vee asked.

"He hasn't come in the last two days, and we haven't heard anything from him. He's not picking up his phone. It's very unusual."

My stomach flip-flopped, and I instinctively jammed my hand into my pocket to clench the shards. Were we too late? Had Jet Su's agents already gotten here ahead of us? My skin crawled, and I glanced around the room. Chrissy was wincing, and I gritted my teeth, thinking of what might have happened.

Vee was nonplussed. "We'd be happy to check in on him and let you know."

The woman looked relieved. "That would be very helpful. Thank you."

"Okay, we'll just need his address," Vee said nonchalantly, grabbing a piece of paper and a pen on the woman's desk.

"Oh, um, I can't do that..." she stammered.

Vee gave me a sharp look. I took a breath to calm my nerves and stepped up next to her. "If you don't want us to check on him personally, that's okay. We won't need his address. Perhaps just his emergency contact phone number. I'll punch it in my phone."

"Emilia. Yes. That would be good."

She clicked on her computer and started doing a search. While she did, I nonchalantly leaned over with my phone out.

"Here it is," she said.

I stretched my arm out over the desk, hoping the phone would take a good photo of the computer screen without being noticed. She leaned in, and I snapped the picture, then pulled back slowly.

She read the number, and Vee wrote it on the paper.

"Thanks," Vee said, and turned.

Before we left, Gonzo said, "I'm hungry. What's the best food around here?"

I asked her in Spanish, and she lit up. "The *humitas* around the corner are the best!"

We thanked her and went around the corner. Sure enough, the *humitas*, Chilean tamales, were fantastic. I couldn't help but eat three different types—chicken, pork, and spicy vegetable.

While we sat, I looked at the photo I had taken. The address was blurry, but it was there. A few of the characters may have been iffy, but there were only a few options.

We piled back into the minivan and drove another forty minutes to what we figured was Miguel's house.

It was on the less respectable side of town, run-down with flaking white paint. All the homes were single-story concrete affairs, with tall walls and foreboding metal bars protecting the front doors. We rang the doorbell, and a short woman peered out of the curtain at us.

She opened the door a crack. "*Sí. ¿Puedo ayudarté?*" She had a quiver in her voice and revealed only a peek of an eye.

With a soft tone, Vee spoke gently in Spanish. "Maybe you can. We're looking for Miguel. Could we speak with him, please?"

The door cracked slightly to reveal a sliver of the woman inside. Her eyes darted between us. Distrust was etched into her features. "He's not here," she said flatly, her voice thin and tired.

Vee didn't flinch. "Oh, that's too bad. We were hoping he could help us with a problem. You see, we heard about his amazing feat on the news with the truck and the whole miracle. We think he could help us with a very important matter."

The woman's expression tightened, her fingers gripping the door like she might slam it shut at any moment. "Go away." She let the door close. "There is nothing for you here."

"Wait!" Vee's urgency bled through her calm façade. She stepped forward, but not too close, her hands held out, palms up in a gesture of peace. "Emilia, please. We think we can help."

For a moment, the woman hesitated. Her grip on the door slackened, but the wariness in her eyes didn't fade. She looked as if she were teetering on the edge. Then she closed the door completely.

Vee gave me a piercing look. "We could use a little luck now, Mitzy."

"Wait!" I called in Spanish. I stepped forward and pulled a shard from my pocket. "Did he have one of these? It's important. Far more than you can imagine."

Emilia peeked out the curtain on the door, and her eyes went wide.

A moment later, we heard two different locks being unbolted, and she gave me a critical stare. "How do you have that?" Her eyes were red, and mascara dribbled down her cheeks from crying.

Vee took over again. "Is something wrong? What happened to Miguel?"

She broke down crying. "I don't know. I think he's been kidnapped! Or worse, killed!"

"Dear God," Vee said, and gave her a hug.

We stood around awkwardly as the two strangers hugged each other, then Emilia pulled away and brushed herself off. "Please, come in for tea."

Her home was simple and looked disheveled, with clothing on the floor and dirty dishes on the table. She looked around at the disarray as if in shock and immediately apologized and started picking things up.

"Not a problem, dearie," Juliette said, and stooped to pick up dirty clothing and tote them off to the laundry room. She bustled about, tidying up the room and bringing dishes into the kitchen.

Emilia gestured to the old, faded green couch. "Please sit. I'll make the tea."

She went into the kitchen, and the sound of clanking dishes reached us. Juliette joined her shortly afterward, and we could hear the sounds of dishes being cleaned.

When she returned with the tea, Juliette stayed in the kitchen, clattering away at the dishes and pots.

Emilia glanced at the kitchen as if to go back, and Vee grabbed her hand. "Please, sit. Juliette would love to take care of it. Come. Tell us about what happened to Miguel."

She sighed, and a single tear fell down her cheek. Vee gave a head jerk to Chrissy, who scrambled up and returned a moment later with a box of tissues. She spoke in Spanish, so Vee and I had to translate for everyone else later.

Emilia's eyes were distant as she spoke, the words heavy with sorrow. "Miguel works in construction. He's always a hard worker, good at his job. One day, about six weeks ago, something changed. He was digging at the site—same as any other day—when something caught his eye. He climbed out of his backhoe and picked it up."

Her eyes flicked to the shard in my hand, and she shuddered. "It looked exactly like that rock piece in your hands."

I exchanged a glance with Vee, who leaned closer, her voice soft. "What happened then?"

Emilia let out a shaky breath, wringing her hands. "At first, it was nothing. He thought it was just a relic, maybe something old and valuable. But after a few days... he started changing. He had more energy than I'd ever seen, like he was running on pure adrenaline all the time. It was... unnatural."

She paused, her voice catching in her throat. "Then, the strength came. He was lifting things that no normal man could—concrete blocks, beams, entire sections of scaffolding—like they weighed nothing. He had to be careful not to do it in front of others, because people started talking. They were calling him a miracle."

Vee caught her eye. "Did *you* hold it?"

"Yes." Her hands clenched into fists, knuckles white. "When I held it... I had visions. I saw things. Things I didn't understand. Premonitions of things to come. At first, the visions were good, that Miguel was destined for greatness, and helping many, many people. But then the visions changed."

She broke down, sobbing into her hands.

Vee gently rubbed her back. "What did you see?"

Emilia's voice quieted. "Impending danger for Miguel. The problem is, I didn't know from where!"

She started crying into a tissue, and Vee continued to rub her back. The rest of us sat around awkwardly. I quietly translated some of what she'd said to Chrissy and Gonzo.

"Go on," Vee said. "What did you sense?"

"They would come and go, these visions. Some of them happened, while at other times, it was like a glimpse of a possibility. But the night before Miguel saved that woman, I had powerful feelings. On the one hand, I knew he would save someone's life. And on the other, I sensed he was in great danger."

She sobbed. "But what could I do? How could I have stopped all of it from happening?" She turned to Vee. "Do you think he's okay?"

"When did he disappear exactly?" Vee asked.

"After he saved that poor woman pinned by the truck, he was on the news. When he came home that night, I was so proud of him. But I knew his life was in danger. I just knew it. I told him to call in sick, but he refused. The next morning, he left for work and didn't come home."

She cried again, and I translated for the others. Juliette came in with some freshly baked biscuits and some cheese. After setting the tray on the coffee table, Juliette sat on the other side of Emilia and patted her shoulder.

"There, there," she cooed in Spanish. "All will be well."

"Will it really?" Emilia asked.

Juliette frowned and then looked at me. "What say you, Stanley? What will you do for this young woman?"

I recoiled, suddenly put on the spot. "Um… That is…" I stammered, mind racing for options. What might help her? I glanced at the shard in my hand, and on an impulse, I held it out. "Here." I leaned over to her. "Hold this. What do you sense?"

She took a deep breath and reached out a shaky hand to take the shard. At first, she frowned. Then her eyes glossed over, trance-like. All at once, her face brightened, and she sat up. "He's alive! I'll see him again. I just know it."

She blinked rapidly, then nodded slowly. "Yes. I'm sure of it. He's not dead. Only held captive. He'll return to me within the week." She turned to me. "Thank you for letting me see. Thank you." She started crying again, only with a smile.

"Do you think he still has the shard?" I asked.

Vee scowled at me. "Mitzy!" she scolded.

"What?" I lifted my hands innocently. "I'm just wondering."

Emilia shook her head. "That rock is far gone from our lives. And good riddance!"

"Gone?" I asked. "To where?"

She shook her head. "I don't see it anymore. It was taken from Miguel. Perhaps it's still in Santiago. But that's all I see."

With pursed lips, she reached over and passed the shard back to me. "Thank you for allowing me the chance to hold this. You have helped put my mind at ease. And now I never want to hold it again."

With that, we ate the fresh biscuits and had our tea. We made idle chitchat with her, then after half an hour, politely went on our way.

When we got back to the minivan, Bobby asked us where to go.

Everyone turned to me, and I looked at my watch. 12:30 p.m. "Let's just head to the café."

As we drove, Gonzo looked out the window, lost in thought. "Do you think the shard has left Chile yet?"

We considered, then Chrissy said, "I think it's still here. If Miguel is truly going to come back to Emilia, that means the agents still have him somewhere, and possibly with him, the shard."

I frowned. "But how would we even *get* a shard from the Preservation Society? They're ultra-powerful."

"Unless," Vee turned back and looked at me with a wry smile, "we were incredibly lucky."

As I looked at her, I found myself smiling back. "I have no idea what to do next."

She shrugged. "Hasn't hindered us yet."

I slowly nodded. "Indeed."

Café Literario was more library than eating establishment. Overlooking a river next to a park, with shelves of books taking up over half the building, it felt like a quirky, out-of-the-way place perfect for a clandestine meeting.

We found a table at the back and sat with our *pan batido* and coffees when an elderly gentleman stepped up to our table. He exuded elegance and sophistication, wearing a well-tailored gray suit and sporting a well-trimmed haircut with a graying goatee.

"Stanley, I presume?" he said with a smirk.

"Yes. Please, have a seat." I offered him a free chair.

He glanced left and right before sitting with us. "I hear you would like intel on the local Preservation Society. They're not a large group here. Their local headquarters is quite close."

Vee cocked her head. "How large is 'not large'? How many people are we talking about here?"

He wagged his head. "Perhaps forty or fifty. Now—" He raised a hand. "I'm happy to provide intel, but I would like something in return."

"Like what?" I asked.

He smirked. "How are you at breaking into buildings and accessing computers?"

I glanced at Gonzo and grinned. "Actually... We may be *really* good at that sort of thing."

Chapter 16

"I will provide you with intel only if you can install this flash drive onto a Preservation Society computer," Mario said, holding up a small thumb drive.

"Tell us more." I glanced at Vee to make sure she was following. Her tactical mind would ensure we didn't miss anything.

The well-dressed man leaned forward with his phone out for us to see a map of our location. "Their headquarters is a mere two blocks from here. They go under the public-facing name *Fundación de Desarrollo Cultural*."

He flipped to a photo of a bland-looking office. "If you can get inside without being noticed, you'll need to get into one of the back rooms. They usually keep five to ten staff there during the day, fewer at night, unless they're having big meetings, but those are rare. Any of the computers there will do. You'll need to unlock it before inserting the flash drive, and the software should be self-explanatory. Just click 'accept' and it should install what I need."

Gonzo was tapping the table nervously. I glanced up at him, and he gave me a look as if to say, *I know you're going to ask me to do this.*

I gave him a matter-of-fact shrug that communicated, *Of course I am.*

Mario looked at me closely. "What more do you need to know?"

I looked at Vee. She was deep in thought. "If we do this for you, what sort of benefit do we get?"

He placed the flash drive on the table. "I'll tell you whatever I can of the Preservation Society."

She pursed her lips. "Don't you think it would help us more to know that before we try breaking into their headquarters?"

He gave her a wry look. "I can't help you much more than I have for the mission. But you do this, and I'll have access to a lot more answers to any question you might have about them."

Vee turned to me and gave a slight nod. I fingered the flash drive. "Okay. Let's do it."

Mario stood. "Message me when you have an update. I'll make sure I'm available all day."

When he was gone, we quickly came up with a basic plan. We would pare the team down to me, Gonzo and Chrissy. Gonzo would try to turn all three of us invisible. My luck would keep us safe and on track, and Chrissy's enhanced listening would help us know what was going on.

Gonzo looked pale. "If I'm going to do this, I need *way* more practice turning myself and you guys invisible. And if I'm constantly holding onto you guys, how do I hack into a computer?"

"Good points," I nodded. "So, let's find someplace secluded and see what we can do."

We left the café and found a quiet part of the park, obscured by trees and bushes. It was a crisp spring day in the Southern Hemisphere, and we were all wearing jackets. Even so, Gonzo held a shard and immediately grew clammy. He closed his eyes, then held a hand toward Chrissy. "Okay, let's do this."

The two of them turned invisible, and we waited as Gonzo tried different grips and ways of holding both the shard and Chrissy at the same time. Then, he brought me into it. With some experimentation, he figured that the best combo for all three of us to benefit was to hold one shard in each hand while also gripping our hands, holding the same shards. Chrissy and I both felt the effects of the shards at the same time, and all three of us were able to remain invisible.

After half an hour, Gonzo looked ragged. "This is exhausting," he complained. "I've only just started using these things, and already I'm tired. I'm getting better with the vertigo, but it feels like it's sucking me dry."

"What do you need?" Chrissy asked with concern.

Gonzo wiped his face. "A sandwich. And maybe a neon sign that says *Invisible Guy at Work—Please Don't Trip Over Him.*"

We strolled down the street to the building with the headquarters, then grabbed a sandwich across the street and watched the building. While we sat there, a few people in dark combat-ready clothing left the building. Otherwise, it seemed like a boring downtown office.

When we were almost finished, Vee got my attention. "Now, remember, you can't be seen. No matter what. They don't know we're in Chile, and we'd like to keep it that way. Get in, do the computer job, and see if you can learn more about the shard they stole from Miguel." She turned to Chrissy. "Keep your ears alert to any conversations."

Just then, two dark-clothed agents walked up to the building and entered. One of them was clutching a bag that caught my eye. "Those guys." I pointed. "We should follow them. Come on."

Leaving Vee and Juliette at the table, the three of us rose and went around a discrete corner where we turned invisible, then crossed the street and entered the office building as quickly as possible. *Fundación de Desarrollo Cultural* was on the third floor, and we rode the elevator up, feeling the tension rise as Gonzo's hands grew clammier. I tried not to think about what would happen if Gonzo released our hands, like at the airport. I could only imagine there would be cameras everywhere.

The glass doors to the office opened to a bland layout, with an empty front desk, cubicles with a few people at desks, and a back door that the two men were walking toward with purpose. We followed as quickly as we could while trying to be quiet. As we passed a woman at one cubicle, I noticed she didn't stand out from any other office worker. No black clothing. No visible combat-ready training. Even a little rotund. It was reassuring that not all the Preservation Society were field agents.

One of the field agents keyed in numbers at a touchpad, and the back door opened. We walked briskly, and I put a foot out to stop the door from completely shutting behind them.

Carefully, we edged the door open and slipped inside. One look and we definitely felt like we were in the headquarters of a secret magical society.

The hallway beyond was dimmer, lit by strips of recessed lighting that hummed faintly overhead. To the right, wide glass windows revealed a tactical training room where a pair of agents sparred in silence, their movements sharp and disciplined on the padded floor. Past that was a long row of doors labeled in discreet lettering—*Logística, Comunicaciones, Monitoreo Nacional.* Through one window I glimpsed a wall of monitors, each displaying different regions of Chile in real time, red markers flaring on maps of cities and highways. A pair of analysts hunched over their desks, headsets pressed to their ears, their voices murmuring in clipped Spanish as data scrolled across the screens.

The two men we were following didn't pause; they carried the bag with the ease of practiced routine, leading us deeper into the heart of the HQ. We slipped past an open operations room, where a digital map of South America glowed on a massive screen and a few field agents studied it, pointing out areas as if planning future missions. Finally, the men stopped at a reinforced door at the end of the hall. A keypad and card reader blinked red beside it until one of them swiped his badge. The lock clicked open, and they stepped into a small, steel-walled chamber lined with lockers.

One of them turned to the other as they strode to a locker and spoke in Spanish. "Did you hear, Jet Su himself is coming for the artifacts?"

"Are you still looking for that promotion?" the other man asked.

"Once he sees our success, I'm a top candidate." He gave a glance at the locker next to him. "Let's get this thing locked up."

He pulled out a key from around his neck and unlocked the locker to reveal a small black safe with a keypad. He pushed some buttons on the safe, each producing an identical *beep*. Seven beeps, and it opened. He unzipped his bag and put something small inside the safe, then closed it and locked the locker.

"All good. Let's go." They turned and left, leaving the three of us invisible.

Chrissy's voice was a whisper. "I could make out some of their thoughts, but not all. It's an artifact. Either the shard or something else important. And the key code. It's a significant date. Six digits and a pound sign. I caught that much. But what the numbers are, I didn't catch."

"Come on," I urged, dragging Gonzo closer to the locker with the small safe.

At the door, I pulled out the skeleton key from my pocket. For the last couple of days, I'd gotten into the habit of keeping it in my pocket. Now I understood why. Without seeing it, I knew as soon as I brought it near the keyhole the key was transforming. I could feel the key wiggling as it changed shape to fit the slot exactly. I inserted it, then twisted and heard the satisfying *click* as the door unlocked.

With my one free hand, I scooped up the small safe—it was probably about ten pounds, a foot wide, a foot deep, and half that tall. As soon as it left the floor of the locker, it disappeared.

My heart was thumping in my ears as I shut the locker door. "We should get out of here as quickly as possible. We just need to get that thumb drive inserted into an open computer."

We cautiously opened the door and looked around. Nobody seemed to notice the unusual door opening. We walked slowly, Gonzo's hands now slick with sweat. He squirmed, our grip feeling more and more awkward as we both held the shard.

"Not long now, buddy," I urged with a forced whisper. "Keep holding."

"This is killing me," he whispered back. "I'm tapped out. Can we hurry?"

I looked desperately for an open computer. None were to be found. "This way." I led them till we found an open door to a room that read *Comunicaciones*. "There."

The room was empty, with computers and screens lining a wall, all of them turned on. We walked inside and scanned the computers till I found one that looked hopeful, with a USB slot. I fumbled awkwardly in my pocket for the drive, the safe crooked under my arm biting into my ribs, and my jostling was enough to put Gonzo over the edge. The shard slipped out of his hand long enough that I blipped back into sight.

My heart leaped into my throat. A quick glance showed cameras in the corners. I was caught on video.

I gritted my teeth. What was done was done. No use worrying about it further. I still had the shard in my hand.

With a burst of confidence, I completely let go of Gonzo's hand and sat down at the computer, putting the lockbox on the desk next to me, trying to keep the shard palmed out of sight from the cameras.

I inserted the drive, accepted the installation of the malware, then waited as it loaded.

"Hurry," Gonzo urged.

My breathing was forced, and I wiped my hands on my pants. The clock ticked away. *Come on, hurry*, I silently begged.

In what felt like far too long, the software finished installing. I closed the window, removed the drive, grabbed the safe, and reached out to where I figured Gonzo stood. A moment later, I went invisible again.

"Let's go," I whispered.

No alarms were going off as we tiptoed back the way we'd come, past the different analysts and to the door. Thankfully, it was unlocked from the inside, and we pushed it open, slipping into the mundane-looking office with cubicles.

Not far to go now. We tried not to make any noise as we walked back toward the entrance. Every scuff of Gonzo's feet had me wincing, but none of the office workers in their cubicles noticed, and no alerts went off.

We got through the front doors, then back to the elevator.

"Can we relax yet?" Gonzo asked.

"Better not," I replied. "They probably monitor the entire building, whether it looks mundane or not."

It felt like an eternity before we emerged and crossed the street back to the sandwich shop.

"Let's get out of here," I said to Vee and Juliette. "Now."

It was over an hour before I felt back to normal again. We were far across town at a bar, growing emboldened with liquid courage. Empty beer bottles littered the table as the five of us sat at a back table, with the small lockbox sitting in the middle of it. Gonzo looked more relieved than I'd ever seen him. His t-shirt was still drenched at the pits, but he looked beyond happy to be sitting safely with us.

He raised his beer, and for the fourth time, gave a toast. "Here's to Team Invisibility: powered by luck, sweat, and mild panic attacks."

"I'll say it again," I chimed in. "You really pulled through, big guy. I know that stretched you. That whole B&E wouldn't have been possible without you." I raised my glass. "Here's to the man who redefined stealth—invisible body, *very* visible smell."

We clinked glasses with laughter and enjoyed the moment until Mario showed up shortly thereafter. He bore the same elegance as before, but now he exuded excitement. As soon as he sat at the table with us, he leaned in eagerly.

"It worked! We have access to their systems thanks to you. And hopefully, they won't notice it for a while."

"Why did you want that, anyway?" I asked.

He stroked his graying goatee. "Let's just say, it will be helpful to stay one step ahead of the agency. You will quickly find that the Theurgica in Chile is a little more... how shall I say, *unrefined*, than other parts of the world. More cutthroat. Vying factions and such. It will pay handsomely to outmaneuver the watchdogs."

"So, tell us about who's after us," I pressed. "Jet Su."

Mario leaned back and pulled out a small tablet from an inside pocket, then began scanning it. "Jet Su. Commander,

Inter-House Investigations Directorate." He glanced up at us. "Big title, that one. Means he can open up pretty much any door anywhere." He went back to scanning.

"Let's see. According to this, he's based in New York City. He's successfully shut down major crime syndicates around the world. Oh... I didn't realize." He glanced up at us. "He's the one responsible for the dissolution of Jersey House. My, my. He's quite the heavy hitter."

Vee was furrowing her brow. "What can you find out about his more recent activity? Is there any mention of what he's been up to?"

Mario frowned. "I don't have any clearance to look at anything beyond just surface-level findings. But let me see what I can dig up." He scanned, then typed and read.

While he was busy, my mind wandered. On the one hand, I was unbelievably encouraged that we'd broken into a Preservation Society headquarters, albeit a small one. It was a sign that we could take things into our own hands. But thinking about someone powerful enough to shut down an entire house... it felt daunting.

Mario broke through my thoughts. "I can't see much more on what he's up to, except that I see the call to the entire agency to find you lot." He glanced up. "All five of you are listed, with photographs and descriptions. It says your last sighting was in Paris."

Chrissy sighed in relief, but I winced. "Yeah, but that'll change now that they've seen me."

"What do you mean?" Mario gave me a serious stare.

"We were invisible for most of the operation, but when I installed the malware, I was visible. We also stole this lockbox, so they know I'm here, and that I have it."

Mario's face paled. "That means my software won't last long at all before they figure it out." He glanced around nervously. "It won't be long before Chile is swarming with international agents, all from Jet Su's reserve." He swore quietly. "I need to wrap up with you quickly and have my team see if they can prolong the time it takes for them to discover our malware. Anything else pressing?"

Everyone turned to me. "Well… one of those guys said Jet Su himself is coming here. So, is there somewhere we can lie low for a bit?"

His eyes grew wide. "You must leave Santiago. Tomorrow morning at the latest."

"Where can we go?" I asked. "Robert mentioned Chile has some safe pockets from the Preservation Society. Is that an option?"

Mario nodded. "Yes. Yes. You could find one of them. The closest would be Cortez, a couple of hours north of here toward the Inca Lagoon." He stood and gave the lockbox a look of distaste. "Good luck. And thanks for getting us into their system, albeit briefly."

With just a slight pause, he turned and left, leaving the five of us sitting around the table.

Juliette was staring at her glass sullenly. The others were watching me, waiting for me to say something.

I shrugged. "Let's try some decent food and get an early rest. Something tells me we'll have a long day ahead of us tomorrow."

We enjoyed a nice meal, with three kinds of ceviche. But the whole time, there was an aura of tension at the table. We were all eager to turn in early, get a good sleep, and get as far away as possible with that lockbox.

The next day, Bobby V picked us up at eight o'clock, and we struck out. Unfortunately, Cortez wasn't on any of the maps we could find, so we decided we'd just start heading for the Inca Lagoon and see what happened. It was a lovely day, and we drove along small country roads while I tried dozens of different six-number combinations on the lockbox while holding the shards. Part of me was expecting it to just open, what with all the lucky breaks we'd been having. But it remained locked as we wound past small towns and wineries, leaving Santiago far behind.

Gonzo shook his head. "If your luck doesn't just open it, you need a system. Chrissy said it was an important date, right? You need to think of all the possible important dates. The nice thing is, if it really is a date, it limits the first digit to zero or one, and the third digit to zero, one, two, or three, and that's limited as well. Narrows it down for sure."

I nodded. "We'll have to do some digging into big dates for the Preservation Society, as well as Ancient Egypt. It could be anything."

The countryside blurred by as we passed another small town. Juliette started singing, and on a whim, I passed her a shard. She held it and sang a little folk song. Soon enough we felt our spirits lift as the aches and tiredness from all the stress and travel dissipated.

Chile is beautiful. Surprisingly, it looks a lot like the western U.S. with the arid climate and tall mountains, but with concrete buildings and many vineyards. After a while, I stared into the glyphs on the shard.

What do I need to do? I asked myself. *Do we already have the third shard, or is something else in this lockbox?*

About halfway to the Inca Lagoon. Robert called. I put him on speakerphone.

"Stanley. Good to hear from you. How did the meeting with Mario go?"

"He asked us to break into the Preservation Society HQ to install some malware. We got in and took a lockbox that looks like it might have the third shard. Can't open it without the six-digit code, unfortunately."

"Well!" Robert replied. "Quite the feat. And what are you doing now?"

"Well," I winced. "I was captured on video, and we know Jet Su is heading this way, so we've decided to try to find one of those safe havens you mentioned."

"Very good plan. Excellent idea. Better than flying out immediately."

"What's the update on your end?" I asked. "Did you go to the Library of Congress?"

He began bubbling with excitement. "I've found the book, Stanley! It's everything we'd hoped for."

Everyone perked up. "Like what?" I asked.

"The prophecy is here. And so much more. It goes into great depths on pieces of this puzzle. I can't believe this level of scholarship exists."

"Can you check it out?" Gonzo asked.

"Unfortunately, no. Hello, Gus. Is everyone else there?"

"Yes," I said. "You're on speakerphone. So what will you do?"

"I'm going to be taking lots of photos, I'm afraid. Two-hundred-thirty, to be precise. But no matter. It's well worth the effort. I believe we'll have the answers we've been looking for."

"Do me a favor and send me a picture of that prophecy," I said. "I want to study it."

"Of course. And Gus, how's the progress on the software to translate the inscriptions?"

Gonzo frowned. "It's going okay, I guess. I can't figure out how to get it to rely on known word associations while also guessing at possibilities. I'm missing something, but not sure what."

"Keep at it, lad," Robert said. "The Prophecy of Ramessesnakht might be able to help. We've got both the original pictures of it and a translation in this book. If we feed that new information in, it most certainly will be of aid."

I brightened. "Hey, did you see any other writing like on the *insides* of the shards? With the magic stuff?"

"Oh yes. But none of it is translated. However, I wonder if we have enough to make sense of it if Gus can get his algorithm working."

"Sounds good."

Robert paused. "You know, the ancient Egyptians were a curious lot. They often had major factions who saw the world completely differently. It can make translation difficult when we're using multiple sources. For example, did you know there were people who didn't even believe the river would flood?"

"Seriously?" I recoiled. "How is that even possible?"

"Indeed." He paused. "You might even say… that they were in de-Nile."

We were silent for a moment. Chrissy started laughing first, and then the rest of us joined in. The car filled with joy, Gonzo slapping his knees happily.

"On that note," Robert said with a chuckle. "I bid you adieu. Good luck."

I was feeling better, even though we were on a road completely far from anything, not a human in sight. How would we ever find a town that wasn't on any map? I stared at the shard in my hand with frustration and was almost tempted to tell Bobby to turn around when there was a sudden loud burst and the van wobbled.

"Flat tire!" Bobby called out as he swerved to the side of the road.

We sat patiently while Bobby puttered around in the back, scrounging in the minivan's trunk. He came back to the front and opened the passenger door, gesturing to the glove box in front of Vee.

"Could you pass me the manual, please?"

Vee handed it to him, and he began leafing through the pages. Soon enough, he was cursing, or at least I figured that's what it was, since he was using Chilean words I'd never heard before.

I got out and stretched, as did the others. "What's going on?" I asked.

He shook his head with chagrin. "I'm so sorry, my friends. I don't seem to have a car jack to put the spare on. I don't know why!"

He was beside himself. "I've never used it. I can't imagine why it's missing. Come look, Stanley. Can you find it?"

I could not, not even holding both shards. And neither could Vee. So, we started waving at oncoming cars. The first few didn't pull over, but finally one did. It was a nice-looking young guy named Ricardo who was driving a beat-up dusty Buick. He got out and asked what was up.

Bobby bowed his head. "Thank you for stopping. It should take only a minute. I have a spare, just no car jack. Can we use yours?"

"Of course," Ricardo said. He pulled the jack out of his car and helped raise the minivan. He even helped remove and install the spare tire.

Before he left, I asked, "Have you ever heard of a town called Cortez around these parts?"

Ricardo squinted. "I was about to say no, but actually, maybe I have." He peered into the distance, the snow-capped peaks creating a glorious backdrop to our broken-down scene.

"You know, I could have sworn I visited a town named Cortez to make a delivery once. But now that I'm trying to remember it, the memory is hazy."

"Here," I said, handing him my smartphone with the map open. "Whereabouts do you think it was?"

He shook his head as he panned around the map. "Definitely north of here, but not toward the lagoon, more toward the coast." He squinted. "Pampita, maybe." He pointed and handed the phone to me. "If it exists, my gut tells me it's either near there, or it *is* there. But who knows." He shrugged. "Sorry my memory is so faulty."

"No problem. Thanks so much."

We piled in and drove for another ten minutes. The whole time I watched my phone from the back seat. "This is the spot. Turn left at this road here."

Twenty minutes in, I said, "Turn right here."

Not long after, we were far from any other town, utterly in the middle-of-nowhere Chile, driving past yet another dirt road, when I felt my gaze drawn to the north.

"Here," I called out. "Turn right down this dirt road."

We went about a mile and came to a hand-painted sign in Spanish that read: *Cortez, Población 365.* And underneath it, in a darker scrawl, *Cada persona tiene su día:* Every person has their day.

Cute, I thought. But what about leap year?

Bobby shifted nervously, his knuckles white against the steering wheel. "You sure about this, Boss?"

"Why?" I was instantly curious. "Something bothering you?"

"Didn't you read the sign?"

"What about it?"

"It... do you think it's okay to go there when they have such warnings about trespassers?"

I looked at Gonzo. "Did you see it?"

He shrugged. "Whatevs, dude. It's in Spanish."

Vee eyed me critically. "It said: Cortez, population full. Visitors not wanted. Trespassers beware."

I smiled. "Ah. *That* sign." My sci-fi brain was going into hyperdrive. Illusions for certain people only? Anything could be possible. But why did *I* see more welcoming words? Or was it because while holding the shards, I was no longer mundane?

Either way, I was now more eager than ever. "Keep driving. It doesn't apply to us."

"Okay..." He didn't sound convinced.

We rounded a curve, and Cortez revealed itself like a secret oasis, nestled snug between the mountains with a river that wound through, sparkling in the afternoon light. On the surface, it looked like any picturesque village you'd find in the Chilean countryside: modest homes, narrow dirt roads, and fields of crops lining the outskirts. But there was something else—a trait I couldn't quite put my finger on.

The first sign that something was off was a group of two dozen kids engaged in a paintball war in a park on the edge of town. Bright splashes of color exploded into the trees and onto the kids as they dashed around jungle gyms and a small fort. I blinked as the entire fort lifted off the ground, hovering twenty feet in the air, kids shooting down at the ones on the ground.

But a teenager on the ground transformed into a giant octopus, twenty feet from tip to tip, its vibrant orange body standing out on the dry, grassy terrain. The giant octopus moved swiftly across the field, tentacles snatching plexiglass shields from kids, who were laughing and screaming like this was all normal. You'd think all that elevation would give the kids on top a serious advantage, but the octopus was surprisingly fast at blocking shots and stood guard over the others impressively.

"Is that—?" Chrissy started but didn't finish her thought.

Bobby's jaw was open. "*Dios mío!*" he whispered.

I swallowed. "So... this isn't a regular village."

We sat there in stunned silence. The van idled as we watched the octopus move brilliantly—leaping and shrinking—blocking with one tentacle and picking up a gun and firing into the fort with another.

Bobby's sharp intake of breath cut through the quiet. "Uh oh."

I snapped my head around. A dust cloud billowed in the distance, growing larger with each passing second. A massive, armored car was barreling straight toward us, a nasty-looking turret mounted on top. The gun on it glinted menacingly in the sunlight.

Bobby turned and grabbed my arm with wild eyes. "Time to leave, Boss."

I didn't answer right away but waited for a sense from the shards. "No." I shook my head. "Not yet."

Vee glanced back at me, then eyed the shards in my hand and gave a tight-lipped nod. "Are you ready for this, Mitzy?" Her voice wavered.

I felt my throat tighten. I wasn't used to *her* being the one relying on *me*. It felt all wrong. "We'll see."

The massive car pulled up in front of us. That armor looked really thick. And yes, there was some dude with sunglasses and a black bandana riding on the top with a massive gun pointed right at us.

And then they just sat there.

My heart thundered in my chest, and I questioned just about every decision I'd made in the last two weeks that had led to this moment. Never in my life had I expected to be in some random Chilean village with a massive gun pointed at me, with nobody else in the world knowing where we were, and no idea what we were even doing there.

I glanced at the shards, realizing as if for the first time just how much I was relying on them. I instantly formed a guttural love-hate feeling about them, wishing I'd never seen them in the first place while simultaneously marveling at how incredible they were. And then, in the next split-second, I felt a calm sense of resolution, recognizing I had to continue moving to make things make sense.

So, I opened the rolling side door of the minivan and walked out, trying to look as casual as possible, hand in my pocket, not wanting to draw attention to the shard I was gripping.

I lifted my left hand and gave a wave, armpits sweating instantly. "Hi. I'm Mitzy. We're here looking for answers to some questions." I spoke in Spanish, since we were far from the big city.

The passenger door creaked open, and out stepped a woman, who immediately commanded attention. Her movements were fluid, almost predatory, as she surveyed me with dark, unreadable eyes. She was striking—beautiful in a fierce, untouchable way—her sun-kissed skin and sharp features catching the light. A pistol hung casually at her hip, and a nasty-looking tactical knife on her thigh, worn with use.

She wore a tight-fitting black shirt with a half-buttoned brown long-sleeve over it and rugged green cargo pants caked with dirt stains. She held herself like Vee—someone who could take you down using just her hands. She strode toward me—animal-like, elegant, fierce.

"Mitzy, you say? You got past our protections. Who are you with? You *do* know you have mundanes with you?"

"Yes, yes. I know." I realized then that she must have some way of seeing that I had power and couldn't tell it was coming from the shards. I felt the urge to babble. "We've been investigating this shard, with extraordinary characteristics nobody seems to know anything about, and a powerful person from the Preservation Society has sent agents to kill us many times over the last couple of weeks. We followed a trail that led us to Santiago for another shard, and when that didn't pan out, we followed other clues that led us here."

I didn't know why I divulged all of that. But that's what came out. Thankfully, it seemed to work, because she gave me a little smile.

"Well, then." She eyed me over again, and I felt suddenly naked. No idea why. I wondered at that moment if she had X-ray vision of some sort.

She put her fists on her hips and stared at the people in the car more closely. She waved me over. "You can ride with us. Your friends can follow."

She opened the rear door of the armored car, and I slowly walked over and looked inside. A scruffy-looking Latino with well-worn combat clothing and a gun strapped to his chest sat behind the wheel. Okay then.

I waved for Bobby to follow us, hesitating for just a moment before climbing into the armored car. The air inside was thick. The leather seats were cracked and worn. The driver barely glanced at me, his face shadowed by a ragged baseball cap. The woman slid into the seat next to me, her presence looming like a storm cloud, and the car did a U-turn.

"So…" I forced a casual tone. "Either of you have names?"

The man let out a low, gravelly chuckle, but said nothing.

"Maria," the woman said, her voice soft but sharp, like the edge of a blade.

"Unique," I retorted without thinking.

"Ha!" She flashed a smile at me with nice-looking teeth, then grew firm again instantly.

But that smile changed everything. Through all the intimidation, I saw a brief glimpse of her as a warm person who was just doing her job, and I wanted to break the ice with her. But how? I blurted out the first thing that came to mind. "Cortez doesn't really have three hundred sixty-five people, does it? What do you do during leap years?"

She chuckled. "I've said that very thing. No, we're over four hundred now, Mitzy. But the idea still stands—everyone's voice is heard equally in Cortez, no matter the age or social status. It's what makes us unique."

"Even visitors?" I prodded.

The man scoffed, and Maria said, "No. Not visitors." She considered for a moment. "Until they prove themselves."

For the rest of the drive into town, I kept wondering what it would take to prove myself to her. I can't even explain how important it was to me at that moment.

As we rolled deeper into Cortez, it looked... normal. But there was something—an energy that permeated just under the surface—that made me look more closely. For all the strangeness we'd just seen, the village itself seemed like any other sleepy town tucked away in the mountains. The narrow streets were lined with concrete homes and small businesses scattered with corner stores and dusty restaurants. The market stalls buzzed with quiet activity, locals seemingly oblivious to the armored car passing through their midst.

But something gnawed at me, a nagging feeling that I couldn't shake. I kept scanning the streets, the homes, trying to put my finger on what was bothering me. Then it hit me.

There were no walls. No bars.

Everywhere else I'd seen in Chile, every house we'd passed had tall walls, gates, iron bars on the windows—a necessary defense against crime. But here the homes were open, unguarded, as if there was no need to protect themselves. As if the village feared nothing from the outside.

I wondered about it for a moment but then thought of the fact that Maria was surprised that mundanes had gotten as far as we had. That, and the fact that they'd showed up in an armored car, and my curiosity at the lack of household protections, were quickly sated.

"So..." I stammered, wanting to make small talk, but somehow my tongue felt like it was glued to the roof of my mouth. "Do you enjoy living here?"

Maria didn't respond right away. I felt like her eyes bore into me for a moment. "I do not have an answer for you, Mitzy. It is what it is."

"Um... okay." Not exactly reassuring. My palms were slick with sweat, and I felt the familiar prickling of anxiety creeping in. Why did this conversation feel like walking on a razor's edge? "So... what do you guys do here?"

"We live. We eat. We die."

It was like cotton balls filled my mouth. I couldn't find words, but I knew we could have a decent conversation. I just knew it. I clutched the shards, hidden out of sight, and my fingers vibrated. I felt a headache throb, but I did my best to ignore it and tried another tack.

"I mean, you've got all this preparation for outsiders. You must do more than just live out here. And you have to stock these stores with stuff. You must leave sometimes if mundanes don't come here for deliveries."

"Yes. Yes. Of course. We will show you everything, Mitzy. In due time. But first, you must explain yourself and your friends to the leadership."

"The Theurgica Leadership?" I asked.

"Not exactly. It's our town's leadership. Although some in the past have been members of the greater Leadership."

"Of course." I was nearing the end of my understanding of these people. But then I realized I'd dropped mention of our foes earlier and she hadn't blinked. "And the Preservation Society?"

The driver spat out his window.

Maria spoke coldly. "They haven't been able to come through our protections in nineteen years, and we're going to keep it that way."

"Wonderful." I leaned back into my seat and breathed deeply. That's when I knew the shard had led us right yet again. We were probably in the safest place ever from those thugs.

I gave a little chuckle to myself happily, and Maria said, "This makes you happy, doesn't it, Mitzy?"

"Yes, Maria. Yes, it does."

Maria's lips curled into a faint smile, though there was nothing comforting about it. "You're feeling good now, Mitzy. But just wait. You'll have to go on trial and answer to the leadership soon enough. And as for your friends..." She paused, letting the weight of her words sink in. "If you can't give a compelling reason not to, their memories will need to be wiped clean."

My stomach dropped. "Wait, what?"

Maria's gaze flicked to mine with a cool intensity. "This town is protected for a reason. Outsiders don't get to leave with what they've seen—unless we allow it."

The pit in my stomach deepened, and I clutched the shards like a drowning man gripping a piece of driftwood. The brief sense of safety I'd just felt evaporated in an instant.

I knew something had been too easy about this place. I just hoped they'd let me keep holding onto the shards during the trial.

Chapter 17

The room was stifling. The pressure of dozens of eyes fixed on me. The leaders sat at one end of the table, their expressions blank but judging, waiting for me to stumble. I could feel the shards pulsing in my hand, the edges biting into my palm, but instead of offering comfort, it made my heart race faster. Members continued to arrive, but nobody said a word, including Maria and the eight other people who stood or sat on the fringes.

When the twelfth member of the leadership was seated, the eldest leader, a man in his seventies who looked like he hadn't smiled in decades, tapped the table with his knuckles.

"State your name and purpose here," he said, his voice cold, devoid of any warmth.

I swallowed hard, my mouth dry. The shards pulsed more fervently, and I felt a familiar ache pounding in my head, like it was being squeezed, but I didn't ease up. My mind raced, battling between the truth and the lies I'd started rehearsing. I struggled. Should I tell them the full story? But then they would know I was mundane, too, and might wipe my brain along with my friends. I dreamed up wild, extravagant explanations. I considered what might save us. I tried willing the shards to work. Why weren't they working? I had no idea what to say, and everyone was staring at me. Were the shards broken? Were these people blocking their power? I was second-guessing everything.

And then, to my left, I heard Maria's voice: "Just tell them, Mitzy."

I took a deep breath and decided to just dive in. "I… am a mundane."

A collective intake of breath echoed around the room, and the leader's eyes narrowed. He looked at Maria and she shook her head *No*. He glanced at me with raised eyebrows. "Go on."

"The name is Stanley Mitz. My friends call me Mitzy. I didn't have powers till just last month, when my friends and I were watching a meteor shower, and one of them landed. Along with the rock was this little shard."

In that moment, I had the instinct to separate the shards and keep one of them in my left hand below the table as I raised the other shard in my right. "Holding the shard instantly gives mundanes traits, as we have discovered over these last weeks. It also enhances the power of anyone touching it. But we were foolish and posted a video online. The very next day, two thugs from the Preservation Society came after it. They tried to kill me to get it."

At the mention of the Preservation Society, the heads bobbed. I knew then I'd taken the right tack. I gained gusto. "With our newfound powers, we survived the encounter with them and followed clues from the shard. We've learned a good deal about it. One side is written in Ancient Egyptian Hieratic, the other sides in an old language of magic. We also know that there are more shards. We believe they are scattered around the world."

At that, a few people in the room leaned forward in interest. I gained confidence. "We followed a trail to France, finding resistance and encounters with agents under Commander Jet Su's leadership. We aren't entirely sure what they plan to do if they can get all the shards, but it can't be good. We know they already have two or three, and they are stopping at nothing to get more. Although they've tried to kill us many times, we've always gotten away. Finally, in Paris, we visited the Theurgica and learned more of your society."

I paused. I was avoiding saying too much, but also didn't want to lie—not after our encounter with Edward Peacock. What if they had a way of seeing through lies, like he could? "We figured out there's another shard in Santiago and came here looking for it. We don't want Jet Su and his minions to have any more, for fear that they plan something awful."

"Another shard? How many *are* there?" asked a younger member, who was peering at the shard in my hand.

"We believe there are six in total. They would fit together perfectly." I held back information—just in case I needed leverage later. "We were right that there was a shard here, discovered by a man who would gain incredible strength when he touched it. The man was kidnapped. We arrived a day too late and spoke with his wife. Holding our shard, she could see into the future, and knew that he was alive but held hostage."

My eyes panned the room at the serious faces. "We had to see if the shard was still in Santiago. We couldn't let them have it, so we broke into the Preservation Society's headquarters to see if we could find it, and to install some software for Mario Camiletti. We didn't find it, unfortunately, but we did install the software. We escaped, but now they most likely know we're in Chile. We knew we needed help. Mario is the one who told us about Cortez. We wanted a haven from the Preservation Society, a place where we could lie low and prepare to take them on without being constantly on the run."

I paused. "The shard led us here to you. I don't know yet what you can offer, but I trust the shard's power. And so, my friends and I come to you asking for your help to take on the people after us and gain some understanding of our circumstances."

I stopped talking and held my breath. Every gaze bore into me, but I felt surprisingly calm, now that I'd said my piece. It was up to them. The room was filled with anticipation, and I absentmindedly traced the etchings on the shard's surface, hoping that it would still somehow save me from losing my memory. I realized then that we'd done so much living in the last few weeks that it would be tragic to lose memory of it.

The elder broke the silence. "Leave the shard here and close the door behind you. We'll call you in when we're ready." He gave a sharp nod to Maria, and she approached me. My heart dropped at losing a shard, but I quickly pocketed the one in my left hand, placed the other one on the long table, and stood.

Without a word, Maria escorted me out of the room and shut the door behind us. I kept my hand on the shard in my pocket. When the latch clicked, she turned and eyed me up and down. Her eyes glittered with something I couldn't quite place. Curiosity? Amusement? It was impossible to tell. She leaned against the doorframe, her arms crossed casually, but I could feel the tension in the air between us.

"Something isn't adding up."

"And what is that?" I tried to look nonchalant, hands in pockets.

"If you only have power when holding the shard, then why do you still have power now? Hmm?" She spoke softly, but her voice was laced with challenge.

"Maybe it's a residual effect?" I tried.

She shook her head, staring at me sternly. "That's not it. You clearly have power pulsing through you, even now." She tilted her head, her gaze piercing. "What's your secret?"

I gave her a lopsided grin. "Secret? You've cracked it—I'm just naturally amazing."

Her lips twitched, almost betraying a smile, but she held firm. "Amazing at what? Bluffing?"

"Maybe." I shrugged. "You'd be surprised how far dumb luck can get you."

She leaned closer, the glint of amusement returning to her eyes. "Dumb luck or not, you're still standing here, which is more than most can say. But something tells me there's more to it than that." Her eyes flicked to my pocket. "A second shard, perhaps?"

"If I had another one, do you think I would tell you?"

She smirked. "No, probably not. You're clever. I'll give you that."

"Clever? That's a first." I grinned. "Usually, I'm called other things. Some of them are pretty colorful."

"Oh, I can imagine." She arched a brow. "Still, I'm keeping my eye on you."

"Is that a promise?" I raised my eyebrows playfully.

She scoffed. "Something tells me you're going to be a handful, Mitzy."

I sighed dramatically. "That's what it says on my Yelp reviews."

She smiled wryly. "I'll be sure to leave an honest one."

I was enjoying our little chat, but then suddenly thought of our predicament. "Do you think they'll wipe our brains?"

She shook her head at me. "It's not as bad as you think. We don't turn you into vegetables. We just make you forget about this place."

I raised my eyebrows. "And forget about you?"

She held back a smile. "And why would that matter?"

"It would be a pity," I said lightly, though the words hung between us with surprising weight.

"This is true." She sized me up, as if considering something. "Well, I don't know what they'll decide. But your story is certainly unique. And as you say, why would the shard lead you here if it weren't for a reason? I can think of a few good reasons, off the top of my head."

"I have a confession to make," I blurted.

"And what is that?"

"The shard didn't exactly lead me. It's just, everything seems to go my way when I'm holding it. But I don't know why. It's not like some magical power guiding me. It just sort of… happens. Just plain dumb luck."

Her smile grew. "I know. I'm aware of your trait, after all."

"You know it?"

"Yes. Although I've never seen it before, I could put two and two together to figure it out. I suppose you could just call it like you did—luck. There's more to it than that, but you have the gist of it. You need to train to use it better, just as one can train to improve how they use any trait."

"Train? Like how?"

She changed her stance to the balls of her feet, knees slightly bent. It was casual, but I could instantly tell she could pull some fight moves on me in a split second. "There are many disciplines to sharpen the body, mind, and senses. It is a lifelong endeavor."

Before I could respond, the door opened. A middle-aged woman beckoned me in, and I took the same seat as before.

She sat down at the seat three away and leaned in. "We have agreed unanimously to allow you to stay in Cortez for the time being, to assess the situation more fully and gain more understanding of this shard you've brought. In the interim, we will teach you what we know and see whether you are worthy. If not, no harm will be done to you. We will clear your memories and send you on your way. You may, however, be crucial to a deep secret someone within the Preservation Society is working to control, and we must learn more. And so, it will be a relationship of mutual benefit, for the time being. Does this agree with you?"

I was thrilled. No mind wiping. A chance to learn from them. And most importantly, a respectable appearing folk who very well could take the shards off our hands forever so we could return to normalcy. The whole thing seemed perfect, but something tasted bitter to me.

At first, I couldn't place it, but then I realized... even with my life in danger, I was really enjoying being lucky. I didn't *want* to part with the second shard in my pocket. I didn't want to forget about the Theurgica, either. I glanced at Maria. These people could train us and enhance our understanding. And I realized with a start, *that* was what I actually wanted—not to be done with the whole thing altogether. I couldn't pinpoint when that shift had happened, but I realized then that I was hooked on the adventure and the mystery. I didn't want to have my mind wiped and go back to my mundane job in Montana.

But in order for us to stay involved, we would have to prove ourselves worthy. Somehow. I clutched the shard. It was my safety net to ensure that would happen.

"Yes. That works for me," I said. "And my friends?"

"They may stay under the same stipulation. If they prove to be unworthy, they will be sent on their way unharmed."

"I see." I nodded, wondering how all of us had any hope of proving ourselves worthy by their standards.

What did that even mean?

She held her hand out. "And we'll be wanting that other shard in your pocket, I'm afraid. We can't have you wandering around with powers you can barely control without being monitored. I'm sure you understand."

Chapter 18

Bobby didn't make the cut. Since he'd never held a shard in the first place and had no part in our story except driving us around, he was sent on his way with a minor scrub of the last few hours of his memories. As for the rest of us, we were all on probation. If we proved ourselves individually, we could stay.

Everyone spent a few minutes with the leadership separately, and then we gathered in the entryway to debrief.

The air in the room was still heavy after the leadership's decision, but no one said it out loud. We were walking a fine line between proving ourselves and having our memories wiped clean. I caught Gonzo's eye, and his expression mirrored my own—a mixture of relief and unease.

"They took both of the shards?" Chrissy asked, her voice low. "Will they keep them?"

I shrugged, trying to play it cool, but my mind was racing. "They didn't say. They want us here, but they're holding all the cards now. We have to be careful."

Vee bored into me with her eyes. "Careful isn't going to cut it. We need a plan. How—exactly—are we supposed to prove ourselves? Do you have any idea what they're looking for, Mitzy?"

Her words hung in the air, and I felt the full weight of the situation pressing down on me. There was no roadmap, no clear path to safety. One wrong move, and everything we'd fought for could be erased.

"That's just it," I complained. "I don't actually know. And nobody is telling me anything. But they want us to stay because the shards are obviously significant. I didn't tell them everything. We still hold some cards." I tried to sound confident, but without the shards, everything felt... off. The emptiness in my pocket was a constant reminder that we weren't in control anymore.

"Not many, from the sounds of it." Vee huffed.

I could see her frustration, but what was I supposed to say? I was flying blind, the same as the rest of them. But more than anything, I didn't want to admit how much I missed the shards already.

Gonzo was looking at the pile of our luggage. "So, where did they say we were staying? Do we have to lug our stuff over there?"

"I'm not entirely sure. They said they'll send someone over soon. Just sit tight."

"Hmph!" Vee sat back and folded her arms.

"It's not so bad," Chrissy said. "If we hadn't come here, we'd be hanging out in Santiago getting pursued by Jet Su. Not to mention, we may have found a good home for the shards. And… we also get to learn a lot of awesome stuff about the Theurgica and these powers."

Vee gave her a skeptical look. "That sounds great, assuming we don't get our minds wiped."

"Well, that's true." Chrissy scrunched her nose and gave me an apologetic look.

Juliette sat with folded hands. "There, there, dearies. You'll be okay. Whatever happens. You have your whole lives ahead of you."

Gonzo frowned. "But how much of our memories will they wipe? I don't want to forget all we've been through so far."

Vee gave me an accusatory look, and I just shrugged. "Well… they didn't say exactly…"

A man in his fifties showed up, looking elegant in an unwrinkled button-down light-blue collared shirt, and a tightly trimmed, mostly gray goatee. He spoke English fairly well.

"Ladies and gentlemen. My name is Juan Carlos, and I will be your host for the duration of your stay here. Anything you need, you will bring to my awareness."

"Nice to meet you," I said, standing and offering my hand. "I'm Mitzy. This is Gonzo, Vee, Chrissy, and Juliette."

"The pleasure is all mine," he said with a polite bow of his head. "Now, there are baseline behaviors we expect from all those who live in Cortez. It is my job to educate you on these things." He paused. After we all nodded, he continued. "Shall we walk and talk, so that I can take you to your homestay?"

"Of course," I said, glancing at Gonzo. He rolled his eyes and stretched his arms, preparing to lug his gear. His luggage consisted of a fairly heavy suitcase and backpack, which held his new workhorse laptop.

Juan Carlos didn't lend a hand as we walked out of the air-conditioned building into the bright outdoors, laden down with our backpacks and rolling luggage. He led us through the narrow streets of Cortez, his polished shoes clicking against the concrete, a stark contrast to the rugged surroundings. He walked with an air of practiced calm, as if nothing in this village could touch him.

"Cortez is a place of balance," he explained, his voice smooth and measured. "We protect ourselves by staying unified, but make no mistake, outsiders are rarely welcome. You will need to earn your place here."

I glanced at Vee, who was already sizing him up. He didn't seem like much of a threat, but there was something about his detached demeanor that was hard to nail down.

"And how do we earn our place?" I asked.

Juan Carlos didn't miss a beat. "Every member of Cortez must pull their weight. Your first duty is to learn the shape of this place and share what you know of the shards. But knowledge alone won't keep us alive. If you are to remain here, you must be tested. All of you will undergo training—in your unique traits, and in self-defense. We cannot afford weak links. Attacks can fall on us without warning, and when they do, every man, woman, and child must be ready. Only through discipline and unity does Cortez endure."

Vee perked up. "What sort of training?"

She's a glutton for physical challenges. Have I mentioned that?

Juan Carlos waved with an open hand, as if he were showing off something important. "It will depend on the individual, the trait, and what is lacking. The top goal will be to make your trait work for you, and to harness its power effectively in any circumstance. We will give you each an individual assessment, and the leadership will set you up with a personal trainer who suits your needs."

Vee was grinning. I just shook my head. Sounded like a lot of work and not a lot of fun. Although I was curious about what Maria had said to me earlier. How would a trainer help me with *my* trait?

Juan Carlos continued. "Cortez boasts a good, diverse set of traits. Even though traits are passed down through a family line, often mixing two traits in marriage results in a new one emerging in the offspring. Our strongest area is in imbuing objects with trait characteristics."

"Like making magical objects?" Gonzo asked, bright-eyed. He was huffing and sweating to keep up with the rest of us.

Juan Carlos eyed him skeptically. "I suppose… This trait has been our biggest asset in fending off the other houses, and although it makes us unique as a community, it isn't rare. We are… how would you say… small potatoes?"

"Yes, that sounds like the correct expression," Gonzo said.

As we walked through the streets, the surrounding buildings seemed frozen in time—concrete walls, peeling paint, narrow doorways that looked like they hadn't been touched in decades. Yet here and there, flashes of modernity broke through—a solar panel on a rooftop, a sleek, digital lock on a weathered wooden door.

Chrissy was peering at a house. "Many of these buildings look like they're from the last twenty years, but there are also plenty more that look really old. How long have you folks been here?"

"Oh, not long at all." Juan Carlos turned to face us, walking backward for a moment. Not a drop of sweat anywhere on him. "My parents came here in the sixties and were among the first to arrive. They fled the domineering grip Rodriguez House has on the Preservation Society in Santiago."

I perked up, my love for history piquing my interest. "The Preservation Society must have pursued them. Maria said that they haven't broken through in nineteen years, but that means they did before that."

Juan Carlos nodded. "It was Rodriguez House at the lead. And yes, they have always had a powerful grip on the Society. They found us and tried to infiltrate us to take over our stash of artifacts. But they were tricked and bested three times. Over the years, some have died on both sides. Truth be told, I believe they are powerful enough to squash us if they truly desired it. But there is no purpose for that. And the Preservation Society is not *that* evil, even if controlled by Rodriguez House."

"What's their name supposed to signify?" I asked.

"They preserve life for our kind. They protect the secrets we hold and ensure news of our people does not seep into mundane society. But the members of Rodriguez House are a ruthless bunch, and in Santiago, agents act more like a mafia. If you were in Paris, then you would have been in the realm of Maison Lumière, one of the Great Houses. They have a significant, although more amicable, grip on the Preservation Society, partly because so many houses are represented there."

Chrissy frowned. "It sounds like the Preservation Society is ultra-powerful but controlled locally."

Juan Carlos nodded. "Indeed. Agents hold incredible positions of power across the world, among mundanes and among our people in the Theurgica. As an organization, its resources are practically endless. But at the local level, they are limited by the houses. It is rare that the international Preservation Society has any real influence."

The truth of his statement sank in. How powerful was our foe? Jet Su seemed to have an influence all over the world. How many agents were at his disposal? Were we dealing with two dozen? A hundred? A thousand? I was itching to write to Mario to ask, but refrained, fearing he'd think we'd already asked too much. I'd have to do my own digging at some point.

Juan Carlos pointed at a tiny white house with peeling paint and a faded orange door. "This is where you will stay. There are two bedrooms. You will have to share."

I glanced at Gonzo. The guy snores like a chainsaw. I gave Vee and Chrissy an exaggerated, pained look, and Chrissy laughed.

Juan Carlos opened the door, which had been unlocked. "One room has two bunk beds. The other two singles. Please settle in, and I will come to check on you later. There is a grocery store down the street, so you can purchase food for dinner. And there are also restaurants around town you can visit if you end up staying."

We told him thank you and made ourselves at home. Chilean homes are small, and this one was on the crumbly side. The walls and floors were all concrete, and the windows rattled in their frames with every gust of wind. The furniture was a hodge-podge of old, mismatched pieces from the seventies, their upholstery worn thin and stained in places, with patterns that might have been vibrant decades ago but now just clashed. A lumpy couch sagged in the middle, its faded floral print obscured by a patchwork of fraying throws. The wooden chairs around the rickety dining table creaked ominously whenever anyone sat down, their varnish peeling and revealing splintery edges. The beds were little more than squeaky metal frames with thin, uneven mattresses, topped with scratchy, threadbare blankets. But we had a place to stay safe far from Jet Su and the Preservation Society, and our minds weren't getting wiped. I thought it was a great success. And I didn't even have my lucky shards.

After we settled in, we gathered around the table in the creaky chairs. I sat with the lockbox trying six-digit combinations. The repetitive beeping filled the small house.

As usual, Vee took charge. "Tell us everything that went down, Mitzy. How are we supposed to prove ourselves?"

I sighed and replayed what I'd just been through. "Like I said before, I'm not sure."

"We can figure this out." Vee drummed her fingers. "Come on. We're all smart. Ideas. Anyone. Throw them out."

"Okay..." Gonzo said with a cocked head. "Perhaps they want to see if we're worthy to have traits when we hold the shards, so we have to be good at our thing."

"Good. Good. More ideas." Vee waved her hand.

Chrissy was next. "They are impressed with how we've survived this long against the Preservation Society. It's our gumption that will make the difference."

"Yes. That's good. And that we found them. All that is important." Vee was getting excited.

I sat musing. "I think it's more holistic than all that."

"Do tell." Vee gestured with an open hand.

Everyone gave me their full attention.

I considered my words. "I think... something Maria said to me is coming to mind. That learning a trait is more than the power itself, but honing the physical, mental, and all the senses."

"Hmmm." Gonzo scratched his neck. "They were impressed with you. Your power—sorry—your trait got us here, but now they have the shards. So, how can we even learn our traits?"

I shook my head. "I don't know. But they know we don't have traits without the shards, so there will be other ways to prove ourselves. Listen. Maybe it's just proving we're trustworthy. So, we could just kind of go along with things?"

Vee shook her head. "You're not lucky anymore, Mitzy. You can be pretty loosey-goosey, and this is one of those times. Your plan is weak."

I nodded and immediately felt like a fool. My plan so far had relied fully on the shards. Without them, I was naked and directionless, like a rudderless ship at sea. There was a hole in my thinking with that emptiness, and I felt my mind get cloudy with indecision.

Vee was drumming her fingers together. "The key will be to show that we're capable. Nobody show signs of weakness tomorrow. We must give it our all, no complaints..." She eyed Gonzo, who gulped and nodded. She turned to me. "And no impulsive lolling about at the whims of the wind. We need to be firm. Strong."

"Yes, boss," I said.

She rolled her eyes at me, then turned to Juliette, who was sitting quietly at the end of the table. "What do *you* think?"

Juliette shrugged. "I think I should get some groceries and start making dinner."

"Great idea!" Gonzo leaped to his feet. "I'm starving. I'll come with you."

They were gone for over half an hour. Juliette struggled to find groceries to make French fare with Chilean options, but she managed. That night we ate well, a French onion soup with salad, cheeses, and Chilean bread. It was the best we'd eaten in days, but Juliette frowned. "I will need to make my own bread. This leaves much to be desired compared to a true French baguette."

Gonzo dipped the bread into his soup and gave her a goofy grin. "Maybe. But this is possibly my new favorite soup. Did I ever tell you I love you?"

She beamed. "Not since the last time I cooked."

Juan Carlos came to check on us after dinner, but by then we were so exhausted from jet lag and all that had been going on, we bid him adieu so we could conk out early. Before he left, he stood in the doorway and got our attention.

"Tomorrow is a big day for all of you. It is a day of proving yourselves and beginning your training. Get a good rest. You will want to bring your best."

With that, he was gone, and we settled into our beds.

Except I was excited.

It doesn't happen to me often, but when I'm overly exhausted and something sparks my mind, I get my second wind, and my whole body is raring to go. So, within minutes I heard Gonzo's chainsaw snoring in the bed across the room, and I was wide awake, mind racing, wondering what the next day would bring.

I lay frustrated in bed for an hour until I finally gave up and walked outside. It was a gorgeous, starry night. Honestly, it kind of reminded me of Montana when you get outside city limits. Big skies, surrounding mountains, and perfect views of the stars. Only they were all wrong.

I'm an educated guy, but having never been to South America before, I forgot that the view of space would be from the other side of the planet. I was looking for Ursa Major (the Big Dipper) and Orion, which are always front and center in Montana, no matter what time of year or where they were in their nightly rotation, and they weren't anywhere. And then I glanced at the moon and was taken aback again.

It was upside down.

How come nobody ever told me that in school? I don't know. It's one of those things that makes you realize the world is way bigger than you'd ever imagined.

I laugh now, because here I was uncovering this entire secret civilization of people with powers, sci-fi, magic, whatever you want to call it, and I was impressed with the Southern Hemisphere stars. In some ways, it was like everything was happening all at once, and I was on a totally different planet. It certainly isn't the one I grew up on. And that's when it hit me.

I was nervous, because I didn't want to forget any of this.

My life was turned upside down. Heck, the world was turned upside down, and I didn't want to... no, I *couldn't* go back to the way things were. I had to prove myself, no matter what. But my trait was the hardest to figure out. Maybe Gonzo could learn to turn invisible quickly, and Vee could do something badass with hers, but me? How do you practice being lucky?

I walked through the village, trying to find calmness, but I was anxious through and through, and my body was still on French time, so it was confused anyway. And that's the state I was in when I met Pepe, a dirty kid with tattered clothing who threw a rock at me.

And who knew a thing or two about luck.

Chapter 19

"Hey, mister!" Pepe called to me in a thick Chilean accent.

"Why'd you throw a rock at me?" I was more surprised than anything. It wasn't a big rock.

"You're gonna walk past the best thing in Cortez tonight. Stupid gringo."

"Oh." I walked over to him.

He was about ten or eleven, dark complexion, thin and wiry. His short-sleeved shirt was probably white at one point, and even in the moonlight, I could tell it was nearing brown. He was barefoot, and he had one hand on his hip, the other raised with his finger wagging at me.

Tsk. Tsk. He scolded. "You don't wanna miss this, gringo. Come on."

Pepe darted through the moonlit park like he'd done this a thousand times, his bare feet making no sound on the ground as I struggled to keep up, my shoes scuffing loudly on the dirt and gravel.

"Hurry," he whispered, his eyes gleaming with mischief. "Almost there."

We reached the edge of the park, and I crouched beside him, heart pounding in my chest. "What am I even looking for?"

"Shh!" Pepe raised a finger to his lips. "There," he whispered, pointing into the darkness.

It was a bird. But no, that doesn't do it justice. It was large, with golden feathers shimmering in the moonlight, waddling along between the bushes. I sucked in a breath.

"Come on!" he whispered, and staying hunched over, he darted to a nearby bush to watch.

I followed him, mimicking his posture.

The extraordinary golden feathers were metallic-looking, and every time they caught the moon they flashed beautifully. When it briefly turned toward us, its eyes flashed with hints of red, yellow, orange, and white. And then it looked right at me. I froze in place, riveted by its stare. The air felt heavier, the world quieter, like something was about to happen.

Pepe stood next to me in the flash of an eye, watching the incredible creature. "If he likes you, you can follow him to find gold," he said quietly. "But if he doesn't... well, he'll lead you to places you can't come back from."

A chill ran down my spine. "Is this some kind of test?"

Pepe shrugged, but there was something unsettling about the way he smiled. "Everything here is a test, gringo."

I watched the bird for a moment as it ruffled its feathers, creating golden flashes and sparkles. "Have *you* ever followed him?"

He shrugged. "Only once. When the leaders asked me to, so they could buy a bunch of army stuff." He watched me keenly, never taking his eyes off of me.

"What's it called?"

"Alicanto. He lives in the mountains and comes into town from time to time."

"How did you know he'd be here?" I asked.

Pepe just gave me a mischievous smile.

The Alicanto waddled off, and Pepe said, "Well, mister. If you want gold, now would be the time to follow him. If he likes you. If he doesn't, he'll lead you over a cliff."

"What are *you* gonna do?" I asked.

"Nothing. I just wanted to see him again. It's been over half a year."

"Well, then I'm doing nothing too."

That seemed to make him happy. I held out my hand. "My name's Mitzy. What's yours?"

"Pepe." He shook my hand, a good grip for a young kid.

I followed my instinct. "Are you lucky, Pepe?" I used the Spanish word *suerte*.

"*Lechudo.*" He snorted. "That's what my *mami* calls me. I'm just great at finding things."

I'd never heard that word before, but I nodded. "Can you teach me how?"

He scoffed. "Stupid gringo. There's nothing to teach."

My lips formed a tight smile. "Okay. Then, I'll just watch."

"Whatever." He gave a wave. "Come on."

I followed him to the other side of the park till we came to a creek. I was taken aback because there were glowing orange-yellow stones scattered throughout.

"What are those?" I gaped.

"Lava," he said with a mischievous smile.

"Ha!"

Pepe started wading in, and I quickly took off my shoes and rolled up my pants to follow. He reached his arm in and pulled out a rock, holding it up to the moonlight. "This is a nice one. Very smooth. Here."

He tossed it to me, and I caught it, then admired it. What sort of properties of rock make them glow at night? I wondered.

Pepe reached in, up to his armpit, and pulled out another one, admiring its bright orange glow in the moon. He glanced at me. "Well, gringo? Get some rocks."

"Yeah. Yeah. Of course," I half-mumbled, and got my pants wet wading past my knees. I reached in to grab one, and half of my shirt got drenched. It wasn't a super chilly night—cold enough that I wondered why the heck we were doing this, though. But I'd been holding the shards for a couple of weeks and was used to being ultra spontaneous, so I just went with it.

He pulled out three more rocks that glowed beautifully and peered over at mine. "How many have you got?"

I looked at my rocks. Not as nicely shaped as his, but they were okay. "Three."

"Okay. Let's go."

He pattered out of the creek and back toward town, walking quietly.

My clothing squelched as I followed. I think, deep down, I was hoping his trait was going to rub off on me, making it easier for me to prove myself. So, I followed him like he was a magic talisman, blindly allowing him to lead me on.

We got into town and turned down a side street. The town was a good two miles across from end to end. We walked in silence toward the center for nearly twenty minutes, bathed in the moon's light. As we walked, I kept imagining what Pepe might be leading me toward. I glimpsed around, wondering if someone was watching me, and measuring me up for worthiness.

When we showed up at a faded red house, Pepe walked around to the backyard, then to an open window. My skin crawled awkwardly as I imagined how this would come across to the Cortez leadership—walking behind people's houses at night when I'm trying to prove my worth, and on my first night? It was feeling wrong. All wrong. I missed my lucky shards like a drug.

And then I heard the crying.

Pepe and I peered inside the open window. A child, no more than six, was sitting up in bed.

When Pepe's glowing orange face showed up in the window, the child stopped crying and said, "Pepe! I knew you'd come."

Pepe just grinned. "Paco. I brought you some little suns. See?" He held up his rocks and gestured for me to do the same.

Paco's face lit up. Pepe placed them on the windowsill. "Now listen, Paco. They only work in the moonlight, so leave them here at night, but you're going to have to get used to them not working when the moon isn't out."

"Okay." The little boy nodded seriously and wiped the tears from his eyes.

When we'd placed them nicely, Pepe gave a little wave. "Okay, Paco. See you tomorrow."

We ducked down and he put his finger to his lips, listening. When the room was silent, he gestured, and we left quietly the way we'd come.

I watched Pepe curiously for a moment as we walked down the street. He looked at me and I turned my eyes forward. "What now?"

He stopped at the corner, fists on hips, and cocked his head. He turned to the right. "This way, gringo."

We went two blocks and came upon a stark white dressy blouse on a lawn. Pepe reached down, picked it up, and continued walking for three houses. He paused, looked around, then crossed the street, walked to the backyard where clothing was hanging up to dry on a clothesline, and reached up to pin the blouse on the line, but he wasn't tall enough.

"Give me a hand, gringo," he said.

I pinned the blouse on the line, and we left the way we'd come.

Then, suddenly, he stopped and turned to me, fists on hips. "Go to bed, gringo. You have a big day tomorrow."

"Yeah, I guess I do." I looked around. No idea where I was.

He pointed. "That way. Four blocks, then turn right and go six more. Go. Go."

He shooed me away, and I walked back to my lodging in wonder. He was a bossy little guy, but how could I not be sucked into his vortex of a world? In a brief amount of time, he'd made two—no, three if you counted me—people's lives better. In comparison, when I held the shards, everything felt so random.

I found where I was staying and crashed. By then it was midnight, which is like 4 a.m. in Paris. In the morning Juliette doted over us, making omelets-to-order, with fresh herbs and perfect little sprigs for garnish. How she found all that in Cortez was beyond me.

After eating, Juliette stood before us, her apron tied snug around her waist, a serene smile on her face. "Now listen, my dearies," she said, her voice gentle but firm. "Don't you get all worked up and anxious about proving yourselves today. What will be, will be."

She looked at each of us. Her gaze softened as she stopped on Chrissy. "Believe in yourself, darling. You're far more capable than you know."

Then, her eyes settled on me, and I felt a flicker of nervousness. Her smile faded, replaced with a look of quiet concern. "And you, Mitzy," she said, her voice dropping. "You need an anchor."

I blinked, confused. "What do you mean?"

"You've been floating through this adventure, relying on that shard to carry you," she continued. "But luck isn't enough. Not for this."

I opened my mouth to protest, but she held up a hand. "You must find something real to hold on to. Otherwise, you'll always be drifting, and the luck will only take you so far."

Her words hit harder than I expected, and I nodded, though I wasn't sure I fully understood. What was she asking me to find?

I didn't have time to ponder on it, because Juan Carlos was knocking at the door. We quickly got ourselves ready and followed him down the street back to the town hall where I'd first been grilled.

Gonzo was called into the conference room as the rest of us sat in the waiting area. I watched the doors, hoping beyond hope he wouldn't say anything foolish, trying to imagine what they would ask him. My hands grew clammy, and I rubbed them on my pants. Chrissy caught my eye. She was biting her lip nervously and gave me a weak smile.

It felt like an eternity had passed. It was probably only ten minutes, really. A fifty-something military-looking guy, with chiseled biceps and a white T-shirt tight enough to see his pecs, entered the building. Without a pause, he walked into the conference room, then came out a moment later with Gonzo following dumbly behind him, looking pale. Gonzo gave us all a feeble wave and followed the buff guy out the door.

"Juliette," a woman's voice called from the open conference room.

Juliette stood, straightened her yellow floral dress, then gave me a gentle smile, eyes filled with warmth. When the doors were shut, I turned back to the entry doors where Gonzo had gone. "Was that his trainer?" I asked no one in particular.

Juan Carlos spoke from four seats away. "He will be with Eduardo for his first day of training."

"Oh." I could only imagine how a slovenly guy like Gonzo would fare against that kind of training. I cringed. Were they picking training for us based on our weaknesses?

Before Juliette emerged, a sweet-looking young woman arrived, wearing a red floral-print dress and humming softly. She went into the conference room and emerged with Juliette in tow. Already the two of them were smiling and enjoying chitchat as they left the building.

At that point, my original theory was thrown out the window. And then they called my name. I wiped my hands on my pants again and noticed for the first time that my scalp was itchy. I stood and was immediately lightheaded. I paused, holding the back of the chair, my mind churning. I desperately wanted the shard. I craved it. I didn't think I'd pass without its luck. And what was it Juliette had wanted from me, anyway? My mind was racing a hundred miles a minute.

The same group of people sat at the table and gestured to an open chair. The room felt colder than before, the weight of their stares pressing down on me like I was buried alive. I sat and wiped my hands on my shirt.

"Mitzy," the old man began, his voice low and steady. "Why are you here?"

"I... don't know." I stammered, hating how weak I sounded. "I mean... I do. I'm here because of the shard, because of—"

He cut me off with a shake of his head. "That's not what I asked." I could feel every set of eyes judging me.

My stomach twisted, the room spinning slightly. I felt the familiar weight of failure creeping up on me, like the time I'd botched that internship. It had seemed like my dream job, history software for elementary kids. I'd taken the initiative, adding some *real* history—the stories behind the dates and names, and everyone had supported me—but when the teachers saw it, they flipped out. The software got pulled. The company lost loads of money. And I lost my job.

I opened my mouth, but no words came out. The silence stretched on, unbearable. They were all waiting for me to speak, but I had nothing. Sitting at that table, I realized that everything I'd ever done since the internship felt like a copout. Until the shard. With it, I was charged with purpose. But without the shard, without its luck... I was just me. And "me" wasn't enough. I'd fooled them with my luck-induced spiel, and now, without it, what did I have?

I felt fully exposed—naked.

"I don't know why I'm here," I finally admitted, the words barely above a whisper. "But I want to learn. I want to understand this world, the shard, the power it holds. And... I want to stop the wrong people from getting their hands on it."

The silence was heavy, but this time it felt different—like they were listening.

Then, a thirty-something woman said, "He needs a seer."

Everyone nodded their heads and the older man said, "Done." He typed on a tablet in front of him, then turned to me. "Mitzy, do you want to hold the shards again?"

I felt deep eagerness grip me but contained myself. "Of course. It has helped us a lot."

"You may have your chance. Not today. Tell me what you've discovered of the language."

"One side is ancient Egyptian Hieratic. At least, it's from that era and that part of the world. We have a friend back in Montana, an Egyptologist, who has more in-depth knowledge. We're working to translate it." I threw that in, hoping maybe if we proved important, we'd have a better chance of not being brain-wiped.

The older man nodded. "Good. Good. We will get to that. But first. You will undergo intense training. You will be pushed to new limits you did not know you had, so we can know what you are capable of. You may get along with your trainer. You may not. Regardless, you must work hard to do all they send your way. Do you understand?"

"Yes." I began imagining what kind of trainer I'd have and Gonzo's buff military guy came to mind. I cringed, wishing once again for the shard to sway things in my favor.

The woman next to me eyed me calmly, her voice even. "We've picked someone who will see through all your pretenses. Someone with strength and skill far beyond what you've ever encountered. Understand?"

I steeled myself, my palms sweating again. "Yes." We sat in silence then, and I wanted desperately to scratch at my scalp but resisted. The more I held back, the more it itched. How far away was this person, anyway? How long did I have to wait?

Finally, mercifully, the door to the conference room creaked open. And my jaw dropped wide open.

Chapter 20

"Wipe that goofy look off your face, Mitzy." Maria had a fire in her eyes. "You have a long way to go, which means a lot of work for both of us."

Maria's sharp tone cut through my euphoria like a blade, snapping me back to reality. "Yes. Yes. Of course."

But that fire in her eyes? It wasn't just intimidating. It was magnetic. Even when she was stern, I couldn't help but be drawn to her. Why did I still feel so lucky to be assigned to her, even now that the shard wasn't giving me luck anymore? I tried to look composed. I felt a pull between us, like invisible threads keeping me in her orbit. I could still picture the subtle shift of her expression when she smiled at me the day before, and it was hard not to smile, even though she was now all business.

She led me to the top of a hill on the outskirts of town with a few scattered trees and some rocky outcroppings. The wind carried the scent of pine and fresh earth, sharp and cool against my face. Nearby, the kids' fort was no longer in the air but hunkered down in a big grassy field. Two lookout towers were visible on similar, taller hills, farther south from where we'd driven in. I was surprised I hadn't noticed them coming in. Or had they been concealed by magic? Below, the village sprawled out peacefully, with a creek winding lazily through the fields. A stark contrast to the tension building in my chest. Even up here, with the entire world stretching out below us, all I could focus on was Maria—how her every movement was precise, controlled, and watching me like a hawk.

Maria stood facing me, waiting until I gave her my full attention. "You have no center, Mitzy. You need to find your center."

"What's that mean?" I asked.

She shook her head. "Exactly. You have no idea. We will start with breathing. Without proper breathing, nothing else will work. Breathe deeply with me."

We took deep breaths through our noses. I mimicked her, lifting my hands as I breathed in, lowering them as I breathed out. A few minutes of that, and I got lightheaded, but I said nothing. I was going to prove myself to her with every ounce of my being.

She started walking around me, scrutinizing me. "Keep breathing, Mitzy."

I felt so confused. Breathing? That's what we were doing? What was she looking for? Her hand pressed against my forehead. "Straighten up."

I straightened immediately, my breath catching in my throat for a second. I felt her eyes on me, watching every movement, every breath. She pressed her palm against my chest, just above my heart, and I felt the warmth of her touch seep through my shirt. My breath hitched, and I struggled to keep it steady.

"Your chest is too tight. Relax." She pushed me back slightly, adjusting my posture until my pelvis tilted forward, forcing my spine straight. It was all so… precise.

Her hands moved with care, but there was something intimate about the way she corrected me, like she knew exactly how to handle my body. Every change sent a wave of awareness through me. I couldn't tell if it was just the training or if it was *her*. I tried to focus, but my mind kept drifting to the closeness between us, the warmth of her hands, the faint scent of her skin.

She tapped my leg next. "Move your feet apart a little."

I obeyed.

"Feet must be rooted," she said, her tone soft but commanding.

She stood back, watching. I wondered what she was seeing. She shook her head in disgust. "You're still breathing through your chest," she scolded, pacing around again. "You need to go deeper, Mitzy."

I tried. I really did. But every time I thought I had it, she would correct me again. It wasn't natural to breathe in this way, and it sure as heck wasn't easy to change something so basic. My mind raced, searching for the right rhythm, but it felt like I was getting it wrong every single time.

After a while, my legs started shaking. I tried in vain to keep them steady. I didn't want to let her see how much I was struggling. I mean, breathing? It shouldn't be this hard. But the more she corrected me, the more I realized how wrong I'd been doing it. The frustration bubbled under the surface, but I kept it in check.

By noon, my legs were jelly, and every muscle in my body screamed for rest. But Maria kept at it, watching me, relentless, as if she hadn't noticed—or cared—that I was about to collapse. My stomach grumbled, but I kept breathing. In and out. In and out. The sun bore down on me as it passed the shade of the tree and sweat dripped from every single pore of my body. I realized with a start that not only was I achy and hungry, but I was jet-lagged. I questioned if this was even helping, or if Maria was just trying to break me down. She was dogged, her voice cutting through my exhaustion like a whip. I was ready to snap, my mind a mess of hunger, frustration, and weariness. And yet, I didn't stop. I couldn't stop. I wouldn't let her see me give up.

She rapped my chest. "Diaphragm, Mitzy. You're using your chest again. You must go deeper."

My stomach gurgled. "How's that?" I asked, managing a grin despite the exhaustion.

She shook her head, but smiled, just a flicker. "Keep going."

And just like that, the pressure eased, if only for a second. I realized then that she wasn't just there to push me to my limits for the sake of it. There was something driving her, too. Maybe it was the same thing that had pulled me to her from the start. Maybe she really wanted me to succeed, and was doing her all to make sure I would?

The tension between us shifted, almost imperceptibly. I stood a little taller, breathed a little deeper. "How's this?" I asked, my voice more confident now.

Maria looked me up and down, appraising me with those sharp eyes of hers. "Better," she admitted. "But can you keep it up?"

I grinned, the strain of the morning still weighing heavy on my muscles, but my spirits lifted by the minor victory. "I don't know if I'll ever keep up with you, but I think I can handle this for a bit."

Her eyes twinkled briefly, that same mischievous glint I'd seen when we first met. "Well then, time for the next step. Spread your legs like this."

She took on one of those kung fu stances. I tried to mimic her, and she winced. "No, no. Front leg slightly bent, back leg straight, at a forty-five-degree angle. Yes. Better." She came over and tapped my rear leg. "Make a line between the legs, your body facing straight. Every move, your whole body should be upright and you should breathe as we've been doing. Think of a plumb line going from your core up through the top of your head, always straight up and down."

I stood in the pose as she'd instructed, waiting. She took up the position next to me with the same foot forward. "Now, take a step. Like this. Swivel front foot, step forward, and now the other is in front."

I tried, and she winced. "Clumsy, but that's the idea. Keep trying. Another step. Good. Don't lose your breathing though! Okay. Continue."

We walked, one slow step at a time. A half hour of that, and then the step varied. This time the front leg was straight, and the back squatted down, a real kung fu move if you ask me. That one took me longer, and when I had that, she also had me involve my arms, and I was getting it. I was learning kung fu!

I've never had an interest in martial arts. Ever. Well, that's a lie. I won a free lesson of taekwondo at a supermarket drawing as a teenager and showed up, tried it out, and never went again.

So, that was my exposure. I figured it wasn't for me. I could exercise other ways. But at that moment, something shifted in me, and I felt excited about learning a new thing.

But it was grueling. The entire afternoon went on in the same way, and our lesson plan was as slow as molasses. By six o'clock, I felt like I had done little, but I *was* holding eight different poses, moving slowly, and breathing in a way that Maria didn't criticize.

Finally, the sun started setting and Maria let me take a break as she looked at the vibrant colors in the sky. "Good work, Mitzy. Better than I thought you'd do."

I was guzzling down a long drink of water and wiped my mouth. "Is that right? And what did you expect?"

She smirked. "You're not the most disciplined man, from what I can tell."

"Hey! I resemble that remark!" I grinned, pretending to take offense.

She laughed. "Come on. Let's get some dinner."

Even though I was utterly exhausted, her minor compliment had me feeling pretty good, so as we walked back into town, I had a bounce to my step.

"So, they said you're a seer? What does that mean, exactly?" I glanced at her nervously, hoping she'd answer.

"Just what it sounds like. I see things."

"Yeah. Well, in English, that word usually means someone who can see into the future."

"No. Not me." She focused ahead, not glancing my way.

"Hmm." I felt like she might talk, since we were apparently going to dinner, so I pressed for more. "What kinds of things do you see?"

She glanced over at me. "I see traits—in people and in things. They have an aura. And different traits have different types and colors of auras, so if I've seen something before, I can usually tell when I see it again."

I tried to imagine it. "What do you see when you see me? What color am I?"

"Yellow."

I beamed. "That's a cheerful color! And what does it do, like emanate out, or does it make some sort of shapes?" I waved my hands around.

She watched me with a smirk as I jutted my hands out from my head like antlers. "A bit of both. When you held the shards, your trait would swirl around a bit, always emanating from your center. But it was raw power, uncontrolled."

"Do you see things with everyone?"

"Everyone here. Yes."

I furrowed my brow. "Doesn't that cloud your vision, seeing auras all the time?"

She scoffed. "I don't see them all the time! Nobody can do that."

"What do you mean?"

She raised one eyebrow at me. "Power isn't limitless. It takes a lot of work. With training, people can use their traits more powerfully and for longer, but everyone has their limits."

"So, it just runs out?" I scratched my head. "How does it come back?"

She rounded some large rocks, and we walked through a field of wheat. "A good night's sleep will recharge your energy. Although any amount of rest helps. And being centered makes the process go faster."

I pursed my lips. "Can you see when I'm centered?"

"Absolutely." She gave me a wry smile before turning back to see the scraggly path before us. "And you're mostly terrible."

I chuckled. "I didn't have a decent teacher before."

She glanced at me, and I gave her a wink. She rolled her eyes while trying to repress a smile. I considered. "Can you tell when someone is using their trait?"

"Absolutely. It glows brighter."

"And when they run out of power?"

"Yes. I see their core color and shape, but it's quite dim."

I was now really curious. "How did I compare to others when I was holding the shards?"

She considered for a moment as we passed the first house on the outskirts of town. "Most people use their trait sparingly, to reserve it throughout the day. You, on the other hand, were like one big blotch. It's not something I usually see in people. You're clumsy. When you held the rock, you were always using it. Very undisciplined. No center."

I mused on that for a moment. "What are you teaching me, exactly?"

"Tai chi. I may teach you more things, but you must know the basics before moving forward."

"And the shard…" I nodded to other folks walking past the other direction before continuing. "What do you see about it? You said you can see power in things."

She shook her head. "When items are used, I see them light up. I see nothing when they're not in use. However, that… shard… I saw nothing at all from it. It was as if it were completely invisible to me, and all the power was coming from within you. That's why I didn't know you were mundane. We have items that can boost power for a time, and even some to help lengthen how long. But I've never seen anything like that shard."

"Very curious," I said, wishing I could get my hands on the shards again.

We turned and walked another block, then entered a small restaurant I hadn't seen before. The peeling sign above the door read: *Flora Cantina*.

"Good evening, Auntie," Maria said, with a wave to a woman in her fifties.

There were almost twenty people seated at tables, and no chairs left for us, so we went up to the counter and sat on two stools. "We'll take the rustic potatoes." She turned to me. "Do you like spicy?"

I shrugged. "Sure. Just not too much."

She gave a nod to her aunt. I noticed a glass door refrigerator filled with beer. "Are we off duty now? Want a beer?"

Maria gave me a little smirk. "Are you buying, Mitzy?"

"Of course." I grinned at her.

Her aunt didn't even bother waiting for me, but grabbed two random beers out of the fridge. I glanced at the menu on the wall and was surprised to see things like pizza, hamburgers, and salads. "What's the best thing on the menu?" I asked.

"The chicken pesto pizza. By far."

"Let's get one of those," I said to her aunt as she served our beers.

We clinked bottles and took a swig. "So, Maria. What do I have to do to prove myself to the people of this town?"

She shook her head with a smirk. "Just getting straight to the point, aren't we, Mitzy?"

I shrugged. "I don't want to mess this up."

"Well, if I told you, you'd probably do worse. So, you'll just have to go through the process."

"How long?"

She scrunched up her nose. "If I knew you were going to grill me, I might have turned down the beer."

"Okay. Okay. Just curious. Let's change the subject. Tell me about Pepe. Do I have his trait?"

She gave me an appraising look. "How do you know about Pepe? You only arrived yesterday."

"I couldn't sleep, so I was taking a walk and met him. He showed me an Alicanto."

She took a sudden intake of breath. "You saw the Alicanto?"

"Yeah." I gave her a curious look. "Is that a big deal?"

"Yes. Yes, it is." She cocked her head and looked at me for a moment, took a drink, then said, "You and Pepe have a similar trait. Yes. However, Pepe's is more about finding things. You both have yellow auras, but quite different in scope. Also, Pepe is much better at using his trait than you are. And he cares about people."

I frowned. "What's that supposed to mean?"

She shook her head. "When's the last time you went out of your way for someone else?"

"Oh, well, of course. I've been doing that all week!" I was feeling offended.

"Oh really? Did you benefit from the so-called help you gave them?"

"I just offered to buy you dinner!" I said defensively.

She raised her eyebrows. "Mmmm?"

I almost gave her a snappy retort, then bit my tongue. Was she trying to strike a nerve with me? Was this still proving myself? I changed the subject to safer topics.

"What does *lechudo* mean?"

She smirked. "Lucky devil, I suppose."

"Ha!" I grinned. "And what do you think about me?"

She gave me a sideways look. "Perhaps it suits you."

I relaxed. "Tell me about Chile. This is my first time here."

She began talking, and I stopped being pushy with my questions. We ended up having a nice dinner. I learned that there were vineyards all over the place. I guess I'd never really realized just how much wine comes out of Chile. It's a lot. In fact, they had a pretty decent little vineyard right there in Cortez.

That's when I realized—besides the one from outer space—both shards were found in places known for their wine. I suddenly had a deep curiosity about bringing the shards into contact with wine. I was tempted to ask Maria if I might see the shards again, but bit my tongue. I annoyed her earlier with my probing questions. Better to leave it. For now.

After dinner, we stood outside and talked a little longer in the beautiful evening air. I couldn't help but get lost in her large brown eyes and her sparky smile, and I didn't want the evening to end. Not yet.

"You really haven't left Chile?" I asked.

"No," she replied. "But it's a large country. And I've seen a good portion of it. Make a guess, how does the length of Chile compare to America's width?"

"Oh…" I eyed her suspiciously. "Of course, I'd thought America would be longer, but now you have me wondering…"

I considered maps I'd seen, then flashed a smile. "There's an app for this! I've seen it. Every map projection has to distort the sizes of the countries, so the app lets you drag countries around to see their actual size. It's shocking for Americans that Greenland is actually quite small, and India takes up most of America."

"You're stalling. Just make a guess." Her smile beamed, and I melted.

"I guess... that... they're the same! Chile north to south is the same as America, east to west." I raised my eyebrows expectantly.

She pouted. "Not fair. You're *lechudo!*"

I opened my mouth wide. "You mean I'm right?"

She laughed. "Almost. Chile is 4,270 kilometers and America is 4,313. A difference of forty-three!"

"Wow. So, you do have a lot to see in this country."

She giggled and slapped my arm. "That's what I've been trying to tell you."

I grinned. Her eyes caught the light, and for a moment, the rest of the world faded. It was just the two of us, standing in the evening quiet. My heart raced, and before I knew it, I was leaning in, drawn to her in a way that felt inevitable. My mind screamed at me to stop, but the pull between us was too strong to resist. I just wanted to taste her lips, to see if the connection I felt was real.

Her hand came up, pushing me away gently, and the look in her eyes wasn't harsh. It was... pained. "No, Mitzy. It will never work." She didn't say it with anger, but with a quiet sadness.

"It won't?"

"No. You are passing through, and I belong here, with my people. And I do not believe in dating around. I believe in long-term commitment."

"Ah." I took a step back, the rejection hitting harder than I'd expected. I tried to put on a positive face and knew she'd see right through me. "I see." I nodded, trying to keep my voice steady.

She smiled, a faint, wistful thing, and turned away before I could say more. "Good night, Mitzy."

As I watched her walk off, the weight of her words settled in. It wasn't an outright rejection. And there was something in the way she'd looked at me, that lingering glance before she turned. Maybe I was just seeing what I wanted to see. Maybe not.

Whatever was between us, it was a training relationship for now. Still, as I headed back to my house, I had a slight skip to my step. But when I opened the door and saw Chrissy's angry eyes, I shriveled up quickly.

"What? What happened?" I asked.

"You!" She pointed her finger at me accusingly. I glanced over her shoulder to see the other three seated at the table with empty plates, and one plate at the table boasting a nice-looking salad, chicken, and rice.

"What is it?"

Her eyes flared, her face dark. "Here we are, being told we'll get our minds wiped, and every day we have to prove ourselves individually, and then you don't show up for dinner or answer your phone and we all get to thinking. Wondering. Did Mitzy get sent home? How thoughtless of you!"

"Oh." My face grew slightly red. I fumbled my phone out of my pocket and saw all the messages. It had been set to Do Not Disturb mode. Oops. "Um. Sorry? But hey, I'm okay."

Vee watched me with a smirk. "Loosey-goosey. Mitzy, you're like a walking disaster waiting to happen. One minute, you're all in, the next you're off chasing who knows what. You never know what's going on with Ditzy Mitzy."

I put on a smile. "Sorry to worry you, Chrissy. But I'm okay. I have Maria as my trainer and I took her out to dinner."

She rolled her eyes and flapped her arms. "Oh. That makes it all okay, then." She turned her back on me with a *humph* and strode away, sitting down at the table with an over-exaggerated plop.

I tried to move on casually, but Maria's words hung in the air.

When was the last time you went out of your way for someone else?

I wondered. Had she seen something I should pay attention to? But I didn't want to deal with it just then.

I gave Gonzo a knowing smile. He shrugged wearily. He looked exhausted.

"What did you do today, buddy?" I asked, as I sat at the table and politely started eating my second dinner. I noticed a mostly drunk bottle of Chilean wine on the table and poured myself a small glass.

His voice wavered, and he barely looked at me. "Grueling. Terrible. Nonstop. My body feels like it's been pulverized in a meat processor, and that's *after* taking painkillers. Dude. I don't think I can handle this."

"What did you do?" I was starting to feel worried about him.

Vee rolled her eyes. "Pah-leese!" She shook her head. "He took a walk."

"Ugh!" Gonzo drooped his head. "You make it sound like such a little thing. It was epic! We hiked. And we kept going… and going. According to my phone, I went *ten* miles!"

I did a little mental math. "But… that's only a few hours, isn't it?"

"Uphill!" he complained.

I glanced at Vee, then back at my buddy. "One direction. Then downhill the other." I was beginning to see why Vee wasn't taking him seriously.

He lifted his head. "On the positive side, all that time walking gave me a thought on how to approach the AI software to decode the shards' messages." He brightened and stood, walking toward his laptop. "It's actually so straightforward, I wonder why I hadn't thought of it before. Eduardo, my trainer, was constantly trying to push me. And somewhere along the hike, he pointed at the top of the mountain and said it was taking forever. That got me thinking."

Vee and I shared a smirk as Gonzo returned to the table. He opened his laptop and started navigating while he talked. "I've gathered a diverse dataset of Hieratic glyphs and made sure it's annotated, based on translations that have been done. I'm using edge detection and segmentation to preprocess images, so the algorithm will have a better time at parsing new ones. And I've used a convolutional neural network for image recognition."

He paused and opened his hands grandly. "But what I *didn't* do was to account for historical context. The *time* element. I tagged authors, but not the era. I wonder if I did that—even if I just honed it down to the century—if things would come together."

He turned back to his computer and started typing furiously. I marveled at how a man who'd looked so weak and pathetic a moment earlier was suddenly fired up. It made me smile.

I turned back to Vee. "What did *you* do today?"

She pursed her lips. "I played Go." She was serious. Stoic.

I brightened. "Sweet! You're great at Go." That's actually how I met her back in college. We were both in the Go club in our sophomore year, and found that we were similarly matched, although Vee's incredible math brain seemed to win more often.

"Well, not today. I didn't win once."

I pondered. "How many games did you play?"

She shook her head. "I lost track. I played all day."

"Oh." I saw where this was going. I turned to Juliette. "How about you?"

She gestured to the kitchen. "I taught children how to bake French pastries. I have saved a few for you once you all have finished dinner."

"Is that all?" I asked.

"No, we meditated quite a bit and focused on our breathing. It was quite peaceful, actually."

Her breathing training sounded nothing like mine. I wondered about the varied experiences we'd had. "Chrissy?"

She shrugged. "Rock climbing."

"What? Like, with ropes and pulleys and things?"

"Yes." She frowned. "I hate heights." She brightened. "But I love my trainer. Kali is her name, and we get along great."

Vee leaned back. "Has anyone besides Gonzo had any new learnings they'd like to share?"

"I do." Everyone turned to me. I pushed my plate back and raised my wineglass. "Maria can see powers in people and in items with powers that are in use, which is a pretty nifty trait. But, as far as the shard goes, she can't see anything about it—at all—just that the holder of it has powers."

"So, the shards are… different somehow," Chrissy said.

"Yeah. She said she's never seen anything like them." I took a sip of wine. "Makes me wonder just what the heck these shards are. They're clearly something this whole… Theurgica… knows very little about. Also, I have another thought about the shards. I realized today that both the French and Chilean shards were found in places with vineyards. Do you think there's a connection?"

Everyone considered a moment. Chrissy spoke first. "But didn't Miguel's wife say he found it digging at a construction site?"

Juliette tapped her wineglass in thought. "The construction site was near vineyards. There are indeed many in this region. I've been paying attention, since I have one myself."

I considered for a moment. "How near the construction site?"

Juliette nodded. "The site itself was an enormous building, but there was one nearby. Perhaps the land *used* to be a vineyard?"

We sat in silence, digesting the new information, when Gonzo smacked a key on his laptop and sat back. "Guys… I think it's working."

"Really?" I paused and set my wineglass down.

"Well, I'm going to send this to Robert right now for his thoughts, but... this looks like some real sentences. And it lines up with the early work Robert was doing on it."

Everyone leaned forward. Vee craned her head around his laptop screen. "So tell us then. What does it say?"

Gonzo stretched his arms. "Both of the shards mention a place that is possibly called the Theurgica. And their purpose... is to save it."

Chapter 21

"Come on, Gonzo, quit stalling and read it!" Vee snapped. Her eyes flicked to the laptop screen, impatient as always.

"Okay," Gonzo said. "But just know it's not overly detailed. It's more of a launching point. And there are a lot of blanks where one or two glyphs aren't translated." He cleared his throat. "This is from the first shard. Among the…" he hesitated, "probably something like strong magic-people, there lies a great… vessel, with the power to… make all things right. The righteous holder of the… I think it's all the shards connected… must bring it to the… probably high place—to save the Theurgica and all… well, probably all the people everywhere. Invoking the spell with noble something the righteous one will… probably rid the world… of all something, sickness, something about weather, and natural disasters."

I cocked my head. "Interesting. Still some gaps to plug, but it sounds convincing. And the other shard?"

He nodded and read: "The righteous one must pass the… trials?… and I think something about growing internally in a certain way… until the something or other time related moment. According to something like maybe weather, the… again, I think it's referring to all the shards combined… must be lifted until something is something. But be warned, unless something or other is said, is… well, is done a certain way, I guess, the righteous one will surely die and bring something like terrible devastation… for hundreds of years. Then it says something about doing this thing with a certain type of internal character trait, or the Theurgica will be no more."

Vee scowled, throwing her hands up. "Great. It's missing all the useful stuff. We're basically left with 'something something doom.'" She shot a glare at Gonzo. "Tell me again why I should be impressed?"

"Ah. But this is a start." Gonzo lifted a finger. "There's still a lot here. And that's how translating ancient stuff goes. The more obscure words are the last to figure out."

"Duh," Vee said. "Doesn't make it better, though."

"Now look. There's a lot here." Gonzo was eagerly rereading the cryptic translation. "The Theurgica could be in danger, and I bet it has to do with how the shards are used. There's a noble, righteous person who has to be involved, and if it's done wrong, it can lead to natural disaster." He looked at me. "Like that volcano you keep talking about back in the day." He sat back. "Do you think the people here can help read this stuff?"

"No." I shook my head. "They didn't seem to know anything about the shards. And when I passed them off, everyone looked just as curious about them as us. I think it's so ancient, even if it comes from the Theurgica, it's like any historical language." I was getting excited about the shards again and wishing I had them in my hands. I wondered how long before I could touch them again, if ever. I glanced at the lockbox sitting not too far away. Perhaps the third shard? I had to figure out how to open it.

Gonzo's computer blipped, and he scanned it. "Robert already responded. He thinks it's quite accurate so far. He says it confirms his interpretation that the combined shards are the items that need to be brought somewhere to save the Theurgica. He just couldn't translate the word, but let's assume these shards are the topic of their own writing. That means they're important to the people of the Theurgica."

"How did your software know the word Theurgica?"

"Oh, I fed it that." Gonzo turned to me. "I didn't know it would call a particular glyph that word, but I defined Theurgica as a hidden magical world within our own. Looks like that was the best word for it."

"There's something I don't get. Doesn't something seem… off?" Chrissy had a furrowed brow, arms folded. We all turned to her, and she continued. "If these shards are so ancient and powerful, why are they all showing up now? What's changed? Why now, after thousands of years?" Her voice dropped, tension thickening in the air. "It's like something's waking up."

We sat quietly for a moment, then she continued. "Ours just fell from outer space a few weeks ago. Miguel's was discovered not too long before that. Juliette, when did you discover yours?"

She shrugged. "It's been far longer than that. A full year."

"Still." Chrissy gained energy. "A year. But in the context of three thousand years, which is how old these things probably are, it's like no time at all. What's making them all show up now?"

"Magic."

All eyes turned to Vee, and she gained energy. "None of these people call it that. But let's face it, this whole Theurgica is like a world of magic right under our eyes."

Gonzo scoffed. "People are quick to label anything they don't understand as magic."

"Maybe. But if you think of it in that light, it changes things, doesn't it? This is a magical artifact, and the wielder of it has to go somewhere to cast a spell. Hmm?"

We all mused for a moment. Gonzo waved her away. "Maybe you're right. Maybe our concept of magic today came about because of these people. None of them have used the word. And frankly, I think they're an alien race that's been here for all these years, living right under our noses."

"Ugh. What difference does it make?" Vee rolled her eyes. "You and your sci-fi theories. Magic. Sci-fi. They're the same, aren't they?"

"No, they're not!" Gonzo shot back.

"It doesn't matter," I cut in, raising my hands in a placating gesture. "What matters is the Theurgica is real. And the shards are important. More important than anyone in Cortez knows. The fact is, if Jet Su knew we brought the shards here, he'd come after them, and bring as many thugs as he deemed necessary. This is a big deal. We have to be smart about this stuff. But we know way too little."

Everyone sat quietly for a moment, then Chrissy said, "We should all do our own digging. We should learn more about who's after us, and what they might want with the shards."

We all agreed and faced the next day charged with purpose. But it turned out to be much harder to glean information than any of us had expected. All of our training picked up much as the first day had gone, only more intense, each being pushed in our own way. Vee moved from Go to sparring, and it turned out her opponent, Victor, a thirty-something quiet man, was equally talented at that. Gonzo spent half his day hiking and then got into breathing and tai chi. Chrissy also spent half her day focused on tai chi, as well as challenges like climbing a wobbly rope ladder to the floating kids' fort, more rock climbing, and walking on a line strapped between two trees. Juliette got out into the vineyard and the different farms to give advice in the morning, then spent a few hours doing tai chi and meditating, and finally helped with cooking in the late afternoon.

Maria kept the intensity cranked up for me with a relentless regimen of tai chi and added in what felt like military-style exercises—jumping jacks, pushups, crunches, and anything else that pushed me to my limit. She wasn't the type to let me off easy. Every time I thought I'd earned a break, she'd be right there, demanding more.

"Ten pushups. Now," she ordered, standing over me with that familiar look of calm control, as if my exhaustion was irrelevant.

My arms were trembling, sweat dripping from my forehead, but I dropped and started counting them off. The first few were manageable, but by five, my muscles were screaming. Every rep after that felt like lifting a mountain, my body shaking violently as I pushed through.

"Keep going, Mitzy," she said, her tone firm. "You've got more in you."

I gritted my teeth and forced out another one, then another, until I hit eight. My arms nearly gave out as I collapsed onto the ground, panting for breath. But she gave me less than a minute to catch my breath before I was doing jumping jacks, then back to holding tai chi poses.

I didn't think it was possible to do so many pushups in one day, but Maria had a way of breaking past what I thought were my limits. Even when I could only manage four or five at a time, she had me doing them so often that by the end of the day, I'd lost count. Hundreds, maybe. It felt endless.

Maria stayed serious all day, and didn't seem in the mood to lighten up whenever I tried. I wondered if I'd offended her with the kiss attempt, but couldn't think of a way to broach the subject.

Finally, mercifully, the training ended, and I guzzled the last of the huge jug of water. My legs shook, and I imagined how nice a cold beer would taste. As we walked back to town, I said, "Want to grab a drink? I'll buy again."

"No, thanks." She avoided my gaze.

"Oh, are you busy?"

She was stoic. I couldn't read her. "What's wrong, Maria?"

She steeled me with a look. "I don't need a reason. Not today."

I felt my heart drop. "I shouldn't have tried kissing you yesterday."

She shook her head. "It doesn't matter. We need to focus on your training. Go enjoy the evening with your friends."

It felt like someone stabbed me. But then, I'd already figured she was out of my league. I'm not ugly, but not really handsome either—just an average guy with an oversized belly. But... I realized then, even if we never had a chance of being together in that way, I was still really enjoying her presence when she was "off duty." And I also wanted to ask her more questions.

"We can still share a drink now and then, can't we?" I asked.

She surprised me with a slight smile. "Perhaps. But not today."

I reconvened with my friends that night, thankful at the very least that none of us had been cut. But Gonzo was going stir crazy. We tried another handful of dates, but the lockbox was still offering no solutions. We even tried prying it open, but gave up almost instantly.

Gonzo huffed. "We can't get this open, and there's nothing left to work on for the algorithm. It's all in Robert's hands now. I need to watch something! There's this lame-o old TV here with only one channel, and it's garbage. Mitzy, do you think you can figure out a way for us to watch a movie? It's been ages since we watched a B-movie together."

That got me thinking. We had cell service, which meant we could do a hotspot. I wasn't sure if the town had internet, but the signal on my phone was semi-decent. "Let's see what we can find. Come on."

The two of us took a trip to a tiny thrift store and dug up a dented Xbox game console with a single worn controller. Now, here's where I used my ingenuity and my geeky tech skills. I figured out how to tether the console to my cell phone as a hotspot to get it online. Then, even with a mostly weak signal, I set up a new Xbox account, downloaded a casting app, and then Gonzo's phone could stream onto the TV. It was perfect!

It was weak internet, like I said, so the picture wasn't the high definition we were used to at home. But the TV was such an old clunker, it didn't really matter. In no time at all Chrissy had made up a batch of popcorn and we were streaming the 1996 film, *The Arrival*.

It's actually not a terrible movie, I will say, and we ended up watching it without turning it to mute and dubbing over the words. Charlie Sheen plays the lead, and he's great. I have no idea why Gonzo picked that film. It was on our list, but still. Maybe he instinctively had a feeling. It was about aliens living among us unbeknownst to regular folks, just like our current situation.

And it got every single one of us thinking.

Now, in the film, the aliens have this crazy global warming agenda to raise earth's temperature so it's more suited to them, and humanity dies off. Charlie Sheen goes about uncovering the plot, finding the secret hideouts of the aliens, and trying to stop them. I say trying because he really isn't successful, but it's still a cool story idea.

And it felt awfully close to home.

When the film ended, we sat there awhile, then Vee said, "Who are these people in the Theurgica, anyway? And what's their agenda? These folks in Cortez seem nice, but what if they're aliens, like Gonzo's theory, and planning on taking over our world somehow?"

Chrissy shook her head. "It sounds like they already have. Think of what we've learned of the Preservation Society. They have these magic-like powers, and they're all over the world in places of power. If it's us versus them, we've already lost."

"Damn," Gonzo said.

I was thoughtful. "Maybe. Yes. But maybe it's not so straightforward. Think about Edward Peacock."

"What about him?" Vee asked.

I grew animated. "His house seems like a neutral party among the Great Houses. Makes me think it's much like any other society, where some have nefarious agendas and some work for good. He was even willing to take us mundanes into the Theurgica. I can't imagine someone from the Preservation Society doing that."

"What difference does it make?" Vee asked. "If there are those who have bad intentions, that's what matters. We need to stop them."

I shook my head at her. "I agree. But you weren't in that first meeting with the Cortez leadership. They despise the Preservation Society. I think we can trust them with the shards."

Vee paced, her agitation growing. "We can't just sit here twiddling our thumbs while they decide what to do with us. They took the shards from us, and you think we're safe? They threatened to wipe our memories, Mitzy. We should get the shards back and protect the world from *all* of them. How do we know what the translation of the shards is about? What if it's not just the Theurgica that's at risk, but the *entire* world?"

"I don't know." I tried to be calm, to not match her energy, because that never works with her. "And yes, they took the shards, but as a precaution. They have enemies. They don't know us from Adam and Eve. The whole proving ourselves, maybe it's just that? We're not proving we're awesome at certain skills, but that we're trustworthy. If we turn on them, and try to steal the shards, that'll be all the proof they need to wipe our brains. Let's just hunker tight for a few more days."

"And then what?" Vee was frowning. "Mitzy, you're not the best planner. Admit it. You're so go-with-the-flow that you miss things right in front of your face. We need to be prepared to make a move. If they wipe my brain, I'm useless. Same for all of you." She stared us down till we had no choice but to nod in agreement. "We need to get those shards back into your hands to make sure we're on track."

"Can't we just wait to see what they do?" I pushed. "They seem like they'll give us a chance if we prove ourselves."

"Mitzy, you need to hold those shards. Every day you're not holding them, bad things can happen. We need your magical luck. Without it, and without a solid plan, we're like a ship lost at sea."

Instantly, I knew she was right.

I breathed deeply. "Okay. I'll try my best to get my hands on the shards again."

She smiled. "Atta boy."

"But... let's be a little patient about it. We've only been here three days. And we have a potential shard right here in this lockbox. Let's give it at least a week before we do anything rash." I gave her a pleading look.

Vee stopped pacing and turned to me, her eyes hard. "Five days. A week at the most. No more. We don't have time to wait around for them to decide our fate. We *all* work on learning where the shards are being kept. And when the time is up, we get the shards, and make sure Mitzy's luck is guiding us. Is everyone in?"

"Yes," Chrissy said.

Vee gave each of us stares, and we all nodded or voiced our agreement. She relaxed. "Okay then. Plan is set. Now, we just need to figure out what date opens that lockbox, and keep learning about the shards in general." She pointed at me. "Didn't Robert send you something about that prophecy? Is it important? Or relevant?"

"Yeah... The prophecy." I pulled out my phone. "Robert just sent it to me today, and I haven't had a chance to read it yet. Shall I read it aloud?"

"Of course." Vee sat at the table, and we gathered around as Gonzo cracked open another bottle of wine.

I cleared my throat. "Behold the Prophecy of Ramessesnakht, High Priest of Amun, Oracle of the Temple, Voice of the Divine." I continued the rest of the translation.

In the supremacy of His Power,
May he live, reign, and prosper,
A voice in the night awoke,
Under the eye of Amun-Ra, a Stone of Power,
Whose heart beats with the pulse of the Nile,
Shall awaken and bring about
The beginning of a new era for all of humanity,
A time of awakening to true power and knowledge
and insight and glory.

The Great Stone shall be the harbinger of tidings,
And stretch its influence on the far reaches of humanity,
From one side of the earth to the other, it shall overcome
And all will know its overwhelming power.

It glows as the midday sun's ferocity,
Not for the faint of heart to wield,
The power of the dragon will consume its prey

Whether good or evil, all shall know its touch,
And none shall hide from its devastating effect.

Woe to those of impure heart who dare to wield the Stone!
If the sacred is profaned with greed,
Three centuries of calamity shall befall all of creation,
War shall rise and blood shall flow,
Brother shall turn against brother,
father against his offspring,
And the meek shall flee to the caves for refuge.

The earth shall quake with deep anger,
Cities will lie in devastation,
Thebes will fall to ruins and become rubble,
Babylon will erupt into flames
and be completely destroyed,
Not a single great nation shall prevail,
As Geb awakes and fire spurts from long dormant depths,
Volcanoes shall cover the earth in fire and darkness,
For an age and half an age to come.

The coastal cities will fall to great waves,
Monstrous in height, greater than the tallest buildings,
They will drown and die,
Like specks of dust in the wind,
Or flowers in the garden,
Once glorious, now wilted and dead forever.

Osiris shall withdraw his hand
and creation shall groan with famine,
The drought shall destroy all sources of hope
For those who have not stored their grains in full.
Pestilence shall come
and kill the weak and the strong alike,
A man working in his field
shall fall and die among his withering crops,

None shall be free from its touch,
And only a small remnant shall persevere.

Yet, hope remains,
for the Righteous One may still be called
To hold the Great Stone and call upon its power
True of heart and mind and tongue,
Keeper of the flame.
Seeker of the good.
Savior of us all.

No one breathed as I finished reading. "So speaks the prophecy of Ramessesnakht, High Priest of the temple of Amun. May the wisdom of the gods guide us in our guardianship of the sacred."

When I finished reading, everyone sat at the table quietly.
Vee broke the silence. "Ho - lee shit."
Gonzo nodded his head. "My sentiments exactly."
Chrissy ran her fingers through her hair. "This is apocalyptic stuff, guys. What have we gotten ourselves into?"
Vee breathed deeply. "That Great Stone—it's got to be the combination of the six shards. Right, guys?"
"Seems likely," I responded. "If Ramessesnakht is indeed the one who inscribed on the shards and wrote this prophecy both. You can see from the image the glyphs are nearly identical. It's got to be him."
Vee tapped the table with her fingertips. "Is there anything from your historical digging that's gotten you thinking? Other connections?"
I pursed my lips. "You know… there are some odd coincidences. I've already mentioned the big volcano that erupted in Iceland around the same time. And this is also written around the time Moses and the Israelites wandered in the desert for forty years. Who… I might add, is attributed with writing the first five books of the Bible while they were there. As

in, the Bible was started at the same time as all of this. And it was the end of the era of great pharaohs. During the time of Ramessesnakht is when they dwindled. It makes me wonder if the shards were created, or brought to this planet then, and it changed the course of history all over the place."

As I spoke the words aloud, I wondered about how God fit into all of it. Everything we were uncovering seemed so outlandish—so otherworldly. It didn't fit with the boring church services with sterilized versions of God I'd grown up with.

Vee was frowning and staring at me. "This is good digging. It also makes me think we can't let those goons get the shards again. At all costs. We don't want another era of history with volcanoes and famines. One week, Mitzy. That's it. We get the shards and let your luck guide us. No excuses."

I audibly gulped. Even though Maria was being tough on me the last two days, I was really enjoying my time with her, and to be honest, I would have been okay with doing the same routine for another month. And if we pushed to get the shards sooner, would that label us untrustworthy, and get our brains wiped?

I just hoped my luck would kick in again and Vee could be happy soon. If not, I might just wake up in my bed back in Montana with no memory of the last couple of weeks. The idea of it tasted bitter. Something I couldn't let happen, no matter what.

Chapter 22

Over the next four days, as we continued to grow in our individual challenges, I looked for opportunities to ask about the shards, but it felt impossible. Every time we gathered at night to debrief, none of us had made any progress with the shards. No new knowledge. No understanding of what the people were doing with them. It gnawed at me. Every moment seemed to slip through our fingers.

And then, on Friday night, I had a breakthrough with the lockbox. I'd been routinely going through important Egyptian dates, entering each one in quickly, and when I couldn't find any more dates from the era of the Ramses pharaohs, I expanded the search.

The moment came as I went back in time over two hundred years to Tutankhamun. I reeled when I punched in the date of his death on April 6, 1323 BC—040623.

Chrissy had been sitting across from me and looked up from the book she'd been reading when the satisfying sound of the door opening filled the quiet room.

She squealed with delight. "You did it!"

Everyone gathered around as I slowly opened the door to the safe, to reveal… not a shard. Some other old-looking green stone. My heart dropped. All that hope and expectation were dashed. Even so, it was important. We knew that much at least.

I pulled it out and looked it over. Tutankhamun was renowned for being buried with many magical items, but something told me this wasn't special for that reason. The disc was smooth and cool in my palm, its polished green surface catching the dim light like ripples on water. The reverse side was etched in tight Hieratic lines, faint but deliberate, wrapping around the center in a spiral.

Gonzo already had Robert on a video call, and as I held it up, the professor said, "Green in Egyptian lore meant rebirth and protection."

Chrissy's brow furrowed. "But why a disc?"

Robert was quick to reply. "Smooth, round stones were sometimes symbolic 'solar discs.' A green disc could be a symbolic sun of rebirth, placed in his tomb for safe passage into the afterlife." He paused. "Take a picture of the writing and send it to me, please. And get it going with your program, Gonzo."

Gonzo obediently snapped a few photos and got to work translating. With his new algorithm, it wasn't long before he had something.

He cleared his throat. "Okay, everybody. This was a lot easier than the shards. Here's a pretty decent translation.

The lamb shall bear the curse of the One.
Through his innocence, the fire is bound.
The sacrifice is made, and the gate shall hold.
May the young king walk in light,
And may the gods receive this offering."

We turned to Robert, who looked thoughtful. "Interesting. Most definitely seems to refer to King Tut, who died as a child. He wasn't deemed a significant pharaoh compared to others, but there remains to this day much speculation about him. This could be a talisman of sorts, blessing him in the afterlife."

I was puzzled. "But if that's all it is, then why was it in Santiago? And why was it being locked away by the Preservation Society, where Jet Su himself was coming to get it?"

We all grew thoughtful for a moment. "Perhaps," Vee began, "it is a piece of a puzzle. Maybe this wasn't just writing about King Tut but predicting the time to come. What does that mean, 'the gate shall hold'? I have a feeling there's a correlation."

Chrissy shivered. "The lamb... it's not just about Tut being young. Lambs are sacrificed. Innocence slaughtered to protect others."

Gonzo glanced at the disc again. "So maybe the kid-king wasn't just blessed. Maybe his death was *used*. Bound into whatever magic kept this 'gate' shut."

Heaviness settled over me. A boy cut down, turned into a symbol, maybe even fuel for something cosmic. I couldn't shake it. The lamb. Innocence turned into the price of survival. Did it have something to do with the shards and the Prophecy of Ramessesnakht? Was one of us going to wind up being a "sacrificial lamb" if we saw this mystery through to the end? It left me uneasy.

The next day, Maria continued to push—tai chi, breathing exercises, fitness drills—by then she was also teaching me jujitsu, which was thrilling. But none of it seemed to get me any closer to the answers I needed. I was growing stronger, sure, even learning to fight now, but the clock was ticking, and Vee's deadline loomed larger every day.

As evening approached and we walked back to town, she said, "Tomorrow is Sunday. No training."

I perked up. "Do you go to a church?" There were three in town: two Catholic and one Protestant.

"Yes. The Church of Jesus Christ of the Saints of the Ultimate Days."

I blinked. "That's a mouthful."

"Yes." She smiled at me. "Service starts at nine."

"Do I need to dress up?" I asked.

She smirked. "What do *you* think, Mitzy?"

That night, before heading home for dinner, I tried to find a nice outfit, but all the stores were closed. I breathed deeply and stood in the *Wuji* stance, feet slightly parted and knees slightly bent. I took a few deep breaths, taking in the dusty street and imagining I still had luck. Then, hoping for the best, I knocked on the door of the thrift store a few blocks from the house.

The owner was an older woman who scrunched up her nose at me as she opened the door. "We're closed." Her deeply wrinkled face gave a gentle smile. "Come back on Monday."

"Please. I need an outfit for church tomorrow," I pleaded.

She scrutinized me up and down, then shook her head and waved me in. She pointed a knobby finger toward a brown jacket on a wobbly rack. "That one."

It was an old, poorly fitting suit jacket, but it would do. I quickly found somewhat matching slacks and a collared shirt, paid her extra, and made it back just in time for dinner.

In the morning, I was actually nervous. First off, I'd never been to a Catholic service before, and had no idea what to expect. Second, I worried about how I'd come across to Maria. And third, I realized on my way there that probably her entire family would be present, and that made me even more uptight.

The building wasn't old like in Europe, but it was beautifully designed with stained-glass all along the left and right walls, and one large arched window showing a dove descending on Jesus in the middle. About seventy people sat in the gleaming wooden pews, and an organ was playing a stodgy tune. I saw Maria sitting with eight others. I cautiously walked up to the pew next to her and waved. She gave me a slight nod and turned back to the front.

I've been to a few different church services, but this was something else entirely. Sitting, standing, kneeling—there was a rhythm to it all, but one I definitely didn't know. The Spanish washed over me in a jumble of words I only half understood because of the different lingo and Biblical references, and I mimicked those around me, hoping I wasn't doing anything too stupid. At one point, I was sure I knelt when I wasn't supposed to, and a few people gave me sidelong glances. Great, just what I needed—more embarrassment in front of Maria and her family.

I tried following the sermon, but I struggled to keep up with the formal and obscure words and grew bored. After the novelty had worn off, it was just another dull church service. I practiced my breathing and sat up straighter. Interestingly, it felt like the room grew a little brighter, the stained-glass depictions more vivid. The priest said a word I didn't know, and it caught my ear. Curious, I pulled out my phone to see the translation of the word.

Cordero. Lamb.

There it was again. The image of the lamb in the big apocalypse mural in Bordeaux flashed into my mind. Something about the lamb stuck out at me, and my mind started racing. Could it have significance to the mystery of the shards? First, King Tut is a sacrificial lamb. Then, the Israelites got away from four hundred years of slavery in Egypt by sacrificing lambs. Then, Jesus. Was the lamb imagery somehow relevant to what we were trying to figure out?

My curiosity kept me listening, and although the rest of the service felt like rote religion, I lasted through it. When the service ended, Maria and her crew rose to leave. I stood and approached her.

I lifted my hand weakly. "Hi."

"What did you think?" she asked.

"Um..." I scrunched up my face. "It was kinda boring?"

She stifled a laugh. "Ah, Mitzy. So honest. Did you learn anything?"

"Yeah." I waved my hands in frustration. "What's with the lamb? What was that about?"

She gave me a questioning look. "So, you *did* pay attention. I would ask Father Romano."

"Okay then, I will." I pursed my lips and nodded.

She smiled gently and went on her way, chatting with another woman her age—a cousin? Sister? Who knows?

Father Romano was standing at the back of the sanctuary, and I approached him. "Please, Father, can you explain to me about the lamb? My Spanish is not so good."

He gave me a gentle pat on the arm. "Ah, child, the lamb is Jesus' crowning glory."

"And why is that?"

"He took the humblest of actions, going to death on a cross, and sacrificed himself like the lambs that the Jewish people would sacrifice. Except it was himself. And because of it, God glorified him."

"Huh." I shook my head. "But it's all symbolism, right?"

Father Romano's smile was gentle, but there was a sharpness in his eyes. "Yes. Of course. How else can we understand God and his actions without metaphors? There is no other way, for our only experience is of this physical world. But symbols point to deeper truths. Just because something is a metaphor doesn't mean it's not real. The lamb is a symbol of sacrifice, but the power behind that sacrifice is very real."

"But... what about otherworldly stuff? I mean, the Theurgica. How does all that fit in?"

His expression didn't change. "Our world has always been connected to the mystical. You don't need to look far to see it. The lamb may be a symbol, but the forces it represents are as real as the ground beneath your feet."

"But what about... how do the mystical and the natural work together?"

He just gave me a wry smile. "My son, have you read the Bible yet?"

"Um... no." I shook my head.

"The Bible... describes God with metaphors. But it also explains a world where the mystical is real. Miracles happen. Magic is a reality."

"Magic?" I raised my eyebrows.

"Have you heard of the church at Ephesus?" he asked. When I shrugged, he went on. "They practiced great magic, the older ways, not like the traits we have today, and as a sign of their devotion to trust in God and not themselves, they burned all of their spells. According to scripture, it was worth fifty thousand pieces of silver, or around five million U.S. dollars today. That was a big commitment."

I reeled. "Why would they do that?"

He held his hands out. "To show they could rely on God and not magic. You see, my child, our traits are not our greatest strength. It lies in our character and in our faith."

"And the lamb?" I pressed. "If it's a metaphor for Jesus dying, how is that strength? Seems more like getting killed as a weakling."

The priest gave a wry smile. "Yes. A weakling. As it says in the letter to the Corinthians, the Greeks wanted wisdom, and the way of the lamb appeared like foolishness, while the Jews wanted strength and power, and his way came across as weakness. But the way of the lamb was the only way to make him worthy, even if it makes little sense to you and me."

I left him with my mind awash with ideas and nowhere to land.

When I got back, Gonzo was sitting with a smile on his face on a lawn chair under a tree in the shade. "What's up, Mitzy?"

"Hey, Gonzo. Enjoying the day of rest?"

"Yeah." He grinned. "It's great." He stood and stretched. "But I'll be honest with you—I never thought I'd say this—but I think I miss the exercise a bit."

"What?" My eyes widened. "Invasion of the Body Snatchers! Who are you, and what have you done with my best friend?"

He laughed. "Calm down. Look at this." He lifted his shirt. "I've tightened a buckle on my belt. A couple of weeks running around on this adventure, including some serious exercise, and I've lost some weight. It feels good. If this keeps up, I'll need new pants!"

"Well, that's pretty cool." I looked down at my own belly. I certainly wasn't anywhere near as large as him, but I, too, was feeling more fit with only a week of intense exercise. If I kept it up for a month, would I be buff? The idea appealed to me.

But when Monday rolled around, Maria didn't show up. Instead, I had training with Gonzo's stern instructor, Eduardo, who didn't want to go outside at all but practice on mats in a gym. Eduardo was stern, silent, and clearly not interested in pleasantries. He quickly let me know he didn't think I was making any progress at all and constantly critiqued me. He focused entirely on jujitsu. He said tai chi was for beginners, and I needed something more useful. That's when I realized how much I was enjoying my time in Cortez because of Maria.

I finished the day bruised, battered, utterly exhausted, and low on energy. I missed Maria more than ever and wondered what had happened to her? Was this the new norm?

When I got back to the house, I learned the others had kept up their similar routines, but Maria had shown up at their training and watched for an hour or more. Eduardo's training left me lifeless, and I crashed early, but also rose early. As the sun rose, and Juliette's sweet singing came from the kitchen as she prepared us eggs and freshly baked bread, I couldn't help but think I could tackle the day. But I got Eduardo again and ended that day in more misery than before.

My whole body ached, and I wondered if I would even be able to move in the morning. What had happened to Maria? And Vee's deadline loomed.

The next morning, we gathered around the table with oatmeal and coffee, and Vee leaned in close, her voice low and intense. "This is the day, Mitzy. If nothing new comes to get us closer to the shards, we take matters into our own hands."

The weight of her words felt like a slap across the face. "Have none of you had any luck?" They all shook their heads. I felt torn. "But I haven't talked with Maria for two days, and Eduardo is a concrete wall. I can't get through to him."

"Today is the day." She pierced me with a serious look. "If nothing new happens, we search the town tonight."

I went into the day edgy, my body sore from days of relentless training. I breathed a sigh of relief when I saw Maria smiling at me.

"Ah. Maria. Good morning," I said brightly.

"Good morning." She gestured. "Mitzy, I'd like you to meet Susanna." A twelve-year-old girl stood and gave me a small bow of her head.

"Um... hello, Susanna."

"Susanna will be your sparring partner today. Let's go up the mountain."

"Oh. Okay." I didn't have more words. What was she trying to prove? The girl wasn't even up to my shoulders in height. I was probably double her weight.

But as soon as we started sparring, I realized my foolishness. Susanna moved like lightning, her slight frame darting in and out of reach with a precision I hadn't seen before. Within seconds, she had me on the ground, staring up at the sky in disbelief.

"No way," I muttered, scrambling back to my feet. But before I could get into position, she was at it again, knocking me flat with a swift kick that left me gasping for air.

The cycle repeated—over and over—until every bit of pride I had was trampled into the dirt. Susanna wiped the floor with me. Over and over. Ugh. It was awful. To be beaten up by a little girl so soundly, after feeling good about my progress—it just stung in the wrong ways. I did occasionally get the upper hand, but every time it was because of me outweighing her, not because of skill.

It was a tough day, and there was never a suitable moment to talk to Maria. By evening, she said, "Good day training. Let's call it." We packed our water and bags and walked down toward town. Every moment felt like an opportunity slipping away. The silence between us was heavy, and I kept stealing glances at her, searching for an opening. But Maria's expression was unreadable; her mind was clearly somewhere else.

I couldn't stand it any longer. The weight of Vee's deadline, my failure with Susanna, and the mystery of the shards—all of it was pressing down on me, and I needed answers. Or at least, I needed something.

I sidled up to her, leaving Susanna to trail behind us.

"What do you see in me today?" I asked, trying to sound nonchalant.

She raised her eyebrows at me. "You're gaining control."

I cocked my head. "A center?"

"Yes, Mitzy. A center. A spark of your trait."

"Wait, what?" I was suddenly distracted. "Like, my power? I have it? But I'm not holding a shard."

"No, you are not."

She was so cryptic sometimes!

"And... do I have my luck?"

"Some. You could do better."

My mind was reeling. "But I'm not holding the shard..."

She shrugged. "I see what I see."

"Where are the shards, anyway?" I asked. I regretted the straightforward question almost instantly.

Maria scowled at me. "You know better than to ask that, Mitzy."

"Okay. Okay. You're right. But listen. We can help decipher them. Have your friends tried? We have knowledge about them. We're working on the translation. And I'm *lucky*. Don't you think it would be good for me to hold them, with all the people after them?"

"We are counting on that." She gazed ahead as we entered the village.

"You are? What about wiping our brains?"

She rolled her eyes. "Mitzy. You will not have your memories of this place erased. You are no longer mundane. I don't know how that happened, but it did. And on top of that, you have proven to be worthy."

"When did I do that?" I was confused.

"I still think you're a self-centered smarty-pants. But one with a good heart."

"Is that so?" I gave her a grin. "This calls for a celebration. Let me take you to dinner. Somewhere nice."

Maria raised an eyebrow, her lips twitching into a half-smile. "I have plans."

"Plans?" I echoed, giving her my best innocent look. "Well, that's a shame. I was going to treat you to the best this town has to offer."

She didn't take the bait, but there was a glint of amusement in her eyes. "You'll have to save your grand gestures for someone else."

"Or," I said, thinking quickly, "you could come over to our house and try Juliette's French cooking! She's really incredible, and you can get to know the others a bit."

She narrowed her eyes at me, and I continued. "It will be the highlight of your week. I promise."

She pursed her lips, then stopped and stared me in the eyes with an intensity that made me pause. "If I come over tonight," she said, her voice firm, "you have to promise me something."

I swallowed. "Anything."

"No questions about the shards. No probing, no trying to get information. Just dinner, and nothing else. Can you do that?"

I put my hand on my heart and raised my other hand. "Scout's honor. No shard talk. No probing. Just dinner."

I realized then she'd have no idea what scout's honor meant, but she studied me for a moment, then gave a nod. "Alright then, Mitzy. I will join you and your friends for dinner tonight. It had better be as you say. For you *and* your friends."

"I guarantee it," I said. And in that moment, I believed it. I had every best intention of the night being a perfect gathering with the six of us. And with her comment that I was exhibiting luck, I just knew it would all go well.

At least, that was what I told myself, anyway.

Chapter 23

As soon as I stepped inside, Vee poked my chest and said, "Well, Mitzy? What about the shards?"

My stomach twisted. *Not now.* I widened my eyes and tilted my head slightly towards Maria. "I've brought a dinner guest tonight, everyone. You remember Maria?"

Maria had a smirk on her face as she looked at Vee. "Veronica Velasquez. Good evening to you."

Vee winced. "Maria. Please. Enter." She put on a stone-cold face. As soon as Maria passed, she mouthed stuff to me animatedly, but I had no idea what she was trying to tell me.

I sidled up to her nonchalantly and whispered in her ear, "I'm lucky again. Even without the shards. It's all good."

She appraised me then, with a look like she was impressed—like I'd actually done something right in her eyes. That felt like a relief, although it didn't last.

"So, Maria..." Vee picked right up. "How's our training going?"

"Fine." Maria gave me a look as if to say, *told-you-so.*

"Um..." I floundered for a moment. "Look, guys, let's just have a meal together and not talk about stuff that Maria's not allowed to talk about."

Vee put her hand on her hip. "And what would those topics be?"

"Our training, for one," I answered.

"That's not really true," Maria said. "I can tell you that you're all doing well in your training. And have proven that you are trustworthy. None of you have shown any reason to wipe your memories of this place. And from seeing Mitzy's beginnings of exhibiting a trait, I wonder now about the potential of all of you."

Chrissy took an audible breath, and Gonzo perked up. "Really? Without holding the shard? How is that possible?"

Maria shrugged. "I don't know. I can only assume that holding the shard has an irreversible effect. What is that wonderful smell?"

Juliette was stirring a pot over the stove, wearing a yellow-and-green-smudged apron. "Simple dinner tonight. Pesto pasta with shrimp and pomegranates, and a side of butternut squash bisque. Fresh baguette and cheese to accompany."

"Yum!" Gonzo licked his lips. "Juliette, have I ever told you I love you?"

She beamed happily. "Every day I cook."

"Baguette?" Maria peered into the open kitchen. "Where did you buy that?"

"Oh, dearie." Juliette shook her head. "I made it from scratch."

"See?" I nudged Maria. "I told you we have incredible food here."

She looked impressed, and I thought it was all going to go well, but then Vee started talking again. "Why is our training so varied, anyway? Mine doesn't seem useful at all."

Maria sighed. "You are all missing key elements to be successful with your traits. If you're going to have a trait, you must wield it wisely."

"What am *I* missing?" Vee looked defensive. "I'm excellent at Go and martial arts. Just because you pitted me against someone who's better than me doesn't mean I'm going to do poorly with my trait."

Maria's lips curled into a knowing smirk. "You fight like someone desperate to prove something. Your ego is in the way."

Vee's hands clenched at her sides, and for a moment, I thought she might throw a punch. Her eyes locked onto Maria's with a fury that could cut glass. "What's that supposed to mean?"

"It is what it is. You must know your place to be here, Veronica."

Vee winced. "And what place is that?"

"Among the rest of us," Maria gestured with open hands.

Vee studied her. Her eyes blazed. "What are you trying to say?"

Maria pointed at her, inches from her chest. "You're no better than me, Veronica. In fact, in some ways, I am your better."

Vee swatted Maria's finger away, nostrils flaring. Maria's reaction was immediate—a quick foot-sweep aimed at knocking Vee off balance—but Vee danced back, her movements sharp and controlled. She lunged for Maria's arm, but Maria twisted smoothly, deflecting the grab with a subtle kick that met Vee's block with a hollow *thud*. Their movements were fluid and practiced.

The tension in the room tightened. A near-visible thread stretched between Vee and Maria, pulling tighter with each passing second. Vee's eyes flared, her breath coming faster, and her muscles coiled like springs ready to snap. She launched herself into a high kick aimed straight at Maria's head.

Maria sidestepped and blocked Vee's kick with a smooth, almost effortless sweep of her arm. Her other leg moved simultaneously, sweeping low toward Vee's feet, forcing Vee to stumble. For a split second, I thought Vee was going down, but she twisted mid-fall, her body bending with athletic grace into a cartwheel that brought her right back to her feet.

Her eyes blazed hotter, her frustration building with every block Maria put up. There was no pause, no breath. Vee rushed forward, two quick steps closing the distance, her left fist swinging at Maria's face.

"Stop!" Chrissy's voice broke through, but it was like throwing pebbles at a charging bull.

Vee's punch met Maria's forearm with a sharp thud. Maria deflected it easily, already expecting the follow-up punch from Vee's right hand. She blocked it too, her focus unbroken, and in a fluid motion, she grabbed Vee's arm and pulled her forward, trying to trip her.

But Vee twisted out of the hold, yanking Maria's arm with her as she turned. The movement was more forceful than strategic. Maria stayed calm, her eyes sharp. She held onto Vee's arm, pivoting her own body to flip Vee over her shoulder. For a moment, it seemed like Maria had her, but Vee pushed off, twisting in midair, landing on her feet with a thudding grace. No one breathed.

Vee's movements became faster, harder. Each punch and kick was aimed at breaking through Maria's defenses. But Maria saw each attack coming. She blocked with a steady rhythm—down, then up, her feet staying firmly planted, her face composed, as if she were calculating the energy in every hit, biding her time.

Vee came in again relentlessly—left punch, right kick, another punch—her frustration fueling her strikes. Maria didn't falter. She blocked each blow, her eyes narrowing as if she could sense the building rage in Vee's moves. And then, just as Vee's right fist flew toward her face again, Maria didn't block but pulled Vee's arm forward, using her momentum against her, and struck.

Her fist sank into Vee's gut, hard and fast.

Vee let out a small gasp, her body recoiling, her face flushing a deep red as she stumbled back, winded. Her breath came in harsh, shallow bursts now, her eyes wide with shock and fury. But the blow only seemed to stoke the fire burning inside her. With a growl, she surged forward again, her strikes wild and fierce, each one filled with the anger of someone who refused to lose.

But Maria was ready. She caught each punch and parried every grab with the precision of someone who knew they had already won. Vee's frustration reached its peak, her movements growing more erratic, less controlled, until Maria saw her opening.

In one swift motion, Maria swept her leg out again, this time connecting solidly with Vee's ankle. Vee tumbled, her body hitting the floor with a dull thud. But true to form, she rolled immediately, leaping back to her feet. Her stance remained defiant, but Maria stood poised, barely winded, while Vee's chest heaved with ragged breaths.

I watched, frozen, my chest tight as the fight escalated. Part of me wanted to stop them from sparring, but something about the raw energy between them held me in place. Was it Maria's confidence and calculated attacks? Or was it Vee, fighting like she had something to prove? Either way, I couldn't look away. I couldn't decide if I wanted one of them to win, and my fascination kept me glued.

And then, Maria's defense sent Vee flying backward, and she knocked a lamp off a counter, which sent it to the ground, shattering into a dozen pieces.

"Enough!" Juliette's voice cut through the tension like a knife from the kitchen. She didn't even bother turning around, but the command in her tone was unmistakable. Both women froze, fists still raised, chests heaving. The sudden silence was thick, broken only by the faint clatter of a spoon against a pot.

Maria was the first to lower her hands, her eyes never leaving Vee. Vee hesitated, nostrils flaring, before she, too, relaxed her stance—though I could see the frustration still burning behind her eyes.

Vee glanced at the kitchen. "Sorry," she said weakly.

"You'd better be." Juliette wagged her finger. "You just proved her point, dearie. Now, come sit down and take a sip of this lovely Chilean wine. It's a Cabernet Sauvignon, and aged well, I might add."

Vee held Maria's stare for a moment. The tension mounted, then dissipated as Vee went to the table and sat down. She drummed her fingers on the table until Gonzo poured her a glass of wine, and she took it with a sigh.

"That's the spirit, dearie," Juliette said as she began laying the food on the table.

We all gathered around the table and poured glasses. I lifted a glass and said, "A toast, to making it this far, and unlocking mysteries together."

I was trying to sound coy, but Vee gave me a stare like I'd said the wrong thing. I tried to figure out what it was—maybe just the fact that Maria was there? Anyway, I let it go—she was in a serious mood, and I hoped having a nice dinner might snap her out of it.

Gonzo raised his glass with a grin. "And here's to emotional growth, physical training, and only *mild* interpersonal violence."

He looked at Maria and Vee, then took a big sip. "We're doing great."

I chuckled and dug into the delicious food.

Maria guarded her words through the entire meal, while Vee held herself coolly and barely spoke. It was not the pleasant dinner I'd hoped for. No new breakthroughs, and not even a great connection between Maria and the rest of the gang. Although partway through the meal, Gonzo started doing a blowfish impersonation, and most of us at the table laughed and started enjoying ourselves.

I say most of us, because throughout the evening, Vee kept mouthing things to me. Most of the time, I couldn't tell what she was saying, but the gist was clear. She wanted me to dig for more information about the shards. But what could I do? As the evening went on, Vee grew more and more agitated, and I became more and more unsure of myself. I just wanted to do the right thing, but what was that exactly? Where was my luck?

In no time at all, Maria said her goodbyes, and I walked her outside. We stood on the street for a moment, the stars twinkling brightly.

"Sorry about Vee," I said.

"What for? It's not your fault." Maria stood a few feet from me, poised to leave.

"I suppose. But I'd hoped she would be more civil. Thanks for coming to dinner. I told you I could restrain myself."

She smiled at me, and my heart melted. I didn't want her mad at me, and it made me happy to no end that she seemed alright. "You are on the right track, Mitzy. Just be careful to keep your motives pure. This would have been a better night if you'd done that."

"Sorry," I said. "You know, I just want to help. I'm really lucky when holding them, and it seems like we could use that. Jet Su seems pretty formidable, and, last we heard, he was coming to Santiago. I'm sure by now he's figured out we're somewhere in Chile. He'll be looking for us, and the shards."

"I know," Maria said quietly. Then, she sighed. "I was keeping any news of the outside world from you so as not to distract you, but you should probably know. He hasn't left. In fact, he's now brought in a dozen of his top agents and taken over the Chilean Preservation Society. We're watching it closely."

My heart squeezed. "That's what I'm talking about. I feel like I would trust you guys to just leave the shards here, but what are the chances he'll track them down? Would you be able to handle him without luck?"

Maria was quiet.

"Also," I continued. "We've learned things about the shards. Big things. It's not just important to Jet Su and the Preservation Society. It could be important for saving the Theurgica, maybe even the world."

"I wondered about that," she said calmly. She looked up at the stars, and I looked, too, barely seeing them, mind racing.

Maria broke the silence. "You have far to go with your training, Mitzy, but you've got the right idea. It's not up to me, but I'm going to suggest they let you and your friends train with the shards and help work on the mystery. We've learned some things as well."

"You have?" I perked up.

She chuckled. "It's not for me to say. But yes. I'll inquire in the morning and let you know tomorrow."

My heart leaped into my throat at her faint smile. She was looking at me, her eyes twinkling, and I felt a spark between us, just for a moment. "Okay," I said weakly.

She smiled sweetly. "Goodnight, Mitzy." She turned and left.

I stood there dumbly for a while, then started walking down the empty street in the other direction, the cool night air like a balm on my skin. Above me, the stars were scattered across the black expanse like pieces of a puzzle I would never be able to solve. I stopped, letting the silence settle around me. No sound but the distant hum of the village and the gentle rustling of the leaves in the breeze.

I tipped my head back, staring up at the Southern Hemisphere constellations. How many times had I wished on stars as a kid, dreaming about being special, about having a purpose? And now here I was—caught in something way bigger than I ever imagined, with powers I didn't understand and a future that felt more uncertain than ever.

Did Maria really believe in me? I glanced down the street where she'd walked off, her silhouette still etched in my mind. For all her cool exterior, there had been something different in her eyes before she'd walked off. A softness, maybe? Or was I just seeing what I wanted to see? I realized then that—whatever was building between us—she was my key to navigating Cortez. My only genuine connection.

That's when I realized I hadn't seen Pepe all week. Was he still out and about on his nightly escapades? I decided this would be a good night to find out. So, I started wandering down the street in the opposite direction. And frankly, I didn't want to face Vee, so any excuse would have appealed to me.

I retraced my steps to the park where Pepe had shown me the Alicanto, but it was dark and empty. I kept walking till I got out of the park and started entering the wilderness. I climbed the mountain overlooking the small town of Cortez.

It was a gorgeous night, with the moon just peaking over a ridge, and the lights of the village below. I found a rock to sit on and gazed over the view, happy to be away from anybody telling me what to do. I like nighttime hikes. I used to take late-night walks with my family growing up in Wisconsin and Illinois, and in Montana, I began enjoying night hiking on open trails with the lights from the sky to guide the way. Something about being outside with no one else there and the wonder of the stars always drew me in.

I realized I was struggling with the whole concept of the Theurgica. After watching that sci-fi movie about aliens taking over the planet, I had serious doubts. But I was starting to really enjoy the whole adventure immensely. Yes, it's not great having people with powers trying to stab you in your sleep or chase you down and steal some magical artifact from you. But at that moment, within the safety of Cortez, I was reflecting on the last few weeks with an almost romantic flavor, and it felt exhilarating and mysterious.

And I was truly lucky! I was going to have things go my way for the rest of my life... unless it wore off. And I couldn't let that happen—I had to keep training. The sheer thought of being lucky forever got me thinking I had to stay in Cortez more than ever. I wondered how Gonzo, Chrissy, Vee, and Juliette felt about it now that they knew we had the potential to have powers without holding the shards.

And then I had a pang of realization—Maria had told me she was going to recommend we get to hold the shards again! I needed to let my friends know the good news.

I headed down the mountain, and that's when I saw a shimmer. I jerked my head to get a look. There it was—the Alicanto, in all its golden glory. It was a marvelous bird, similar in body to a peacock, with long tail feathers, but colorful red and gold, like I would imagine a phoenix.

I stared, wondering what to do. It looked at me, then started walking around the mountain. I took a step, then faltered. Should I follow it? It paused, looked back over its shoulder at me, as if beckoning, then continued.

That's all I needed. I took off and followed the dazzling bird over the rocky terrain. We went along the mountain for twenty minutes, then it disappeared into a cave. The tunnel glowed as it descended, and I tried to decide what to do. It was glowing enough that I figured I'd be able to see, but the idea of being in a cave at night with no flashlight and nobody knowing where I was freaked me out. So, I looked around, trying to commit to memory where I was. I saw a tree with a split trunk and a few distinct boulders, then retraced my steps back the way I'd come.

By the time I got back to the house, Vee was fuming mad. Nobody wanted to be around her. I guess I hadn't thought of the fact that she'd been waiting for me to go back inside to debrief, and instead I was gone for over an hour.

Oops.

"So… I began. She eyed me with a glare from her seat at the table, and I cleared my throat to speak to the entire room, not looking Vee in the eyes. "I have good news and bad news. First, the good news." The others looked up from the couches. I tried to look happy. "I spoke to Maria, and she's going to recommend that we train with the shards again."

Vee's voice was icy. "*Maybe* good news. If she *recommends* we train, it doesn't mean it will happen."

"Still," I burbled cheerfully. "It's what you wanted. And we got it. I'd call that a huge success. Also, I found a gold mine."

Gonzo perked up. "What do you mean? Something awesome?"

I chuckled. "Well… it is that, too. I mean literally. I found what's probably a mine of gold. So, if we need more money, we can just go get it there."

Vee rolled her eyes at me. "Mitzy, you're impossible."

Chrissy folded her arms and gave me an appraising look. "So, you're lucky again, huh? That's awesome. I wonder what's happened with you that hasn't happened with the rest of us. Is it because you held the shards more?"

"It has to be," I said, instantly reminded of the moments where it felt like using the shards was twisting me up inside.

"Look," Vee said sternly. "I don't know if you guys are remembering… we still don't know who to trust. Right? People are literally trying to kill us. I got beaten up in an alleyway. Let's not forget all of that. We need to hold our cards close. Play it safe. I'm sure many people here are trustworthy, but are *all* of them?"

When none of us answered, she continued, "Exactly. We know next to nothing. And these folks in Cortez haven't helped fill in the gaps in the slightest. So, let's put this into perspective. We're treading on very unstable ground here. We must go carefully. With open eyes."

"Yes. Yes. Of course." I winced. "And the bad news is… pretty bad, actually." When nobody prodded, I continued. "Jet Su is still in Chile, looking for us. He's brought a dozen of his top agents and taken over the Chilean Preservation Society."

Vee didn't say a word. Her eyes narrowed, calculating.

"Which means, of course, we need all the training we can get." I held my hands out to Vee, fingers laced, pleading. "Please, please, please… can you try to be nice, and work with them for a while? I don't want to mess up my training. I'm positive that's what's helping me to have this power. And I definitely don't want to lose it."

She nodded slowly. "Of course. You have my word. But all of us need to be aware. Things can change in an instant. Be ready for it."

I looked at the others and saw Chrissy and Juliette nod, but I could see Gonzo's gears turning. "Gonzo? What's up?"

"Oh." He glanced at me. "Robert messaged us while you were out. Says he's been followed closely ever since he went to the Library of Congress. And then, when he got back home, his house had been broken into and everything was strewn about."

"Damn." I stared vacantly. "Is he okay?"

"Oh, yeah." Gonzo waved it off. "He's fine. Just wanted us to know he's going to have to be careful. All of his paper documents were rifled. Some were taken. They must know he knows a lot. But a chunk was digital, so he's optimistic they don't know *how* much."

Gonzo's words hung over me. The feeling of safety I'd been feeling in Cortez was thinning. It felt like the clock was ticking, but to what end, we didn't know.

I went to bed restless and wanting more answers—hoping that somehow my luck would lead me to them. Because that's all any of us had to go on at that point.

Chapter 24

I never imagined my training would involve being trapped in a racquetball court while balls were whipped at me faster than I could dodge. But apparently, that's how you help people train to be luckier.

The racquetball flinger, or whatever that cannon is called, shot those things out at over 140 kilometers per hour, or so I was told. Whatever it was, they stung big time.

The cannon swiveled around randomly, so balls went zipping in every direction. Every quarter of a second, there was another sharp crack as one ricocheted off the wall, and I could barely keep up. I'd been hit fifteen times in a row.

"Ow!" I shouted, wincing as another ball smacked into my shoulder. Sixteen. Why I was keeping track, I have no idea.

The balls stopped.

Maria walked onto the gym court, her expression unreadable. "Mitzy, you're trying too hard to dodge."

"And?" I gave her a look like she had to be kidding. One of them had left a stinging red welt on my cheek, and it hurt like the Dickens. "I'm supposed to just stand here and take it?"

She sighed, shaking her head. "No. You need to stop thinking so much. Find your center. Move as your body tells you. Luck isn't something you chase—it's something you let happen."

"Easy for you to say," I grumbled. My whole body throbbed from where the balls had already struck. This was supposed to be about luck, right? So far, I was just feeling sore.

"Here." Maria held out a shard to me and my eyes brightened. "See what it feels like with this."

My hand shot out before I even thought about it. The moment my fingers wrapped around the shard, I felt that familiar buzz of energy spread through me, like an invisible shield. It was intoxicating, that feeling of power. I couldn't help the sigh of relief that escaped me.

"Okay," Maria said, stepping out of the line of fire. She gave a small nod to the guy running the cannon.

I bounced on my toes, ready this time. The machine whirred to life, and the first ball zipped past my head. I didn't even have to think about it. My body just moved, light and fast. The balls came faster, and I dodged them with ease. It was like I could feel where to be—like I knew where each ball was going before it even left the cannon.

For a minute, I thought I had figured it out. I was untouchable. And then one clipped my arm. I faltered, and then another smacked into my leg.

The world came back into focus, and I stopped, shaking my head in frustration. "Damn it!" The next ball hit me square in the chest, knocking the breath out of me.

Maria's voice was calm. "Close your eyes. Focus. Take a deep breath."

I grimaced, but did as she said. The shard hummed in my palm, and I felt a rush of positive energy flow through me. I shifted into a tai chi stance, trying to find my center. The next ball zipped by, missing me entirely. My body moved in sync with the rhythm of the machine. I flowed through tai chi positions quickly and sporadically, in a random order, and the balls didn't even graze me as I danced between them.

When the cannon stopped whirring, I opened my eyes and straightened up, panting but unscathed.

Maria walked back out to me with a big ol' smile on her face. "Now that you know what it feels like, let's see you do it without that shard."

I glanced at the shard in my hand longingly. Without it, I was nothing but a sitting duck. But I sighed and handed it back to her. I felt the loss immediately, like a light switch being flipped off inside me. The power and confidence were completely gone, and with it, the majority of the luck.

Meanwhile, the other guy gathered up the balls. That was super cool. His power was something to do with wind, and the balls would all roll back to him with a gentle breeze along the floor.

The cannon started up again, and I closed my eyes and found my center once more doing rapid tai chi. A ball grazed the top of my head. I tried to ignore it. Another smacked into my side. I grimaced, but kept going. Then, one hit me square in the nose and my focus shattered.

What followed was a barrage of balls, each one pelting me worse than the last. By the time the cannon was turned off, I was hunched over, gasping for breath, my entire body aching.

Maria walked back onto the court and looked me over. "Much better, but still sloppy. Hold the shard. To get the feel for it again."

For the next two hours I practiced hard, holding the shard, then giving it back, then holding it again. Every muscle in my body burned with exhaustion. I could barely see out of one eye, which was swollen and throbbing. I was a sweating, hot, steaming mess. And yet, admittedly, I was getting better and better.

By noon, Maria gave me a once-over, her face unreadable. "Go take a shower, and let's watch your friends."

I brightened and went to wash up. The first person we observed was Juliette. She had already been practicing with the other shard all morning, and was out in the gardens with an old gentleman. As they walked along, the plants would perk up and look more nourished and healthy.

When Maria saw the plants, she gave a smile. "Lorenzo has the same trait as Juliette. He's showing her how to use it more effectively. Her energy is all over the place, but when she focuses, she can be more effective."

Maria paused to turn to me with a look of wonder. "That shard is truly incredible. Anyone who holds it, their trait lights up. And Juliette... she had no glimpse of a trait last night at dinner, and now, you wouldn't even know she was mundane. She looks like one of us."

"Sounds good," I said, touching my swollen eye. "So... can I ask her to use her trait on me?"

Maria stifled a smile. "Go ahead."

The next friend we went to watch was Gonzo. His trainer watched him turn invisible with a stern expression.

"Quicker," he demanded.

Gonzo gave me a sheepish look before vanishing again, a little faster this time.

I grinned. "You've got this, buddy. You've got superpowers!"

Gonzo beamed, disappearing instantly with his next try. His trainer seemed unimpressed.

"Good. Now for the next challenge," he said, leading us into a gym set up as a cluttered children's playroom with a few structures built with wooden bricks, a suspended hula hoop, jungle gym bars, a slide, and a seesaw. Five people with large mesh bags at their sides filled with six-inch dodge balls were waiting.

"Your next task," the trainer said, "is to cross this room without being hit by a single dodge ball."

Gonzo took a breath and blinked out of sight. The room fell silent as the ball throwers listened intently. Then, a scuffing sound, and one of them threw their ball. It bounced off an invisible person, and Gonzo blipped back into view.

"Again!" the trainer said.

He tried twice more but was hit each time.

Maria winced beside me, and I whispered, "Can you see him?"

"No," she said. "Although if I focus on where I know he is, I can occasionally see a glimmer of his aura."

We heard a clatter of blocks falling and Gonzo came into view, looking disappointed.

With barely a glance at Maria, I ran out to him. "Let's team up. You make us invisible, and I'll make us lucky."

Gonzo's face lit up with relief, and we both disappeared. It was disorienting. I could barely tell where I was, let alone avoid anything, and I realized the depth of the challenge Gonzo faced.

We whispered a quick plan. Throw blocks in opposite directions to create a distraction. We launched the blocks, and the dodgeballs flew wildly as we tiptoed across the gym. The throwers all stopped to listen.

"Over here!" Gonzo called from the other side, grinning.

The trainer nodded. "Good. Now try alone, with no help."

As I patted his shoulder and turned to leave, Gonzo grabbed my hand and gave a squeeze. "Thanks, Mitzy."

"You bet." I gave him a thumbs up, then went back to Maria, hoping I'd built his confidence.

As I'd hoped, when he went the next time, he moved quieter, smarter. When the dodgeballs flew, he didn't reappear.

After a full minute, I whispered to Maria, "Do you know where he is?"

"Yes." She nodded slowly. "But only because I'm looking for him. He's getting better at fully disguising himself, even from me."

"Nice." I smiled.

Ten seconds later, he emerged on the far wall, sweaty but victorious, smiling ear to ear.

"Woo-hoo!" I shouted from across the room.

He gave me a thumbs-up, then leaned on the wall. "Tell the X-Men I'm ready... but only if there's a subclass for stealth-based introverts with questionable stamina."

I grinned, and Maria grabbed my arm. "Come on. Vee should have a shard by now."

We walked out of the large room and down the hall into a smaller room with mats where Vee was sparring with an agile guy in his thirties. As soon as I saw them, I was reminded of old Bruce Lee movies I'd seen, where adversaries would take flying kung fu leaps far higher than humanly possible, and a single punch could send three men tumbling to the ground (to the sound of garbage can lids clattering).

Vee moved with intensity, launching herself at Victor with a force that seemed unnatural. She clenched the shard, and I could see the effect—her muscles tightened, her body poised like a predator about to strike. She leaped into the air, far higher than any normal person could, her foot swinging in a powerful arc aimed straight at Victor's chest.

But Victor was ready. He sidestepped with a swift, fluid motion, and Vee landed hard, her foot slamming into the mat with a force that shook the floor. She wasn't just moving fast—she was stronger, heavier, every strike carrying the weight of a sledgehammer.

"You're too slow," Victor said calmly, dodging another punch that would have knocked him across the room if it had landed. "You're relying on your strength too much."

Vee's eyes narrowed, frustration flashing across her face. "What's the point of this power if I'm not going to use it?" She lunged at him, her body twisting midair as she aimed a kick at his head.

Victor ducked just in time, and Vee sailed over him, landing with an almost graceful roll. But the second her feet touched the ground, she was charging again, each step heavier than the last. It was like watching a boulder gain momentum—powerful but unstoppable in the wrong way.

She swung hard, her fist carrying enough weight to put a hole in a wall, but Victor sidestepped once more, letting her punch slam into the air.

"You're thinking too much about the shard," he said, his voice calm. "Stop relying on it to do the work. Control it."

Vee's frustration mounted. She gritted her teeth and leaped again, this time boosting herself with more power, her body becoming impossibly light mid-jump. She soared into the air, aiming to land a kick from above, but Victor barely flinched. He moved just enough to avoid her, and Vee crashed down hard, the floor vibrating beneath her.

I could see it in her face—she was getting angrier, the coil inside her winding tighter with every miss. She was powerful, but it wasn't enough. Her fists clenched, her breathing grew ragged, and her movements became more erratic as she tried to land a blow.

Victor dodged again, this time sweeping her leg out from under her. Vee hit the ground hard, and for a moment, she didn't move. Her eyes squeezed shut as she lay there, gasping for breath. I could see her knuckles whitening as she gripped the shard tighter, like it was her lifeline.

"Get up," Victor said, his tone softer now. "You're stronger than this, Veronica. But you're fighting like you have something to prove. Power is nothing if you can't control it."

Vee opened her eyes, staring up at the ceiling for a moment. Her chest heaved, her whole body tensed. Slowly, she lightened her grip on the shard, her hands trembling. She sat up, but this time, she didn't leap to her feet. She stayed there for a beat, catching her breath, something shifting behind her eyes.

Victor watched her carefully, waiting.

When Vee finally stood, it was different. Her fists were loose, her body more relaxed. The frustration was still there, but it was simmering, not boiling over. She took a deep breath, steadying herself, and raised her hands into a fighting stance. The shard was still in her hand, but the tension in her grip was gone.

"Ready?" Victor asked.

She didn't respond. She just nodded, her eyes focused, her breathing steady.

This time, when she moved, it wasn't with brute force. She adjusted her body's mass with precision—lightening herself to move more quickly, then increasing her weight only when needed, her strikes sharper, more calculated. She landed softly, immediately shifting her weight to dodge Victor's counterstrike.

Victor launched, throwing a punch aimed at her ribs, but Vee expected it. Instead of trying to block with sheer strength, she sidestepped, light on her feet, and struck back with a sharp jab to his chest.

Victor staggered, surprise flashing in his eyes.

But Vee didn't stop. She didn't smile or celebrate. She was in control now, and it showed in every movement. When Victor came at her again, she used the shard's power with purpose—leaping, light as air, dodging his strikes effortlessly, then shifting her mass just enough to deliver powerful hits without losing her balance.

Each move was smoother, more efficient. The wild, erratic energy from earlier was gone. Vee wasn't trying to overpower Victor anymore—she was outmaneuvering him, using her abilities strategically.

The fight went on, but the dynamic had shifted completely. Victor was the one on the defensive now, forced to dodge her quick, precise strikes. Vee's power wasn't just raw strength anymore—it was refined, controlled.

Finally, Victor stepped back, breathing hard. He gave her a small nod of approval. "Good," he said. "Now you're fighting with skill, not just force."

Vee stood tall, her chest rising and falling with deep, steady breaths. She didn't gloat. She didn't need to. The look in her eyes said it all—she had found the balance between power and control.

Standing next to Maria, I took it all in with wide-eyed awe. I whispered, "What's Victor's power, anyway?"

She cocked her head. "It is difficult to explain. Let's just call it agility."

"So, he's super agile?"

"Of mind and body both. Yes. Something like that."

I turned to Maria. "Is he using his trait right now?"

"Off and on," she said. "He's learned to preserve it well, so it lasts most of the day."

I frowned. "Do you see Vee using her power?"

"Yes." She nodded. "I can see what sort of attack she's planning on doing when she uses it. To someone like me, it's like a broadcast."

I brightened. "Hey. Maybe *you* should spar with her while she holds a shard? You could really teach her some things."

She gave me an appraising look. "All in due time, Mitzy. Let's go see Chrissy. Gus should have finished his turn with the shard by now."

We left the building and walked down the street, turning in at the school. It was two stories, and took up half the block, with a playground next to it. We went to the loudest room with the youngest kids. They were gathered around tables, chattering with each other as they worked on different arts-and-crafts projects. And there was Chrissy, standing in the corner, holding the shard, a look of great pain on her face. A woman with angular features stood and watched her from across the room—I assumed it was her trainer, Kali.

I could only imagine. If it hurt her to hear anything the first couple of times she held the shard, all that chatter would be awful.

I gave her a wave with a look that tried to say *I'm sorry*.

She gave a little wave back, teeth gritted.

"What's the point of this?" I asked Maria.

Maria smirked. "I'm sure you can figure it out, Mitzy."

I thought for a moment. "She's got to learn to deal with her power, no matter the circumstances."

"That's a start," she said.

I thought longer. "She can even hear people's thoughts when they're quiet. Do you think she could hear thoughts in this noisy room?"

Maria grinned at me. "Now you're thinking, Mitzy."

I shook my head in wonder. Would Chrissy ever be capable of that? She sure looked awful. I'll say that much.

I smiled at Maria. "Now I feel like you let me off easy."

"Ha! Just you wait." She radiated warmth, and I felt my heart skip a beat.

I tried to look nonchalant. "Bring it on."

She just shook her head and scoffed. "Oh, Mitzy. You forget I'm a seer. No use hiding things from me."

Once again, I wondered just how much she could see. "Are there more seers here?"

"In Cortez? Yes. Many, in fact. Traits often run in the family. My auntie is a seer. You've met her."

"And what does *she* think of me?" I asked with a foolish grin.

She just smiled at me.

That night, when I walked into the house, Vee wasn't angry or uptight. In fact, she looked happy—a rarity these days. I was surprised.

"Hi, Vee," I said cautiously.

She smiled, a glimmer of her usual fire in her eyes. "Hi, Mitzy. Showing up on time for dinner tonight?"

I grinned back, but something about her calmness made me wary. "Wouldn't miss it. I wanted to hear all about how trounced you were today."

"Ha!" she scoffed, crossing her arms, but still sparkling with energy. "Not entirely."

I grabbed a cold beer from the fridge and made my way over to the couches where the others were lounging. I sat next to Vee, observing her carefully. "So, what changed?"

She paused, gazing upward as if searching for the right words. "The key to controlling the power is in breathing and using your chi. But for me… since I already know those things, I had to learn something else." She hesitated, her eyes flicking to me before looking away. "I had to learn to not take everything so personally."

There it was—the vulnerability. Vee rarely let her guard down, and hearing her admit it felt like a shift, but there was something else lurking beneath the surface. I could tell she wasn't done wrestling with it.

I leaned closer. "I saw that change in you. It was pretty incredible to watch. Did you know he was using his trait when he sparred against you?"

"I figured." Vee shook her head. "He moves faster than anyone I've ever sparred with. He reads my moves before I make them. It was frustrating, but it made sense once I realized he had an edge." She sighed. "He's still better than me, but at least I don't feel like I've been beaten all week for nothing."

"Nice to see you in a better mood," I said, taking a swig of my beer. "Still itching to leave?"

Her eyes flicked to mine, studying me for a moment. "No. We've passed whatever test they had for us. They're teaching me valuable lessons. And since they trust us with the shards, I'd say we can stay as long as they let you hold them as often as possible, to ensure we're lucky."

The tension in her voice was subtle, but it was there. Despite her words, I could tell she wasn't entirely convinced that everything was as safe as it seemed. I leaned back and clinked my bottle with hers, but my mind was buzzing.

Chrissy's voice broke through, more serious than usual. "Now we just have to figure out the mystery of the shards."

I paused. "Yeah. That, and everyone against us. How many agents does Jet Su have involved? And is there anyone else?"

Vee frowned, her gaze sharpening. "Do you think he has more than the dozen he brought here to Chile?"

I nodded slowly. "I think so. At the very least, if he can put us on a Most Wanted list in Paris, I'm sure he could gather agents anywhere in the world. I wish we knew more about this whole Theurgica society…" I paused in thought, then sighed. "I've held off contacting Edward Peacock because I don't want us to owe him another favor. But it's our only real connection to any of these answers." I pulled out my phone.

"Is it worth the risk of another favor?" Chrissy asked.

I winced. "I'll have to take my chances."

I got onto my phone and sent Edward a message: *Quick question—do you have any idea how many agents exactly are after us? Also, is Jet Su working with anyone else? Mitzy.*

As I hit send, the phone felt heavier in my hand, like I'd just made a deal with the devil. I tucked it away, but the unease lingered.

Juliette's voice rang out from the kitchen, breaking the tension for a moment. "Dinner! Everyone wash up and come to the table."

I licked my lips, grateful for the distraction. Dinner was never a dull meal in our temporary home, and I looked forward to it every day. But as we fell into our usual routine, a creeping sense of uncertainty gnawed at the edges of my thoughts. Robert was under tight scrutiny, and the threat to us was very real, albeit distant. If he were kidnapped and tortured, would he give up our location? It made me want to learn as much as possible about the shards as quickly as possible.

Halfway through the meal, Edward sent a text. As I pulled out my phone, my face dropped and everyone quieted.

"What is it?" Chrissy asked with concern.

I shook my head as I read the message aloud: "Jet Su has multiple teams searching for you in Chile. If you're still there, watch yourselves." I looked up with a wince. "I guess I'm not surprised. But still..."

Everyone sat quietly. Gonzo shook his head. "There's no way he'll find us here, right?"

"I don't see how," I drawled. "We know they can't track the shards themselves, or they'd have found them all easily. And our phones are all new numbers. Unless he somehow knows my number through Edward?" I shook my head. "No, Edward wouldn't do that. And Robert wouldn't possibly give us away... willingly. So, I think we're safe."

"For now," Gonzo said quietly. "Unless Vee is right, and not everybody in Cortez can be trusted."

As we finished eating around the table, I couldn't shake the feeling that time was running out. The calm we'd found in Cortez was fragile, and I knew better than to get too comfortable.

Later that night, as I sat alone, I decided I'd borrow Gonzo's laptop and dig deeper into Robert's files. I hadn't gone through all the photos of the *Mystic Secrets of Egypt* book, and something told me there were clues we'd missed.

Because who knew how long our circumstances would stay like this?

Chapter 25

The next morning, just after sunrise, Juan Carlos knocked on the door. Most of us were up, and we gathered around.

He spoke with practiced elegance. "Today, you will take a break until one o'clock, at which point, the leadership would like to meet with you to discuss the shards."

I lit up. "What are we going to talk about?"

He eyed me casually. "They would like to share information with you." He paused. "Take the morning to rest. Meet at the conference room you went to when you first arrived promptly at one o'clock." He gave us all a brief look to ensure we were tracking, then turned and left.

That entire morning, something nagged me. Chrissy noticed me pacing and turned from her book. "What's up, Mitzy? Everything okay?"

I frowned and sat next to her. "Not sure. I had weird dreams last night, and something feels... off."

She sat up. "Do tell."

I sighed. "Have you ever had dreams where you woke up and it had felt so real, it took you a while to reorient, and know where you were?"

"Sure. Rarely, but yeah."

"Well..." I started. "Without going into all the weirdness... In the dream, I was standing on red, cracked earth, the heat shimmering in waves around me. There were kangaroos, hundreds of them, bounding across the landscape. I could hear their feet hitting the ground—like drumming. And in the distance, there was something, some presence, drawing me in. It wasn't clear, but I felt it in my chest, like I belonged there. Urgently."

I hesitated, and Chrissy nodded encouragingly. "It sounds like it impacted you."

I frowned and touched my forehead. "I woke up feeling strange, like my head was buzzing, and I couldn't shake the feeling that my dream meant something. With everything going on, it didn't seem far-fetched to think that my luck, or something more, was trying to tell me something important." I gave her a sheepish look. "But now that I'm explaining it to you, it sounds silly."

She gave me a knowing smile. "We've all had a lot on our minds. It's been a pretty serious time. It's okay to be silly, now and again."

I smiled back at her, but inside I squirmed with unease. Something wasn't sitting right with me. I had a feeling that the conference with the leaders would be a turning point, an important one, and that we were running out of time. But it was all just a loose hair, not concrete, and it made me stir-crazy. I took a long walk to clear my head. I wanted to be in a good mental space for the big meeting.

Even after my walk, I couldn't shake the dream from my mind. It felt like more than just random images. Maybe it meant something, but I didn't know what. The only thing I knew for sure was that whatever was coming, we had to be ready for it.

After lunch, we filed into the conference room, the air thick with anticipation. The long table dominated the space, and sitting at its center were the two shards, their etchings casting reflections on the polished wood. Our trainers and the leadership sat around the table, their expressions solemn.

I couldn't help but feel a chill as I looked at the shards in that space. They seemed to pulse, alive with power, and for a moment, the room felt smaller, heavier. I couldn't shake the feeling that something was off. It wasn't just nerves about the meeting. I felt like we were being pulled toward something bigger, something we couldn't control. The shards sat there as if they were waiting for us to unlock them, and that nagging feeling in my chest wouldn't go away.

Alberto, the seventy-year-old chairperson, drew our attention by clearing his throat. "First, congratulations." He eyed each of us. "The five of you have proven your worth. You are test cases, helping us understand what the shards are truly capable of." His eyes settled on me, sharp with curiosity. "Stanley, you are of particular interest to us. You've exhibited your trait even without the aid of the shards. Which begs the question, could the same happen for the rest of you, with more exposure?"

I shifted in my seat as his words hung in the air. "Stanley, you were the keeper of the shards when you first arrived. Did you hold them a lot?"

"Yes," I replied. "It was mostly me, and not the others." I thought back to the headaches and other side effects I felt when holding both shards together. Were those moments when the shards were changing me permanently?

"I see." He drummed his fingers together. "We've seen a pronounced increase in anyone's trait when they hold them. What isn't clear is the shards' origin, their purpose, and the motives of the people after them. We have a few ideas, but first, I'd like to hear from you. Please," he lifted his hand. "You said you were working on translating them?"

Gonzo glanced at me, followed by the others.

I hesitated for a moment, then held out my hand. "May I hold a shard?"

Alberto nodded, and as soon as the cool surface of the shard touched my palm, a wave of calm washed over me. The tightness in my chest eased and the swirling thoughts in my head slowed. The constant tension that had been gnawing at me for days—gone. Not that I suddenly knew what to say, but I wasn't worried about it anymore.

"We are deciphering the writing on them, and it's significant."

Everyone at the table perked up. "Gonzo," I said, "can you pull up what you've got so far?"

He smirked, pulling out his smartphone. "You know I can."

Gonzo's voice filled the room as he read the most recent translations aloud, each phrase landing like a stone in still water.

I watched the faces around the table—eyes narrowing, brows furrowing, fingers tapping against the table in thought. You could almost see the gears turning in everyone's heads, each piece of information slotting into place.

After reading the shard translations, I explained the Prophecy of Ramessesnakht and Gonzo read it as well. When he finished, the room buzzed with unspoken questions, but Alberto didn't leave them hanging.

"Now," he said, "it's our turn."

He pressed a button, and the projector flickered to life. On the screen appeared an image of the two shards. "You can see from the way they fit together that there are six in total. If we include the one taken from Chile, then that leaves three unaccounted for."

"Two, actually," I said. All eyes turned to me. "One was stolen from a museum in China. I mentioned it to a Preservation Society agent in France, and she seemed to know about it, right, Chrissy?"

"Yes," Chrissy said. "She also thought of the one in Chile, and... something more." She soured. "I think by now they may have three."

"That leaves one left." I held my hand out to Alberto to continue.

He changed the slide to a map of the Mediterranean. "The origin of the shards is... elusive," he began. "Just as you've conjectured, we believe they originated from Egypt three thousand years ago because of the Hieratic script on one side. It's possible they were created before that, and the Hieratic was added afterward."

I mused on that for a moment. The thought hadn't occurred to me. Would that explain why two of the sides were so different?

Alberto pointed at the map. "Ancient texts describe unique ways of combining powers when creating artifacts with spellwork. It's something lost to us today, but I wonder if that is how the shards were created."

He flipped the screen to an illustration of a large group of people in robes in an ancient-looking stone room with several symbols and torches everywhere.

"We know only some things of that era of history, but one thing is certain—the people in power were not as shy about using their traits in front of others. There were far fewer of them in those days, and they were looked at as gods. And with such power and resources at their command, the things they did are legendary."

He paused and turned to me. "Stanley, do you have anything you'd like to add about the shards' origins before we move on?"

"Yes," I replied. "We're nearly certain they're from the High Priest Ramessesnakht during the reign of Ramses IV or around then. At least the Hieratic side is in his handwriting."

I recounted to the room much of my knowledge, trying to keep it brief. I'd uncovered a lot of factoids that weren't necessarily relevant.

I paused. "But what I don't know is how and why they were even created. Why are they all over the world? Do you have any light to shed on that?"

"As far as why they were created, it's hard to guess." Alberto moved to another slide—a picture of a glowing fly swatter. "Creating artifacts is quite a common trait. We have many people in Cortez who can create artifacts—essentially imbuing an item with a trait. Simple items are easy. If you have someone who can float, you can bring them and the item together, and transfer some of their power into it. My trait is to do this, and as I imbue the item, I pour the intention of how it's used. For this fly swatter, it took me only an afternoon. Imbue it with a little wind power, and the intention, and flies will always get hit with subtle little pushes of your will as you're swatting them."

He gestured to a slide of a remote control with multiple buttons. "More complex items, like ones with settings and options, are much more difficult, and require more thoughtfulness and procedure. An object of great power takes months, even years, to perfect, and even then, it wears down and has limited usage."

He pointed to the shards. "These artifacts are the most powerful any of us has ever seen. They're a completely different category altogether."

"But why were the shards so spread out?" Chrissy asked. "And why are they just now surfacing? Especially the one that fell from outer space. What's that about?"

Alberto pursed his lips. "It's almost as if—"

"As if what?" Gonzo was leaning forward eagerly.

"As if they were intentionally separated and hidden to the farthest reaches of the earth. It wouldn't even surprise me if one were sent into space, with the assumption it would be impossible to retrieve, but it got stuck in our orbit and was knocked back to earth."

"And the reason they're showing up now?" Chrissy asked eagerly.

A woman's voice cut through the room. "A powerful spell."

All eyes turned to see Chrissy's trainer, Kali, a lithe, middle-aged woman with sharp features.

She explained. "We have no spellwork in Cortez, but it's commonly known among some Houses. There were eras in the past when it was far more prevalent, and now the mysteries are kept by very few. If any House could accomplish such a task, it would be the House of Eldritch."

"Isn't that the one in London?" I interjected.

Kali scoffed. "They certainly originated there, but they're all over the world." She pursed her lips, her tight cheekbones looking even more angular. "The House of Eldritch is known for spells. They can control and protect things in ways that none of us here could dream of. I wouldn't be surprised if someone discovered a spell to awaken the shards somehow. I've heard of more farfetched things."

"How do spells work?" Chrissy asked.

Kali straightened. "They use the language of magic to draw on the aether. The wording must be precise and uninterrupted, which is why, even if one were to see magical runes, like the ones on the two inner sides of the shards, they're useless to most of us."

I cleared my throat. "I don't think House of Eldritch is behind this."

Everyone turned to me. "It's Fulton House. Or at least the U.S.A. Jet Su is in New York, and I'm pretty sure he's with Fulton House. He's the one who ordered everyone to go after us for the shards."

Alberto began typing. "We have been doing some digging on Jet Su. He is not someone to be trifled with. And yes, he's with Fulton House."

I was itching. "What can you tell us?"

He shook his head. "He has commanded the Preservation Society for many years now, with a reach that extends to any country. He has hundreds in his division. And multiple squads of field agents. From what we've read, he has a reputation for ruthlessness. Shoot first, ask questions later. He can phase his body between material and amorphous, making him impossible to harm, and the people he's amassed for his teams are nearly as impressive."

The screen flashed through news headlines:

Commander Jet Su Freezes Accounts of Cairo House in Overnight Raid—27 Agents Detained Without Warning.

Mystery in Mumbai: Inter-House Investigations Directorate Seizes Entire Dockyard, Finds Contraband Relics.

Beijing Sweep Nets Dozens of House Operatives—Jet Su Claims 'Routine Audit,' Critics Call It a Purge.

Commander Su Shuts Down Jersey House Over 'Financial Misconduct'—Sources Whisper the Raven's Hand Behind It.

London Left Reeling After Su's Directorate Exposes House Moles Inside Parliament Security.

Gonzo's face was pale as the screen flashed through a dozen different articles. Each one added another squeeze of tension to my already writhing guts.

Chrissy's voice quavered. "With someone like that on our tail..."

Suddenly, the shard pulsed, almost like a shock of electricity so abruptly I almost dropped it. "Oh!" I exclaimed and jerked my head up. Something was about to happen.

"What is it, Stanley?" Alberto asked.

"I—I don't know," I stammered. "Something bad—"

Before I could finish my sentence, a sudden, high-pitched alarm broke through the room's silence. Everyone in the room froze, glancing down at their phones and smartwatches. Whatever message had come through was enough to send over half the room into motion, chairs screeching back as people scrambled to their feet.

"What's going on?" Vee's voice cut through the chaos, her body already tensing as if preparing for a fight.

Alberto's face darkened as he quickly pulled up a live feed on the screen. The grainy footage showed the main road into Cortez, where four black Suburbans kicked up a cloud of dust as they sped toward town.

"We have visitors," he said, his voice grim. His fingers danced over the keyboard, zooming in on the convoy. "Uninvited ones."

He glanced at Maria. "You stay here."

She nodded, biting her lip.

He quickly typed a message, and everyone's phone blipped again. He stared at the shard on the table for a few seconds. "Stanley, you hold both of the shards."

I reached out and grabbed the other shard. The two naturally connected, and instantly I felt a surge of positive energy course through my body, tingling from my toes to the top of my head.

Alberto pulled his hand through his hair as he watched the screen. "This is the moment of truth." He looked at Maria squarely in the eye. "If Jet Su gets the shards, everything we've fought for will be in vain. You understand?"

"Yes, sir," she replied, voice curt.

He turned to a dark-skinned man down the table. "Javier, time to meet our visitors."

He changed seats to the end of the table as Javier fiddled with a box in the middle. "Ready, sir," the man said.

With a nod, a light came from the center console and covered Alberto. On the screens, a large hologram of Alberto appeared on the road in front of the Suburbans, from his chest up.

The vehicles slowed, then stopped. When Alberto spoke, we could faintly hear his voice echoing outside.

"Greetings. Why do we have the pleasure of receiving a visit from the Preservation Society after nineteen years?"

Jet Su emerged from a Suburban, flanked by two other men, all wearing tight-fitting black combat fatigues. Seeing him on the screen made my stomach churn. He held himself poised for action, a man who'd overcome any obstacle. A man who would never stop till he had what he wanted.

"You are... Alberto Gonzalez?" His voice was cold. Precise.

"Yes. And I know who you are, Commander Su. Your reputation precedes you."

Jet Su cocked his head. "You know why we are here. Give us the fragments of the Stone of Amun-Ra, and we'll be on our way."

"We have no such things," Alberto replied.

Jet Su quirked a smile. "Ah. But I know that's not true." He paused. "Is Stanley Mitz there with you now? Put him on."

My eyes widened. Alberto signaled subtly with his fingers, and the broadcast went on pause. On the big screens, we could see it didn't shut off to the outside world, just held his face. He spoke to me urgently. "No matter what, he can't have those shards. We will fight. It's inevitable. So, what does your luck lead you to? Quickly now."

My head was buzzing. *What the hell. Why not?*

I stood and walked over to him. "I'll do it. He knows we're here, anyway."

Alberto nodded at me and whispered. "The longer you keep him talking, the more time we have to get people into position. We could use even one more minute." He signaled again, and the stream continued, to see me pull up a chair next to him.

"Jet Su," I said as casually as I could. "You're shorter than I thought you'd be."

He smirked. "So… we meet at last, Stanley. I've always wondered what it would be like to meet someone like you. I hope you don't take offence, but we'll need those fragments." Before I could get a word in, he raised a hand. "Oh, I know. You'll probably resist, thinking you're doing the world a great service. But two things."

He raised a finger. "First, it's inevitable that we'll wind up with them." He looked at the hologram almost apologetically. "Sorry. And second." He lifted a second finger. "We're *not* going to blow up the world, or some nonsense. I know that's what you're thinking. But we're going into this with far more knowledge than you. We're actually going to make the world a better place."

He held open his hands. "So, what do you say, Stanley? Give them up peacefully, or will we need to kill a few people along the way? Which is it?"

The whole time he'd spoken, I'd worn a lopsided smile. "Let me guess—this 'better place' world you're talking about has you and your cronies on the top of the food chain, while the poorest of the poor suffer?"

He shrugged. "Perhaps. But if the world is better off, what does that matter?"

I scoffed. "I guess it depends on how many of the little people you squash along the way."

"Details. Details. Look, are you going to work with us nicely, or are you willing to pay the price for being difficult?"

I glanced at Alberto. He gave me an imperceptible shake of his head, as if to say, *Do not give him the shards, no matter what.*

I cocked my head and tapped my wrist. *Are we good on time?*

Alberto gave a tiny nod.

I turned back to the projector. "So far, your willingness to kill innocents is a *little* bit of a red flag for me, if I'm totally honest." I shrugged. "Come and get 'em, Commander Killjoy."

He and his men scrambled back into their Suburbans and kicked up dust as they headed toward Cortez.

The feed cut, and Alberto nodded at me. "Well done. You bought us enough time for a full defense."

Maria's knuckles were white as she gripped the edge of the table. "How do they know the shards are here? We've been so careful..."

Alberto's jaw clenched. "There's only one explanation," he said, his voice low. "We have a spy."

The words landed like a slap. Maria's eyes widened in disbelief. "A spy?" she echoed, shaking her head. "That's impossible! Everyone in Cortez was born and raised here."

"Loyalty can be bought," Alberto said darkly, glancing around the room at the people left, his eyes lingering a second too long on each face. "We send people out of Cortez every day. It takes only one to be lured by something more tempting than loyalty. It doesn't matter now. What's done is done. The shards must leave Cortez. Now."

He locked eyes with me firmly. "Stanley. It will be a nearly impossible task."

A low rumble, like distant thunder, reverberated through the floor, followed by the sharp crack of an explosion. I whipped my head toward the screen. One Suburban was lifted off the ground, sent spinning through the air like a toy, flames licking at its undercarriage. For a moment, my breath caught—but then, impossibly, the vehicle righted itself, hovering for a beat before gently settling back onto the road.

The doors of the vehicle flew open, and people dressed in black poured out like a swarm. Some were armed with weapons. Others had nothing in their hands but carried themselves with quiet, deadly confidence.

One of the unarmed figures stepped forward and lifted his hands. A blue crackle of electricity surrounded him. It raked outward, building up strength, ready to be unleashed.

My stomach dropped. "Well. There's Bruno."

"Who's that?" Maria whirled on me.

I sighed. "Bruno Marx. He tried to kill me in Montana. He tracked us all over France. Nearly killed Vee. So, not my favorite person."

Alberto brought us back. "You must take to the mountains and get to the sea. Maria. Kali. You guide them. Take whatever you need and stay hidden. Don't turn back. Don't worry about us. We can take care of ourselves. When they realize the shards are gone, they'll leave us. Go!"

Maria gestured, and we followed her out the door. As we exited, another explosion erupted in the distance. We glanced to the town entrance where smoke was rising. People were running around everywhere.

Many were bustling in and out of a large brick building nearby, and Maria took off on a run, leading us there.

The place was full of nervous energy, everyone moving quickly and efficiently with practiced precision. Most stood in line waiting their turn to get into one of four different rooms. Others were calling out orders and directing. We stood in the third line.

"What are we doing?" I asked.

Kali was standing next to me. "Gearing up."

We barely had time to process what was happening before it was our turn. The room was packed with gear—rows of water bottles, goggles, shields, even fishing poles. One entire wall gleamed with weapons, everything from knives to rifles, their cold steel reflecting the harsh lights.

Kali pointed to a wall filled with packs. Each of us grabbed one quickly. My hands were shaking, but I forced myself to focus. This wasn't just about survival. This was about protecting the shards.

Gonzo suddenly seemed pained. "Oh! I left the freeze-gun back at our house. And I definitely need my computer."

Maria gave him a hard look. "We must leave immediately. But your house *is* on the way. You will need to get your things as quickly as possible."

She filled a backpack with a few things and shouldered it, then handed a wooden staff to Vee, a foot-long sheathed dagger to Chrissy, and a wristwatch to me. "Let's go."

We ran down the street, breaking into a sweat instantly. We arrived at our house panting and wheezing.

"Two minutes," Maria said sternly.

The five of us ran into our rooms, and I grabbed things as quickly as possible—a small solar phone charger, my wallet, and a travel waistband filled with euros. I tossed a few pieces of clothing into the backpack and turned to go, then noticed the skeleton key. *Can't leave that behind.*

In a blur, we raced after Maria toward the mountains. Gonzo quickly fell behind. The next to slow were me and Juliette. By the time we were heading up the mountain, Maria was fifty yards ahead of me, and Gonzo was a good two hundred yards behind us all.

"Maria!" I called out. She stopped. "We can't all go at that pace."

She frowned as she jogged back to me. "Mitzy. Why aren't you holding the shards?"

"Oh, sorry." I quickly fetched the shards out of my pocket and held them.

She scowled. "Ach! Remember your training. Find your center. Quickly now."

I closed my eyes and did the breathing exercise she'd taught me. My whole body tingled, and increasing pressure formed in my head. My insides squirmed, unsettled, but the energy was positive, and I welcomed it.

Vee broke my concentration by exclaiming, "Shit! They're flying over the town."

I was tempted to open my eyes, but Maria's voice calmed me. "Focus, Mitzy. Breathe."

I heard an explosion and screaming in the distance. I tried to tune it all out and simply be present in the moment. That's when I remembered I'd been at that very spot only two days before.

I opened my eyes, suddenly alert and energized. "There's a cave that way. We can hide there."

Just then, Gonzo caught up to the rest of us, sweating and panting. I passed him a shard. "Go invisible, buddy. And try to keep up. The rest of us will hurry from one hiding spot to the next. Let's go!"

He put his hands on his knees and gasped for air. "Ooookay," he wheezed between breaths, and blipped out of existence.

Even though crazy magical thugs were after us, something about the situation had shifted for me. I felt great. I was on fire. Alive. Energized. And confident. We dashed to a rocky outcropping, then crouched down, shielding our position from the view of town.

I glanced around. "Where's Kali?"

"Here." I heard her voice and turned, but she wasn't there. In her place sat a weathered, rusty-colored fox.

I didn't even blink. "Great. And I hear Gonzo."

He was so noisy, I was thankful he wasn't trying to sneak past anyone. He plopped down next to us, gasping for breath. I risked a glance over the boulders at the town. Smoke was coming up from seven different locations now, and people were running in the streets.

"Ready, Gonzo?"

"One... more... minute," he rasped.

I took the time to breathe deeply. I noticed I'd been hunched over and sat up straighter. Maria spritzed something into the air. I waited till I was centered, then stood. "Okay. Let's go."

We dashed across the rocky mountain face for a few minutes, then I pulled us aside at another rocky outcropping. I glanced around the area, looking for the familiar split tree by the cave I'd encountered late at night a few days earlier.

A minute later, when Gonzo arrived, we took off around the mountain until we reached the cave of the Alicanto. Without pausing, I went inside and waited for the others.

"What is this place?" Chrissy asked.

"I assume it's a gold mine. I followed the Alicanto here the other night."

Maria shook her head. "Impressive, Mitzy. And that was without a shard."

I grinned. "I was wondering why I'd need gold out here in Cortez. I guess I just needed a hiding spot."

"Or maybe both," Chrissy said with a coy smile. "Let's go see where the gold is."

"Wait." Maria held her hand out. "Alberto assumed we would trek across this mountain to a small town where we could find a ride. There are many towns along the coast where we could enlist a boat and head elsewhere. But I want to know... Mitzy, what do *you* think?"

At that moment, I wished my trait were more like some magical guidance telling me exactly what to do. Instead, although I felt great, my mind was blank.

I blinked at her, wondering what to say.

I opened my mouth, but no words came out. How was *I* supposed to know what we should do?

I tried to breathe deeply, and find my center, while everyone watched on. Gonzo's breathing finally calmed down, and he passed the other shard back to me. Instantly, a renewed burst of energy flowed through me, but rather than giving me inspiration, my head started pounding.

As we crouched in the cave entrance, it hit me: holding these shards was no small thing—it was a responsibility, one I was still trying to figure out how to handle. My trait was powerful, sure, but I didn't fully understand it yet. How could I protect everyone if I didn't even know what I was capable of?

I closed my eyes, searching for that calm, that instinct I'd been training to tap into. My mind drifted to Pepe—how he seemed to roll with whatever life threw at him, trusting his gut without overthinking it. Maybe that was the key. Maybe I needed to stop *trying* to control everything. Maybe I just needed to trust myself and start... doing stuff.

Loosey goosey, as Vee would say.

"Let's check out the cave first and then cross the mountain to the next town when it's darker."

"Do you think we'll find gold?" Chrissy asked.

I grinned at her. "There's only one way to find out.

Chapter 26

Maria winced as the frantic crackle of the radio filled the cave, the chaotic sounds of battle filtering through the static. Shouts, explosions, and the distant hum of something mechanical all blended into a sickening noise. Kali, fully human again, darted to the cave opening and used magically enhanced binoculars to scan the way we'd come.

"What's happening?" Chrissy asked, her voice tight with worry.

Maria's grip on the radio tightened, her knuckles white. "There are casualties," she hissed. "On both sides. Jet Su has brought in elite fighters. The village is overrun. And I'm not there to help."

A chill settled over the group, the weight of her words pressing down on us. The fate of Cortez hung in the balance, and we were hiding in a cave.

Kali came back to us, her eyes dark with concern. "They won't stop till they have the shards. Rodriguez House has left us alone for all these years. But now…"

"They won't find us yet," Maria interjected, her voice lacking its usual steadiness. "Alberto's buying us time. But soon enough, he'll meet with them and tell them the shards are gone." She turned to me. Her expression was deadly serious. "Mitzy, we must be on the move as quickly as possible. With their combined traits and gear, there's no telling how quickly they'll be able to trace our path."

"Can we prevent it?" I asked.

"Some." She pointed to her backpack. "I've been covering our tracks with a removal spray that gets rid of traces of the power we use. But it doesn't cover up tracks or smells. If they have someone good at tracking, or if one of them can transform like Kali here into a creature with a keen sense of smell, they could find us. We have little time."

I turned to Kali. "Could *you* find us here?"

She laughed a little. "Most definitely. As a fox, I could smell you many kilometers away."

I gritted my teeth, glancing toward the cave's mouth where the fading light cast long shadows. "Something tells me we shouldn't leave the cave till it's dark. What time is it?"

Maria scoffed. "You have a wristwatch now."

"Ah." I glanced down. "Four-thirty. That leaves us with about two hours. By the way, what's the wristwatch do?"

She smiled playfully. "It tells time."

I laughed, and everyone chuckled along with me. It suddenly felt nice to have a break from all the stress. "What *else* does it do? I assume it was in that special gear room for a reason."

"Twist the crown to the right and it'll protect you and those closest to you with a small force field. It's effective for at least one attack, maybe more depending on how weak the attacks are. Twist it to the left and it'll give you sight like mine for about ten seconds."

I was immediately curious and twisted it to the left. Maria and Kali immediately lit up with auras. Maria looked like a greenish yellow haze, top to bottom. Everywhere she looked, I could see yellow-green traces of her aura leak and envelop the thing she looked at. Kali was more like a faint red glow in a sort of fox-human form. Nobody else had auras of any sort. Then I looked at myself.

I was glowing bright yellow. A massive blotch of brightness, overpowering to look at. It was incredible. That's when I realized just how powerful those shards are. Here I stood, born mundane, and showing more power than either of the natural-born Theurgicans present. I couldn't believe it, even after everything we'd been through. It boosted my confidence in my ability.

Maria shook her head and sounded exasperated. "Mitzy, use it sparingly. You only have so many uses before it runs out of power."

"Ah. Sorry."

I realized then that she knew I was using it, because the watch was leaking out the same chartreuse aura that she had, and it was seeping toward everything I looked at. And just like that, it ended.

Chrissy was holding out the long dagger. "What's this do?"

Maria tilted her head. "Have you heard of the singing sword?"

"Yeah?" Chrissy looked at it curiously.

"It's kind of like that. It has a personality of its own. And yes, it will talk… and sing when it's excited. You must invoke his name to call him to action—Rafael. Be polite to him, and he will protect you."

Chrissy's eyes widened as she held it.

Vee was next. "What about this staff?" It was a little taller than her, around six feet long.

Maria's eyes turned to the sturdy hickory stave in Vee's hands. "An exquisite creation, thanks to Alberto himself. Whatever you dream of will develop off the tips of either end. People have made blades or even brooms appear. But it must stay attached. No bullets or the like."

Vee was gripping the staff and flowers appeared at the top. "Very nice."

She plucked a flower, and it dissipated into thin air.

Maria shook her head. "Just know that the effectiveness of these objects will wear off after repeated use, so use them only when necessary."

"Okay." I stood and stretched. "Let's go look for gold."

Just then, the radio started crackling and Maria said, "You guys go. I'm going to stay by the entrance to keep watch and listen to what's happening."

"Alright." I almost started heading down, but I paused. "If we find gold, do you have anything in that pack of yours that could extract it?"

She shook her head. "No. Oh, wait." She took the pack off and rummaged through it. "Maybe this." She handed me a small stir stick.

"What's it do?"

"It might not work. It's used to purify things. I grabbed it for drinking water, but whatever you think of could probably be purified. It's worth a try, I guess."

I took the stir stick, and we went on our way, leaving Maria, Kali, and Gonzo, who wasn't a fan of enclosed spaces.

The cave was a maze of jagged rocks and narrow passages, the floor uneven and treacherous. Every step was a calculated risk; one wrong move, and you'd be on the ground with a twisted ankle—or worse, tumbling down into the unseen depths below.

My mind kept drifting back to the sounds from the radio. To the people dying in Cortez while we stumbled through the dark, searching for something as trivial as gold. Each step felt heavier than the last, as if the weight of what was happening was pressing down on us all.

Our phone flashlights, which had seemed like such a good idea, were way too weak to see any appreciable distance compared to an actual flashlight. I gripped the shards more tightly, and they hummed pleasantly in my hand. There had to be something we could do, right? I looked at the others for inspiration, then smiled.

"Hey, Vee. Can you turn the end of your staff into a flashlight?"

"Ha! Mitzy, those shards make you seem like you're actually smart or something!"

I laughed. In the next second, we had a beautiful light source guiding our way. And it's a good thing, too, because there was a drop-off about twenty feet in front of where we'd been that went down and down and down, farther than even the flashlight could see. *Lucky I thought of giving us better light when I did.*

We nervously edged around the drop-off and kept going. Then, when the cave widened and multiple passages with stalactites and stalagmites opened up, I pointed randomly to a passage. "That way."

In ten minutes, we saw it. A gorgeous vein of gold that ran through the wall, from floor to ceiling.

Chrissy was ecstatic. "Gold! Mitzy, this is incredible."

I've gotta admit. I was pretty happy. Not that we were prepared to carry out a hundred pounds of gold or anything. But that we'd stumbled into it like that was incredible.

My heart raced as I pressed the stir stick to the vein of gold. For a moment, nothing happened. Then, slowly, the rock seemed to melt, liquid gold oozing out in thick droplets. They fell to the ground, solidifying into perfect, gleaming nuggets. It was mesmerizing, hypnotic, watching wealth literally fall from the walls.

Drop. Drop. Drop. Money literally pooling at my feet.

Vee's voice broke through the fog. "Mitzy, stop. We don't need that much."

She was right. I tore my gaze from the gold and straightened. The four of us filled our pockets and some of our bags till they felt weighted plenty, and there was still a little bit left.

"Let's leave the rest here. If we ever come back, we'll find the vein more easily."

We walked back laden down and soon enough could hear the crackle of the radio.

"How bad is it?" I asked when we reached the group.

Maria's voice was low, almost a whisper. "It's bad, Mitzy. At least fifteen dead. We're a small town—that's too many. I just hope the children…"

My stomach twisted. I'd never heard Maria's voice sound so hollow. Here we were, pockets heavy with gold, while the people who had given us refuge were losing their lives. A sharp pang of guilt shot through me. All that gold suddenly felt meaningless.

"I'm sorry," I muttered, feeling the weight of their deaths settle on my shoulders. In that moment, something shifted in me. What if it was Alberto who'd died? Or Pepe? Or Maria's aunt? All those good people, dying because we'd shown up with the shards. It was wrong. Jet Su and his thugs were evil. We couldn't, ever, let them get the shards.

I steeled myself at that moment. I would do whatever it took to keep the shards from those people.

I trotted over to the entrance. The sun was setting. It wasn't completely dark, but we'd probably be safe. I went back to the group. "Let's go."

We gathered our meager belongings and headed out. Kali ran ahead as a fox. I still hadn't seen her transform. I was secretly super interested to see if it was similar to how that kind of stuff happens in the movies.

Maria led us, and we took off over the mountain, crossing back and forth to make the traversal easier. About midway up, we started walking around, rather than heading over the peak. Every ten minutes or so, she'd pause and spray her concoction into the air. Gonzo used the pauses to catch his breath. I felt for him. Despite all his training the last week, he was still not fit for a full trek. Poor guy. I was honestly surprised I was doing so well myself, because a couple of weeks earlier I'd have been struggling like him.

Soon enough, it was pitch black out, with only stars and a distant moon to guide us. Maria was insistent that we not use any lights, so it was very slow going. Either that or risk a sprained ankle. Half an hour in, the moon had risen enough so that we could find our path easier, and we picked up the pace again.

The trek over the mountain was slow, every crunch of gravel underfoot making me flinch. With the stars and moon our only guide, it was hard to shake the feeling that we were being watched, that at any moment one of those elite fighters could swoop down on us, using thermal imaging to pick up our heat signatures. Every twenty to thirty minutes, I would notice Kali in human form, watching behind us with those ordinary-looking binoculars. I would peer into the dark, but the naked eye could see nothing.

Two hours in, the faint glow of lights appeared on the horizon. Relief washed over me. The village was smaller than Cortez, with just a handful of homes lit against the inky night sky. We wound our way down a rough path, exhaustion tugging at every step. By the time we reached the edge of town, around eight o'clock, the weight of what we were carrying—both literally and figuratively—felt crushing.

Maria stopped in the middle of the street, turning to me with an expectant look. "Well, Mitzy? Which house do we get a ride from?"

My stomach lurched. "Oh, yeah." I'd forgotten how much of the plan was counting on me. A surge of frustration bubbled up as I looked around, scanning the dimly lit houses. There was no voice in my head, no magic sign telling me which door to knock on. I was just... guessing.

I clenched my fists, trying to tune into the shards' hum. This was my trait. My responsibility. My head pulsed, and I ignored it. I took a deep breath and let instinct take over, my feet carrying me forward. I walked up to the nearest house and almost knocked on the door, then held my hand, turned around, and went to the next house. The shards hummed, and my body tingled.

Everyone followed me, not questioning anything. I started walking up the sidewalk to the next house with the light on, then turned around and crossed the street, walking up to the house there. I rang the doorbell.

The door creaked open, revealing a man in his fifties, his face lined with suspicion. "What's going on?" he asked in Spanish, his eyes narrowing as he glanced between us.

I tried to keep my voice steady. "We'll pay you handsomely for a ride to a port town with a harbor

He peered past me to everyone I was with. "How many are you?"

"Seven."

He considered. "Show me the money."

I reached into my pocket and pulled out a single gold nugget, holding it up so the dim porch light glinted off its surface. His eyes widened, and a small, greedy smile crept onto his face. "Let me see."

I handed it to him, and he bit into it, then turned to me brightly. "What are we waiting for? I'm ready when you are!"

I suppose one of those gold nuggets, considering market value, was worth around four or five hundred bucks. In hindsight, I could have pulled out one or two hundred euros. But whatever. I was lucky. I was just doing things. Money was losing its meaning. In a matter of minutes, we were piled into a van driving down a dark road toward the coast.

As we rolled down the highway, I felt the tension mounting. The only sound was of Chrissy and Kali chatting in the back seat, too quiet to be heard above the engine, although from the sound of it, they were talking about personal matters, so I politely ignored them. About twenty minutes out, we hit cell range, and Maria immediately dialed Alberto. I couldn't hear his side of the conversation, but the way Maria's face tightened told me everything I needed to know. She muttered a few words, her tone low and strained, before hanging up.

"What did he say?" I asked quietly from the next row, afraid of the answer.

Maria leaned back in her seat, her hand covering her face for a moment before she answered. "Not good. The attackers have killed sixteen and lost ten. At least the shards are with us. Alberto met Jet Su and explained to him we've fled with them. They've agreed to a temporary truce. But... there's no telling how it will end. Jet Su sounds ruthless and impatient. He insists on knowing where we went." She paused, glancing out the window as if searching for answers in the dark. "With a spy in Cortez... who knows who we can trust? Alberto told me not to tell him any details about us. You know, in case they have some magical means of learning it from him."

"I'm sorry," I said.

She looked at me, then slowly nodded. "Thank you, Mitzy."

We arrived at the coast in half an hour, then drove down the highway toward bright lights in the distance, passing many small towns and beach resorts. Eventually, we arrived at a decent-sized town with three-story buildings and a large marina. The driver dropped us off at a rustic two-story hotel near the city center and we waved goodbye.

After we booked our rooms, Maria went off to find a boat that would take us to Valparaiso in the morning, and Vee and Chrissy decided to join her and check out the town. Kali went up to the roof to keep watch, and Juliette called it an early night. So, since it was just the two of us, Gonzo and I unpacked our minimal belongings and went downstairs to the hotel restaurant to see if we could find any food.

We ordered just before they closed down the kitchen—two seafood specials complete with calamari, shrimp, and fish, all deep-fried and delicious. Accompany that with a few cold beers, and it was perfection after a long day. It didn't take long before we were calmed down and completely loosened up.

"You know, Mitzy," Gonzo said, leaning into his bottle. "This isn't just some sci-fi adventure. It's real. People are dying because of those shards, and I bet you…" He wagged his finger. "I bet you it's going to unfold into something profound. You just watch, Mitzy. That's how it always goes. What do you bet we're going to have to save the world?"

I scoffed. "Save the world? You've been watching too many movies, man. We can't save the world."

"Couldn't." He pointed at me, eyes suddenly sharp. "Not before. But now…" He paused grandly, then gestured. "Now, we have powers. Mitzy, we're special. And these shards." He gestured to hand him one, so I passed it over. He peered at it in the light. "The inscription says these are important for preventing catastrophe. This is big. Bigger than us, bigger than Cortez. Even if we didn't plan on being in the middle of it, we are. And we're going to have to make a choice."

I stared at him, the weight of his words sinking in.

He started wagging the shard at me. "Come on, admit it, you agree with me. We're going to use them to save the world."

"Pshaw!" I waved him off. "Come on. How realistic is that? I think they're a part of some big important scheme. But our way of saving the world is to keep the shards away from Jet Su and his thugs, not use them."

"Nope." He shook his head vehemently. "You've got it wrong, Mitzy. We won't be running forever. Mark my words, one day, we'll be taking these shards and doing something important with them. And it'll make all the difference. And when we do, I'm putting it on my résumé. Skills: stealth infiltration, world-saving, light emotional trauma."

I had a retort, but I held my tongue. I was trying to be more thoughtful, even after a few beers in. And as I held my tongue, I realized Gonzo may be right, so I just nodded, then raised my bottle. "Here's to saving the world."

We clinked, then Gonzo sighed deeply. "I never wanted any of this, Mitzy. Never wanted a life of adventure. All those good people of Cortez, killed. I'd rather be drinking piña coladas on a hammock at that beach over there without a worry in the world."

"Yeah, I get you. But... don't you just feel... I don't know... more alive than before?"

He paused in thought for a moment, then cracked a wistful grin. "I sh'ppose that's true." He was slurring his words.

I cocked my head. "Well, I do think we should book it out of here as quickly as possible. I was looking at the map on my phone, and Valparaiso is only a two-hour drive from here, so Maria must want to take a boat for some sort of way to mess with their magic-tracking abilities."

Gonzo waved me off. "Yeah. Yeah. But actually... whatever. You're lucky, man. You're *lucky!* Think about it. You can do anything. You're invincible." He raised his bottle in salute, then downed it. He waved down the waiter, who brought us two more beers. "I'm just saying," he continued. "Whatever you want, man, you can probably do no wrong."

I shook my head. "No way, man. That's not how it works."

He leaned back. "Prove me wrong. I've seen you giving eyes to Maria. I bet if you gave her a little romantic gesture while holding the shards, everything would go your way."

I thought of it and lit up. "Yeah. You're right! I should do that." But as soon as I said it, I was second-guessing myself. Did I really want it to be luck that made a relationship work? Wasn't that what was happening with Deborah less than a month earlier?

"Ooooh! Check it out!" Gonzo pointed at a small TV on the wall where some guy was reeling in a monster-sized sea fish, when a voice cut through the calm behind us.

"Do you really think it's smart to be getting drunk when people are trying to kill us?"

I turned sharply, my stomach dropping. Maria stood behind us, her arms crossed, a hard look on her face. Chrissy and Vee were with her, neither of them looking pleased. Gonzo's eyes went wide. "Shit!" He fumbled with the shard and passed it to me. "Here. Quick. Hold it."

I took the shard from him, then turned back to the girls with a ridiculous, over-large smile. Surprisingly, they laughed. Vee shook her head at me. "You're so obvious. The both of you. You think holding that shard means we won't be angry with you?"

I gave a sheepish grin. "Couldn't hurt, I suppose."

She chuckled. "I suppose." She waved the waiter down, gesturing for three more beers, and pulled up a chair, as did the others. "Whatcha talking about?"

"Oh... saving the world, that kind of stuff," I said nonchalantly.

"Is that so?" Chrissy asked. "In what way?"

"Well, think of this." Gonzo leaned in and gained excitement. "The message on the shards is all about protecting the Theurgica from certain doom. What's the reason Jet Su is all worked up and sending all these agents after us? Probably *not* trying to protect the Theurgica, I bet. But to control it!

Although... come to think of it... protecting the Theurgica is in their very name. Preservation."

Did I mention he was drunk by this point? He tends to ramble. The conversation around the table shifted from tense to lighthearted as the beers flowed and the night wore on. We started talking about everything. Our powers, the shards, and even the craziness of our situation. But after a while, it wasn't the specifics that mattered. It was the laughter that finally came after days of tension, the easy way we slipped into jokes and stories.

For a moment, it felt normal, like we weren't running for our lives or holding the fate of the Theurgica and possibly the entire world in our hands. Gonzo, as always, started rambling about conspiracy theories while Chrissy shared a few stories from her childhood, her eyes lighting up in a way I hadn't seen since this whole mess began.

And then there was Maria. I caught her glancing at me more than once, a small smile playing at the corners of her lips. It wasn't much, but it was something—a spark, a connection. She wasn't just the stern leader who had taken charge of our safety. She was... part of us. One of us.

I gave her a look, and she met my gaze, holding it just a second longer than usual. There was something unspoken there, something that made my heart skip a beat. So, yeah. That was cool.

Chapter 27

The knock on the door came at 6 a.m., a thunderous pounding that jolted me awake. I shot up, still tangled in my sheets, heart racing.

"What! What?" Gonzo groaned from the next bed over, his voice muffled by his pillow.

Bleary-eyed and disoriented, I stumbled to the door, my head pounding from the night before.

Maria stood there, her eyes sharp, scanning me and then Gonzo. "Be quick now. They're here."

"What?" I shook my head, trying to clear the cobwebs. "Who?"

"Jet Su. They've found us. We leave in two minutes."

Jet Su. My stomach clenched at the sound of his name. And he'd have with him Bruno Marx—the man who had nearly killed me back in Montana, the one who seemed to delight in making me his prey. The air in the room felt suddenly thin, pressing in around me.

Gonzo swiveled in bed, now wide awake. "What?! How?"

"No time to explain." Maria was already heading away. "Be ready in two minutes."

It's amazing how quickly you can get ready when you think your life depends on it. In just a few minutes, we were fully dressed, with everything stuffed in our bags. I gripped the shards as they pulsed in my hand, vibrating with energy, as if trying to warn me. But nothing could quell the knot of fear twisting in my gut.

As we staggered down the hall, Gonzo held his head. "I'm ninety percent sure I made a blood pact with a bottle of vodka last night. If I start speaking in ancient tongues, just roll with it."

I chuckled. Although we could be killed within the next hour, Gonzo could still make me smile.

We met up with Kali in the hotel lobby. Her eyes were serious and calculating. "It's too late to run for it on the main street. They must know where we are. They're coming right toward the hotel."

I stared at her, the words barely registering. "How?"

She shook her head. "They must have followed our trail through the mountains and found our driver from last night. We never told him to keep quiet about us—not that it would have mattered."

It suddenly struck me that Kali had probably stayed up all night keeping watch, and I experienced an intense feeling of gratitude mixed with selfishness. Here I'd stayed up late having fun while someone else was watching my back. My head was pounding, and I wasn't sure if it was the shards working or the hangover. Or a bit of both.

Chrissy, Vee, and Juliette showed up with their backpacks and saw our faces.

"Too late?" Vee asked.

Kali nodded. "Three black Suburbans are heading our way. They could have us surrounded any minute now."

Vee's eyes darted to the front glass doors. No sign of anyone yet. She glanced at me. "Top goal is to keep the shards away from them. Is there a boat ready?"

"It will be." Kali nodded. "Maria's headed there now." She fidgeted with the buttons on her jacket. "I'm not a fighter. I'm not tactical. I thought we had more time, or I would have switched places with Maria. What should we do?"

Vee gripped her staff. "Turn into a fox and get the lay of the land. We'll head out the west exit and see if we can make for the docks through the residential neighborhood. Can you find us in fox form?"

She nodded and gave a wry smile. "Most definitely. I can smell you from quite a distance." She gave us a knowing look, and lingered on Gonzo.

He smelled his pits. "What? That bad?"

Vee was all business. "Let's go." She took off down the hall, the rest of us following behind.

I glimpsed Kali transforming into a fox as I turned. It was a pretty cool sight—a nearly instant morph that incorporated all that she was holding. But I didn't have time to dwell on it. I held both shards as I fled down the corridor, willing them to keep us all safe.

Shoot first and ask questions later. That's what we'd been told about Jet Su. Would they use force openly with all the mundanes surrounding us? As Preservation Society agents, their job was to keep mundanes from seeing any hint of the Theurgica. But something told me Jet Su didn't care about such things when it came to retrieving the shards.

Vee was holding the door for us, eyes darting outside. "Go! Go!" She waved us through, then took the lead again, glancing in both directions before bolting across the street toward some bushes outside of a three-story apartment building.

We dashed after her and crouched behind the bushes. Gonzo was already sweating, and my pounding head made it hard to think. I scraped my arm on the branch of the bush and winced, the shards pulsing madly in my left hand.

Vee peered around the bushes. "Shh!" she scolded. "They're here."

I held my breath, trying to hold still.

Vee's voice was a harsh whisper. "Two agents. One is Bruno Marx. They're on foot." She paused. "Bruno's going inside, the other standing guard at the door. Shit!"

"What do we do?" I asked.

Vee gave me a sour look. "We can't run for it. He'll see us. At least we're not inside."

I cringed, waiting for her great tactical mind to come up with something. In that moment, I was so thankful I could rely on Vee, because I felt like a hot mess. She was always meant to be our leader, keeping us safe with her bold moves and tactical mind. But then she turned to me.

"Mitzy, we need your luck now."

My heart dropped. Between my throbbing head and the overwhelming fear filling every pore, I felt the impossible burden of coming up with a solution. I glanced around for ideas and my eyes landed on Gonzo. He was sweating and wheezing, but looking a lot less freaked out than I felt.

He gave me a smile and cocked his head. "You look like you've got an idea."

I slowly nodded. "We need a distraction." I held out a shard to him. "Time to use what you've learned this week. Go invisible, get away from here, and come up with something—anything—some way to draw them away from us. Don't let them get close to you. As soon as they're near, turn invisible and hide. Even Maria can't find you invisible unless she's looking super closely. Stay invisible and head to the docks. Worst-case scenario, Kali can find you with her keen sense of smell."

He took the shard. The look in his eyes was firm. "And what if *they* have someone who can smell me?"

I sighed. "Use your judgment."

Vee patted Gonzo's arm. "Try not to wake people up. No explosions. Maybe find something with wheels, so you can make a speedy getaway. Ready?"

He grinned at her. "The G-man was *born* ready." He winked at us and blipped out of existence.

And then we waited.

The minutes crept by. Vee peered tensely around the edge of the bush from time to time. My mind wandered. How would we know what Gonzo's distraction was? Would it be obvious? I shouldn't have doubted it.

A loud engine revving pierced the early morning quiet, and Vee leaped back to her lookout spot and gave a chuckle.

"What is it?" I asked.

"He stole a motorcycle," she said. "And a nice one at that. A Beemer."

I laughed nervously. "I guess I should have expected no less."

A moment later, as the motorcycle engine rumble took off down the road, Vee said, "The coast is clear. Let's go!"

We followed her, dashing around the apartment and down the sidewalk of the residential street. Our backpacks clunked with every step, and my thoughts turned to worry about Gonzo. *Can he outwit Jet Su? What if they have distance attacks he can't avoid?*

We ran two blocks past apartments with gates, then turned toward the coast. Juliette and I lagged, but not terribly. There was no sound from the motorcycle now, and my mind filled with anxious thoughts. *Come on, Gonzo. Outwit them. You've got this.*

Around the next corner, the apartment buildings were replaced with quaint shops and restaurants lining both sides of the street. Only three blocks to go to get to the docks, and then Juliette twisted her ankle.

"Oh!" she called, grasping the ankle, and we stopped and gathered around.

"How bad is it?" Vee asked.

She winced and put some slight pressure on it. "So sorry, my dears. It's going to slow me down." She grimaced as she hobbled, and Vee leaned in and draped Juliette's arm over her shoulder.

We'd barely begun moving again when Kali appeared around the corner. She held up a hand. "They took the shard from him."

My heart dropped. "Is he okay?"

She nodded slowly. "I think so. I'm guessing he leaped off the motorcycle before it slid, so he looks scuffed up, but otherwise fine. They've got someone watching over him, and the rest of them have spread out."

I breathed a sigh of relief.

Vee turned to me. "Two priorities now. We rescue Gonzo, and we get the last shard out of here."

I gave a terse nod. "Lead the way."

Kali peered around the corner, then turned left and trotted down the sidewalk. We followed as quickly as we could with Juliette's injury, then crossed the street and slowed. Before we reached the corner, she stopped and turned toward us. "He's around this corner, sitting on the sidewalk."

I nodded and steeled myself to confront the agent guarding Gonzo, but something felt off. The shard started pulsing almost painfully, as if I wasn't using it right. The feeling was confusing. It felt like sharp jolts of electricity. I held it out, peering at it. Something was amiss.

But what?

And suddenly, from nowhere, a person appeared.

Jet Su.

He walked through the wall of the building next to us, and in one fluid motion, he nimbly snatched the shard from my fingers.

I reeled in shock.

Vee was already in motion, swinging the staff in a deadly blow to his head. Her staff passed through as if he wasn't there. I knew then there was no way we'd be able to take the shard from him with his trait. He could make it as if it didn't exist.

He scoffed. "Sometimes, if you want a job done right, you must step in and do it yourself."

I was dumbfounded and speechless. All that effort, and it was over in an instant. He'd walked over me and my luck trait as if it were nothing.

"You'd better not have hurt Gonzo." I blurted. "And what's so important about these shards that you'd kill sixteen people in Cortez, not to mention let ten of your agents die in the process?"

He gave a wicked smile. "Oh, we have grand plans. Marvelous, world-changing plans."

I grew desperate. "We've been translating them! Do you know what they say? It's world-ending stuff. You can't just throw caution to the wind."

He shook his head at me. "We have our own linguistics experts. Once we have them all, we'll be able to put the pieces of the puzzle together."

So, they don't have all six shards yet, I thought absently as I tried to form other words. How could we get the shards back?

Vee tried swinging her staff at him from behind, but it phased through again, as if he could predict every blow. I heard Chrissy whimper behind me.

An elderly couple came out of a building and saw us, then nervously turned in the other direction. The city was waking up. He wouldn't possibly kill us in front of witnesses… would he?

Jet Su tapped his chin in thought, as if he was in no rush. "You, Stanley, have an interesting trait. It's very curious. Because you're always successful, even though you appear to be untrained." He peered at me. "It must be how you eluded my agents in France so many times, and Montana before that."

I held my tongue, and he eyed me with scrutiny. "Could it be? Could it be… luck?"

I must have given away something, because he brightened. "Oh, my. This is quite incredible. Luck has resurfaced! I thought that trait was all but gone for many centuries. Fascinating. And from a mundane, no less."

He stared at me, deep in thought. "Someone like you could do so much. A trait like yours… is too rare and strategic to go to waste." He nodded, mostly to himself. "You will hear from me again. And your friends…"

He gave my friends a passing glance. "If you were ever to be convinced to use your trait for something useful, I imagine you wouldn't want them dead." He paused and gave me a knowing look. "For now."

With that, he turned and walked around the corner toward the agent standing over Gonzo. Vee tried swinging another blow at him, to no avail. She slumped as he walked away unscathed, and a moment later was picked up by a black Suburban.

Chrissy broke the spell of my shock. She ran around the corner toward Gonzo, who was sitting on the sidewalk, back to the wall of a laundromat. The motorcycle was on its side, scraped up thirty feet down the road.

"Are you okay, Gonzo?" she asked.

His jeans and jacket were ripped at the knees and elbows with patches of blood forming from his wounds, and his hands were scraped, but he looked otherwise unharmed. He gave her a weary nod. "Yeah. *No problemo*. A little fall. Nothing big. They stole the shard, though." He gave an apologetic look at me as I arrived.

"They took mine too," I said, the guilt washing over me. How come I did nothing when the shard was pulsing differently at me? If I'd followed that lead and done something random, I might have avoided being an easy target. But I'd stood there dumbly.

I realized then that Maria's training hadn't been enough. Just over a week, and sure, I was improving, but I wasn't fully in tune with my trait. Instead, I put all our lives at risk.

As if reading my mind, Chrissy turned to me. "It wasn't your fault," she offered gently. "How could you have predicted he'd come through a wall?"

"I knew," I said stoically. "The shard pulsed at me differently, and I just stared at it. I knew something was up, but I stood there like an idiot."

Everyone went quiet then, even Chrissy. None of them understood, and they all knew it. The burden of losing the shards felt heavier than ever.

Kali approached us, hanging up her phone. "Maria's on her way. I've filled her in." She glanced from one of us to the other as we stood around woodenly. "What? What happened? He's okay, right?" She gave Gonzo a concerned look.

"Yeah, I'm okay," Gonzo replied. "We're just… sad about losing the shards."

Her eyes bore into him. "Perhaps. But sixteen of my friends and family died yesterday. You," she gestured to us all. "You've all survived to tell the tale."

"It doesn't matter." Gonzo shook his head. "We survived, but for how long? What will happen to our world?"

She frowned at him, lips pursed. "What do you mean?"

Gonzo shook his head. "The shards have the power to change the world. I'm sure of it. Why would they constantly refer to the power of Amun-Ra—the god of sun, weather, and the hidden forces of creation? We're talking about world-changing important. It's in the lines of the Prophecy of Ramessesnakht. I have it memorized, I've read it so many times. 'Under the eye of Amun-Ra, a Stone of Power, whose heart beats with the pulse of the Nile, shall awaken and bring about the beginning of a new era for all of humanity. A time of awakening to true power and knowledge and insight and glory.' And later it says: 'Three centuries of calamity shall befall all of creation.'" He gave her a pleading look. "Does that sound like a little thing to *you*?"

He went on with more conviction. "None of us knows for certain, but I figure it means our world will be changed forever. The power of Amun-Ra, with Jet Su. Think about it. Even for a second. What will he do first? It's ultimate power in the wrong hands."

He stared into the distance. "Yes. Sixteen people died. And if we don't get those shards back, their deaths will be meaningless."

He gave a sigh and rose to his feet. Brushing himself off, he gestured to his motorcycle. "We'd better get after them before they go too far."

"Wait. What?" I reeled.

He raised an eyebrow at me, as if daring me to disagree. Just then, Maria showed up, panting. She saw our posture and turned to me.

"What's next, Mitzy?"

I blinked at her in surprise. "You're asking *me*?"

She cocked her head. "You may not be holding a shard, but you're lucky. I see it. So… as I asked, what's next?"

I glanced at Kali. "Do you think they've gotten far?"

"Let me check," she said, turning instantly to the building next to us and leaping up the wall. She clambered up quickly, using a drainpipe for grip, while not placing too much weight on it. As she clambered up the side of the building, I marveled at how she made something I would find completely impossible look so effortless, then wondered if she had an artifact of some sort that was helping her.

We craned our necks as she disappeared over the top. A moment later, Maria's phone rang.

Her voice was terse. "They haven't left town yet. Two of the Suburbans are parked just down the street by the hotel, and the third is on its way to join them."

All eyes turned on me and I pursed my lips as I took in Juliette's twisted ankle and Gonzo's scuffed up knees. It would have to be a smaller group of us. But what would we do?

Gonzo grinned and patted my shoulder. "You're still lucky. Maria said. Don't forget it."

Vee was eyeing me. "Do you have a plan?"

I pursed my lips. "I need some way to block Jet Su's power long enough to take the shards from him. At the very least."

Maria took off her pack and pulled out a small sphere. "This can block anyone's powers for a full minute. It's a one-of-a-kind, powerful artifact."

I blinked. Then, I glanced at the motorcycle. Then back at my friends. I could see the glimmer in Gonzo's eyes, and a faint smile lifted at the edges of his mouth as he saw my face. Soon, I mimicked it, a small smile turning into a grin.

I glanced down the street. "Who's got the most experience driving motorcycles?"

Chapter 28

Maria cut the corner sharply and revved the engine, flying down the street far faster than I'd ever been on a motorcycle before. If it weren't for the fact I was lucky, I'd have been freaking out that we weren't wearing helmets. Well, that, and the fact we were off chasing the most powerful villain I'd ever imagined on a wild goose chase.

Maria's phone buzzed in my hand, and I clenched her body with my other hand as I tucked my head against her back and put it to my ear.

"What've you got?" I asked.

Kali's voice came through, muffled by the wind. "They're heading east, probably toward Route Five on *Avenido Caupolicán*."

I shouted Kali's message to Maria, and she gave a terse nod, then revved the engine and swerved around a slow-moving truck. It was 6:30 a.m. and the city was just beginning to stir.

A minute later we turned onto the bigger avenue and saw three black Suburbans ahead.

"Get right up next to them!" I shouted.

Maria nodded, and we shot forward. As we neared, I pulled the small spherical item with a single button out of my jacket pocket.

We had a plan, however shaky. Before we'd ridden off, Maria had handed the sphere to me and given me a five-second explanation. It had only one use, primed by pushing in the button and twisting it to the right. Upon impact, it would be like a no-magic grenade, blocking most forms of traits for a full minute within a ten-foot radius of the impact. She mentioned no other details, but as we swerved around a pothole and hurtled toward the Suburbans, I knew our only chance of stealing the shards back was to block Jet Su's power.

My hand holding the sphere fidgeted with it, feeling the contours as I thumbed lightly over the button. Teeth clenched,

I took a deep breath and glanced over her shoulder. The rear vehicle was only twenty feet away. I pressed the button and twisted—locked and ready. Now, to find Jet Su.

As we pulled up next to the right side of the rear Suburban and I looked at the agents, I had a flash imagining myself from a bird's-eye view. Maria was highly skilled and trained, but I was a bumbling fool, tearing on a wild chase that made no sense. A thrilling and ridiculous situation that would probably get me killed. The thought of it actually made me chuckle and crack a smile. If luck could somehow make this work out... maybe I could do anything?

We edged up to the passenger side window and saw Bruno Marx sneering at me. His window lowered and my mind scrambled.

I couldn't use the sphere on him. I couldn't waste it. It was our only chance against Jet Su.

He lifted a hand, his eyes crackling with blue energy. My pulse quickened, and I wrapped both arms around Maria, clenching her jacket with my free hand.

And then, two things happened simultaneously. Maria braked, and a blue bolt of electricity shot out, missing us by two feet and exploding into a parked car. I gripped Maria, thankful her trait allowed her to see other people's powers in use. One second delay and we'd have been dead.

She throttled the engine, and we sped past the rear Suburban up to the next one in line. We pulled up to the passenger window, and there was Jet Su.

Now or never!

I lobbed the sphere, praying it would hit. In the same breath, Maria slowed, giving us space. I watched, almost in slow-motion, as the sphere sailed through the air and landed on the windshield. A direct hit!

One minute. That's all I had to use my luck and steal the shards from him—an ultra-trained killer who could have the shards hidden anywhere.

I suddenly realized the futility of the task. I clenched my teeth. How was I going to steal them from him? Was this the moment I got killed?

Maria revved up next to the window, but Jet Su didn't roll it down. He gave me a smirk and a slight shake of the head. Casually, he leaned his head back and spoke to the people in the rear seats. The rear window went down and a woman nonchalantly raised a rifle barrel toward us.

"Get closer!" I yelled instinctively.

Maria swerved right up to the Suburban, and I reached out to grasp at the gun. The woman looked confused for a second as I grabbed the barrel, then we hit a bump, and I nearly fell off the motorcycle.

The gun went off, a single shot flying wild, as Maria corrected and swerved, then dodged a pothole. The jiggle sent me leaning to the right in a heart-pounding moment where I thought I'd fall off the motorcycle.

In that moment, another shot rang out, and I swear the bullet went right past my head.

I was dizzy and panicked, and clutched Maria, pulling her. She tried locking her legs on, but the leaning weight put her off balance and she slowed the bike to correct. In a moment of pure terror, I felt us teetering onto our side.

Time slowed down, and I was almost certain our right sides would be scraped and ripped open on the street. The bike wobbled, and Maria slowed further, popping a foot down and shoving to rebalance us.

A third shot rang out right in front of where we'd almost been. If Maria hadn't slowed, it would have hit one of us. But we were completely unscathed.

Maria grabbed at me with her right hand, the bike wobbling as she pulled at me. A bright blue flash of electricity from behind slammed into where we'd been heading, then the rear Suburban passed us.

My brain was a mess. How had we survived all of that? How could I even dream of stealing the shards back? What was I, insane?

Maria slowed to a stop, the Suburbans driving off ahead of us.

The motorcycle engine died down as she took a deep breath and repositioned herself on the seat.

"Are you okay?" she called back.

"I'm alive," I responded. "Do we still have time?"

"No." Her voice was terse. "By the time we catch up again, the effect of the artifact will be over. Jet Su will have his full power back."

My heart sank. "That's it, then. We lost our chance. There's no way we'll get the shards back now."

She twisted until she could see my eyes. She didn't say a word, but looked me up and down. Pursing her lips, she gave a slow nod. The sound of the Suburbans leaving echoed down the street, and with them, our only chance of retrieving the shards and preventing potential catastrophe.

Catastrophe.

Global havoc.

The words from the prophecy rang out in my head.

Three centuries of calamity for all of creation.

Or was it just an old dusty prophecy that had nothing to do with this moment? I held onto that thought.

Yes. Lots of prophecies have been given. Most are long passed. This couldn't be about us now. There was no way.

Right?

But then, I thought of how the shards had suddenly appeared after three thousand years, and I felt my heart constrict. Who was I fooling? There was a tiny chance it wasn't about now. More than likely, though, this was it.

The apocalypse.

And I was practically powerless to stop it.

I wondered for a moment if we'd recognize the world-shaking devastation or if it would come gradually. I imagined everyone I know and love dying, even if I somehow survived because of my luck. The weight of the implication felt suddenly unbearable.

Maria furrowed her brow. "What next?"

I felt a nervous laugh well up and I snorted. "Am I still lucky?"

"Yes." She gave a slow nod.

I took a deep breath. "Then… we try again."

Chapter 29

Maria gave a sharp nod, her eyes narrowing with resolve. The engine roared, and we sped up, weaving through traffic until we caught up to the convoy.

"Pass on the left!" I called. Away from Bruno Marx's electric attack.

We hurtled toward the Suburban, and as we passed, the rear window was already down with a rifle tracking us.

Maria braked suddenly. Multiple shots rang out. She gunned it and braked again, barely dodging another shot. With a reckless burst of energy, she gave it her all, and the motorcycle shot past the Suburban, gunshots echoing behind us.

The agent leaned out of the window, taking aim and shooting, but Maria swerved as we closed in on the second vehicle, its tinted windows gleaming ominously in the streetlights. We pulled up behind it, preventing the shooter behind us from taking a shot and risk hitting the other vehicle.

This was it. Jet Su's vehicle, and with him, the shards. But how could I get them without the sphere? His trait was impossible to tackle. There was no way I could take the shards directly from him. He'd just make himself and the shards substance-less.

But his Suburban wasn't able to do that. My mind raced. Could I take out the entire vehicle?

That's when I saw it—a massive truck barreling toward us in the opposite lane, its headlights slicing through the early morning light. My gut churned, but I trusted the instinct that hit me.

"Cut in front of the truck!" I yelled, gripping Maria's waist tightly.

She didn't hesitate. With a fierce twist of the handlebars, Maria veered left, straight into the path of the oncoming ten-wheel commercial vehicle. The truck's horn blared—a deafening, furious sound—and its brakes screeched in protest as it swerved violently, trying to avoid the collision.

Everything seemed to slow as the truck's front end slammed directly into Jet Su's Suburban's left bumper with a thunderous crash. The SUV crumpled like a tin can, its frame folding inward under the sheer force of the impact. Shattered glass and twisted metal flew.

The rear Suburban didn't stand a chance. Unable to brake in time, it plowed into the wreckage, its hood crumpling against the lead vehicle. The chain reaction left both Suburbans mangled, their hulking forms sprawled across the road in a heap of destruction.

Maria whipped the bike back into the proper lane, then slowed and turned around with a fluid motion. The roar of her bike's engine swallowed my pounding heartbeat. Behind us, the aftermath was chaos. Pieces of the vehicles were strewn about everywhere, a single stunned agent stumbling from the wreckage, disoriented and slow to react.

I took in the devastation. "Holy crap, Maria. You pulled it off."

"*We* did. Come on. We don't have much time."

We drove up to the wreckage, eyes scanning Jet Su's vehicle.

My heart suddenly stopped.

Jet Su stood calmly, watching us unscathed from the side of the road. He'd phased at impact and gone through all of it without a scratch.

The lead Suburban was turning around, and I knew we only had a moment before the recovered agents would be on us.

"He's truly unbeatable," I mumbled.

Maria's voice cut through my lack of certainty. "He needs to recharge, just as any of us do. Even holding the shards, he won't use his power constantly. He's not used to using the shards yet, I can tell."

I took in the new information, then had an inspiration. "Let's come at him from two angles." Without waiting for her response, I leaped from the bike and scrambled behind the wreckage, out of his line of sight.

Maria bit her lip as she watched me, then revved the engine and drove around the truck, circling it before heading back toward Jet Su.

She drove straight at him, eyes flaring. She got nearer, and he didn't budge. He even held the shards out, as if tantalizing her with them. The motorcycle hurtled straight through him, his body phasing at the precise moment it would have impacted, and Maria drove completely through him and hurtled past.

The entire time his focus was on her, I was creeping up behind him. The moment she passed through, I paused for one brief heartbeat, then grabbed at the shards.

Contact!

With desperation, I pulled the shards from his hand. Jet Su whirled on me and kicked. His face twisted angrily.

I blocked feebly, barely remembering my training as he kicked again, then punched. I blocked and tried to dodge, then stumbled on a strewn door from the Suburban and went tumbling head over heels.

I rolled and came to my feet, the car door between us.

He shook his head. "Incredible. Your trait." He chuckled. "It's magnificent. So unpredictable. And always in your favor."

He leaped suddenly over the car door with a flying kick aimed at me, and I blocked it weakly and moved to the side just in time. He leaped in, punching aggressively, and I stumbled, hands landing on shards of glass.

Desperately, I threw the glass at his face, and the pieces flew right through him harmlessly.

He scoffed. "You have no idea how to fight someone like me. It's inconceivable how you're still here. The Raven will *love* to know about this."

My eyes darted as my mind raced. But the shards in my hand pulsed warmly, and I felt an unnatural confidence well up, even from my inferior vantage point on the ground. My free hand landed on a two-foot jagged piece of metal and I picked it up.

The sound of Maria's approaching motorcycle grew louder. He smirked and leaned over me, his eyes piercing into mine, a mere foot away from my face. I tried to get a good grip on the piece of metal, but it was jagged and uncomfortable to hold. I couldn't possibly use it as a weapon without slicing my hand. Why was I even holding it?

His voice was gloating. "What could your luck possibly do to save you now?"

As if on cue, a bright blue bolt of lightning flashed toward Maria from behind, and she swerved just in time, causing it to arc just to her side and crash into a nearby parked car. The car exploded, fragments flying right toward Jet Su.

He phased, and the pieces passed through him toward me. I instinctively raised the piece of metal in my hand to protect my face, and a few pieces of metal embedded themselves into it.

Jet Su's eyes darted toward the attack.

Now's my chance!

With a burst of energy, I threw the hunk of metal at him and leaped to my feet, racing toward the sidewalk and Maria. Jet Su, quick to react, was fast on my heels.

She slowed, and I jumped on the seat behind her, then we took off again. I felt Jet Su's hand brush against my back, grasping for a grip.

"Go! Go! Go!" I shouted.

We passed the last intact Suburban just as it arrived on the scene.

Jet Su was sprinting after us.

I turned to look, and the sight of his intensely furious face brought another round of panic.

"Hit it! He's a fast runner!"

Maria obediently gunned it, and the motorcycle reached the end of the block. As we slowed to turn to the right, Jet Su almost gained on us. I could see the fury in his eyes, and he grasped at me again.

I punched at his arm, and he grasped, then got a grip on my jacket sleeve. Incredibly, he kept up with us and almost pulled me off the bike. Maria slowed, feeling me wobbling and losing balance.

Frantically, I kicked at him and caught his knee. He let out a grunt and released my arm, and Maria sped up again.

We zipped down the side street, Jet Su sprinting a mere twenty feet behind us, then we turned again, headed straight toward the docks. He was fast, but once we had a straight path, we gunned it and flew well over a hundred kilometers an hour, leaving him in the distance.

We went a few blocks, then turned off and took another side street, hoping to lose him. Once he was out of sight, I felt my heart thump more calmly. Then, I laughed.

I held up the shards in my left hand and laughed and laughed and laughed. I glimpsed Maria's face in the side mirror, smiling along with me.

"I can't believe that worked!" I chuckled. "That was incredible! And dang, Maria—nice maneuvering."

I could almost hear Maria's grin as her voice carried over the wind: "We make a good team, Mitzy. Just don't get too comfortable—this ride is far from over."

Chapter 30

We found the others where we'd left them.

As soon as the engine died down, Gonzo raised an eyebrow. "Please tell me that look in your eyes means we won."

I climbed off the motorcycle. "We did. And we brought souvenirs." I held out the shards with a wry smile.

He gave a low whistle. "Tell me about it later?"

"Yes," I replied. "There's no time now. They've still got a working vehicle and Jet Su is sprinting after us. They could be here any second."

I took Juliette's hand. "Maria, get Juliette on the boat. We'll be close behind you."

Vee helped me load Juliette up behind Maria on the motorcycle. They took off down the street as the rest of us broke into a run the last few blocks to the docks.

Gonzo immediately fell behind. As we turned down a narrow alley, I passed him a shard. "Here, go invisible!"

As soon as he took it, his form blurred and shimmered out of existence. But I didn't stand around watching. Chrissy, Vee and I took off as fast as our feet would carry us down the alley, then another street and turned to the last stretch to the boats.

As the three of us were racing down the docks, a familiar prickle raced up the back of my neck, like static electricity clinging to the air. I skidded to a stop just as a black Suburban screeched to a halt behind us.

"Everyone down!" I shouted, diving to the ground just as a blue arc of lightning ripped through the air, slamming into the boat nearest us. The wood splintered and exploded into a shower of debris, sending waves rippling through the marina.

I glanced to my left and right, where Chrissy and Vee were laid out on the docks. Chrissy looked a bit beat up. But otherwise, we were okay.

The doors of the Suburban opened, and two men dressed in black combat fatigues stepped out. One was a scruffy, burly man, and of them was Bruno Marx.

His eyes locked onto mine, and a smile curled his lips. "Did you really think you could run forever, Stanley?"

His voice sent a shiver down my spine. Jet Su might have had ideas to keep me alive, but I didn't get that sense from Bruno. He wasn't just there to retrieve the shards. He was there to finish what he started... with me.

"Come on!" Maria shouted from the boat behind us. "He needs to recharge." I got to my feet and sprinted toward her. The boat she'd chartered was a two-level mini yacht with the name *Santa Ana* on the side. Maria helped Juliette climb aboard. The motorcycle sat parked nearby.

We ran all out when I felt the shard surge a pulse of warning through my body. "Down!" I shouted, diving to the dock. Semiautomatic rifles with suppressors rang out with muffled retorts, and a bullet whizzed over my head.

"Oh!" I heard Chrissy gasp behind me.

I turned in dread to see her lying on the dock, holding her left hip. I crawled over to her, bullets continuing to fly toward the others at the boat. I didn't have time to worry about them.

As soon as I got to Chrissy, I scrambled in front of her and turned on the protective force field from my watch.

I did just in the nick of time, because two bullets shot right at us. The invisible bubble absorbed the bullets, then dissipated, the bullets clanging onto the dock in front of me.

"How bad is it?" I asked, eyes scanning her body.

"A graze," Chrissy said, clenching her teeth. "I'll manage."

"Get to the boat," I urged. "Keep low."

The shard pulsed, and I felt my insides squirm with power. In a flash of instinct, I stood.

Bruno was slowly walking toward me, holding his rifle casually. The other agent strode just a few feet behind. Back at the Suburban, a woman was setting up a long-range rifle on a tripod.

Bruno smirked. "I hear Jet Su figured out your trait, Stanley. Luck. It explains a great many things."

I glanced over my shoulder to see Chrissy almost to the boat. Satisfied, I gave him my full attention. "What of it?"

He scoffed. "Luck has limits. Do you even know what you're wielding? The power of the fragments isn't consistent. Nor is it bottomless. There will be a crack in your defense."

I wavered. As he said it, I knew deep down there was truth to his words. "I've been training." I tried sounding confident.

"Ha!" He stepped toward me slowly, methodically. "You think that will save you? You've been a thorn in my side ever since I first met you, Stanley. I'm going to really enjoy tearing you apart."

His eyes crackled with blue electricity, and I knew he was ready for another attack. But I waited. "Can we negotiate?"

He laughed. "It's too late for that." He lifted his arm and pointed at me.

I almost leaped out of the way, but something told me to wait. I stood poised… watching his eyes, waiting for a sign. Eyes locked, there was a moment where I felt his hatred, and something in me felt defensive. I didn't deserve that. And I would fight him with everything I had to prove myself worthy.

With a surge of energy, I leaped to the left, but my foot caught on a loose board and I tumbled. My brain processed it all in slow motion—falling to the dock just as another blue arc of lightning danced through the air, crackling as it snaked to where I'd been leaping toward. The energy slammed into a crate, exploding it and sending fragments of wood everywhere.

I rolled to my feet and stood in a tai chi pose. A moment later, I was joined by Vee. She stood next to me on the balls of her feet, holding the staff with a blade at one tip, and a shimmering force field at the other.

"You think you're going to have all the fun?" she said with a smirk.

I smiled, lips tight.

The second thug raised his rifle, and Vee lifted the shield side of the staff just in time as he fired off a couple of shots. The bullets clanged into the temporary shield, clattering to the dock harmlessly as the shield dissolved.

"There!" she yelled, grabbing my arm and diving behind a crate.

The two men approached us slowly, rifles raised. With a pang, I suddenly thought about the woman at the Suburban with the long-range rifle. She could pick us off one at a time. I took a risk to glance at her, and saw her frozen in place, bending over partway.

Gonzo! He must have used his freeze-gun on her. And hopefully, if there were other agents in the Suburban, on all of them.

I turned to Vee. "We just need to get Gonzo to the boat, and then we can leave. He's close." I pointed at the frozen woman by the Suburban.

Vee gave a slight nod, then peered with the edge of her vision at the two approaching men. She held up a finger to me, signaling me to wait. It grew eerily quiet, a gentle wind cooling my sweaty face. The sound of a squeaking plank nearby cut through the silence.

One of our attackers.

With a sudden burst of energy, Vee leaped from behind the protection of the crate toward the second attacker. She whacked his rifle away, then jabbed with the blade. He barely blocked it in time with the rifle butt, but Vee swung and knocked the rifle out of his hands, then cut at his feet.

He danced away in the nick of time, then began to transform, his skin taking on a silver sheen. She jabbed again, and he didn't block. Instead, the blade ripped through his shirt and bounced harmlessly off his now-metal body.

With a grin, he took the opportunity with Vee off-balance, swung a thick metal arm and knocked her onto the dock. The blow was clearly powerful, far more than a normal one, and Vee flew a good six feet. But she rolled with it, and came to her feet, staff at the ready, a new bruise forming on her arm.

Meanwhile, Bruno took three steps and pounced toward me behind the crate. I tried dodging, but his fist connected with my jaw, sending me sprawling across the dock.

With a gasp of pain, I landed, using both hands to catch myself. The shard went skittering across the boards.

My heart lurched. Without the shard, the air around felt suffocating, charged with danger. I scrambled, trying to grab the shard, but Bruno's boot came down on my hand, pinning it to the dock.

In a flash, I saw my imminent death—a quick shot to the head with no luck to protect myself, and it would all be over. But the sound of a shot didn't come. Instead, I heard a high-pitched voice call out from the boat. "*Who summons me?*"

I dared a glance to see that Chrissy had drawn the talking blade. Rafael's voice rang out, a theatrical tone that didn't match the danger of the moment. From the corner of my eye, I caught a glimpse of his absurd little face—eyes, mouth, and all, floating in the shimmering steel.

"Chrissy," she replied, unflinching. "Rafael, I need your help against those bad guys." She pointed.

"*Say no MOOOOORE!*" Rafael sang, and leaped from her hand, flying toward the attackers.

As the blade neared Bruno, he sent a jolt of electricity in its direction and swiveled to the side to dodge. The blade swiped at him twice. He danced out of the way. It passed him and headed toward the metal man.

While Bruno was distracted, I scrambled the last two feet to the shard and snatched it up. Then, with no other ideas, I got to my feet and took up a jujitsu position.

Bruno smirked and took up a similar pose facing me, his rifle slung on his back.

His eyes weren't crackling, so I figured I had time. But I knew then that luck was only going to get me so far. I had to rely on my own skills. But how could I take on someone so experienced with so little training?

Maria shouted from the boat, "Hurry!"

Bruno snapped a left hook toward my face.

I reacted instinctively, raising my right arm in a smooth block while stepping to the side, using the movement to redirect his momentum. I grabbed his wrist with my left hand, pivoting to guide his arm away from me.

Bruno was quick—he countered by twisting out of my grip and lunging for my arm. I shifted my body weight to avoid his grasp, then took a step to the right to reposition myself and pulled him through.

With his stance slightly off-balance, I stepped in and I aimed a sharp palm heel strike toward his chest. My hand connected, but the impact lacked force.

Bruno smirked, grabbing my extended arm. He twisted with incredible strength and executed a throw, sending me crashing onto the dock. The wooden boards groaned under the impact as I hit the ground. Pain flared through my body, but my training kicked in—I slapped the ground with my free hand to absorb some of the fall and immediately rolled out of the way.

His boot slammed into the boards where I'd been a moment earlier, the sound clamoring through the morning air. I scrambled to my feet, keeping my hands up and my weight centered, facing him once again.

I got a glimpse, then, of the metal man battling Vee and the floating dagger. Rafael whizzed about and struck again and again, but all he was really doing was distracting the man from giving Vee his full attention. Vee whacked again and again with the staff, doing no damage. Her face was taut, and she scowled at the staff as if it wasn't doing what she wanted.

Then, one tip lit up into a flame and she grinned. She pointed it at the man and sent out a burst of flame. He lifted an arm to shield himself and took a step back. Vee stepped into it, flooding him with fire, and the metal began to glow.

I couldn't watch, though, because Bruno took a step toward me, his eyes crackling with blue energy.

"You know," I said, trying to sound calm. "You can't win."

"Hmph. And why is that?" He took one more step, now a mere six feet away from me.

"Because..." My mind raced, thinking of what I could say to distract him. I glanced around the dock, looking for ideas, and saw boat debris nearby. The glint of a mirror caught my eye, and instantly I thought of my first encounter with him. "Because you're a bad guy."

"Ha!" He scoffed and raised his hand.

In that instant, I dove and rolled for the mirror, grabbed it, and in one fluid motion, lifted it and held it up toward him. The air crackled with energy and blue electricity snaked out from Bruno's hand toward me, hitting precisely at the mirror and bouncing back in an instant, slamming into him and sending him flying across the dock.

He flew back and landed on his back, then skidded to a stop, lying inert. I stared, wide-eyed. *It worked!* I was incredulous. But I didn't have time to reflect. Vee was still battling the metal man with the floating dagger.

I stood and brushed myself off, considering my options, when suddenly the metal man froze in place and Gonzo appeared, sweaty, his overstuffed backpack weighing him down.

I grinned. "Nice work. Let's go!"

He gave me a weary wave and trotted over. "What's the rush? I was just starting to bond with the homicidal tin can."

I grinned as we turned to the boat. "Yeah? Well, maybe send him a postcard."

The three of us ran to the boat and piled in.

"Go! Go!" Maria shouted to the boat driver, who needed no urging. He ignored the wake speed limit signs and took off at full throttle.

"Okay, Rafael" Chrissy called. "Come back." The dagger immediately obeyed, flying back to the departing yacht.

But Bruno was already sitting up. With a slight shake of his head, he pulled the rifle off his shoulder, took a knee, aimed, and fired five shots in quick succession. One of them hit the back of the boat, and another whistled past us. The other three landed in the boat. I had no idea where they hit, but I heard shrieking, and I clenched my jaw, wishing my luck could do more than just protect myself.

It was then that Jet Su arrived. He sprinted past the frozen woman with barely a glance, headed down the docks. I watched anxiously as he came to Bruno and shared a few words. Then the two of them leaped into a nearby speedboat.

I wrenched my gaze away from them to see who'd been shot. Vee was clutching her right shoulder, blood seeping down her shirt and staining most of it. And Kali was lying on the floor of the boat with two bullet wounds, one to her stomach and one to her chest.

"Juliette! Take the shards!" I yelled, passing her mine, and ripping the other one from Gonzo's hand to pass to her.

She quickly knelt down next to Kali and started singing. I watched in quiet anticipation, wondering how fast the healing could work with the power of two shards fueling it.

My eyes were riveted on Kali when Maria said, "Oh no."

I wrenched my eyes away to look at where Maria was focused. My stomach lurched. A speedboat was following us in pursuit—a fast boat that looked like it could gain on us quickly. And at the wheel was Jet Su.

Chapter 31

"Shit! Shit! Shit! Shit! Shit!" Gonzo said, scrunching up on the floor. Which is pretty much what I felt too. I just didn't say it.

Chrissy bent over Kali, her hands trembling as she pressed down on the wounds. Tears streaked down her cheeks, her breath coming in ragged gasps. "The bullets—" Her voice cracked. "They have to come out. We can't—" She shook her head so hard her eyeballs probably rattled. "Juliette, please, you have to get the bullets out!"

Juliette's voice wavered, the melody barely holding together as tears welled in her eyes. Her voice wavered as she choked back sobs, clinging to hope, but every note felt like it was slipping away.

My mind reeled. Without the shards, I felt hollow. Useless. Every instinct told me I needed them. My fingers twitched, aching for their weight in my hand. Could I do this without them? In less than a day of using them nonstop, when I wasn't holding them, nothing seemed to make sense.

But I still had some luck without them, if it hadn't run out yet. I just needed to find my center. So, I closed my eyes, took a deep breath, and tried to clear my thoughts.

I lit up. "Maria! The purifying stir stick!"

Maria's hands moved frantically through her pack, tossing items aside until she found the stick. She thrust it at Chrissy, who grabbed it desperately. Slowly, painfully, the first bullet wriggled its way out of Kali's body. Every agonizing second felt like an hour.

A shot rang out. Our pursuers' boat cut through the waves, getting closer with every second. The crackling of electricity in the air felt palpable. They were coming, and we were running out of time.

Kali gasped, her chest heaving as she fought for breath. For a moment, her chest heaved, a flicker of life, hope—then came the final, rattling exhale. Her body stilled, the light in her eyes flickering out.

Juliette kept singing, her voice trembling, tears spilling freely down her cheeks. The melody wavered, cracked, but she didn't stop. Not until Chrissy knelt beside her.

"She's gone," Chrissy said, wiping her eyes.

The words shook me to the core. My universe spun as I watched Chrissy's shoulders shake as she cried. I couldn't take my eyes off of Kali's lifeless form, struggling to accept the reality that just hours ago, she'd been standing watch, protecting us.

Chrissy took a deep breath and closed Kali's eyes. Then, still crying, she patted Juliette's shoulder. "Come on. Let's heal Vee."

I stared at Kali's lifeless body, wrestling with my thoughts. I was completely fine, the luck from the shard protecting me, while I was useless to keep everyone else safe. How was it *I* was being asked to lead them? It wasn't fair. I shouldn't be in that position. I wondered why I hadn't made sure Bruno was knocked out. I'd simply been thrilled that I'd had the idea to hit him with his own attack. Like a fool, I'd run off. I could have at least taken away his gun. And now this. Murder, right in front of my eyes. Part of me felt shock and sorrow about Kali's death, and part of me felt a deep anger at being put in this situation. It wasn't fair.

Vee was stoic. She didn't even wince when Juliette asked her to remove her hand. With the stir stick to pull out the bullet and Juliette's trait, Vee was on the path to healing, but that didn't change the fact that our enemy's boat was slowly gaining on us.

When I saw Vee would be okay, I moved up next to Maria. "What should we do?"

She eyed the boat with a steely glare. "You're the lucky one, Mitzy. But if you have no ideas, then I will do what I can. I didn't pack a long-range rifle, but I packed a handgun. When they get closer, I can take a shot."

I glanced at the backpack on the floor. "None of your fancy artifacts have long-range attack capabilities?"

She looked at me with pursed lips. "None as effective as a gun."

At that moment, I realized our driver had been yelling at us the whole time. I'd just blocked it out. He was hysterical, shouting something about how his precious boat was ruined, and who the hell were we, and yada yada yada.

I called out to him, "Hey! Calm down. We'll pay you in gold for your boat. Just get us out of here."

"Gold?" He looked at me with incredulous eyes. "You think that's going to make up for endangering my life and damaging my boat?"

"No, but it's all we can do for you. It's not our fault bad people are trying to kill us. We didn't know this was going to happen."

Somehow, my retort shut him up, and he turned back to focus on getting us out of there. By then, the speedboat was closer, and Bruno had the rifle on a little tripod aimed at us. He was watching the boats bob up and down, then fired a shot. It whistled a few inches from my head, close enough that I heard the bullet whiz past.

"Yikes!" I ducked down. "Can you shoot back yet?"

"Not yet," Maria said calmly. "Handguns have a much shorter range, and it's very difficult on waves."

I stood next to her at the rear of the boat, watching the speedboat get closer and closer. How close did we have to be to shoot a handgun? How could anyone shoot accurately in such choppy waves?

The boat got within range and Maria lifted her handgun, aiming at the other boat. She held herself rigidly, but she oscillated up and down over the choppy waves. She tried taking a shot, and it went way off target.

She grunted in frustration and continued holding the gun, trying to steady herself.

Bruno fired a shot, and it went to the right, then another that went high, and then a third that grazed my ear.

"Ow!" I shouted and crouched down, grabbing my right ear. It stung terribly, and I looked at my hand, covered in blood, before holding the car again.

My mind raced, thinking of ways to deal with him. Everyone but Maria was now crouched low, out of sight. I did the same, not wanting to be hit again. Luck or not, I was shot, and it hurt, even though it was just the outside tip of my ear.

Just then, an electric blast lit up from his boat and slammed into ours, sending it reeling. The boat sputtered a moment, then picked up speed again. Their boat was now thirty yards away.

"Take a shot!" I shouted to Maria, my voice cracking with desperation. Every nerve in my body screamed at me to keep low, out of sight. I watched her from my vantage point, crouched below the railing.

She held her gun steady, kept her left eye closed, and fired again. Nothing.

I looked at my friends, all crouching low or on the floor of the yacht, hiding. We were all protecting ourselves. But it wasn't doing anything. One of us needed to step up and take on Bruno and Jet Su. Maria was trying, and for that, I was thankful. But I wondered how it could possibly be enough. I watched her, impressed that she could even do what she was doing. She was so brave. Braver than all the rest of us.

She was the perfect person to rely on. *Better her than me*, I thought.

But then I immediately had the opposite thought.

I glanced over at Vee. She was leaning back on the cushions and breathing evenly, no longer clutching her wound. Juliette's healing had taken care of the worst, and even my ear had stopped stinging.

"Juliette, pass me a shard."

She reached over, still below the line of sight, and handed it to me. Then I held my other hand out to my right. "Maria, the gun, if you would?"

Without a pause, she passed the gun to me. I took a breath, then stood up, making myself an easy target. I'd never held a real gun before, not even once. So, I just held the gun out at arm's length and aimed in the general direction of the speedboat. My hand was shaking. I wasn't used to this—not guns, not shooting, not any of it. But I trusted my luck. I had to.

Closing my eyes, I exhaled slowly, focusing on the steady rhythm of my breathing. The sound of the speedboat's engine roared in the background, getting closer, closer...

With one last breath, eyes still closed, I shifted my aim slightly toward the sound of the speedboat's engine. Then, I pulled the trigger.

For a split second, nothing happened. But then the world erupted in a deafening boom. Fire and debris shot into the sky, the heat from the blast searing my skin even from the distance. The shockwave hit the water, sending ripples crashing into our boat. For a second, I couldn't think—just the ringing in my ears and the sight of the wreckage.

I blinked, stunned, as chunks of the boat scattered into the waves. My ears rang and my hands trembled. For the first time since all of this began, I felt something new, a strange mix of pride and certainty. Maybe I wasn't a hero. But I would not be afraid to fight.

Maria's eyes were wide. "That's... impossible."

I gave her a big grin. "Or... highly unlikely?"

"But... how?" Her mouth was open as she stared at the wreckage.

Gonzo had regained his senses, and was craning his head up over the railing, eyes wide. "Boats don't blow up from a single gunshot except in the movies. The only way you could blow up a speedboat like that is to hit the fuel tank, and that's usually under the deck or seating area in the back. The bullet would have had to ricochet off of one of the metal poles of the frame. Not just a lucky shot. Ridiculously lucky. Stupidly lucky." He grinned at me. "Pure genius."

I laughed and handed the gun back to Maria, and she instantly put the safety on and pulled out a pair of binoculars. "Stop the boat," she ordered.

We stood and watched the wreckage. Bruno would have died instantly, but Jet Su...

There was no sign of anyone, and we held our breaths.

"Do you think he could survive—" My voice trailed off.

Maria was tense. "He might have phased at the first blast, if he was lucky. But any time I saw him use his trait, the phasing only lasted a couple of seconds at the most. I don't think he could have survived."

Don't think he could have survived.

The words hung in the air. Uncertainty. But also hope. Hope that we were done with the fear and running. Maybe forever.

Maria watched closely with her binoculars as we rocked on the waves. Seconds ticked by. Then minutes. No sign of life.

But what if...

She kept watching, and time continued to tick by, her search vigilant.

Finally, she lowered the binoculars. "He's gone."

I exhaled slowly, a weight lifting from my chest. "He's really gone?"

"Yes," she said. Although her eyes lingered on the smoldering debris. "Let's go."

The driver turned the engine on and we continued on our way south along the coast.

"You did it, Mitzy!" Gonzo said happily, clapping my shoulder. "You're no longer just my best friend—you're my lucky charm. If I could keep you in my pocket, I would."

I gave him a playful punch. "Too cramped, but thanks for the sentiment. Not bad, yourself. Running around invisible, freezing bad guys. Dude, you're a superhero."

He gave me a grin. "G-Man, saving the world. Oh, yeah."

But then, his smile faded as his gaze caught something, and I turned to see Kali's dead body lying on the floor of the boat. We'd won, but at what cost?

Chapter 32

A heavy silence settled over the group as the boat cut through the choppy waves. Gonzo leaned against the side railing, his gaze distant. Juliette sat cross-legged near Vee, her hands fidgeting with the hem of her jacket. Chrissy had her arms wrapped tightly around herself, her face pale and streaked with tears.

For a moment, no one spoke. We were alive. We'd won. But it didn't feel like a victory.

"We should take care of Kali," Chrissy said softly, her voice breaking. "She deserves—" She couldn't finish, turning away as fresh tears welled in her eyes.

Maria nodded grimly and gestured for Gonzo to help. Together, they laid Kali's body gently across the bench, covering her with a spare tarp they found in the boat's storage. It was a poor substitute for a burial, but it was all we could do for now.

I stood apart, my hands shaking as I stared at the water. My ear still throbbed from the graze of Bruno's bullet, but I barely noticed. The adrenaline was wearing off, and the enormity of what had just happened began to sink in.

We'd done it. Somehow, we had survived.

But winning never felt so heavy.

Maria stepped beside me, her presence grounding me in the moment. "You okay?" she asked softly.

I shrugged, unable to meet her eyes. "I don't know. I should feel relieved, right? But I don't."

She nodded, her gaze steady. "That's normal. Victory doesn't always feel like you think it will."

I looked at her, searching for something to say, but the words wouldn't come. Instead, I just nodded, and she placed a hand on my shoulder.

"Take a minute," she said. "Breathe."

I did as she said, closing my eyes and inhaling deeply. The salt air filled my lungs, sharp and bracing. It helped—just a little. Enough to feel the beginnings of clarity.

"We should feel safer now," Juliette said, her voice small but firm. She looked around at all of us, her tear-streaked face defiant. "But why don't I?"

Maria and I exchanged a glance. She wasn't wrong. Even with Jet Su and Bruno gone, there was an undercurrent of unease that none of us could shake.

"Because this isn't over," Maria said quietly. "Not yet."

I felt it too. A faint, gnawing sensation in the back of my mind, like the moment before the storm clouds break.

Then, my phone buzzed in my pocket. In the chaos, I'd forgotten about it entirely. Pulling it out, I saw several missed texts from Edward.

My stomach sank as I opened them.

4:41 a.m. *Found out who's really after you guys. Jet Su is only his Preservation Society pawn. He goes by The Raven. Top guy at Fulton House. I'll do some more digging.*

5:48 a.m. *Bad news. This Raven fellow is a big deal. Top dog. He keeps out of the limelight, so I've never met him myself, but sounds like he's got special privileges within Fulton House. His base of operations is in New York, but he has influence everywhere.*

6:55 a.m. *Hate to be the bearer of bad news, but The Raven has the Fulton House Preservation Society in his back pocket. And pretty much endless resources. I have done deals with him and didn't know it. Everybody has. His influence is everywhere, quietly, and none of us knows about it. He's attracted some of the top talent of the Theurgica. Sorry, but you lot are buggered.*

The phone slipped from my hand onto the deck with a dull clatter. Everyone turned to look at me, their faces filled with concern.

"What is it?" Maria asked, her voice sharp.

I swallowed hard, my throat dry. "It's not over," I whispered, the words tasting bitter. "Jet Su and Bruno were just foot soldiers. The real threat—the one pulling the strings—is still out there."

Maria's brow furrowed. "Who?"

"The Raven," I said, my voice trembling. "He has total control of Fulton House's Preservation Society. And he has resources and connections everywhere. According to Edward…" I hesitated, my hands shaking. "According to Edward, we don't stand a chance."

For a moment, no one spoke. The weight of the revelation pressed down on us like a lead blanket.

Maria broke the silence, her voice steely. "We've faced impossible odds before."

"Not like this." I stared at my hands. "He has everything. Power, influence, money. We're nothing compared to him."

Chrissy spoke up, her voice trembling but firm. "Maybe. But we have something special as well." When I was quiet, she frowned. "It's not just you, Mitzy. It's all of us together. And Kali gave her life for the cause. We have to honor that."

Her words hung in the air, sharp and cutting. She abruptly strode across the boat and pulled the tarp off of Kali's lifeless body. "Before we do anything else, we need to say some words over Kali. We need to recognize her… and her sacrifice… before we say anything else."

The driver turned off the engine and joined us as we obediently gathered around Kali's body in somber silence. My mind was blank. The shock was still dissipating.

Maria cleared her throat, and we all looked at her. "Kali. A wonderful person. Reliable. Friendly. Excellent teacher. Leadership member for almost ten years…" She paused. "I would count her among my closest friends. She was sacrificial and giving to the end. God bless her soul. Amen."

"Amen," I said. It struck me then that Maria was an enigma. Both relying on magic and believing in God in one breath. How did she make sense of that?

Chrissy went next, her eyes full of tears. "Kali trained me in ways I didn't know I needed. It was brief, but we became friends.

She had a sweet soul, loved kids, and helped me face my fears. I am forever grateful to have known her." She choked on her words and shook silently.

My heart got stuck in my throat. I had no idea Kali had made such an impression on Chrissy, and it made her death that much more painful. I looked around at the others. Nobody else had known Kali for long enough, but I felt like something else needed to be said.

I cleared my throat. "She stayed up all night, keeping guard, while we were hanging out and enjoying ourselves. Kali was a good person. She sacrificed herself for us, and for that, I honor her."

Everyone nodded quietly, even the owner of the boat.

"Amen," I said awkwardly.

Chrissy wiped a tear, then she and Gonzo wrapped Kali in the tarp again and the boat took off south.

The thrum of the engine filled the space as we bobbed over the waves of the South Pacific, the rhythm hypnotic as we each held our own thoughts. I stared at the distant shore, then at the sea's horizon. Endless paths. Endless possibilities. Some good. Some bad. Did Kali's death have any meaning, or was all of it meaningless? What was the point of it all? And was God a part of this craziness, or just an ancient construct to help people make sense of the pain and the loss?

I turned to Maria. She was at the back of the boat, eyes glazed in thought.

I sat down next to her and blurted out, "Tell me what you think about God."

She gave me a puzzled expression. "That's an odd question."

"I mean, how does this whole thing work? With God and magic? Do you pray?"

"Of course."

"So, if God already knows what's going to happen, what's the point?"

She gave me a wry smile. "Ah, Mitzy. You see God as a puppeteer, don't you?"

"Um…"

She shook her head. "God may know all but doesn't control all. Father Romero explained it to me like this: At one extreme, you could think of God as someone controlling puppets, who makes everything happen exactly a certain way. And at the other extreme, God is like an old-style watchmaker, who created a beautiful watch, wound it up, and now is sitting back observing it. On the puppet side, you've got people who think God makes bad things happen in order to punish sinners. On the other hand, you've got those who think God isn't involved in our lives. He just kicked off creation and is now sitting back. Father Romero says God is more like a parent than any of those metaphors. God wants to be involved in your life but also wants you to grow up and learn to deal with some hard knocks on your own. It's a balance. So, to answer your question, yes, Mitzy, I pray. Sometimes I wonder if my prayers are mostly to change myself. But even then, it's worth the time."

When she finished, my mind was lost in thought. "Thanks," I mumbled.

We sat in silence for a few minutes. I had a lot to think about. But now that the action had calmed down, I realized I hadn't had my normal cup of caffeine.

"Coffee?" I asked her.

She shrugged. "I'm pretty sure the boat owner packed a thermos."

We went over to him, and he pointed at the thermos. The others saw us and gathered around, filling small cups and passing them around. While I was passing cups out, the owner began ripping into Maria.

"This is completely unacceptable! One hundred percent. How are you going to pay for the bullet holes and other damage to my beautiful boat? Plus, the stress you just put me through. I'll have you thrown in jail."

I stood in front of him, hands out. "Look. We're sorry. But we'll pay for it."

"With gold?" He scoffed.

I rummaged through my pack and filled a sock with a couple of pounds of gold nuggets. Probably fifty thousand dollars' worth. I passed it to him.

He calmed down a lot.

We sat then, with coffee and the gorgeous views, and it felt almost as if the action and danger had never happened. We were just a few good friends on a luxury cruise. But Maria interjected, not letting me live in my little perfect fantasy moment.

"We're heading to Valparaiso. After we touch base there, what's next, Mitzy?"

I felt my stomach lurch. Again?

Once again, they were looking at me for some incredible, magical insight. The whole thing tasted bitter. Especially when I had no answer. I looked at Maria, wondering what to say. Why was she asking this of me? It felt unfair. So unfair.

But nobody said anything, and the moment dragged on. I looked into everyone's eyes. They were all still counting on me. I looked at the tarp at the back of the boat with Kali's lifeless body. I couldn't possibly make any more decisions and put any of the rest of them in danger. Now that we knew our real adversary, an ultra-powerful Theurgican, we knew the odds were impossible. How many more had to die before we wised up? As I sat with it, the answer became obvious.

"Somewhere safe," I blurted out. I turned to Maria. "We either need to bury or give these shards to someone more qualified. I'm done with them. Too much killing, shooting, and running."

Maria's eyes bored into me. I felt like squirming.

"Look," I said. "I love all the training and the excitement, but my favorite moments these last few weeks have been hanging out with you guys, same as back before all of this went down. I do love solving mysteries, but I just killed a couple of guys! Gonzo, you know what I'm talking about, right?"

"Definitely." He put his arm around my shoulder. "We've gotta get the shards somewhere safe and get out of here—out of this danger zone. And I miss my computers, man."

Vee gave me a sour look. "Mitzy, Gonzo, please. All the people in Cortez died for these shards. Don't you want to make it worth something?"

"We have," I said with energy. "We've kept the shards out of their hands. But now that Jet Su is dead, we've probably bought some time. Let's ditch the shards somewhere safe and lie low." I shook my head. "I'll miss the fun moments, but we don't need more people dying. Let's find someone more qualified to keep them safe."

Vee fumed. "You are so selfish! When's the last time you truly got outside of your bubble and did something without getting anything in return?"

"Why are you always so pushy?" I retorted. "Why can't you just let me do what I want and stop telling me what to do? I'm sick of it. All of you. Just let me be."

"Coward!" Vee glared at me.

"Hey, I never signed up to be a hero." I shook my head at her. "You've trained for stuff like this your whole life. Not me. I'm just a normal guy, with no skills to help."

"No skills?" Vee scoffed. "You have plenty, Mitzy. You're just afraid to use them."

"Pah!" I waved her away. "I have geeky skills. I know history. Not how to fight someone. I'm no action hero, and you know it. Everything I've done successfully this last month was because of luck." In a huff, I handed both of the shards to Maria. As they left my hands, I felt a longing to keep holding on, but I figured it was like any addiction. I would be okay after detoxing.

It was an abrupt end to the conversation. And everyone was shocked into silence, including me. Minutes passed by. The shards were gone from my touch, maybe forever. But was my luck gone? I seriously hoped not.

We sped along the water, the shoreline passing by as we made our way south, and no one said a word.

Finally, Chrissy broke the silence. "Guys. If The Raven is this ultra-powerful person, what do you think's gonna happen if he gets his hands on all of them? We can't let that happen. Mitzy, you know deep down that the prophecy that they worked so hard to hide from us is about now. I know it."

She paused, giving me a stern look. "If we're talking apocalypse kind of stuff here, who better to keep the shards away from that kind of evil than the luckiest person alive?"

Her words sat with us. I heard Gonzo sigh, and I glanced over at him. He gave me a look as if he was caving in—tight lips, cocked head, wrinkled forehead.

Chrissy continued. "It's asking a lot from all of us. But think about the meaning of the inscriptions. Even with the gaps in our current knowledge, we all know this is a big deal."

I took a deep breath. "But don't you think the people in the Theurgica with far more experience and power should be the ones to deal with it? If Fulton House is the one after the shards, how about finding someone in another of the Great Houses to protect them? The House of Eldritch can perform spells. Why not them? Why us?"

Chrissy shrugged. "Maybe none of the houses should have them, but a more neutral party. If The Raven is as big a deal as Edward thinks, I bet he could take on another of the Houses. But can he take on luck?"

"Who's saying he can't?" I retorted.

Chrissy sighed. "Mitzy, Gonzo, we're doing something important here. What exactly besides keeping the shards safe, I don't know. But it's worth it to keep going."

"Even if one of us gets killed?" I asked.

The words hung in the air, and we looked at one another. In every pair of eyes I looked into, I knew deeply it would hurt even worse than Kali if they died.

Chrissy nodded slowly. "Even if."

I let out a deep breath. Maria's stare was killing me, and I felt myself caving. I looked at Gonzo and could see he'd already been convinced and was just waiting for me.

Silence hung in the air as all eyes watched me. I squirmed, knowing that if I committed, I'd be all in. I wasn't going to go halfway. And I knew I'd make more mistakes.

Chrissy's conviction pushed me. When I locked eyes with her, she nodded at me. I knew then that she would fight with everything she had to make Kali's death worth something.

I felt selfish, and also thankful. Thankful for friends like her, so loyal, so true, so strong. I wanted to make her proud. I knew I'd probably let her down again, but I decided then it was worth the risk.

"Okay," I said.

Chrissy beamed. "Wonderful."

Maria stood. "Alright. Now, for the hard part."

All eyes turned to her. She looked troubled, like she was holding a weight, and I suddenly wondered if she was shouldering the burden of atoning for all the people who had died.

She passed me both shards and locked eyes with me. "Take a deep breath, Mitzy."

I did. But she cleared her throat. "Not good enough. Come on Mitzy. Are you in?"

"Yes, I'm in," I said.

"I mean it," she insisted. "Are you in? Are you truly in?"

"Yes. Yes! I'm in." I looked her in the eye.

"Good." She paused. "Take a breath through your nose."

I closed my eyes and inhaled, the crisp sea air filling me, and a flash of the strange dream from two nights earlier flitted through my mind. And then it was gone. I opened my eyes again to face Maria.

She fixed me with a firm gaze. "Where to next, Mitzy?"

Without thinking, I blurted out, "Adelaide, Australia."

Her eyes twinkled. "That's my boy."

About the Author

Ephie Risho is the author of *The Elementalists*, a YA fantasy series co-written with his child after a third-grade writing assignment snowballed into a full-blown saga. His *Stone of Amun-Ra* series ups the pace (and the stakes) with ancient mysteries, supernatural luck, and at least one explosion. By day, Ephie leads software design teams; by night, he leads plucky misfits into magical chaos. He's been writing since sixth grade, when his stories made classmates put down their pencils and actually pay attention. He lives in scenic Montana with his wife, two kids, and a strong suspicion that his next plot twist is lurking behind the laundry.

Author's Note

Writing this book has been a blast—and a bit of a whirlwind. I cranked out the first drafts of this and the next novel in just three months (a new personal record, and yes, I am bragging a little). But after early feedback from my trusty beta readers, I wisely let it simmer on the creative back burner. I've learned over the years not to push it when my brain hasn't quite figured out what's broken—or how many subplots I forgot I was juggling.

The book you have in your hands is over twice the length of that first draft. And I love it. Once the characters found their quirks and started improvising their own lines (as they tend to do), I wanted to give them more time on stage.

Small things still make me grin—like naming Bruno Marx. Writing Gonzo was equal parts joy and challenge: he might look like comic relief, but there's more under the surface. Writing "luck" turned out to be its own headache. Early readers pointed out that Mitzy felt like he was bumbling his way through, so I had to dig in and show that his growth, not just his good fortune, was what made the difference. Luck might put the mirror in the debris, but it's up to Mitzy to pick it up and use it.

As with any book, it's never a solo effort. First and foremost, I'd like to thank my wife Michelle, who has supported and believed in me from the beginning. Her deep belief in me as a writer is so encouraging and motivating. She also puts up with a boatload of times where I hide away writing rather than spending it with her, and for that, I'm grateful for her patience.

My friend Jeff Pernell was the brave soul who read the very first draft and helped me untangle the mess. His feedback was crucial to help shape the book. He kept encouraging me that the ideas were solid, even as I struggled over how to gut and rewrite scenes. Some chapters were completely thrown out. Most of the time, many more chapters were added to fill out the story more fully.

I'd also like to give a huge shout-out to my primary editor, Daniel Edelman. Not only is he sharp with words and continuity, he's also the type of guy who'll point out that meteorites hit the ground—not meteors—and suggest a better fight move while he's at it. Every writer needs a good editor. I somehow landed a great one.

I was also blessed in my final rounds of editing to work with Melinda Falgoust. She tightened up the words on nearly every page, reminding me that there's always a way to say it more succinctly. She also helped encourage me to keep working on a few areas, which helped me add the final polish to the book it needed to make the characters consistent and likeable, and the plot to stay engaging.

And finally, thank *you* for reading my books! As much as I love writing, the real joy is sharing stories with people like you. If you enjoyed this adventure, please consider leaving a review on Amazon and Goodreads. Ratings and reviews are the magic beans that help authors grow more stories—and gain visibility. Plus, they make our day. Every single time.

Until the next adventure!

Ephie

Wrath of the Raven, and Other Inconveniences

Don't miss the next book in the Stone of Amun-Ra series: *Wrath of the Raven, and Other Inconveniences.*

The discovery of the shard was only the beginning. Now, Mitzy and his friends are drawn deeper into a web of ancient secrets and shadowy forces. The shard's mysterious powers grow stronger, but so does the danger surrounding it. As the group struggles to stay ahead of relentless enemies, they uncover whispers of an even greater threat: a figure known only as the Raven, whose ambitions could reshape the world.

From hidden sanctuaries to bustling cities, Mitzy and his friends must navigate a perilous path filled with cryptic clues, ancient symbols, and alliances that may not be what they seem. As loyalties are tested and stakes rise, the question looms: will the shards save humanity—or doom it?

Wrath of the Raven, and Other Inconveniences takes the suspense, mystery, and adventure of the Stone of Amun-Ra series to thrilling new heights, promising twists you won't see coming and a battle you'll never forget.

Other books by Ephie Risho

Enter the world of **The Elementalists**, where teens discover powers tied to the elements, and are thrust into battles that test their courage and friendships. Filled with magic, danger, and heart, it's a journey of discovery and destiny you won't want to miss.

Printed in Dunstable, United Kingdom